The Inheritance

Also by Jenny Pitman

ON THE EDGE

DOUBLE DEAL

THE DILEMMA

THE VENDETTA

Jenny Pitman

The Inheritance

MACMILLAN

First published 2005 by Macmillan
an imprint of Pan Macmillan Ltd
Pan Macmillan, 20 New Wharf Road, London N1 9RR
Basingstoke and Oxford
Associated companies throughout the world
www.panmacmillan.com

ISBN 1 4050 4854 9 HB
ISBN 1 4050 8830 3 TPB

5 7 9 8 6 4

A CIP catalogue record for this book is available from
the British Library.

Typeset by SetSystems Ltd, Saffron Walden, Essex
Printed and bound in Great Britain by
Mackays of Chatham plc, Chatham, Kent

To Friendship

Where in the world can a man find nobility without pride,
Friendship without envy, or beauty without vanity?
Here; where grace is laced with muscle,
And strength by gentleness confined.
He serves without servility; he has fought without enmity.
There is nothing so powerful, nothing less violent;
There is nothing so quick, nothing more patient.
England's past has been borne on his back.
All our history is his industry.
We are his heirs, he is our inheritance.

'The Horse', Ronald Duncan

Acknowledgements

Very grateful thanks

to

Nina Clark
for shared opinions and hard work

Liz Cowen
for technical help – Pan Macmillan

Wally Johnson
for his fun criticisms

Peter McCormick
solicitor

Maria Rejt
for guidance

Peter Straus
the academic

Professor Newman Tayler
for his medical help

Alan Walker
for his veterinary help

Jan braced herself as the spooled-up engines gave an enormous roar and the 737 charged down the runway.

'I hate this bit,' she thought as the plane left the ground and climbed steeply towards an iron-grey canopy of cloud. From her seat by the window she watched the earth below as it turned from a landscape to a table-top model; then finally the animated green and brown map disappeared as the plane entered the clouds. For a few moments it was completely enveloped in mist, before it burst through into sparkling sunshine and a serene pale blue sky. As the huge cotton-wool carpet receded below them she nudged Eddie, who was sitting beside her.

'That's more like it,' she said, pointing out through the window. 'Here comes the sun.'

Eddie didn't answer. Nor did he look in the direction Jan was indicating.

'Eddie?'

But Eddie's eyes were closed, his head was jammed back against the headrest and his cheeks were as white as the fluffy clouds below. So were the knuckles of his fingers, which were clamped tightly on the armrests.

'Hey, Eddie! What's the matter? You look terrible.'

She nudged him harder and he opened his eyes.

'I *feel* terrible,' he whispered.

'My God, you can't have the trots already. We've only just left England.'

He shook his head.

'No, no, it's not that,' he groaned through clenched teeth.

His eyes closed again and Jan stared at him. Sweat was appearing in beads on his forehead, his mouth was set tight.

'Eddie, you're not . . . ?'

She tapped him sharply on the wrist, feeling the rigid tendons bracing the grip of his hand on the seat. In the bright sunlight his handsome face was a mask of anxiety.

'You're not *scared of flying*, are you?'

Eddie nodded. 'Bloody terrified, actually. I always have been.'

Jan smiled and lightly stroked the back of his hand.

'I thought you were strangely quiet on the way down to the airport. How come you never told me when we booked the flights?'

'I'm not afraid when it's in the future. Only when I'm in the departure lounge – that's when it starts.'

'You poor old thing. It must have been hell shuttling backwards and forwards to Australia all those times.'

'It wasn't much fun,' Eddie admitted, 'but the drinks trolley helped. As it would do now.'

'Don't be daft. It's seven in the morning. You'll be all right.'

'It's just sitting here, having nothing to do but wait for something seriously unpleasant to happen.'

Jan gestured to Matty and Megan, who were sitting in the row in front. They were busy using the crayons provided by the airline to keep them amused.

'Shall I get you an activity pack? You could keep yourself occupied with some colouring in.'

Eddie smiled at Jan's withering irony.

'Don't take the piss, Jan, it's not funny. I'll be all right in a while.'

She leant across and kissed him on the cheek.

'Cheer up. They'll be round with some coffee in a minute.'

For the next hour Jan kept dozing off. Racehorse trainers are used to early rising, so today's start from Edge Farm in the dawn light hadn't seemed particularly hard. But now she felt extremely tired. Perhaps it was the release of tension: all that lay ahead, as far as Jan was concerned, was two weeks of blissful relaxation.

Jan knew she deserved this holiday, they all did. She had worked extremely hard since the dramatic events of the winter, when justice had at long last been meted out to Harold Powell, and she'd settled accounts with Virginia Gilbert at Leopardstown – if not finally, then at least for the time being. Her reputation in the racing world, as a trainer with a small string but large ambitions, had grown steadily. There had been four or five important races in which her horses had run really well, and she'd come out on top in three head-to-head encounters with runners from Virginia's Riscombe Manor yard. True, their best young animals, her Morning Glory and Virginia's Velvet Dynasty, had not met since Leopardstown. MG had got a terrific second to an Irish horse in a novice hurdle at the Cheltenham Festival, while Velvet Dynasty had been off the course with a dreaded virus. After the Festival Jan had had a magical run of nine good-class winners in a month. Russian Eagle had missed the Grand National – Jan knew he was a bit short of work following a bout of coughing and took an easier route. In an emotional return to Fairyhouse a couple of weeks later, he'd almost taken the Irish National for the second time, valiantly running the winner to a neck whilst carrying a stone more in weight. Eddie hadn't been riding him, in fact he'd not sat on a horse since the car crash eighteen months ago and Jan now wondered if he ever would.

She yawned, stretched and checked the children. They'd both dozed off, their colouring half-finished. Beside her, Eddie was emptying a miniature brandy into a cup of coffee on the hinged table in front of him. An empty bottle already stood next to it: the medicine was obviously beginning to work as something resembling his normal colour had returned to Eddie's cheeks. He looked at Jan, his smile still a little half-hearted, and raised the cup.

'Medicinal,' he mouthed.

She smiled back and shook open her paper at the racing page.

🐎

'Here, Jan, why don't you, Eddie and the kids have my place in the Algarve for a couple of weeks?' Bernie Sutcliffe had said in an expansive manner. 'It's great there – sun, sand, sangria, the lot.'

It was back before Easter and they were in the owners' and trainers' bar at Ludlow racecourse, drinking a bottle of what seemed to be Bernie's favourite brand of champagne – the cheapest available. Jan had happened to mention that she'd never once taken her family away for a seaside holiday.

'Oh, Bernie, we couldn't possibly,' Jan countered automatically. Instinctively she shrank from being beholden to any owner. But at the same time she was curious, wondering what Bernie's place in Portugal was like.

'Yes, you could,' Bernie pressed her again, sounding even more enthusiastic about his brilliant idea. 'It's free the last two weeks of July. Take it then.'

'Well, that's *very* generous of you,' Jan conceded.

Smirking, Bernie poured another glass of champagne.

'Not generous at all, but when I say "free" I mean it's not reserved or anything. I usually go myself in July and I can let you have it at cost. You just pay the staff while you're there. It's a snip in value terms, but it's not expensive anyway, Portugal.'

'Is it near the sea?'

'Course it is, just a few minutes' walk, beautiful beaches and anyway it's got its own pool. Lovely place. Very classy. Very exclusive. Villa Lagoa Azul. In other words: the Blue Lagoon Villa.'

Driving home in the horsebox, Jan had asked Eddie what he thought about Bernie's suggestion.

'The Blue Lagoon? It sounds like a hot Kim Basinger film. Saxophone jazz and sex in the sun are good enough for me.'

'As Bernie would want it to be, I'm sure.'

'Well, I'm completely in favour. The villa sounds dead romantic. And the kids would love the beach.'

In Jan's eyes this was by far the best argument for taking up the offer. Megan and Matty's classmates were always going off on foreign holidays. Several had been to Spain and the Greek islands last year and one had even been to the Gambia, which sounded impossibly distant and exotic. Why should her children be deprived? She chewed her lip for a moment. The question was could she afford it.

'Oh, to hell with it, let's go,' she said loudly, banging the steering wheel with her hands. 'July's our quietest month. The amount Bernie said he'd charge for the villa sounds very reasonable, and a flight to Faro can't be that dear.'

Eddie sat back in his seat, rubbing his hands together in satisfaction.

'It'll be great, babe, I know it will.'

❧

The heat at Faro airport was stifling. Eddie showed the address of Bernie's villa to the taxi driver, who nodded his head vigorously.

'I know this place. We go. Twenty minutes.'

They drove for forty. At first the road was a busy dual carriageway, with glimpses of the sea on one side and of scrubby, heat-parched countryside, with vineyards and olive groves, on the other. Just as Jan was about to ask the driver if he knew where he was going, they turned off the main road and raced down towards the seafront. It was a twisty, narrow street, lined with white-painted houses whose doors and shutters were picked out in bright reds, greens and blues. Cats and chickens jumped out of the way as the taxi flew past. After a few minutes the brakes squealed and the car swept under an arched gateway in a cloud of dust. Jan caught sight of a faded sign on a sun-cracked wooden panel. It read Villa Lagoa Azul.

The taxi driver pulled up on a dusty forecourt in front of a substantial but water-stained concrete building whose main feature was a plethora of balconies rising up several storeys, each identically angled to face in the direction of the sea. Jan, Eddie and the children got out of the cab and looked around.

'This can't be right,' said Jan, squinting up at the building. 'These look like apartments.'

She tried to make the driver understand that he must have taken them to the wrong place, but he insisted he hadn't.

At that moment a couple emerged from the building and strolled towards them. 'Hi, I'm Jim and this is Eileen. You look lost. Can we help?'

Jim was bald and his peeling red skin showed that they, too, were recent arrivals. Relieved to hear English voices, Jan asked if they spoke any Portuguese.

'Not a word,' said the man cheerily in a Lancashire accent. 'Never seem to need it. Not round here, anyway.'

'I'm trying to get the driver to understand that he's brought us to the wrong place.'

'Let's have a dekko at the address.'

Jim took the letter Bernie had sent to Jan, which she had been trying to show the cabbie.

'Oh yes, this is the place all right. I see you've got the apartment above ours. Are you friends of Bernie's? This is one of his fortnights. As it is one of ours too, we see him most years.'

'One of his fortnights? I don't get you.'

'Most of us get three or four fortnights a year here – you know, that's our share. I believe he has three.'

'You mean . . . this is a *timeshare*?'

'Well, the Portu-geezers call it a *mulitpropriedado*, but it's exactly the same thing.'

'Oh!' Jan and Eddie exchanged looks.

'Why's it called a villa, then?' Eddie asked.

The Englishman shrugged.

'Well, there probably was a villa on this site once upon a time. Maybe it was bulldozed to make way for this.'

Jan sighed. Bloody Bernie with his fantasies of grandeur.

'OK,' she said, looking up at the building again through new eyes. 'Where do we find the keys?'

⤜

Bernie Sutcliffe's timeshare apartment was on the fifth floor and, though boasting two box-like bedrooms and a small family bathroom, was largely made up of an open-plan living area with kitchen space and breakfast bar, a Formica-topped dining table with four upright chairs, and a three-piece suite made of bent cane. A sliding plate-glass door separated the room from a triangular balcony at the front. Nor did it have a swimming pool of its own, there was a busy communal pool shared with all the other apartments.

After Eddie had dragged the luggage in, he flopped into one of the cane easy chairs, breathing heavily for a few moments. Then he started laughing.

'And I'd dreamed of a hacienda-style villa with white-coated staff seeing to my every need.'

6

Megan and Matty were running in and out of the bedrooms screaming. Feeling rather vexed, hot and dusty, Jan wandered onto the balcony, where a few parched geraniums in pots were lined up begging for water. She leant on the balustrade. Between the huge buildings she caught a glimpse of the Atlantic Ocean washing against a sandy beach at least half a mile away.

She nodded towards it. 'I bet that's more than a few minutes' walk, or my name's Christopher Columbus.'

Eddie came out to join her, placing his hand over hers on the iron rail.

'Bernie's special rate doesn't look quite so special now,' Jan said. 'What do you think the going rate is for a place like this? I bet he's charging us that and a bit more. The mean bastard.'

Eddie slipped his arm round her waist.

'It doesn't matter,' he said. 'We're all together for our first foreign holiday. It'll be fine.'

'What I really hate is always having to think about money. When is it ever going to come right, Eddie? When are we going to be able to do the things we want to do without counting every sodding penny?'

He leant across and kissed her ear.

'Soon. Now come on. The kids and I'll take the cases into the bedrooms, then we'll get out the beach kit and go off to explore a bit. It will be all right, I promise.'

They strolled through the village and followed signs to the *praia*. Eddie timed the walk on his watch and found it took them all of twenty-three minutes to get there. But the effort was worthwhile. The beach was long and wide, with plenty of space between the other holidaymakers, who clustered in family groups under their big blue parasols. It seemed these were rented from a sun-wizened old local who also ran an unofficial-looking beach bar, where they bought crusty rolls and fizzy drinks for lunch. After their tiring journey the sea was delightful. The children scampered around on the beach, in and out of the waves, and with Eddie's help made complicated sandy defences against the tide, which they watched slowly crumble away as the water inevitably overwhelmed them. They were almost the last to leave in the evening. On the way back to the apartment they noted a small restaurant, called enticingly A Churrascaria Alcatraz, where they went later for a dinner of fresh grilled sardines and vegetables, washed down with Coca-Cola and ice-cold *vinho verde*. It was a hot, stuffy night and back in the apartment, before bedding down, Jan threw open all the windows.

At three a.m. she woke with a start. Her skin felt hot and dry. She'd known that the offshore breeze could double the burning, despite lavish applications of sunblock – but this was not what had woken her. She'd heard something. She strained for the sound again and there it was, that thin whine like a miniature buzz saw close to her ear. Suddenly the sound stopped and she knew the insect had landed and was enjoying its meal. She slapped her cheek, but had no idea if this was the place where the mosquito had chosen to picnic.

Jan soon dozed off but, by morning, serious damage had been done. Her face, shoulders and legs were covered in angry mosquito bites.

'God, just look at me,' she called from in front of the bathroom mirror. 'I've been bitten before, but they've never swollen up like this. I look like I've got the plague.'

Eddie, whose blood annoyingly the little blighters had found relatively unappetizing, did his best to be sympathetic. He used calamine lotion to soothe the bites, then made a pot of tea. Back in bed Jan sipped her tea while Eddie leant on the windowsill, staring idly out into the area behind the apartment block.

'Hey,' he said after a moment. 'Come over here.'

Jan put down the mug and joined him at the window. Eddie pointed into the space below them, a patch of bare, sandy earth, strewn with builders' rubbish – broken breeze blocks, lumps of hardened cement and several rusty rolls of steel mesh. Beyond this an assortment of miserable shrubs and cacti struggled for survival around the edge of a pond, about twelve feet across. She saw that its water was sludgy and stagnant, with a sickly turquoise tinge.

'Jan, I think we've found the blue lagoon,' Eddie said. 'Mosquito paradise.'

Two hours later a wrinkled local woman, who must have been well into her seventies, arrived at their door. Her head was covered by a scarf and she was wearing an old print dress. She spoke no English but pointed to her chest and said, 'Maria', then took them laboriously round the apartment, pointing out the rooms and the fittings like a proud guide.

'*Quarto vivo . . . quarto da dormir . . . refrigerador . . . balcão . . .*'

Finally, Maria indicated a cupboard – '*armario*' – which she opened, dragging out a mop and bucket. She waved the mop in the air before rubbing it a few times across the floor, as if to demonstrate her skills. Then she dumped it back into its bucket, shoved them both back in the cupboard and shuffled towards the wall, where a calendar hung. She rapped with her finger on the next day's date, then headed back to the front door.

'*Até amanhã!*' she croaked, waving goodbye, and they all waved back.

Maria was clearly the 'staff' Bernie had referred to.

Following her departure, Eddie went into the village to buy bread, milk, eggs and other supplies at the *minimercado*, and came back with an extra item in a lurid red and black cardboard box.

'What's that?' asked Matty.

'This is the hi-tech answer to Mum's prayers,' Eddie said grandly as he unpacked his purchase. 'It's the famous, patent Moziradicator.'

'What does it do?'

'What the name says. You plug it into the electricity socket and, with the addition of a chemical pill that sits on top, it spews out something really nasty into the air that mosquitoes can't stand. With this baby doing its stuff we won't get bitten again.'

Matty twisted his face.

'Yeugh! But what about the nasty stuff in the air?'

'Don't worry: to us it's odourless, colourless and harmless. But to a mosquito it's like the worst stink bomb you ever let off.'

It would be fair to say that the Moziradicator was the saviour of their holiday. From that night on the miniature doodlebugs, which were breeding like fury on the Blue Lagoon, kept well away from Jan's window and the rest of the fortnight passed in lazy, and occasionally energetic, contentment. She and Eddie lounged by the communal pool while the children splashed happily in the shallow end for hours. Or they all trekked to the beach and played cricket, frisbee and football with other families and drank beer and Orangina under the blue parasols. At night they had drinks by the pool then ate simply in the apartment, or they went back to the churrascaria for fish, spicy sausages, succulent pork and even on one occasion, to Eddie's great delight, grilled octopus.

Megan pulled a face when he suggested she try it.

'I'm not a *cannibal*, Eddie,' she said with prim firmness. 'It looks like worms.' He grinned at her childlike remark.

All to soon, it was the evening before their last day.

Eddie said to Jan, 'Let's go out after dinner. There's a fado house in the next village. The bloke in the beach bar says everyone should hear fado before they die.' With the help of Jim and Eileen, he had found a teenager from one of the other apartments who was willing to babysit Megan and Matty.

Around nine o'clock they took a taxi and twenty minutes later were sitting at a table in what appeared to be a nightclub, with coffee and brandies in front of them. The performance was to begin at ten. Jan had heard of fado, but had never actually heard it sung and had little idea what to expect. The word, Eddie explained, meant 'fate' and the songs were almost all about love and passion.

Two guitarists came onto the small stage, one carrying a conventional Spanish guitar, the other with an unusual-looking pear-shaped instrument, which Eddie said must be the *guitarra*, an instrument his guidebook told him was unique to Portugal. A breathless hush fell in the room as the *fadista* strode to centre-stage. She was a woman of about forty, tall and slim with shiny dark hair pulled into a tight and complicated braid at the back of her head. Her mouth was painted a vivid red and her eyebrows were curved and starkly pencilled. A black tasselled shawl covered her shoulders over a tight black dress. Her face was immensely proud, her back straight, her arms bare.

'Jesus, will you look at that?' Eddie murmured in admiration. Some other members of the audience shushed him.

For a moment the singer stood surveying the audience haughtily and then the room was plunged into darkness. Out of the shadows the *guitarra* played a short solo introduction before the other guitar joined in with rippling chords. A spotlight suddenly flashed through the gloom to pick out the dramatic figure of the singer, who breathed in deeply and began to croon. Her voice was vibrant, rich, and produced from deep in the throat, though there was nothing raucous or guttural about it. Pure and full, it swelled and faded and swelled again as the stories of her songs unfolded. Jan had no idea what these were, but she knew they were full of hope and anguish. Under the brilliant light the singer's hands clenched and opened in a convulsive manner, until she reached the final dying note of the song, when they at last came to rest against her skirt.

Like the rest of the audience, Jan listened with intense concentration. It was an extraordinary performance, so draining that the *fadista* sang sets of just three songs before disappearing for a fifteen-minute rest. She came back to sing another set and by the time she approached the end of her last sobbing, heart-rending lament Jan was as exhausted as the *fadista*, but she was also filled with a sense of buzzing exhilaration.

Emerging into the open air, a little drunk from the strong brandy and even stronger music, Jan and Eddie heard the sea breaking against the shore and realized for the first time that the fado house stood close to the beach. Eddie took Jan's hand and led her a short way down a path, until they felt the sand yielding beneath their feet. The sound of the breaking waves was clear, unmuffled by intervening dunes or buildings. Under stars that punctured the deep velvet of the night sky, they crossed to the water's edge. Holding hands, they began to stroll beside the foam.

'Is the tide going out or coming in?' Jan asked.

'Going out, you can tell by the waves. Look, they're getting shorter. By the way, what did you think of the performance?'

'I wanted to cry. I think if I'd known what she was singing about I might have.'

'What *do* you think she was singing about?'

'Oh, I don't know. Things she wanted . . . things she couldn't have, probably.'

They walked on in silence, until Eddie turned quickly to face her.

'Jan, there's something I want. Maybe it's time I found out . . .'

She looked at him. His face was now angled upwards, looking at the stars.

'Found out what, Eddie?'

He stopped and pulled her towards him.

'Found out whether I can have it.'

'Oh? And what is it you want that you can't have?' she asked teasingly.

Gently he lifted her hand, guiding it towards his mouth, briefly putting his lips to the tips of her fingers. At the same time he took her other hand in his, then with his unblinking, crystal-clear eyes locked on hers, he said, 'I want to marry you, Jan Hardy.'

Jan gasped.

The brandy and music, and all the accumulated emotion of the evening, made her momentarily dizzy, her knees felt suddenly weak. But it didn't matter. Eddie was holding her close and, as the tears of joy rolled down her cheeks, she buried her face in his shoulder.

'Hey, come on, it can't be that bad a suggestion.'

Jan stood back from him and looked into his eyes. They were fixed steadily on her face and that steadiness made up her mind.

'Well, I say yes, Edward Sullivan. I say yes, you *can* marry me, if you like.'

He reacted with a blink and his broad mischievous grin as he gathered her close again, swaying her gently from side to side. Even when the sea flowed over their feet they still did not move.

'Eddie?' Jan gasped.

'What?'

'There's one thing you've got completely wrong.'

'That is?'

'The sea.'

'What about the sea?'

'It's not going out, it's coming in.'

2

The aircraft in which they were to fly home was delayed coming in to Faro. Waiting in the departure hall, trying to keep the children amused, Jan noticed Eddie tapping into his bottle of duty-free malt.

'Eddie, is that wise?'

'I'm all right. Except that this bloody waiting's killing me.'

She stroked his hair.

'Please don't get plastered before we get on the flight. Can you keep an eye on the kids for a minute? I'm going to ring Annabel.'

Jan headed for a line of payphones on the wall and dialled the number at Edge Farm.

'Hi, Jan!'

Annabel, her best friend and assistant, sounded jubilant, as if she'd just been laughing.

'Good to hear you're happy,' Jan said. 'But think of us. Flight's delayed. We're going to be at least two hours late.'

'Oh, poor you.'

The commiseration was pure politeness. Whatever was making Annabel so bubbly could not be repressed. 'Anyway it doesn't matter,' she went on. 'We're fine. Take all the time you need.'

'If I had any say in the matter,' said Jan, 'we wouldn't be stuck here, I can tell you – in a crowd of strangers with nothing to do.'

While she talked, Jan was trying to keep an eye on Eddie. He had shoved the whisky bottle back into his flight bag and was heading in the direction of Matty, who had wandered off on his own to the other end of the hall.

'Any news?' she asked Annabel, her glance flicking anxiously between Eddie and Matty.

'Well, Gilly's got a bit of a runny nose. I've had the vet out – he said it's nothing serious. Supercall's not been eating up, but I think he's just being silly, missing you, I expect.'

Jan listened to Annabel's report with half her mind – the rest was on Eddie. She realized that her warning about tapping the whisky had come too late and that he was now a mite unsteady on his feet. To reach Matty he was negotiating his way through a group of hungover young men, who were gloomily drinking cans of beer and eating crisps. Suddenly Eddie lurched sideways, struggling to correct his balance. He trod squarely on the gleaming white trainer of one of the men, a large shaven-headed, prop-forward type who had been studying the sports pages of the *Sun*.

The prop forward's voice carried right across the busy hall as he lifted his head truculently from the paper.

'Oi, prat!'

He rose to his full height, which was at least six inches taller than Eddie, and lifted a rigid finger of warning to within a hair's breadth of Eddie's nose.

At this moment Annabel said in Jan's ear, 'And there's one other bit of news . . .' Annabel's voice had turned coy. 'But I'm not sure how you're going to take this.'

Jan wrenched her attention back to the phone.

'Sounds like something bad. What's happened?'

'Look, don't worry. This is nothing to do with the horses and it's nothing bad. At least, *I* don't think it is . . .'

In the departure hall, Jan saw that Megan had taken a hand. She'd run over to Matty, grabbed him by the wrist and was now leading him back towards their seats. Meanwhile Eddie and the prop forward were eyeball to eyeball. Reassured, at least about the children, Jan turned her back on the distraction to concentrate on Annabel's news.

'So, go on. Tell me.'

'I've broken up with Johnny.'

'*Really*, but I thought you and he . . .'

'Absolutely, but it's history now.'

'My God, when was this?'

'Couple of days ago.'

'So, what happened?'

'Someone else happened.'

'You mean, JCB went off with someone else? The cheating no-good toerag! I'd like to—'

'No, Jan, you wouldn't. It wasn't him. It was me.'

'*You*. You went off? Who with?'

'I don't know if I should tell you, not now . . . maybe I'll wait till you get back.'

'Spit it out, Annabel.'

'Oh, God, all right then. It's Ben.'

'Ben who?'

Annabel giggled.

'Ben your brother, idiot. Ben Pritchard.'

Jan almost dropped the phone.

'Ben? . . . You mean, you and Ben? . . . *Ben* and you?'

'Yes, Jan. Either way round.'

Annabel was laughing, but Jan was gobsmacked, unable to absorb the fact that her best friend had got off with her little brother. She groped for something light-hearted to say.

'Well, congratulations. You couldn't have picked a chap from a better family.'

'I know.'

Jan couldn't think of anything to add, so thought she'd better bring the conversation to a rapid close.

'Del, I can't *wait* to hear all about it, but right now I'd better get back to the others. I think Eddie's starting a fight. See you later on, OK?'

She found her new fiancé back with the children again, crouching to unzip his bag and all smiles. The belligerent young men were cracking open fresh cans of beer and raising them in his direction.

'Eddie, for God's sake, I thought you were going to get your lights and liver punched out,' said Jan in relief.

'Oh no. They're a stag party and I stood on the groom-to-be's foot. But I told him we were both rowing the same boat, as I *too* am a groom-to-be. Then it turned out they're all from the Cotswolds.

So now we're the best of mates. Matter of fact, they're having a drink with me, so I'll see you later.'

❧

It wasn't until they were in the air that Jan thought more deeply about the implications of Annabel's news. After all the whisky, Eddie had fallen asleep as soon as they were seated, while Jan, looking down through the small round window at the Algarve coast, had been trying to spot the beach where he'd proposed to her the night before. But, though she could see the strips of sand that ran along the shore, she couldn't decide on which one it was that the life-changing question had been put to her.

This led her to wonder whether Annabel would eventually marry Ben. Her first thought was that it would be a delightful result. Bel's love life had been fairly fraught in the four years that they'd known each other. So if her adored kid brother married her best-ever friend it looked like the perfect outcome, as long as Ben would be happy to settle back into Cotswolds life, or at least agree to be based there.

And yet undoubtedly there would be problems to overcome. First, Johnny Carlton-Brown's company Brit Records was where Ben worked as a top producer. How would the fact that he had pinched the boss's girlfriend play with the injured party? Second, JCB, as he was universally known, currently had three horses in Jan's yard and had recently been talking about getting a couple more. This would make him her second biggest owner after the Irish plutocrat A.D. O'Hagan. But a major part of JCB's original motivation for owning horses had been that he fancied Annabel. The question was, had he got the racing bug sufficiently in the meantime to maintain his involvement? And would he continue to want Jan Hardy as his trainer? If he moved his horses, the financial implications would be serious. And if JCB took them to Virginia, whom he knew socially . . . well, it didn't bear thinking about.

But as soon as the car drove up the steep approach to Edge Farm and stopped on the forecourt below the house, Jan's reservations melted away. Following in the wake of the frantic welcoming rush of the dogs, Fred, Fly and Tigger, Ben and Annabel came out of the house to greet the returning holidaymakers. They were holding hands.

Jan almost burst into tears, clinging to them both and swaying this way and that.

'You two ... who'd have thought it? It's just too good to be true.'

'Don't get carried away, big Sis,' said Ben. 'It's early days, you know.'

Jan sniffed and, letting him go, hit him playfully on the shoulder.

'Early days, my foot. You've known each other for donkey's years. Long enough to have a perfectly good idea of what you want!'

Eddie hugged Annabel too, then slapped Ben on the back.

'Talk about secretive,' he said. 'How long's this been going on, you crafty devil?'

'No time at all,' said Ben. 'Though not for want of yearning – at least on my part.'

'And on mine, actually,' Annabel admitted as the slight tinge of a blush crept over her perfect cheekbones.

Jan laughed and wagged a finger at both of them in warning.

'You do realize, don't you, that you're facing a lifetime of jokes about Bel and Ben the Flowerpot Men?'

They all laughed, and it felt so much like *their* moment that Jan didn't want to say anything about her engagement to Eddie – not just yet.

As soon as she could, she took Eddie aside and whispered in his ear, 'Don't tell them about us. We'll do it tomorrow, OK? I don't want to spoil their moment.'

❦

The next day was Sunday. Jan, Eddie, Ben and Annabel were sitting over the remains of breakfast after the children had run off outside to track down their ponies. Jan and Eddie had told most of the story of their stay in Bernie Sutcliffe's timeshare during the previous evening, with all the gory details about the Blue Lagoon, now renamed Mozzie Marsh. This morning they added the final flourish to it all: the visit to the fado house and that momentous walk along the beach.

Annabel shrieked when she heard that Eddie had proposed and Jan accepted.

Ben just beamed. 'I was hoping it might work out like this. Top news, you two. Fantastic.'

Annabel wanted all the details of the planned wedding. Jan and Eddie looked at each other. They hadn't even begun to discuss it.

'Oh, don't worry, we'll pull all the stops out,' said Eddie grandly as he plastered marmalade thickly across a slice of toast. 'Gloucester Cathedral, massed choirs, the bishop in his mitre doing the honours.'

Ben laughed. 'And don't tell me: the staff from the yard forming an arch of pitchforks as you come out of the west door.'

'And why not?'

Jan laughed with the others, but she didn't want Eddie to get carried away with his cathedral fantasies.

'It'll be a quiet wedding,' she said firmly. 'Just family and close friends. And definitely no pitchforks.'

🐎

Eddie and Ben planned to spend the day giving the horse transporter an oil change and a service, while Jan was to drive over to her parents' home in Riscombe with Megan and Matty. One reason for this visit was to tell Mary and Reg about her engagement.

The children had taken the news that their mum was getting married to Eddie Sullivan as perfectly natural. Jan marvelled at the way kids of their age were able to take remarriage for granted. It was, she supposed, the great variety of the modern family that was the reason. Many of Megan's and Matty's classmates had divorced parents, not to mention step-fathers, step-mothers, and step-siblings, even some of the five-year-olds in Matty's class had second families. She'd laughed when one day she'd overheard a friend of Megan's talking about her four grandmas. It didn't say much for the current value of the marriage contract, she thought, but at least it made it easier for children to accept substitute parents and she had to admit it was far better than having them live in a war zone.

It was different, rather rarer and maybe more problematic, for children to have a father who'd died as Megan and Matty's had. Matty couldn't remember John at all, while even to Megan her father was little more than a blurred memory. Eddie, on the other hand, had become a familiar figure around the place. True, he'd been crocked up for most of the previous year and hadn't always been easy to live with. But with his regained mobility much of his old humour and breezy self-confidence had come back. He would never *be* John or even an approximation – the two men were as unalike as rubber and rope – but she had begun to believe Eddie could be a good father figure to her children. Jan didn't expect her own father to be very demonstrative when he heard the news and he wasn't. He only smiled and gave his daughter a quiet hug and a kiss on the forehead.

'I'm glad for you, girl. You deserve a good man, and I hope he'll be that for you.'

It was Mary's reaction that surprised her. Jan had expected her mother to be genuinely delighted at the prospect of a wedding, even the kind of low-key affair that Jan had in mind. But Mary seemed oddly quiet and detached. It wasn't as if she was radiating disapproval of Eddie. Jan knew Mary had once expressed doubts about his usefulness, not to mention his staying power, but in spite of this she had always rather liked him. Today her mother's oddly detached mood seemed to be a case of having too many other things on her mind.

'That'll be very nice, dear. Yes. That's wonderful news,' was all Mary said. In reality she sounded about as excited as if news of next year's holiday plans had just been unveiled.

Jan thought her mother was actually more focused on attending to the small needs and comforts of her husband. She noticed in particular Mary's insistence that Reg take an extra helping of roast potatoes at lunch, and the way she rushed off to find his cap as he and Jan were preparing to walk up the field to look at his sheep.

Outside, as Jan unlatched the gate to the field, she broached the topic with Reg.

'Mum seems a little anxious, Dad. She's been all right, has she?'

'Oh yes, she's been healthy enough, you know, since they started her on that new medication.'

'I just thought she seemed a little underwhelmed by the news – about me and Eddie.'

'Well, I think she's pleased enough, girl. But I must admit she's been a bit edgy, like, ever since Colonel Gilbert died and we got that letter from Virginia turfing us out of the house. I expect it's on her mind.'

'But that was all sorted out ages ago. There's no way you two can be evicted. You're protected, the tenancy is cast-iron guaranteed.'

'So I keep telling her. She goes quiet for a bit, then a few weeks later she brings it up again. She doesn't like us paying rent to that woman and she wishes we could move. But when I tell her we've got nowhere else to go, she says Virginia Gilbert's out to do us harm, and we'd be better off anywhere else, even in an old folks' home.'

Jan turned to Reg in astonishment.

'Dad, that's bollocks. She didn't say that! Not Mum. I never thought I'd hear that from her. Dad, tell me it's not true.'

'Mind your language, my girl. Of course it's not that she *wants* to live in a home,' Reg emphasized. 'She just doesn't like the idea of paying money to Virginia. She says I should be looking for somewhere else, but I don't want to, of course, because it'd mean giving up the sheep, see.'

They were climbing the hill now.

'But you've been living in that house for donkey's years,' Jan protested. 'For absolutely always, so it seems. You *can't* move out, you just can't, Dad. Shall I have a word?'

Reg shook his head vigorously.

'No, no, girl. Say nothing, stay out of it. Your mother may be quiet, but she can be mighty stubborn when she's on a campaign. My idea is passive resistance, it usually works.'

He chuckled.

'Like that Gandhi feller.'

They were closing on the small flock of Cotswold sheep, the rare longwool breed that Reg had taken up since his acreage was reduced by the Riscombe estate after his 'retirement'.

'So, here are my beauties. What d'you think?'

Jan loved Reg's sheep, which, with their white faces, hornless heads and thick fleecy fringes falling in ringlets over their eyes, looked disarmingly cute. But 'cute' was not a word Reg recognized. He was a countryman through and through, who saw beauty instinctively in how well an animal's adapted form functioned in its environment.

'Dad, they look magnificent,' she said. 'Well cared for and healthy. As I'm sure they are.'

'Oh, you're not wrong. But it's not difficult, not with them. They're the best type of sheep that I know for the conditions in this part of the world – which is why they were bred here in the first place, probably thousands of years ago. Look after their feet and they'll repay you handsomely. They're fine lambers, give a great big clip and they're tough. God knows how they got so badly managed that they nearly fell extinct thirty years ago. Anyway, with luck, the breed's been saved now. That's the main thing.'

As they walked back down the field, Reg brought up something that would normally be of little interest to a non-specialist: there had been new draft regulations published for farmers on the prevention of scab and blowfly strike in sheep.

'They're talking about lifting the compulsory dipping.' He looked sharply at Jan. 'You know what that means?'

'Yes,' said Jan.

She knew precisely what it meant. She had always believed that her sheep-farmer husband had been killed by regular contact with organophosphates, an essential ingredient of the sheep-dip formulae that had been in mandatory use since the 1970s. Since John's death she had kept up as well as she could with the campaign against their use, much of it waged by women who noticed not only higher rates of cancer but also regular depression and mood changes in their menfolk in the days and weeks after the sheep-dipping was over.

'Does it mean we were right all along? I bet that stuff really is a bloody killer, and I don't just mean the maggots either.'

Reg grunted. 'Well, it certainly looks like it. But I doubt you'll get anyone to admit it.'

Driving back in late afternoon, Jan pictured John in his last days. She knew he had died ashamed of himself for leaving her with two bairns to raise – a choking thought that made tears sting her eyes. Oh God, what would John think now about her marrying Eddie? She would dearly like to know the answer to that.

In the evening Jan decided to bite on the bullet over Johnny Carlton-Brown. When she asked if anything had been said about JCB's horses, Annabel just shrugged. When she had split up with JCB he'd not even mentioned that aspect of the matter.

'And to be honest, Jan, it never occurred to me that we might lose the horses. I was just thinking about him and me and Ben!'

Which is why I'm the trainer and she's the assistant, Jan thought to herself dryly, as she dialled JCB's number.

'Hello, Johnny. It's Jan Hardy.'

'Oh! Hello, Jan. Did you have a good holiday?'

So far, so polite.

'Yes. Wonderful, thank you.' She took a deep breath. 'But I gather there have been some quite big developments in my assistant's personal life while I've been away.'

'Ye-es?'

'Which is why I'm ringing. I'd like to know if these, er, developments affect *your* position in any way. I mean as one of my most valued owners.'

There was an agonizing pause. Jan looked in the mirror which hung on the wall by the phone and realized that she had unconsciously screwed up her face, bracing herself for a blast of fury and contempt down the line. But JCB's drawl remained as cool and level as ever.

'Oh, Jan, I never let personal matters impinge on my business decisions. And I regard my horses as part of the business now. Even if I didn't love them to bits, they are such a good publicity vehicle, especially since Brit Records has started sponsoring one or two big races. I'm stepping that investment up in the coming season, did you know? It's been excellent value, so my marketing people tell me. In fact we must talk about this: if at all possible, I'd like to have runners in our sponsored events.'

Still monitoring her own reactions in the mirror, Jan registered an expression of sheer relief as it slid across her face.

'Oh yes, Johnny, we can talk about it, of course, but I must just say again that any final decision on entries has to remain with me. I know which tracks and races will be most suitable for each individual horse. You can easily wreck them running them out of their depth and no one wants that to happen, do they? That said, I always do my *very* best to accommodate the owners.'

Jan put down the phone and offered up a prayer. Maybe JCB was a cold fish. Maybe he'd never really cared too much about Annabel. Maybe he was more interested in making money than love.

Well, all I can say is thank God for that!

3

It was the middle of August, one of those cloudless mornings when everything in sight seemed to sparkle, including the brass weather-vane swinging this way and that over the arched gateway of the stable yard. Their iron-clad hooves clattering on the tarmac, the horses were returning from second lot following their exercise, with Jan heading the string. The rest of the staff followed in orderly fashion as Eddie bustled out of the office to greet them.

'The feed rep just rang,' he called out.

Since he moved back to Edge Farm in the middle of March, Eddie had been playing an increasing role in the management of the yard. He was still not up to riding, nor was he driving on the public highway – a source of tension because he was always taking Joe Paley away from other duties to chauffeur him. But, as his strength and mobility increased, Eddie had effectively taken control of the yard's vehicles, and he was also doing a great deal to help his friend Gerry with the upkeep on the buildings. He could even on occasion be persuaded to sit down in the office and type letters or an invoice, though office discipline was not exactly his strength.

'Bill Johnson? He's coming tomorrow, right?' said Jan, as she reached for the girth strap and unleashed the saddle.

'No, it definitely wasn't Johnson.'

'Oh?'

'I don't really know who the chap was, he wouldn't say, but he wants to call in later. I told him it was OK.'

'But it's not OK,' Jan countered, her hackles rising slightly. 'Why didn't you look in the diary? I've arranged to go over to Gloucester to see that bloke.'

'What bloke?'

'That artist. Horace what's-his-name.'

'Oh yes. Pursival.'

A.D. O'Hagan had arranged to have Russian Eagle painted, as he did for all his more successful horses. He was assembling a gallery of horse portraits at his magnificent home, Aigmont, in County Wicklow. The chosen artist this time was a distinguished painter who lived in Gloucester – Horace Pursival, RA.

'Yes, Pursival,' Jan went on. 'He wants to look at some photos and videos of Eagle in action.'

'Why doesn't he come here? Then he can see the real thing.'

'Apparently he doesn't drive. Anyway, he's invited me to lunch, and besides that A.D. says he's rather prickly and I've got to keep on the right side of him. Likes to do things his way. Which is all I bloody need, still . . .'

'Look, why not leave it to me?' suggested Eddie, as Jan removed her horse's saddle and vigorously sponged the damp sweaty patch beneath it. 'Joe can drive me to Gloucester. I'll have no problem chatting up Pursival, given that I know a lot about paintings. Whereas I'd be no use at all with the feed rep, since I know sod all about what goes in a manger. You, on the other hand, know all about that.'

'And sod all about art. Is that what you mean?'

Eddie grinned cheekily. 'You said it.'

In reality, Jan was relieved. She had been dreading the lunch.

'OK, I'll ring him and say something's cropped up, so I'm sending you instead. If he doesn't like it he'll just have to lump it.'

❧

The feed rep appeared just before twelve. A fresh-faced, well-turned-out young man, he wore a waxed Barbour jacket but didn't look as if he knew much about horses. He introduced himself as Nick Barlow.

'What happened to Bill?' asked Jan.

'He left. I've taken over his area.'

'Left? Just like that?'

'Apparently he's gone off to New Zealand with a girl.'

'*Bill?* But I thought he was married with a bunch of teenage kids.'

'Well, that's what they're saying back at the plant.'

'Fancy old Bill philandering off to New Zealand. How amazing, he seemed so reliable and, well, *normal*, I suppose. Anyway, there's no time to dwell on your predecessor's kinky little ways. How long have you been in the business?'

Nick Barlow coloured slightly.

'Um, this is my first job, actually.'

'I see. So, tell me, what do you know about feeding racehorses?'

'Well, I've got a BSc in veterinary nutrition.'

Jan smiled.

'Not much then,' she teased.

Nick Barlow reddened further and Jan relented.

'I'm sorry, that's a bit unfair. You probably know a lot of theory. But, to me, the practicalities are even more important. Come and see our feed room.'

Jan led him across the yard and threw open the door of the store. Inside were orderly stacked bags and galvanized bins full of equine feed.

'It's vitally important to me to know everything that goes into my horses,' Jan explained. 'And I mean *everything*. The Jockey Club regulations are tough and they're getting tougher, so it's a question of absolute liability: did you know that if someone slips a horse half a Mars bar four hours before a race the caffeine in the bar could be picked up in the dope test? That means the horse is disqualified. And, if it happens to be one of ours, I'm fined as well. It's already happened to a number of other trainers.'

The rep smiled reassuringly.

'Well, I can assure you, Mrs Hardy, our quality control's very good.'

'It'd better be. Because we keep a record, a test sample, of every bag of feed we open, we keep track of every mouthful of food consumed by our horses, and we know precisely which batch of feed it came from. So, for instance, if there's anything that shouldn't be in a racecourse sample, or if there's any other problem with the horse, I can go back to the samples and have them tested. You needn't look so scared. I'm not going to feed *you* to my horses.'

For the first time she noticed that the light in the room had darkened and glanced towards the door. It was blocked by the bulky silhouette of a man wearing sunglasses, a tasselled suede jacket and a check shirt, whose open collar revealed an array of glinting gold neckwear.

'Oh, I didn't see you there!' Jan exclaimed. 'Can I help?'

'Excuse me, ma'am. Sorry to interrupt,' the man said in an American accent. As he smiled, she noted his perfectly white, orthodontically even teeth. 'May I speak with you?'

Jan touched Nick Barlow's arm to indicate he follow her, then crossed to the door. This new visitor was a complete stranger. How long had he been there? she wondered.

'That'll be fine,' she said, 'if you can give me another ten minutes. But would you mind waiting outside in the yard while I finish up here?'

'Gladly, ma'am. My vehicle is parked on your driveway. I'll be right there.'

The outsized American retreated towards the arch, using that bouncing tread peculiar to vast men with big paunches. His straight black hair was streaked with grey and worn in a long ponytail that reached down as far as the small of his back. A slim woman in her twenties – probably half his age – was hovering under the arch, waiting for him.

Jan took the feed rep back to the office, where he ceremoniously opened a presentation folder and cleared his throat. She listened as patiently as she could while he turned the laminated pages and trotted out his well-rehearsed sales rhetoric on a range of new products. Then, completely ignoring what he'd said, Jan opened the filing cabinet where she kept all the records of feed orders made in the current season and adjusted the order for the month to come. She then slipped the file back into the drawer and slammed it shut. Meanwhile Nick Barlow, with a small sigh, filled in on a form all the details she had given him, before handing it to her to sign on the dotted line.

Then Jan opened the filing cabinet again, took out another piece of paper and laid it in front of the wilting rep.

'It's a letter of indemnity. It means that you guarantee to repay to me any prize money that I may lose as a result of your feed being contaminated.'

She pointed to the bottom of the paper. 'You need to sign here.'

Nick Barlow suddenly looked ashen and taken aback.

'Er, is this normal practice, Mrs Hardy?' he asked nervously.

'It is with me. Ask Bill Johnson – oh, silly me, I forgot he's done a flit. Anyway he signed.'

Jan showed him an identical letter from the file signed by Barlow's predecessor. After he'd seen it, the new rep took out a pen.

'Good, that's it for now, young Nick,' Jan said briskly. 'We'll see you next month. In the meantime I'd better find out what Sonny and Cher want. Bye for now. Take care of yourself. You look a bit peeky.'

'My name's Bobby Montana, ma'am, and I have a coupla horses. I'd be obliged if you'd take care of them.'

Even allowing for the considerable presence imparted by his size alone – he stood at least six-five – Bobby Montana was an impressive-looking figure. Though his complexion was sallow, his eyes, on either side of a prominent nose, were the most intense green Jan had ever known. And he kept those eyes locked on hers all the time they were talking. Though the bentwood office chair he sat on appeared much too small for his massive frame, he occupied it with perfect ease and comfort.

'Where are the horses now, Mr Montana?'

'Over in the States momentarily.'

He extended his hand to his companion, who was seated beside him and whom he had neither named nor introduced. She lifted an attaché case from the floor, placed it on her knees and, snapping open the lid, produced two sheets of paper with printed notes about the horses, each with a colour snapshot stapled to it. With a flourish Montana laid these on the desk in front of Jan. Looking at the pictures and the printed details, she saw they were both three-year-old colts, and looked rather scrawny without being completely unpresentable.

'As soon as I have gotten the right place for them over here,' he explained, 'I'll be bringing them across.'

'Have they been racing in the United States?'

'They sure have. Fairmount Park, Illinois.'

'Flat, of course?'

'Yeah, on the dirt.'

'What sort of form have they got?'

He shrugged.

'Not so good, I'm afraid. We figure they need a change of scene. See, I'm a Native American, Mrs Hardy. Cherokee. We know horses. These horses got great chances, great potential – you can count on that.'

'And you want to race them over jumps here?'

'I guess so.'

'Because that's what I do, Mr Montana. If you wanted to race these on the flat in England, you'd need to find a specialist trainer.'

'Right.'

Montana still maintained the fixed eye-contact, suggestive of intense interest in the conversation. But Jan sensed he was more than a little evasive regarding arrangements for his horses in England. She went on. 'Looking at the size of these horses, they would probably only make hurdlers. They are three-year-olds right now, this says.'

'Right.'

'That means they are too young to be steeplechasers anyway.'

'OK, I can dig that.'

Jan paused for a moment.

'Can I ask how you heard of me? Out of all the trainers you could have approached, why me?'

'I've seen your name in the newspaper sports pages, ma'am. That's how I picked you out.'

This was proving more difficult than Jan had anticipated. She'd been expecting Montana to say he'd had a personal recommendation, in which case she could use it to check up on him. As things stood, he could be anything, anybody. How could she tell, for instance, if he'd ever pay any training fees?

'Could you give me the name of the trainer in Illinois?' she asked. 'So I can get more information about your horses.'

'Sure. It's a Canadian guy named Mervyn Sawyer. Genius trainer.'

Jan jotted down the details. She could always phone up this Sawyer man, but right now she had a gut feeling that was still dubious. She certainly didn't want Edge Farm to take on horses without being sure their training fees would be paid.

'Mr Montana,' she began, 'I'm really flattered you thought of me, but at the moment I haven't room for two more horses.'

It was a fib, but she had to make a snap decision about Montana's request. It was intriguing, she had to admit, but she couldn't afford to take the risk. From his clothes, Montana didn't look a particularly wealthy man, though she knew they would not be much of a guide if he was some kind of rock star or eccentric billionaire. For all she knew he could be nothing but a professional chancer and there were always plenty of them around.

'This is a small yard,' Jan went on, 'and the staff can only cope with a limited number of horses.'

Still with his eyes fixed on her face, Montana gave a flicker of a smile and cocked his thumb over his shoulder.

'But I saw plenty of empty stalls out there, ma'am. I guess you're worried about my credit score, right? It should be good, as a matter of fact, but you don't need to concern yourself about that anyways.'

He turned again to the girl and took the attaché case from her. Placing it on the desk, he opened the lid and swivelled the case so that Jan could see its contents. He then flipped up a partition to reveal what was in the bottom. Jan could hardly suppress a gasp. It was packed with bundles of fifty-pound notes. Montana took out two of the bundles and dropped them in front of her.

'I like to pay my dues, cash in advance. Will ten grand in English bills cover it for now?'

Jan picked up the wad of money, which was secured by a paper band, and flicked through it with her thumb. The notes were all fifties.

'Yes, yes, of course,' she stammered. 'I suppose I can't argue with that.'

So it was that Jan agreed to take Bobby Montana's American-bred three-year-olds, which he told her were called Big Freeze and Spring Blow. She emphasized that it would be for an initial trial period, but if they proved themselves on the gallops she would do her best to win some races for him. Montana flashed his frost-white teeth at her and said he would arrange for their transport tomorrow. They would be at Edge Farm within the week.

As they walked out to Montana's car, Jan noticed a Hertz sticker on the back window as she handed her new owner a business card.

'Phone me when you know which day they'll be arriving and I'll have their boxes ready in our isolation block.'

Bobby Montana fished out a card of his own and presented it. Beaming, he took Jan's hand in his enormous paw. 'I thank you again, ma'am. Pleased to do business with you.'

As they drove away Jan glanced at the business card. The address given was Claridge's Hotel, Brook Street, Mayfair.

🐎

'Well, the spondulicks appear genuine,' said Eddie three hours later, holding one of Bobby Montana's fifty-pound notes up to the light and squinting at it. 'I wonder where he got these from.'

Ben and Annabel were with them in the office, and had listened intently as Jan related the curious events of earlier that day.

'Crikey, I can't wait to meet this guy,' Eddie went on. 'I've never met a Cherokee Indian before.'

'Native American,' Jan corrected. 'Not surprisingly I've been wondering about the money too, especially as I saw the rest of it. There were eighteen stacks in that briefcase and I reckon there was another layer underneath. So he's probably still carrying a hundred and ninety thousand quid around with him in cash, can you believe.'

Ben whistled. 'Lucky bastard.'

'The thing is, who do you think he is?' asked Annabel. 'Some rich businessman?'

Jan shrugged. 'He wasn't dressed like the usual article.'

'How about a rich Mafioso?' asked Ben.

'No, he was more like an old-fashioned rock star. Is there one called Bobby Montana?'

Ben shook his head. 'Not that I've heard, but he sounds like a pretty flamboyant character. If he was from the music business, I'd know if he had been successful. What did it say on his card?'

'Nothing much – just his name and address, which is only Claridge's Hotel, by the way. But at the same time he's driving a medium-range hire car. It's all a bit weird, don't you think?'

'No, it's not. It's great,' said Eddie. 'We just shove this lot in the safe and say nothing and, Bob Montana's your uncle, we've got a tax-free stash of money.'

'Don't go there, Eddie. This little lot's going into the bank first thing tomorrow morning, I can assure you of that.'

Jan picked up the wad of notes with the information sheets about the horses that Montana had given her and handed the latter to Annabel.

'He gave me this info on the two horses. They've got crap form, by the way, and they don't look too special, so I haven't got my hopes up high.'

'But, you can't tell from a photograph,' corrected Annabel, glancing through the sheets, which listed the sire and dam lines, birth places and dates, and other details, including descriptions of the two horses' unpromising runs at the Fairmount Park race track.

'I suppose you're right,' Jan conceded. 'Anyhow the breeding appears to be OK, not that I know too much about American bloodlines. So we'll just have to see. Let's hope we're in for a surprise. By the way, how'd you get on with that artist, Eddie?'

Eddie's face lit up.

'Pursival? He's an absolute hoot. Wears a panama hat, silk cravat, linen suit and totters around in matching shoes. He says he was a pal of Munnings, which I don't disbelieve. I reckon he's probably about ninety years old, but after his sixth gin he was back behind the barricades refighting the war against modern art.'

'So what's he want to do about painting Eagle?' asked Annabel, who as A.D.'s co-owner had been taking a special interest in the portrait of the eleven-year-old chaser.

'I showed him the videos after lunch, but he was hardly able to keep his eyes open by then. Anyway, he assured me before I left that Eagle was a damn fine animal and he hoped to do him justice when he comes over to make the sketches.'

'But when's that?' Bel persisted. 'I'd really like to be here when he comes.'

'He said he'll telephone when he's ready. You could go and pick him up, if you like.'

'Good idea. You can work your charm on the old boy and maybe he'll give you his sketches when he's finished with them.' Jan drained her tea mug. 'Right, back to work, you lot. Will you pick out a couple of boxes for the new horses, Bel? Eddie, you can give them a good clean-out and disinfect them tomorrow. They could be arriving here by the end of the week.'

'For a small fee,' said Eddie, folding and refolding the note that he had so carefully inspected earlier, then slipping it into his shirt pocket. 'This'll do nicely.'

'OK, Eddie, but don't spend it all at once.'

'Are you going to contact the trainer in Illinois?' asked Annabel. Jan sighed.

'I suppose so. At least, I can try.'

But, regrettably, it was a long time before she did.

The next morning the bank in Broadway was busy and, with only two tellers at work behind the counter, Jan had to wait almost ten minutes before she was able to pay Bobby Montana's money into the Edge Farm account. When she was finally standing at the window, with her back to the lengthening queue, she heard two customers in conversation as they, too, stood waiting their turn. Their voices were familiar.

'Hello, Rosemary,' said Virginia Gilbert. 'Lovely day again. Come in by bus, did you?'

'It's a minibus, actually. Driven by the vicar.'

'Good heavens! Driven by the vicar? You'd think he'd have better things to do with his time. What on earth happened to the real buses? There used to be – what? – three or four a day?'

'They stopped running fifteen years ago, Miss Gilbert. Now all we've got is the vicar's twice-weekly.'

The second voice Jan recognized as the elderly one of Rosemary Sterry, who lived in a small cottage on the Riscombe estate and was another of the Gilberts' tenants, like Jan's parents. Rosemary was, in fact, one of Mary Pritchard's oldest friends. The two of them had grown up together in the village and, when they were younger, had both worked at the Manor.

Jan was about to turn around and greet Rosemary when the bank teller leant across the counter and said in a low voice, 'I make it nine thousand, nine hundred and fifty pounds. But I'd better check it again, in case I missed one.'

Jan nodded and became absorbed in watching the teller's finger, with its rubber stall, riffling through the notes with bewildering speed, from time to time laying aside the next bundle of a thousand pounds.

'It's all so changed now, isn't it?' Virginia remarked, in her best through-the-nose manner. 'It must be *so* difficult for you all.'

This was not a real concern to Virgina, of course. The fact that she didn't know or even care about the effect the demise of rural bus services had had on the community was proof enough of this. But she liked to patronize her tenants by appearing to share their burdens, laughable as the idea was.

'We manage,' said Rosemary, sounding rather irritated by her landlady's grand manner.

'It was so much better in the old days,' Virginia went on regardless, as the bank teller began on his seventh thousand-pound bundle. 'You know, I shall always remember when I was a little girl. Every summer was just glorious. I spent all my time out of doors and there was nothing but dances and tennis for the grown-ups, and then the shooting parties in the autumn. It was heaven. You must remember, Rosemary, how it was when you used to skivvy for us up at the Manor.'

'You forget, Miss Gilbert,' Rosemary muttered darkly, 'it weren't so nice for some. Leastways, not when Mr Hugo was around.'

There was a momentary pause. Jan felt Virginia stiffen.

'Really, I don't know what you mean, Rosemary.'

Jan's teller had reached the end of her count at last. Neither Virginia nor Rosemary Sterry had noticed her standing at the counter and she hurried out of the bank without revealing herself.

4

Four days later Bobby Montana phoned to say they should expect his horses within forty-eight hours.

'We're looking forward to seeing them,' Jan told him. 'By the way, do you want us to organize insurance? We normally suggest "all risk mortality". The alternative is "loss of use", which is prohibitive. The insurers nearly always argue and never seem to settle on a worthwhile amount. The first cover will at least pay out if, unfortunately, a horse dies for any reason.'

'No need. That's all taken care of, ma'am. I fixed my own insurance in the States. I can assure you those valuable horses are covered every which way.'

Jan told him she would send him her standard letter to confirm their agreement and that two adjoining boxes had been set aside and made ready for the new arrivals. It wasn't strictly true. Annabel had allocated the boxes all right, but, as far as Jan knew, Eddie still hadn't finished cleaning them out.

As soon as Jan rang off, she decided to check and walked out into the yard, where everyone was busy mucking out boxes or grooming their occupants. Jan paused to look at Blue Boar, who was due to run in the evening at Worcester and was having his mane plaited by his devoted lass, Emma.

'Everything OK?' Jan asked.

'He's as good as gold,' said Emma. 'And he's going to win!'

'The bookies don't agree.' Jan chuckled. 'He was twelve to one in the paper this morning. But we've got to keep the faith, Emma. If *we* don't, who will?'

She moved on. A few boxes further along the row she found young Patsy Keating with his particular charge, the temperamental novice, Morning Glory. The horse had recently bruised a foot and had been on light work for the last three days.

'How is he?' Jan asked. 'What's he telling you, Patsy? Does he want to stay on the easy, or shall we have him on the gallops tomorrow and do a bit extra?'

It was a byword in the yard that Patsy's rapport with the horse was so close that the two of them would sit around for hours discussing the meaning of life together.

'Ah, he's not so bad today. The foot's not bothering him the way it did, y'know, but I think we should be steady away for a bit longer, Mrs H.'

Jan found Eddie sitting in one of the two unoccupied boxes earmarked for the new arrivals reading a racing paper. Strewn around him were a bucket, a yard broom, several old dandy brushes and a spray gun hooked up to a container of disinfectant.

'Hi, Jan,' he said cheerily. 'There's an article here which you might enjoy. It's speculating about whether Virginia's going to have to slim down her personal string of horses to pay death duties on her father's estate.'

Jan glanced over his shoulder at the piece. 'Well, she's not got many valuable animals, though I suppose she'd get a good price for Velvet Dynasty. And I can think of one or two ambitious men who'd shell out plenty of ackers to own him.'

'Including A.D.?'

The nip-and-tuck rivalry between the two novice hurdlers, A.D. O'Hagan's Morning Glory, trained by Jan, and Virginia Gilbert's Velvet Dynasty, former inmate of Edge Farm, had been one of the hottest talking points of the previous racing season.

'Yes, as a matter of fact, I'm pretty sure he'd be interested, and if he is . . .'

'We'd get him back?'

Jan shrugged. 'Who knows? But we can live in hope. Now for God's sake, Eddie, get a move on. I've had Bobby Montana on the phone. His horses could be here within forty-eight hours. So get these boxes sorted, toute suite.'

Eddie gestured towards the disinfecting equipment. 'I was waiting for Gerry. He knows how to use this spray.'

Jan sighed.

'Well, I'm sure it's not rocket science and there's a hell of a lot to do before that. It's called old-fashioned scrubbing.' She pointed upwards. 'Every surface, including the ceiling.'

Eddie jumped to his feet and tugged his forelock. 'Yes, Mrs Hardy, ma'am! Scrubbing commences right away!'

But the scrubbing was destined to be put on hold yet again, as Annabel's voice was heard calling across the yard from the office.

'Eddie! Telephone. It's from Australia.'

Leaving Eddie to talk in private, presumably to his parents in Queensland, Jan and Annabel strolled out towards the paddocks. The last of the horses that had been turned out for their holiday earlier in the summer were waiting to come back in to begin the process of getting their rotund bodies fit. One was Johnny Carlton-Brown's Supercall. The two women leant on the gate and watched the nine-year-old cropping the grass.

'Were you surprised,' Jan asked, 'that Johnny didn't take his horses away? I thought he'd never want to have dealings with Edge Farm again.'

Annabel sighed.

'Yes, I did think it was rather odd. And it's a bit, well, *galling*, really. The fact that he's still with us proves he didn't really care too much about me in the first place, I suppose.'

'I'm sure he did at the time.'

'At first it felt like a great relationship. There wasn't any tension between us, no rows, or anything like that—'

'Maybe that's the point, Bel. No tension. No rows. A man like that isn't really on the hook until the bells are ringing.'

Annabel laughed as a light gust of wind caught her hair and blew it across her face.

'I have a sneaking suspicion you're right. He wasn't really smitten, though I couldn't see it at the time. For me it was pretty exciting – the helicopters, the villa in Barbados. But now it seems he was just stringing me along.'

'Bel, there's no "seems" about it. When Ben came along and you two fell for each other, JCB gave up too easily.'

Annabel laughed ruefully.

'I like to think he was hurt, if only because of his pride. But I hear he's moved on pretty smoothly to a new girlfriend now.'

'Oh? Who's that?'

'Some catwalk model of twenty-three.'

Jan placed a hand gently on her friend's shoulder.

'Well, you're better off without him now, don't you think? And, what's more, the good news is we haven't lost any horses from the yard. To be perfectly frank, I was just a *tiny* bit worried about the financial cost.'

The two women strolled back, discussing the timetable for bringing Supercall and the others back into training. But, as they approached the arched gateway to the yard, their conference was interrupted by Eddie heading towards them.

'Guess what? And it's a hell of a guess,' he said, his eyes shining. 'My parents are coming back from Oz.'

'You mean for the wedding?' Jan asked.

'No, no. They're coming next week *and* they're coming to stay, if that's all right. I've already told them it is.'

❧

On the following Monday a transporter containing Bobby Montana's two imports from America rolled up to the yard. Jan and her staff watched, scrutinizing every move as the horses came down the ramp. The first, Spring Blow, a dark bay colt with a broad blaze and three white socks, descended quietly. He was a small, narrow-framed individual, with a gooselike backside and a placid expression in his eyes. Jan was not impressed. His travelling companion, Big Freeze, was another colt, this time a grey. Jan noticed immediately how he gingerly picked his way towards the ground.

'Give that horse a turn over there,' she instructed Patsy, who had Big Freeze's rein. Patsy led him in a wide arc around the forecourt and Jan immediately saw the problem.

'Look at that,' she said, pointing. 'He's as lame as a cat.'

They could all see that the horse was hobbling on his off-fore.

'Perhaps he got a knock on the way over,' suggested Roz Stoddard, one of Jan's longest-standing members of staff.

'Perhaps,' said Jan sceptically. 'Let's hope so. If it's something more long-term, I'd say Mr Bobby Montana has some explaining to do. And just take a look at the bay. I was given to expect a budding superstar, but he's got an action like a crab. If the other one's crippled as well, I'd say we've probably got a couple of real duds on our hands. Bel, get the Polaroid. I think we'd better photograph these before the shit hits the fan.'

Eddie had been unusually flushed and excited at the news of his parents' return from their self-imposed exile down under, an enthusiasm Jan found slightly over-the-top for a man of thirty. He was, she thought, like a boy who'd been told he'd been given an extra birthday this year and his mood had intensified by the following week, when they drove down to meet Ron and Sue Sullivan at Heathrow airport.

'Eddie,' said Jan, with a mixture of amusement and mild irritation at his irrepressible exuberance, 'you're like a kid on the way to the circus.'

Eddie laughed. 'I know, I know. This is only my old folks we're meeting. I've known them all my life. No real cause for undue drama.'

'But you *are* excited!'

'It's true. I'm a bit surprised about it myself.'

'But what's it all about?'

'My dad, I guess. I haven't seen him for over a year and a half, you know. I can't wait.'

'You haven't seen Sue for more than a year either.'

'I know. And I love her to bits, of course I do. But Ron's different.'

'Different? You can say that again.'

'Jan, you just don't understand. He's my main man, you know? He's a one-off. The cockney expression "diamond geezer" could have been invented for Ron. He sparkles and he's worth his weight in gold, but underneath he's as hard as granite. He's always been my hero, always will be. Of course he'd be my role model too, if I could ever get anywhere near being like him.' Eddie sighed. 'But I can't. It's hopeless, especially since the accident.'

Jan knew that the Sullivans had once been wealthy on the strength of Ron's 1970s property empire, but about four or five years back the business had fallen into dire straits. To get himself out of trouble Ron had taken on a huge and seemingly unpayable debt, at an astronomical interest rate, to some highly disreputable contacts in the East End of London. They were, by all accounts, men who would stop at nothing to enforce their will and, when it became clear that the borrowed money had gone the same way as his original fortune, Ron and Sue had fled to Australia, disappearing into the backwoods of Queensland to escape the attentions of the gangsters. What Jan wanted to know was how things had changed to enable Ron to return safely to the UK now. Eddie either hadn't been told the answer or he wasn't letting on.

The flight touched down on schedule and Ron and Sue came into the arrivals hall looking jet-lagged through their Antipodean tans, yet smiling broadly. As soon as Eddie caught sight of them wheeling their luggage, he ducked under the barrier and strode forward to give his father an extravagant bear hug, followed by another, gentler embrace for his mother.

'Well, well, Ed, my boy.' Ron beamed. 'You're a bleeding marvel. No crutches, no stick, hardly a limp. When your mother left you last year, you was a complete wreck.'

'Well, it's all down to hard work, Dad. Physiotherapy and gallons of honest sweat.'

Ron slapped him on the back and then folded Jan into his arms, kissing her on the cheek.

'It's the love of a beautiful woman, son, that's what's done it,' he boomed. 'There's no medical treatment to touch that.'

🐎

For the drive back to the Cotswolds, Sue took the front passenger seat next to Jan, while Eddie and his father talked, seemingly without drawing breath, in the back. At first Sue said little, listening to the men's ebullient conversation and smiling from time to time at Jan. Only once did a shadow fall across Sue's face when Ron alluded to his financial situation.

'Of course I probably shouldn't have come back. But the only place I'm ever going to get straight with these villains is over here. I can't do it in Australia, that's for sure. There's a particularly nasty bloke called Max Barrington. If he finds me, he will definitely have my guts for garters, unless I can straighten him out first.'

'How are you going to straighten him out, Dad? I thought the only way to do that was to come up with the cash.'

'Not necessarily, son. Of course, he stupidly thinks what's owing has to be paid either in money or in blood.'

Jan glanced at Sue, who was now listening to Ron with her eyes shut and mouth set tensely. Jan wondered if this return to England had her wholehearted support.

'But I think I've got a third way, right?' Ron went on. 'I reckon there may be a way of settling this debt without me being taken away in a wooden box.'

'How then?'

'No, no.' Ron laughed. 'I'm keeping shtum about that for the time being. There's people I got to see, *arrangements* to make. Now why don't you tell me about yourself? Are you really going to get back into the antique pictures game, or what?'

Sue opened her eyes and turned to Jan. 'And how's everything at Edge?' she asked with forced brightness, as the men began to discuss the pros and cons of Eddie resuming his old career as a picture dealer. 'I was so happy to read that that disgusting man Harold Powell had got his just desserts.'

The Sullivans stayed just two nights at Edge Farm and then departed for Cornwall, where Sue's sister lived in St Austell. After that the weekly routine at Edge continued as usual, including one or two racing days, a frequency that would gradually increase as the season progressed, until they would be sending out horses to three or four meetings a week all around the country.

Two weeks later Jan had a call from Bernie Sutcliffe, who had not been in touch since she had sent him a cheque to cover the rental of the apartment at Villa Lagoa Azul.

'I got the cheque, thanks. I've just got back from the Algarve myself. Jim and Eileen send their best. And another thing – a little birdie tells me you and Eddie decided to get hitched while you were out there.'

'Well, yes, we did as a matter of fact. How did you—'

'I told you it was a romantic spot. You got a date for the ceremony?'

'No, not yet, Bernie.'

'You'll be wanting professional advice, anyway. I can help. I got a friend who's a genius at that sort of thing. Knows as much about planning weddings as I know about scrap metal, and that's a lot. I'll fix up a consultation for you.'

'Bernie, it's very kind of you to offer, but I don't think it's really appropriate in our case.'

'No, no, it'd be my pleasure. Absolutely. Look, Jan, the other phone's screaming at me, so I got to go. Bye-bye for now.'

The same morning a call came from Horace Pursival, saying he wanted to visit Edge to do the sketches of Russian Eagle for A.D.'s picture. Jan sent Joe Paley to Gloucester in the Shogun to collect him.

Pursival was a scrawny, unkempt old man with a piercingly high-pitched voice. His hair was yellowy-white and his nose and cheeks were a roadmap of purple veins. When he walked, he seemed to stagger every few steps, as if he was about to crash down sideways, but he always righted himself in time. He carried with him a flat wooden case, which apparently contained the tools of his trade.

'I shall have a look around, if I may,' he said, after insisting Jan give him a couple of stiff gins in the sitting room. 'I believe it's referred to as "scouting for locations" in the film business. I propose a classic portrait of the horse in profile with a groom at the head holding the, er, what d'you call it?'

'The lead rein?'

'Quite so. It's the classic pose, goes all the way back to the great horse painters of the eighteenth century, you know. But you still can't beat it.'

They made their way down into the yard and Jan took Pursival across to meet his subject. Joe brought Eagle out from his box and walked him up and down for the artist's appraisal, but the great academician seemed more interested in the passing stable girls than the horse in front of him.

'I've been wondering who we should have posing with the horse,' he announced after a few minutes' observation.

'What about Joe?' said Jan. 'He's his lad. He looks after Eagle day to day.'

Pursival sidled over to Jan, shaking his head with a disapproving expression.

'Oh, no, no. I don't think so at all. I require a more *decorative* figure, you know. Possibly one of the female spirits of the place . . . you yourself, perhaps?'

Jan gasped and quickly nipped this suggestion in the bud.

'Good God, no. I'm afraid I'm far too busy for anything like that.'

At that moment Annabel emerged from the office and Jan called her over.

'Annabel, you must meet Mr Pursival. He's come to paint your darling Eagle.'

As soon as he saw Annabel, the artist's mouth opened and his eyes widened. He extended a mottled claw, which Annabel shook cautiously.

'This is Annabel Halstead,' Jan continued. 'Annabel is my assistant. She's also Russian Eagle's part-owner: she and Mr O'Hagan have a half-share each.'

'Well, well, the part-owner, eh. Couldn't be better.'

5

In September life in the countryside changed gear. The harvest was cut and the rooks flapped down in untidy squadrons from the rookeries to clean up the spilt corn. Church congregations heaped up their offerings of cabbages, marrows and tomatoes, mixed with root crops, baskets of fresh-picked field mushrooms, plums and apples, jars of honey, homemade pickles and jams, all laid out like a patchwork quilt. In time the villagers would be gathering in church to belt out 'We plough the fields and scatter' and the other age-old harvest hymns. Meanwhile, in the woods and hedgerows, sloes and blackberries ripened, and the leaves and bracken grew stiff, their greens fading to yellow as the chlorophyll bled away. The buck deer in the parks and woodland prepared for the rut by roaring at each other under the trees, and the first of the migrant birds assembled ready to fly to their winter quarters in the south.

Scattered through the west of England, a generation of autumn calves was being born, while in studs and farms the last of the season's foals were weaning. Guns were unlocked from their cupboards to shoot duck and partridge. Beagle packs, rather fat from their summer break, emerged to be conditioned in a succession of sharp early-morning meets. Foxhunts, too, opened their autumn season. And, on Jan's gallops, the vapour from the horses' nostrils, and the steam from their flanks, plumed that much more thickly into the fresher air of September's dawn.

The National Hunt season was well under way now. With half her string of horses already fit, Jan sent out runners to meetings stretching from Newton Abbot in Devon to Cartmel in Cumbria. These were routine belt-and-braces events, where she could pick up rewards for her less-talented runners while holding the stable stars in readiness for the bigger prizes to come in late autumn and early winter.

The two new horses belonging to Bobby Montana were far from ready to go into training, for neither had settled down to life at Edge Farm Stables. Spring Blow was listless and had little appetite, but Jan hoped that with a few tempting morsels in his feed and a bit of TLC he would adapt to his new surroundings: after all, she thought, he was an immigrant from another continent and would need to get to know our ways. Big Freeze was more worrying. A fortnight after his arrival he was still lame and Jan's vet Shirley McGregor, making a third visit to look at his legs and feet, was plainly unhappy.

'As you say, he's still walking rather gingerly,' she told Jan. 'At first I thought it was the shoulder, but now I'm not so sure.'

'We thought he might have had a knock on his way across the pond, as no one said anything about it prior to his arrival. But there's been no heat in his legs to suggest that.'

Shirley shook her head with a sigh.

'No. If it was that, something would have developed by now. I'm afraid we're going to have to consider the possibility it's more serious.'

Jan looked at her. 'Like what?'

Her mind was racing through an inventory of possibilities. Of these, Shirley chose to mention one that all horse handlers hold in special dread.

'I think it may be navicular disease.'

Jan groaned. She well knew how disastrous this foot condition could be.

'Oh God, Shirley. Don't say that!'

'I'll X-ray both front feet and do some other tests. Let's hope it's not.'

The vet hurried off to set up her portable machine, while Jan went to find Annabel, who was in the feed store taking samples from the latest delivery by Nick Barlow's company.

Jan gave her the bad news. 'Shirley thinks Big Freeze might have navicular.'

'Oh, no! Poor old fellow, how absolutely horrible.'

'The thing is, if he has, it must have been there before he left America. I mean, he was walking on eggshells when he came down that transporter's ramp.'

'Has Montana said anything?'

'Not a bloody word.'

'Perhaps his American trainer never told him. It does happen, you know.'

Jan nodded. 'Possibly, but I'm wondering if he even knew. If they'd been running the horse on bute, it's possible no one realized anything was wrong. The condition would only show when they stopped giving him the bloody stuff – in other words not until they walked him into the transporter to send him here.'

Phenylbutazone, a strong anti-inflammatory painkiller, is banned in Britain, but is given long term, and legally, to racehorses in some parts of the world, including the United States. Jan hated the very thought of it. The use of bute, she thought, was a cruel abuse of horses because it masked underlying veterinary conditions to enable horses to continue racing. Worst of all, they would then go to stud, where the degenerative condition could be passed down the line to their offspring.

'What are you going to do?'

'I'm going to help Shirley and when she's finished I'm phoning Montana. I want to have this out with him.'

❦

Shirley McGregor left, promising to call the next day when she'd looked at the X-rays. Jan dialled the mobile phone number on Bobby Montana's business card, but there was no answer. She left a message for Montana to call her back urgently, but there had been no return call before dark.

Then later that evening, after dinner, just as Jan finished loading the dishwasher, the phone rang. She was disappointed not to hear the Yank's dulcet tones.

'Jan? It's Sue Sullivan. Is my Ron with you?' She sounded anxious, and rather flustered.

'Ron? No, Sue, he's not. I didn't know we were expecting him.' Jan said, feeling uneasy.

She pressed the button which set the dishwasher churning and took the phone through to Eddie, who was slumped in front of the TV watching his favourite programme, *Men Behaving Badly*. Very apt, Jan thought.

'You weren't,' Sue was saying. 'Not as far as I know. But he's gone off somewhere. I haven't seen him all day. You don't know if Eddie's spoken to him, do you?'

'You can ask him yourself, Sue. He's here.' Jan passed the receiver to Eddie. 'Your mum says she can't find your dad – you'd better have a word. I'm going down to check the horses. I'll be back in a minute.'

On her way down to the yard Jan could hear the wind on top of the ridge bending the pines, which creaked as they swayed. An owl hooted somewhere in the valley below. The horses were for the most part quiet, but when she looked in on Big Freeze he was shifting his legs restlessly, rocking from one side to the other. She checked his manger to see if he had eaten up. He pushed his nose into the cup of her hand after disconsolately chewing the carrot she'd given him.

'You poor old soul,' she said, rubbing his muzzle. 'That little bit you've eaten wouldn't keep a budgie alive. It looks like those sods didn't look after you the way they should. But you're in better hands now. So cheer up, eh?' She closed and bolted the bottom half of the stable door and continued with her round.

'What's up?' she asked Eddie when she got back to the house.

He was sitting, hunched forward on the edge of the sofa, frowning. He seemed to be concentrating on a point in the air about halfway between himself and the TV screen.

'My dad's gone AWOL.'

She sat down beside him and switched off the set. 'Are you sure? Why would he do that?'

'I really don't know. My mum says he left the house this morning in my aunt's car. He was going down to the beach for a walk and he hasn't come back. He's disappeared, gone. Jan, I'm really worried.'

'He might have fallen. Has the car turned up yet?' Jan said, trying to be positive.

Eddie shook his head. 'No, I don't think so. They're going to mount a proper search tomorrow. They're working on the assumption he's had an accident or something like that. But I'm not so sure. Those guys he owed money to are not the Friendly Bank. Jan, I've got to go down there and help look for him.'

'Of course you must. Anyway, Sue will need your support. Poor Ron. To think he might be lying helpless somewhere.'

Jan shuddered as she remembered Colonel Gilbert and how he'd died last year. He'd suffered a heart attack while chasing burglars from his property and had lain in the open for hours in the rain. She mentioned her thoughts to Eddie.

'I don't need reminding of old Gilbert,' Eddie said darkly. 'Sometimes, Jan, you would do better to engage your brain before you open your mouth.'

Shaken by Eddie's outburst, Jan left the room. She hoped Ron's disappearance wouldn't reignite Eddie's depression.

🐎

The next day was Friday. Unable to drive himself, Eddie had ordered an early-morning taxi to take him to the station at Cheltenham, where he could intercept a fast cross-country train to Cornwall. He was waiting for the taxi when Jan kissed him goodbye before she went out with the first lot. As they were hacking up the hill towards the gallop, Jan twisted around in the saddle and saw the cab bumping down the track towards the road, carrying him away. What on earth could have happened to Ron? They'd already spoken to the St Austell police. Was his disappearance connected to the money he owed to those East End gangsters? Or was it an accident? Or some sort of sudden illness? However Jan looked at it, the implications were not pleasant and she felt a sharp twinge of foreboding. In whatever way this was going to affect the Sullivan family, it was going to affect her too.

Later in the morning Shirley McGregor was on the phone.

'The X-rays on Big Freeze are not conclusive, but there are obvious signs in the off-fore foot that may indicate navicular disease. Have you spoken to the owner?'

'He hasn't phoned me back. I'll try him again now.'

Shirley rang off after promising she'd return to Edge Farm as soon as possible to do more tests on Big Freeze. Jan immediately dialled Bobby Montana's number and this time received an answer.

'Hi, this is Bobby Montana.'

'Mr Montana, it's Jan Hardy. We need to talk about Big Freeze.'

Big Freeze's owner took the news about the possible navicular disease calmly.

Jan wondered if he appreciated how serious the situation could be and she pressed him. 'Do you know what navicular is?'

'Sure I do. Like I said, I'm a Cherokee. I know horses.'

'Then you'll be aware that it can result in a complete breakdown in the structure of the horse's feet. I need to know how long it may have been there – if there were any signs of a problem before Big Freeze left the States.'

'No, ma'am. There was nothing that I know of. That's all I can say.'

'Do you know if he was on bute? If this condition wasn't picked up, bute could be the reason. I mean he could have had the condition for weeks, months even.'

'I, er, wouldn't know if he was on medication. I'd have to ask Mervyn over in Illinois.'

Jan felt like speaking to Mervyn Sawyer. She was convinced the horse must have had the problem for weeks and Sawyer had kept quiet about it, if he was aware of it at all. Either way, it didn't reflect too well on this 'genius' trainer Bobby Montana had spoken of.

'I could contact Mr Sawyer myself,' she suggested.

But on this point Montana was firm.

'I want you to leave this to me,' he said. 'I'll talk to him and let you know.'

The yard had two afternoon runners at Uttoxeter and, as this was almost sixty miles away, there was no time left to think about either Big Freeze or Ron Sullivan. Annabel, who was expecting Ben to arrive from London, had already excused herself from going racing on the grounds she had two or three things she wanted to do to clear her desk. Tomorrow she was collecting Horace Pursival and bringing him over to begin work on the portrait of Russian Eagle.

So it was Jan, with Roz and Declan, who took the horses up the M5.

🐎

Soon after they returned home and the horses had been rugged up and fed, Jan was in the office telephoning Eddie in St Austell. It was past six o'clock.

'What news?' she asked. 'Any sign of Ron?'

'No. He's not been found. He's not been in touch, he's just vanished.'

Jan could hear the edge of panic in Eddie's voice, pushing it to a higher pitch than normal.

'Is the search still going on?'

'Yes, of course it is. I just came back to my aunt's to get something to eat. Then I'm going back on the moor.'

'The moor?'

'Bodmin Moor, just north of here.'

'Yes, Eddie, I know where it is. I thought they were searching the coastal path.'

'They were. But then they found my aunt's car, the one he was driving. It was abandoned in a lay-by somewhere on top of the moor. So now the search-and-rescue people are out, helicopters, heat-seekers the lot.'

'How's Sue?'

'She's being strong. It's me that's in bits, Jan. Anyway, I've got to go now. Talk to you later. Bye.'

As the phone went dead, Jan slowly, almost absent-mindedly, placed the receiver back in its cradle. Her mind was racing, fearful about the outcome of the police search. She wondered how it would affect her relationship with Eddie or, indeed, if they would still have one. A million things rushed through her brain, imagining the headlines in the papers. Would there be an overspill that affected the owners' confidence in the yard or Jan? Worse still, if it was to do with gangsters, how safe were she and the kids?

The phone interrupted her thoughts. 'Supper's ready,' Fran said.

'What?' Jan replied slowly. 'Oh, sorry, Fran. I was miles away. I'll be there in *two* minutes.'

In the kitchen Megan and Matty were already eating their supper, which had been prepared for them by Fran, who came in daily to look after the house and the children. Sitting at the kitchen table, with an almost-cleared plate of food in front of him, was Ben. He greeted Jan after swallowing a last large mouthful of baked potato.

'Hi, Sis. Megan's been regaling me with her exploits on Monarch at the Cheltenham Show. Two rosettes, no less!'

He reached over and patted the head of his niece, who giggled.

Ben picked up a paper napkin from the table and wiped his mouth, then rose from the table.

'That was delicious, Fran. I couldn't resist, even though I'm eating out at the Fox with Bel tonight. Enjoy the rest of your supper, kiddoes. I've got to have a talk with your mother. See you all later.'

'Will you play the guitar to us before bed?' asked Megan.

Ben promised and signalled to Jan with a jerk of his head to come through to the sitting room. Hastily pouring herself a cup of tea, she followed.

'Did you have a good day?' Ben asked.

'No, it's been bloody awful. Eddie's dad's gone missing so he's chased off to Cornwall. Montana's horse might have navicular and both our runners were beaten.'

Ben gave her a hug. 'And on top of all that,' he said with a laugh, 'I gather Mr Horace Fusspot Pursival RA's coming tomorrow to make a nuisance of himself with his sketchbook.'

'Precisely. All we need on a Saturday.'

Ben let her go, his expression more serious. 'But what's this about Ron Sullivan?'

Gulping her tea, Jan summarized the situation as she knew it. 'And I've just heard,' she told him finally, 'he still hasn't been found. I'll give Eddie another call on his mobile in a bit. Anyway, what was it you wanted to talk about?'

Ben produced a letter on headed notepaper from his pocket and put it on the coffee table.

'This. I don't know what to make of it.'

The letter was under the letterhead of a firm of solicitors in

Broadway and was headed *The Will of Col. George Gilbert of Riscombe Manor, Riscombe, Glos, deceased.*

Jan picked it up and read it through.

Dear Mr Pritchard,

I write to inform you that you are a beneficiary of the late Colonel Gilbert's will. This news may surprise you, and you may additionally wonder about the long delay between the colonel's death and this notification. However, the colonel's immediate family had asked for the provisions of the will to be kept confidential while certain investigations were carried out, and the will was proved. The validity of the will has now been ascertained and probate is due to be granted shortly. Once this happens the will becomes a public document, so it is incumbent on us now to inform all beneficiaries of their interest.

There are one or two complicating factors about the colonel's legacy to you that may be more easily explained in person. Would you therefore be kind enough to attend a meeting at our offices on Monday, 12 October? Please let us know as soon as possible if this is inconvenient.

The letter was signed by John Mellor, senior partner.

'How extraordinary,' said Jan.

'Isn't it? You don't know anything about it, do you? No local gossip?'

'Nothing,' said Jan. 'What on earth can it mean?'

'Search me. I hardly knew the colonel. He knew you far better – you trained his horses.'

'Yes, he was a good friend to me and the yard generally. It amazed me he kept horses here, when his own daughter was training most of his runners. And he was very encouraging with Megan's junior eventing. He even lent her Monarch when she outgrew Smarty.'

'Didn't he actually leave Monarch to Megan in his will?'

Jan crossed to the mantelpiece, where a pile of correspondence was lying under a glass paperweight and slipped a letter from the top, which she handed to Ben. It was on the same headed notepaper as the one he'd just shown her, and explained that the colonel's will was about to be officially proved and that under its terms ownership of the pony known as Monarch would be formally transferred to Jan on Megan's behalf. It was dated a week earlier.

'This just confirms what Virginia told me after her father died,' Jan said. 'There didn't seem to be any particular secret about it. Probate's taken so long that ownership hadn't been formally transferred from the executors to me until now, but we hung on to Monarch, even though we had to send Velvet Dynasty and the other horses back to Riscombe.'

'So why didn't the solicitors just write to tell me about my legacy? What's this mysterious meeting all about?'

'Well, Monarch's only a pony, and because Virginia chose to tell me we've known about it coming to Megan all along. For some reason she didn't want you to know about this. God knows why.'

Bobby Montana arrived the next day, just as Horace Pursival was setting up his easel in the yard. He was being attended to by Annabel, who Jan could have sworn was wearing just a touch of make-up for the occasion. Taking her new owner across the yard to look at Big Freeze, Jan explained about A.D.'s commission.

'Neat,' was Montana's only comment.

Jan had hoped Shirley McGregor would be there when Montana turned up, but she was acting as official veterinary officer at an agricultural show on the other side of Stroud. Nevertheless, Jan did her best to impress on Montana the seriousness of the situation. For a man who boasted about his Cherokee horse sense, he seemed strangely apathetic.

'Mervyn don't know nothin' about navicular. So I guess he used bute, which would kinda explain things. Anyways, I got the horse well insured. It'll be sad if he dies, but I'll survive, which is more important.'

Jan's whole body seethed, but she managed to contain herself. At this stage, with the horse's future still in such doubt, it would do no good to lose her cool. But she thought Montana had a callously hypocritical attitude, the more so when he went through his pockets until he found a lump of brown sugar, which he held out to the horse in the palm of his huge paw.

'I so like to give them something sweet. Tell them who loves them,' he said. 'Now where's that other friend of mine – Spring Blow? I got another one of these for him.'

Montana did not stay long. After they'd examined Spring Blow, he told Jan he'd be back to visit the horses regularly and that she was authorized in the meantime to OK any treatment Big Freeze needed, as long as it was in consultation with the vet. On his way back across the yard Montana made his way towards Pursival, who was now at work sketching Russian Eagle from various angles, with Annabel standing by the horse's head. Montana hovered for a moment behind the artist's shoulder, looking with a slightly puzzled expression at the work in progress. Standing apart from the group, Jan thought the two men made quite a contrast: the grizzled English artist in his straw hat, tweed suit and brogues, and the sneakered, zipper-jacketed, ponytailed Yank.

There could have been a flashpoint, when Pursival suddenly stopped what he was doing and turned to Montana with a barely concealed look of aggression. But Montana did not flinch.

'Real neat,' Montana said, clapping Pursival lightly on his tweed-clad shoulder. Then the American set off towards his car.

Hurrying after him, Jan just heard Pursival mutter, 'He's a bloody barbarian.'

6

It was much later that evening when Eddie rang again.

'We've been out all day, Jan, and I'm bloody knackered – everyone is.'

'And?'

'I reckon we've combed half of Bodmin Moor and, apart from the car, we've turned up nothing. At least we've got some publicity, now that the local television crews and journalists are camped outside. The police are holding a press conference and they want me to make an appeal for witnesses – any sightings, or whatever.'

'Are you going to do it?'

Eddie sighed. 'Yes, I suppose so. If I don't, the police'll go ahead anyway.'

'It sounds like a good idea to me.'

'I'm not so sure,' he said darkly. 'Certain people might see the item. You know who I mean. The same people Dad's been avoiding. He'd prefer they didn't know he's in England, that you can be sure of.'

'Have you told the police about your concerns?'

'No. At least, not yet. Those gangsters might be behind this and I'm worried they'll do him in.'

'Eddie, that's all the *more* reason to tell the cops.'

'Not if they have already got Dad somewhere.'

'Oh, Eddie,' said Jan a touch impatiently, 'aren't you jumping to conclusions?'

'Yes, I suppose so, but isn't it obvious?'

Not to Jan it wasn't. When faced with a puzzle she would always look for the nearest and least fanciful explanation. Eddie's suggestion that Ron had fallen foul of gangsters seemed to her a conspiracy too far.

She was still uneasy a couple of hours later when she turned on the television. The news bulletin seemed to crawl through a succession of foreign and political stories before the item concerning Ron appeared.

'Police and rescue services are searching Bodmin Moor in Cornwall after a man went missing yesterday morning.'

The image on the screen cut from the newsreader's face to shots of a line of gumbooted policemen and volunteers, ten yards apart, walking across a stretch of moor.

'Sixty-four-year-old Ronald Sullivan, who arrived recently from Australia, is understood to be visiting family in this country. He had left a relative's home in St Austell at about nine a.m., but the car he was driving was discovered much later in a lay-by on the moor, seven miles away, and Ron Sullivan has not been seen since. At a press conference this evening his son Edward made an appeal for any witnesses who may have seen Mr Sullivan or his car in the area.'

The outdoor shots gave way to what looked like the interior of a village hall. A couple of policemen sat on a stage with Eddie. The report cut to a shot of Eddie's face, which was drawn and uneasy.

'My father just went out for a walk,' he was saying, 'and he hasn't returned. He said he was going to the beach at Par Sands, but the car turned up a long way away on Bodmin Moor. We don't know why he should have gone there. We need anyone, anyone at all, who saw him or his car either at Par or on the moor . . .'

The camera cut to a view of a small red car parked in a bleak upland lay-by, with a phone number displayed on the screen below.

'. . . to please contact the police or emergency services.'

The camera cut back to the newsreader, who was now moving hastily on to the next story.

'In Hartlepool a group of schoolchildren have come up with an ingenious way to liven up their lunchtimes . . .'

❧

The next morning, as they often did on Sundays, Jan, Megan and Matty rode over to her parents' home, Riscombe Vale Farm, for lunch. The route went in a more or less straight line over Riscombe Down, the ridge that defined the south side of the valley overlooked by Edge Farm to the north. The ride was along a broad, well-used bridle path and, compared to the snaking six-mile journey by road, it was an easy two-mile hack.

As they passed over the top of the ridge before beginning their descent into Riscombe vale, the riders enjoyed a panoramic view, in bright sunshine, of the part of the Gilbert estate known as Dower-house Farm. This was where Virginia Gilbert's ancient grass gallops were, a lush, wide strip of turf inscribed on the lower reaches of the slope like a number six. Whenever Jan saw that strip of ground, she felt a pang of envy, as her own was a bumpy, tufty, make-do bit of turf. And, unlike her own, the Dowerhouse gallops were rarely out of commission through lack of rain. They had a tenacious ability to retain moisture and at the same time were well enough drained never to be waterlogged, even after a heavy storm.

Colonel Gilbert once told Jan that racehorses had been exercised by his family over this grass for more than two hundred and fifty years, and the ground had never been used for anything else. It had been written into the farmer's tenancy agreement that the grass and turf on the gallops must be looked after as carefully as if one of their own crops were growing there. For years, the house and farm had been let exclusively to one family, who became experts in the task. The last tenant had died twenty years ago and the house had remained empty. Although structurally sound, the property had no central heating, needed rewiring and only had a cold-water supply. The previous tenants had lived in two or three rooms – a sitting room with an open fire, a kitchen with an old range for cooking and a freezing cold bedroom. It was obvious that the money the colonel had needed to invest in refurbishment would have run into many thousands of pounds, and Jan reckoned it would far outweigh any rent he would receive from the property by reletting it. But Jan knew that a really good strip of turf, with just the right degree of springiness, will hold itself in that condition for decades, if it was not overused.

After reaching the bottom of Riscombe vale, it was only a short ride along the road before Jan and the children turned in at the gate of the Pritchards' farm. Hearing the clatter of hooves on the forecourt, Reg, puffing away on his pipe, and Mary in her apron came out to greet them. Jan dismounted and gave her parents a hug before Reg led her horse away, while Matty and Megan followed on their ponies. They were going to hitch the animals in the shade of the barn before giving them a drink. Jan went into the house with her mother.

'Will we see Ben today?' Jan asked, as Mary took her swiftly through into the kitchen.

'He was here yesterday. I asked him to join us for lunch today, but he said he had to get back to London.'

'Did he mention the letter he's had about the colonel's will? Apparently he's got a legacy of some kind, but he doesn't really know what it's about. He does think it's a bit weird, though, because he hardly knew Colonel Gilbert.'

With her back turned to Jan, Mary was already hard at work peeling and chopping vegetables.

'Yes, I know. He did say something about it.'

Mary's voice was low and sounded oddly tense. Jan knew her mother well enough to realize that this way of speaking, with her head lowered to a task as if it required her total concentration, was invariably a sign that the discussion had ended. Jan moved across the kitchen and stood beside her mother, deciding not to press the matter of Ben's interest in Colonel Gilbert's will any further.

'Right, Ma. How can I help?' she asked, rolling up her shirt-sleeves.

As she sat opposite her mother at the lunch table, Jan thought Mary looked tired and physically diminished. The traditional meal of roast lamb and potatoes, with greens, carrots and properly made gravy, followed by blackberry and apple pie with custard, was entirely home-made, as it had always been: Mary would rather starve than dish up a bought pie or gravy made from freeze-dried granules. But the effort of doing everything as it had always been done now seemed to be taking its toll. She had endured more than her fair share of ill health in the last couple of years. She seemed exhausted and preoccupied and Jan was extremely concerned.

While Reg carved the roast and Mary served large helpings of steaming, well-buttered vegetables, Jan told them about the continued absence of Ron Sullivan and the search for him on Bodmin Moor.

'There's a lot of old mine workings up on that moor, so they say,' Reg announced in an ominous voice as he settled into his place at the head of the table. 'Maybe he fell down one of them.'

'Oh, Reg, don't talk like that,' said Mary quickly.

'Well somethin' must've happened to the beggar, if they can't find him after two whole days' searching.'

With that pronouncement the subject was closed and the talk turned to Jan's mysterious new owner, Bobby Montana.

'I don't understand him,' said Jan. 'He comes down regularly to visit his horses, as if he really cares about them. The grey's in trouble with his feet and Montana doesn't seem particularly bothered; but navicular disease is no joking matter. I've already told him that.'

'You're not wrong there,' said Reg. 'More often than not you lose the horse eventually.'

'Well, either he doesn't know horses as well as he pretends or he just doesn't give a damn.'

'I think he really loves his horses,' put in Megan, as she shoved a forkful of food into her mouth. 'He's always got sugar lumps for them.'

'Don't speak with your mouth full, dear,' interrupted Mary.

'Well, he has,' Megan insisted defiantly, still chewing her meat.

'Maybe he's just got complete confidence in my daughter's ability to save an injured horse,' said Reg. 'And, personally, on that score I agree with him.'

'But I'm not a miracle worker, Dad.'

'Have you got it definite, then, that it *is* navicular?'

'I'm going into the surgery to see Shirley McGregor tomorrow. She wants to show me the X-rays of Big Freeze's feet. And she's asked Mickey Reid to call in as well.'

'If she wants the farrier she must think som'ing can be done,' Reg grunted. 'Else she'd be asking for the knacker.'

By the time the last remnants of pie and custard had been scraped from their pudding bowls, the sky had clouded over. As

Megan went out to check on her pony, Jan and Reg got ready to take their customary walk up the field to view Reg's Cotswolds. Matty reverently went to the sideboard and got out the battered and well-Sellotaped box containing Snakes and Ladders. He brought it to the table and solemnly challenged his gran to a game. How many times had she played this with Mary during her own childhood? Jan thought. At that moment a wave of love for her mother swept over her uncontrollably, almost like a physical pain. Suppressing it, she blinked back her tears and hurried out after Reg, who was whistling up his dog Blue to come with them.

'Dad, what's the matter with Mum?' she asked later as they stood at the top of the field contemplating the flock. 'She seems sort of withdrawn at the moment.'

'She's all right,' said Reg. 'It's her nerves, but she'll get over it – she always does.'

'But I'm worried, really worried.'

'Well, don't be.'

'Dad, you can tell me, you know. I'm her only daughter.'

'There's nothing to tell, Jan. Just let matters lie.'

Reg was stonewalling her. Like Mary earlier in the kitchen, Reg had his own way of closing a discussion he did not want to pursue. Jan decided to switch to the other subject on her mind – the same one that Mary herself had refused to discuss earlier.

'What do you think of this legacy Ben's got from the colonel? I mentioned it to Mum and she didn't seem that interested.'

'Well, we don't know what it is yet, do we?' Reg said, with no greater enthusiasm for this topic than he had shown for the other. 'There's no point in playing guessing games, there's been enough of them already.'

He pointed with his stick towards the flock.

'Now, what d'you think of that bonny ewe over there? I like them all, me, but she's my favourite, if I'm honest about it.'

To Jan the favoured one seemed much of a muchness with all the other sheep, but she didn't say so. Instead she put her arm through her father's and gave it a squeeze.

🐎

It was mid-morning on the next day when Jan went down to Shirley McGregor's surgery for the conference about Big Freeze. In the car park she recognized the wiry frame and gap-toothed grin of Mickey Reid, the local farrier who shod all her horses. Mickey was waiting beside his old decrepit Jeep, dragging on a roll-up cigarette.

'Hello, Mickey,' Jan said. 'Sorry to break into your busy day.'

'Don't matter, Mrs H,' said Mickey cheerfully, pinching out the half-smoked weed and dropping it into his jacket pocket as they walked to the surgery door. 'I've just been over at Miss Gilbert's yard. It looks like you might get a chance to have that Velvet Dynasty back.'

Mickey, as usual, was well informed and he knew how the previous year's removal of Velvet Dynasty, whose talent had been discovered and nurtured at Edge Farm, had pained Jan.

'Oh? How's that?' Jan asked in feigned innocence.

'There's talk Miss Gilbert's got to offload some of the old colonel's best nags to pay the inheritance tax on his estate.'

'But she won't get rid of that one, surely,' Jan continued with guile.

'He's one of her best, ain't he? If she needs the money she'll have to. There ain't no choice in the matter. Anyway, there's talk that what the colonel left Miss Gilbert and her brother wasn't exactly what she expected and that they have even tried to challenge the will.'

'Really?'

Jan thought of the complications mentioned by the solicitor in his letter to Ben. Was this what he meant?

Intriguing though all this was, in the surgery Jan's concentration shifted to Big Freeze's sensitive feet as Shirley showed them an X-ray on a wall-mounted light box.

'Look here and you'll see this little spur close to the heel. It can be caused by the horse treading on something like a sharp stone. However, in this case, looking at the navicular bone itself, it seems there's been internal degeneration for some time.'

She pointed to a smudge on the X-ray, which lay alongside the bone.

'See this blood vessel? It's enlarged. If there's damage to the blood vessels within the bone this is what happens, as the tissue tries to compensate for the reduced blood supply. And look here. This seems to be a spur, where the bone has grown an abnormal projection, which is a common sign in well-established navicular disease. Another is the abnormal wear in the toe of his shoe, which I noticed the other day. It looks as if Big Freeze has had this problem some time, though not excessively. If he had, I'd expect to see a different pattern of wear in the shoe. Mickey, the reason I asked you to come in is, if we're going to be able to do anything for this horse, he's going to need special shoeing.'

She showed Mickey a circular pad of rubber about the size of a hoof print.

'It's a shock-absorbing pad which I'm going to get you to place next to the hoof underneath the shoe.'

She gave Mickey detailed instructions about the particular way she wanted him to pare the feet and refit the front shoes, using the protective pad. Then she turned to Jan.

'Give him supplementary cod liver oil and Naviloc for the pain. We'll leave him a few weeks on walking exercise and see if there's any improvement.'

And meanwhile, thought Jan, these vet's bills are mounting and Bobby Montana's ten thousand cash advance is gushing away.

As the days went by, Eddie rang Jan every evening, but there was still no news about his father. On Sunday night the search for Ron again made the news, but it then dropped off the agenda. As the press forgot about Ron Sullivan's continued disappearance, the police abandoned their systematic ground search and began to speculate openly that Ron had disappeared deliberately. Eddie tried his best to put them off this theory, which in fact was too close to what he thought himself, until, that is, he discovered the basis of police reasoning: they sniffed the presence of another woman in the case.

'It's totally fucking loony,' Eddie bellowed down the line at Jan. 'They think he's done a sort of Bill Johnson, you know, like your sodding feed rep who pissed off with a floozy. I know there have been others in the past, but he wouldn't do that again. But they won't listen, the bastards. Anyway, I don't care what the police are thinking. I'm going to keep on looking for him. And I wouldn't be a bit surprised if I hear from our friends in the East End before too long.'

'But what are you going to do on your own?' Jan asked, full of foreboding.

'I'll probably go up to London. Remember Ron said he'd got people to see and arrangements to make. My mum says he was away in London for a couple of days before he disappeared. He was up to something and I want to find out exactly what that something was.'

'Oh Eddie, I wish you'd tell the police what's been going on!'

'No way. They're not bloody interested and it's too risky. This is something I have to do by myself.'

🐎

Two days after this conversation, days in which the work of a busy yard masked Jan's anxieties about Eddie, she called in at George Machin's butcher's shop in Riscombe. Rounding the corner of the small car park just off the High Street, she almost bumped into Rosemary Sterry. After recovering from the near collision, Rosemary nodded at Jan's purchases.

'Been into George's, have you?'

'Yes, I always buy my meat there.'

'That's right, girl. Good butchers are like good dentists, my old dad used to say. Never change until you're sure you've found one better. Though it's hard enough to find one at all these days. What with these superstores, it's all prepacked, you know.'

But, having met Rosemary by chance, Jan didn't want to talk about meat. 'Have you seen my Mum recently, Rosemary?' she asked.

'Oh, aye, I was in for a cup of tea on Monday.'

'How do you find her? She doesn't seem very happy to me. I think something's bothering her.'

Rosemary shrugged her shoulders.

'I've known Mary a long time. We were kids together. And we

worked as daily 'elps at the manor, you know. Your mother's had her trials in the past, and I reckon recent events have served to remind her, like.'

'Remind her of what? I don't follow you.'

Rosemary looked at Jan, as if weighing something up.

'Oh, I don't know. Changes in the village . . .'

'You mean all this talk of the Gilberts selling stuff?'

'Well, ye-es,' said Rosemary cautiously. 'It could cost people's jobs, could that.'

'That wouldn't apply to my parents, though. How could it? Their tenancy is guaranteed.'

Rosemary shook her head and shrugged again.

'Well, maybe it's just the general uncertainty that's affecting your Ma, like. Making her a bit low.'

Rosemary dropped her voice and spoke as if about to reveal a deep conspiracy.

'My Herb says there's strangers been in the village, asking questions about the racing yards hereabouts. Says he heard it in the pub. Scouting out the Gilberts' horses, like as not, he says. Seeing what might be for sale.'

'Really?' said Jan politely. 'I suppose it's possible. Anyway, thanks for that. I really must be getting on.'

Driving back to Edge, Jan tried to make sense of what Rosemary Sterry had told her. What did she mean by Mary's 'trials' in the past? At first Rosemary had spoken as if she was expecting Jan to understand what she was talking about. When Jan didn't, Rosemary had clammed up.

As for the news about strangers asking questions in Riscombe, Jan didn't at first take it seriously, or think that it should particularly concern her. Jan knew that Rosemary was shrewd, but her son's album was plainly a few stamps short of the complete set, as Eddie had unkindly put it after meeting Herb one night in the pub.

7

The next night Jan was even more restless and she found herself pondering on what Herb Sterry had said. She had gone down to the pub to drink the health of Connor, her stable lad, whose birthday it was, and noticed Herb sitting with his pint on a stool at the end of the bar. After the toasts were all drunk and Connor had sung his obligatory party piece, she decided to speak to Herb. She clearly remembered that Rosemary had referred to racing yards in the area, implying the strangers' interest wasn't solely in Virginia's. Perhaps this *was* something she should know more about.

'Oh, yeah,' Herb said, nodding when Jan went over to tackle him. 'They wanted to know all sorts about what's goin' on. That's one of 'em over there, matter of fact. Stayin' in the village, he is.'

He nodded across the room to where a large young man with a shaved head and heavily muscled arms was sitting hunched over a paper. The pub was busy and Jan could only half see the man through the crowd of drinkers. But she couldn't help thinking there was something indefinably familiar about him.

She nodded her thanks to Herb, squared her shoulders and began pushing through the crowd. She decided to confront the man now and find out just why he was so interested in racing yards in the Riscombe area.

'Excuse me,' she said, tapping the enormously meaty T-shirted shoulder from behind. 'Could I have a word?'

The man turned and looked up at her, Jan blinked, then started back out of pure surprise.

'I know you, don't I?' she said. 'What the hell are you doing here?'

🐎

It took a few moments for Jan to put it all together: the delayed plane at Faro, the stag party of young men drinking cans of lager, the groom himself almost starting a fight with Eddie, and then all of them drinking together.

The same groom – by now, presumably, a safely married man – rose to his feet and held out a huge hand.

'Jan, hello! Jason Cobb.'

The hand he held out could have crunched Jan's as easily as a scrap-metal baling machine. Jan took it cautiously and found the grip surprisingly gentle.

'Pleased to meet you properly,' Jason went on, with a nervous laugh. 'Remember, I only saw you across the crowded airport.'

Jan scowled at Jason Cobb, who was at least a foot taller than herself. He had a head that might have been chiselled out of a cliff face, with cropped sandy hair, and a nose that had at some point been broken. At the same time he was obviously not the complete lout he had appeared to be when she'd last seen him. Jason Cobb had manners, when he chose to deploy them, and a cheery smile.

'That's it. Faro – right?' she asked.

'Yes, my stag party; a whole three days wiped from the memory banks, so God knows what I got up to. But of course I do remember the bloody awful wait at the airport on the way home. It was there I met up with Eddie. He's become a mate.'

Jason lifted the remains of his pint to his lips and drained it.

'Here, let me get you a drink.'

Jan agreed to a gin and tonic and sat down to wait for his return from the bar. She was thinking that this obviously wasn't a chance meeting. Herb Sterry had identified Jason Cobb as the one who had been asking questions about the racing yards in the area. And now she discovered he'd 'become a mate' of Eddie's. But how? She remembered Eddie saying something back in August about a 'reunion of the Faro airport crowd' at a pub in Banbury; he'd got Gerry Harris, the builder from the village, to drive him over. Had

Eddie seen Jason Cobb since then? If so, why hadn't he told her about it?

Cobb was back in a couple of minutes with her gin and another pint for himself. Not wasting time on small talk, Jan went straight to the point.

'Jason, I need to be quite frank, I've been wondering why you're here. I'm told you've been making enquiries about the racing yards in the area. So what the hell's going on?'

Jason frowned, as if showing concern at being a nuisance.

'Eddie told me you wouldn't think it appropriate if I made myself known to you. He said you always insisted on keeping your independence.'

'So, I still don't get it. What exactly are you saying?'

'OK, I'll put my cards on the table, shall I?' Jason spread his large hands wide in a gesture of openness.

I used to be in the army, the Paras actually. I came out of the sevice five years ago and started the firm over in Banbury.'

'The firm?'

'Security consultancy. Eddie's hired us – well, me, actually.'

'Eddie? How? He can't afford to hire anyone, he hasn't any money.'

Jason shrugged.

'To be honest it doesn't matter. I wasn't getting any other work at the time, so I gave him tick and said he could pay me eventually.'

'Really. What's he hired you to do exactly?'

'To look after you. Personal protection we call it.'

'Without telling me about it?'

'Well, as I said, he didn't think—'

'You can say that again, he certainly didn't! When exactly was it that he saw fit to engage you?'

'He phoned me last Monday. Said he was in a spot of bother. He told me about the Sweeney family: that's the mob his father owed money to.'

'And I suppose he said he thought they'd rubbed out his dad, or whatever the correct term is.'

'His dad's disappeared all right. He may have slipped away to avoid the attentions of the Sweeneys. Or they might have got to him somehow.'

Jan was unimpressed.

'Jason, this is all too dramatic for me, I'm afraid. I knew Ron Sullivan was in debt to a slightly shady bunch of characters from the East End of London, or Romford, or wherever it was. But I've never heard of the Sweeneys before.'

'I've made some enquiries, Jan. They are a bit more than *slightly* shady. They're a very rough family indeed. My impression is they're making money supplying so-called contract labour, which is probably a front for illegal immigrants and prostitutes from eastern Europe and Russia.'

'I see.'

'Eddie was worried in case they came to Edge Farm looking for him or his dad. So he asked me to keep an eye open.'

Jan took a deep pull on her gin. She was having trouble working out just what went on inside Eddie's head.

'That's *very* kind of him,' she said sarcastically. 'So he hires you, and you go stomping around gangland asking all sorts of questions, and then scurry back down here and camp on my doorstep. Great! I would say that more or less guarantees the Sweeneys will be taking an unhealthy interest in my affairs, wouldn't you?'

Jason looked abashed after Jan's onslaught. 'I didn't think—'

'Marvellous, you didn't think, eh! Well, aren't people like you supposed to think? Isn't that what Eddie is paying you for?'

'What I meant was—'

'Look, Jason, don't bother to explain yourself, let me explain *my*self. I don't need this aggro, I've got plenty of problems of my own, and I'm not about to take on Ron Sullivan's as well. So why don't you just pack your bags and ride that cockhorse of yours back to Banbury Cross? And I don't want you turning up uninvited ever again. Got that?'

Sheepishly, Jason Cobb pulled out his wallet and extracted a small card. He pushed it across the table towards Jan, letting out a deep sigh. 'OK, message received and understood. I won't. I agree this could have been better handled, but Eddie definitely told me I wasn't to contact you myself. Anyway, here's my business card. Take it, just in case I can be of any use to you – and please ring me if the Sweeneys do come calling.'

Jan took the card automatically and got up, tight-lipped, to leave.

'I don't expect they will,' she said. 'Not after I've had a word in Eddie's shell-like.'

🐎

'What the sodding hell have you been up to?'

Jan had phoned Eddie at his aunt's house as soon as she got home. On the drive back to Edge she had become increasingly angry and was now trembling with rage.

'I'm looking for my dad. What's the matter with you now?'

'Mr Jason bloody Cobb security consultant is the matter.'

'Oh, Christ. You've met him then.'

Eddie sounded suddenly crestfallen.

'I've seen him all right, in the pub, Eddie. He's been all round the area making himself about as inconspicuous as a U-boat in Riscombe duck pond. And, by the way, he's told me all about the Sweeney gang.'

'A really nasty bunch of people.'

'Apparently so. But *nothing* to do with me. I won't have you dragging me and my children into whatever dodgy dealings your family's been involved with, Eddie. What were you thinking of?'

'Well, I was trying to protect you. That's all.'

'Oh, really, by getting some half-arsed, unemployable security guy in? Without even *telling* me?'

'Jan, I had to do something.'

'Why, Eddie? Because I'm the defenceless, clueless little woman, sitting at home at the mercy of the bad guys? Is that how you see things?'

'No, not when you put it like that. But I was trying to look after my future wife.'

'Eddie, I don't *want* to marry a people-trafficker, if what Jason Cobb said is right and that's what the Sweeney gang are doing.'

'Well, I'm *not!*'

70

'That's fine, I'll give you the benefit of the doubt for the moment and assume you know nothing about Ron's business affairs. But I'm not getting hitched to the *son* of a trafficker either. Is that clear, Eddie?'

'It's a bit over-the-top, all this talk about people-trafficking.'

'Well, whatever you want to call it, there's far too much murky water for me. I've got my own business to think about and import-ant people like A.D. O'Hagan to answer to. If he finds out what's been going on, he'll think I'm running a frigging circus. I've got employees who depend on me for their livelihood and I've got my children. Eddie, it's bad enough you flitting off all the time – I can't put up with much more.'

'Jan, can't we talk about this?'

'We *are* talking about it. But not for much longer. Eddie, forget about Ron's dubious racket, whatever it was. Walk away. Come back here now, tonight, *please*.'

'Jan, you don't seem to understand. There wasn't any racket. My dad's not a criminal. He was just very unlucky. He took a chance and lost.'

'Yes, and the prisons are stuffed full of unlucky chancers – poor sods who meant well but the cards didn't fall right. I don't think so – it's crap and you know it, Eddie. You need to be honest with yourself for once.'

'But Jan, he's my dad. I've got to help him, save his neck if I can. Then I'll come back – I promise.'

'If those are your priorities, Eddie, go ahead. But don't count on me being around when you get out of jail, or hospital, or whatever it's going to be. I need this grief like a hole in the head. But realistically I'm thinking it could be you that ends up *getting* a hole in yours. Do you understand what I'm saying, you idiot?'

Eddie gave a sigh, which was clearly audible down the line. 'OK, Jan, I've got the message. I'm really sorry I've upset you, but I just can't leave Ron in the lurch. He needs me.'

'Eddie, he may be beyond needing anything. You have to realize that.'

'Yes, I know, but until I'm certain I've got to keep on being there for him, and you know that's the right thing to do.'

Now it was Jan's turn to sigh and reflect. Who was she to argue that Eddie should abandon his family obligations? Wasn't that exactly what she was refusing to do herself?

'OK, Eddie,' she said, steeling herself. 'If that's the way you want it. All I can say is good luck. And – I'm sorry – but, for the moment it's also goodbye.'

She hung up and stood for a moment with her eyelids squeezed tight shut. As the days went by, she would replay that conversation many times over. She had said goodbye to him: in most people's language that was breaking up, breaking off the engagement, finishing with Eddie. Was that what she'd done? The feeling of dread in the pit of her stomach told her something momentous had indeed happened.

🐎

'I've never known a pair have a more on-and-off relationship than the two of you,' Annabel remarked the next day as she and Jan were giving Big Freeze and Gylippus, another invalid, some gentle walking exercise around one of the paddocks on the hillside below the yard.

Jan had to admit that the history of her relationship with Eddie had been an inconsistent one.

'Inconsistent?' laughed Annabel. 'A switchback ride more like.'

Despite the bantering tone, Annabel was clearly disappointed by the news that Jan and Eddie would be apart again, and for an indeterminate length of time. The fact that Annabel's newly minted relationship with Ben had been so fulfilling made Jan hanker for something equally gratifying in her own life. She was tempted to discuss her relationship with Eddie further, but in the end decided against it and let the conversation go in another direction.

'How's things been going with Pursival?' Jan asked. 'He must have nearly finished the great masterpiece by now.'

Annabel had recently been over to Gloucester to sit for a supplementary session in Pursival's studio, which Jan suspected had been completely unnecessary.

'God, he talks as if it were never going to be finished.' Annabel sighed. 'He's quite sweet really, in a bonkers sort of way.'

'He's besotted with you. That's the kind of bonkers he is.'

'Yes, well . . .'

Annabel let the thought, whatever it was, trail away. She was used to people falling insanely in love with her. Jan changed the subject again.

'Has Ben heard anything more about this Colonel Gilbert thing – the legacy?' she asked. 'He's going to the solicitor's next Monday, isn't he?'

Until now Jan and Annabel had only discussed the matter superficially, and she was intrigued to find out what Annabel really thought of this unknown provision of the colonel's will.

'Yes it is, Monday. But no, he doesn't know anything more than the solicitor chappy revealed in his letter, which was almost nothing at all. It's very odd, though, don't you think? Ben's quite worried, actually. He says it's affecting your parents, especially Mary. He thinks that's why she's been so nervous and withdrawn lately.'

Jan thought before answering. 'Well, it's true she's got this thing about not wanting to have to pay rent to the ghastly Virginia Gilbert, or Harry, for that matter. My father tells me she gets in quite a state about it. I can't think why, though. And I really can't make out how that could be linked to whatever it is that the colonel left to Ben, which is probably not worth anything anyway.'

'But what if it *is* worth something?'

Jan shrugged. 'Well, I can see how that might upset my mum, given that the younger generation of Gilberts seems to have such a down on us Pritchards. They are bound to resent someone from our family getting anything substantial from their father's will. Virginia positively spat like a cobra over a small thing like Monarch going to Megan.'

'There's dark talk in the village about Virginia and Harry contesting the will. Perhaps the colonel made a whole series of potty legacies. Maybe he really was senile.'

'Well, he wasn't when I last saw him, which was only a few days before he died.'

The two women fell silent as they walked the horses on. As they reached the top of the rising ground, Jan noticed something and pointed into the valley.

'By the way, talking of switchbacks, look at that.'

A flock of rooks were soaring on a thermal. Every now and then pairs of them would suddenly go into free-fall, tumbling through the air like dancers, or playful wrestlers.

'It's called "shooting",' Jan went on, as Annabel shaded her eyes and squinted heavenwards. 'It's something they do at this time of year, the cock birds and the hens.'

Another couple of birds fell out of the flock in synchronized fall, their wings overlapping and bodies almost entangled, in a head-over-heels descent through the clear air.

'Rooks mate for life, don't they?' said Annabel.

'Yes, I think so. Dad says they're more faithful than humans, and by the looks of it they have as much fun.'

Jan's thoughts returned to Eddie and she felt a strong stab of emotion as she rubbed Big Freeze's mane and turned him towards home. On the way back down the hill, she could still feel it and tears filled her eyes.

🐎

Jan was approaching Riscombe in the horsebox, on the way home from a Thursday afternoon's meeting at Towcester racecourse. In the back were Toby Waller's Nero's Friend, A.D. O'Hagan's Magic Maestro and Bobby Montana's Spring Blow. Jan wished Toby had been there to see Nero win his race. They had bought him as a youngster and he'd turned into a wonderfully brave chaser. He seemed to thrive especially at Towcester, which, with its mile-long uphill climb to the finish, was one of the most demanding National Hunt courses in the country. But Toby was on an extended assignment with his bank in Hong Kong and would have to make do with a briefing from Jan by phone. A.D., on the other hand, had been there in the stands, wincing at Jan's side as Magic Maestro took a huge chunk of birch out of the last open ditch three from home. He had looked full of running and the mistake probably cost him the race, though Jan knew that it had been caused by tiredness and that the horse would improve for the run. A.D., too, had seemed satisfied.

'We'll win with him next time out,' he murmured to Jan as they watched the horse pass the post in third place. 'Just don't tell anyone I said so.'

In his novice hurdle race Spring Blow had given an impression very different from that left by the other two Edge Farm runners. In truth, Jan was only running him because he had been with her for two months now and he had to go out and try to earn his keep. But the horse had never shown real enthusiasm on the gallops – he appeared listless and dim-witted. So Jan wondered if a trip to the racecourse would liven him up. But it hadn't happened and his jockey had pulled him up halfway along the back straight. Jan had been disappointed that Bobby Montana hadn't showed up to watch his first runner in England, but now she was glad about it. To see your horse win was ecstatic; to see him spill his guts for you in defeat could be inspiring; but she knew that to have one pull up, not trying a yard, was one of the most dispiriting experiences an owner could have in racing.

Driven by Declan, the lorry had nudged slowly through the late-afternoon traffic clogging Riscombe High Street, and then picked up speed as it cleared the thirty-mile-an-hour zone. A minute later Jan's parents' house came into view and, as they passed the gate, the telltale flashing of a blue light in the cottage forecourt made Jan dig Declan savagely in the arm with her elbow.

'Stop, stop! Pull up on the verge.'

Jan jumped out and ran through the Pritchards' gate to where the ambulance was waiting, with its engine running and rear doors open. Inside the house Jan found the medics carefully negotiating a stretcher down the stairs on which Mary Pritchard was strapped. Her eyes were shut and her drawn, strained face was a ghastly grey colour.

'Oh, my God, what's going on?' Jan gasped. 'What's happened?'

'And you are . . . ?' panted one of the green-suited paramedics handling the stretcher.

'Jan, I'm her daughter.' She too was breathless, but for a different reason. Her chest felt tight with panic. She caught sight of Reg following the stretcher down the stairs. His face was a mask of bloodless pallor: he looked scared and confused, as if he was confronted by events impossible to comprehend. When Mary finally reached the hall the ambulance men lowered the stretcher to the floor and began to rig up a drip, which fed a vein in her arm. Jan went halfway up the stairs to grab her father and led him down.

'Dad, what on earth happened? Did Mum have a fall?'

Reg's voice was husky from shock.

'No, no, nothing like that. After tea she said she wasn't feeling too clever, so I said go upstairs, my girl, for a lie-down and I'll bring you a hot-water bottle. Well, when I got up to her she was on the floor. She'd just collapsed, like. Nothing I could do about it because I wasn't there, see? So I picked her up and laid her on the bed. Then I dialled nine-nine-nine. They were here really quick and now they say they've got to take her to hospital.'

Jan gave Reg a hug, then went back to the stretcher and stroked her mother's heavily veined hand.

'Mum? It's Jan. Can you hear me?'

Reg's voice croaked behind her. 'She can't talk, Jan. She's been saying nothing. She doesn't know what day it is even.'

'She may not be conscious yet,' explained the medic, speaking gently. 'It's always difficult to know immediately after a stroke.'

'A stroke?' gasped Jan. 'Oh, Mum, what's happened to you?'

The ambulance men lifted the stretcher and placed it in the rear of the ambulance. Jan ran out into the road to speak to Declan.

'You get off back to Edge with the horses,' Jan ordered. 'I've got to stay here. My mum's had a bad turn. I'll ring Bel to make sure she's there to help with everything back home.'

At the hospital, after hanging around in the A and E department for about an hour, a young, trim-looking doctor, who described herself as the trauma registrar, came in and told them that Mary had been admitted and had been made comfortable in the emergency unit. Reg and Jan went up to see her, with Reg standing stiffly in the lift like a sentry in his box.

They found Mary hooked up to various monitors but, despite all the active machinery around her, she lay motionless, her jaw slack and her eyelids closed.

'We'll be keeping her under close observation throughout the night,' the neat young registrar told them. 'The first twelve hours after something like this are crucial, and the most worrying as one is constantly on the lookout for another event. After that, Mary's chances of recovery will gradually increase day by day.'

Reg did not seem to take in this talk of his wife's 'event' and her 'chances of recovery'. Although he tried to protest, Jan and the ward sister decided it would be too much for him to stay at Mary's bedside all night, and Jan took him back down in the lift.

Still holding himself like a guardsman, Reg muttered, 'I'll be back to bring her home tomorrow. First thing.'

Jan didn't know much about strokes, but she knew enough to appreciate there was no chance of Mary going anywhere near her home for the next few days, weeks even. But, struggling to control the emotion in her voice, she said, 'OK, Dad. I'll stay the night with you and we'll both come back in the morning.'

8

Reg felt reluctant to take himself to his usual early bed and waited up late with his only daughter. Jan made him cocoa, stirring in a tot of whisky, and they sat in the kitchen as the black knobbly coals burnt in the range.

The hollow tick of the ancient grandfather clock, audible from the stone-flagged hall, marked the long silences between them. They were waiting for Ben, who was driving down from London and had hit traffic on the Oxford bypass.

'She's been building up to this, you know,' said Reg quietly after a while. 'She's not been herself lately.'

'I noticed, Dad, how confused she's been and not very talkative.'

'Aye. Dwelling on the past, I reckon; brought on by the colonel's death, I dare say.'

Jan thought about this. It was true Mary had been overly concerned with the Gilbert family and with what might happen in Riscombe now that the colonel was dead. Jan thought her mother was unduly worried regarding the prospect of change. For generations it had been such a settled community, though not always a completely contented one.

'Anyway,' said Reg, after another long pause, 'I don't like to think of her in that hospital bed. There's no warmth there, nothing familiar. She should be here, with us.'

'You know that's not possible in the state she's in, Dad. She's far better off where she is. The specialists there know what they are doing. Mum needs their expertise.'

Reg sipped from his mug and stared into the glowing range.

'Well, she's hardly spent a night in hospital afore,' he said after another long pause. 'She won't know what's what.'

'Really? What about when Ben and I were born?'

'Eh?'

'Wasn't she in hospital then?'

'No, she weren't. You were both born here. We had the midwife in. That's what you did then. Miss Loy came on her bike. You was her first delivery, that's how you came by the tea service in the cabinet. She gave it to your mum and said she was to hand it on to you when you reached twenty-one.'

At any other time Jan might have laughed affectionately at this tale. But now it made her sad – a small memory of a lost world, the young days of Reg and Mary, still green in the ways of the world and launched into parenthood by a middle-aged district nurse on a rattling old bike.

'Anyway, Mum probably doesn't even know where she is at the moment,' Jan said after a while. 'So it doesn't really matter to her.'

'But I want her back where she belongs.'

'Oh, I know how hard it is, Dad. It is for me too, but let's just get her well again first, eh?'

Another long, considering silence followed before Reg spoke again. 'If it wasn't for me, perhaps she would be well.'

'Dad, what on earth do you mean?'

Reg sighed and sipped again from the mug, his eyes fixed on the red hot coke in the grate.

'It's just that sometimes I think she judges me,' he said darkly.

'Don't be silly. What has she to judge you about?'

But Reg was not really listening to his daughter. He had turned inwards, attentive to his own thoughts. 'Things that happened,' he muttered. 'Things that were not right. And matters I should have attended to years ago.'

'Dad, what on *earth* are you talking about? Mum loves you more than anything in the world. You are her rock. She's told me that more than once.'

Reg went to sip again, then stopped, and suddenly a fleeting smile flickered across his face.

'Aye, well, maybe. But she's been mine, too.'

At that moment they heard the front door crashing open and slamming shut. Thank God for that, Jan thought, comforted by the arrival of her brother.

🐎

For the next few days they kept a close-knit family vigil beside Mary's bed at Cheltenham General Hospital. Jan had asked Fran to stay at Edge Farm for the duration, so at least she didn't have to worry about the children.

There had been little change in Mary's condition. She simply lay against the pillows with her eyes closed. When spoken to, she gave not a flicker of response. As Jan sat in the bedside chair, she would find herself listening obsessively to her mother's breathing. At times the inhalations seemed heavier and more rapid than at others, as if Mary were experiencing an inner disturbance, as if there were mental activity of some kind. But Jan had no way of knowing if these were worries or wishes, troubled thoughts or happy dreams.

The medical staff remained noncommittal about her mother's prospects. The only message Jan received was that Mary might regain her faculties completely at any time or she might not improve at all. Or she could end up somewhere in between.

'But is she aware of anything?' Jan quizzed.

'I'm afraid, Mrs Hardy, that is something we don't know the answer to.'

The doctor was a smartly turned out but tired-looking registrar, a woman of about Jan's age.

'If she is, she's simply lost the ability to react. But she may actually be unconscious at the moment. We can't be positive one way or the other.'

'You mean she's actually in a coma?'

'Well, yes, that's one word for it. Asleep is another. But it's a good idea to keep talking to her. A familiar voice is a stimulus. It never ceases to amaze me, the body's ability to recover.'

Moments later Jan leaned forward on her chair and, with her mouth close to her mother's ear so Mary could listen to her voice, she just spoke randomly about her life, the horses, the children's schooling, things she'd seen on television like *Coronation Street*, which was Mary's favourite programme. At these moments Jan felt strangely childlike as this was how Megan and Matty would talk to her, chattering about things they were doing in class, or giving long descriptions of playground games or the plots of stories in their books or on television. Furthermore, the children didn't expect any input from the opposite side. Twenty-five years ago, Jan thought, this was how me and Ben often spoke to Mother and now, as an adult, here I am doing it all over again.

On Monday morning Jan did not go to the hospital. Instead, after exercising the horses and cooking breakfast, she got down to some urgent and neglected paperwork in the office. Ben, she knew, had taken Reg in to Cheltenham General before going on to the offices of the solicitor, John Mellor, in Broadway, for the meeting about Colonel Gilbert's will. Jan was finding it hard to concentrate on her race entries and the farrier's and veterinary bills, which had to be sorted before her own accounts were sent out at the end of the month, but to make a mistake could be costly, she knew that. Her mind constantly went back to her mother's frail figure in the hospital bed, and she found herself from time to time wondering what news Ben was getting from Mr Mellor. 'Just get a bloody grip, will you?' she said to herself.

Shortly after midday Jan was back in the house, standing at the kitchen table as she trimmed a bunch of flowers to take to Mary, when she heard the engine of a car, then the slam of its door. Ben came in looking serious, a little grim even.

'Hi, Sis,' he said as he strode over to the kettle, checked it for water and clicked it on. 'I think you'd better sit down.'

'I'm all right. I want to finish doing these flowers before I go and see Mum.'

'No, you don't.'

Ben collected two mugs from the cupboard and dropped a tea bag into each of them.

'You will need to be sitting down when you hear my news. I've just left Mellor and I've also seen Virginia and her no-good brother.'

Jan carried on cutting the ends off the stems.

'It's OK, you can tell me. I'm not going to faint.'

'All right, then, but don't say I didn't warn you, it's absolutely crazy. Mad even, and I haven't a clue why.'

He was rooting around in the fridge looking for milk.

'He's left me Dowerhouse Farm.'

'WHAT? OUCH!'

The shock had made Jan jerk her hand and, in the process nick her thumb with the scissors. 'Dowerhouse? He's left you *Dowerhouse*? Is this a joke?' She stuck the thumb in her mouth and sucked hard to clear the wound.

Ben returned to the table with the bottle of milk and sat down. He shook his head.

'Deadly serious. I am the official owner of Dowerhouse Farm.'

'Fucking hell, Ben! The colonel's left you a whole house?'

'Jan, don't use that language. You know Mother doesn't like it. Anyway, not just the house but the three hundred and fifty acres of land that go with it.'

'Oh my God!'

Jan dropped the scissors and the dahlia, then flopped into the chair opposite her brother, still sucking her thumb.

'What, he left you all the land as well?'

'Yup.'

The kettle came to the boil and automatically snapped off. Ben poured hot water into the mugs and handed one of them to Jan.

'Crikey, you know what that means? Virginia's gallops are on that bit.'

'Yes, I guess that's one reason why she was there at the solicitor's. She's none too happy about the situation, I can tell you.'

'I'll bet she's not. So sweet little Virginia was there to hear all this?'

'She knew about it already, as a matter of fact. But she and Harry arrived later than me.'

Jan clicked her fingers twice in Ben's direction.

'Come on, Brother, I want to know what happened while you were in the solicitor's office. Every detail, mind!'

'Well, to be honest, it wasn't at all what I expected. I think I had it in my head that this was the fabled reading of the will, like you see on the telly on a Sunday afternoon. You know the kind of thing

I mean: in a classic, the gathering of expectant legatees sitting around a boardroom table listening to a doddery old solicitor with mutton-chop whiskers and a starched collar reading out the legacies in a reedy voice.'

'So what was it like in real life?'

'Well, I realize now all that stuff is a bit of a myth. What actually happened is that Mellor saw me in his office and told me that the colonel had added a codicil to his will, and in it he stated that I was to have Dowerhouse Farm. Apparently somehow the codicil had got detached from the original document and Mellor didn't find it straight away. When he did, Virginia and Harry Gilbert tried to argue that it wasn't in order legally and that the colonel's original wishes had always been that the estate should remain whole and stay in the family. But Mellor told them the codicil was properly signed, and had been witnessed by the colonel's doctor from London, so it was in order. So then they resorted to saying their father must have been of unsound mind.'

'What? The colonel off his rocker?' said Jan. 'That is complete bollocks. Nobody was more sane. But you do have to ask yourself why on earth he should make such a codicil. You would think the ghastly Gilberts were right and he would actually want the estate kept within the family. Does the will say why he's picked you out, what his reasoning was?'

Ben shook his head in bewilderment.

'Not a word. I was totally gobsmacked. I asked Mellor, why me? And he just said my guess was as good as his. Then he said he thought the colonel may have wanted me to know the reason, but in the strictest confidence. He told me – and this is the part that really is a bit like something on the telly – that I'd been left a second legacy and that maybe it would give a clue as to what this was all about.'

Ben took a folded sheaf of papers out of the breast pocket of his jacket and began to flatten it on the table.

'What's that?' asked Jan, getting up and trying to grab what Ben was holding. But he quickly whisked the document out of her reach.

'Now, now, Sis, patience,' he said, holding the papers high in the air as he leafed through the four or five pages. 'This is the actual will, with the colonel's codicil. I quote . . .'

He cleared his throat and held the legal papers high in front of his eyes before reading out loud.

'"And I further bequeath to Benjamin Pritchard my metal deed box and its contents, which he is directed in the first instance to open in private."'

'*In private?*' said Jan. 'Why would you have to do that? The plot thickens. Where *is* this deed box anyway? Did Mellor give it to you there and then? Have you opened it yet?'

'No, I can't do that until tomorrow. It's in a vault. I have to meet Mellor at the bank in the morning. We'll retrieve it then.'

'This whole thing is simply amazing. What on earth is it all about? You did say you actually saw Virginia and Harry at the solicitor's, didn't you?'

'Yes. They arrived just as I was leaving, in Harry's ultra-flashy open-top motor. I gather they were also going in to see Mellor to talk about the Dowerhouse gallop, amongst other things, of course. They collared me in the car park.'

'What did they say?'

'Oh, the usual stuff. Virginia sneered at me in her customary and superior way and Harry just seemed rather embarrassed, especially when Virginia suddenly got quite aggressive. She told me not to harbour any ideas about taking the gallop away from her. She said, "That gallop is for our horses, and our horses only. Daddy didn't intend me to be deprived of it." She was going in to insist that Mellor fights me tooth and nail for it. So I just said there was no need to waste her energy as I intended to let her go on using it anyway.'

'Well, if you ask me, I don't see why she should,' said Jan. 'There's plenty of other land she could use, though I admit anywhere else on the estate would come a poor second to the strip of turf at the Dowerhouse, at least in quality. That gallop's absolutely fantastic.'

'So I gather. But I can't just throw Virginia off, can I? In any case you wouldn't want me to *really*, would you?'

Jan's eyes looked skywards as Ben held up the colonel's will.

'It says here that I have to maintain that specific piece of land especially for the sole purpose of exercising racehorses, and that I

must allow Virginia use of it "for a reasonable rent". Mellor says it's
a legal stipulation. So I told Virginia that I was sure we could agree
terms. She looked as if she'd just bitten the head off a toad. She
must hate the idea of paying me.'

'Of course she does. She thinks she's not like the rest of us, who
have to pay our way.'

'You rent your gallop, don't you?'

'Most of it. It begins on my land, but it finishes up on the farm
next door, so we pay just for the use of that bit. Mind you, it's not
cheap.'

'I don't suppose you'd like to switch over to the Dowerhouse
gallop yourself?'

Jan's eyes lit up.

'God, Ben! Try and stop me. It's a thousand times better than
what I'm making do with here. Do you really think I can? Will it be
all right? You know, within the will, I mean.'

'Of course. Anyway, it's only a mile-and-a-half hack from here,
so it's just about the right distance to warm your horses up before
you gallop them, and I can't think of any reason why you and
Virginia shouldn't both use it.'

'Well, I can. As a matter of fact, I can think of two. She doesn't
like me and I can't stand the sight of her either.'

'Who says you have to be best buddies? You can share. And I
tell you what, just to pay her back for being such a snotty bitch, I'll
give you first call.'

Jan gave a gratified smile.

'Thanks, Ben. That would suit me just fine.'

He folded the copy of the will and slipped it back into his
pocket. 'Now, Jan, I have a favour to ask. Will you come to the
bank with me tomorrow? I want you to be there when I open that
deed box.'

'Oh! I don't know if I should. What about the colonel saying
you have to do it privately?'

'Well, he won't know, will he? And having you there wouldn't
really count. The point is, I gather the colonel didn't want any
strangers knowing the truth, whatever that might be.'

'OK,' said Jan. 'I'll be there, but what time? I need to exercise my horses first.'

❦

It was the afternoon when Jan drove to the hospital to collect Reg. They spent a fretful hour together with Mary, whose condition showed no change, before Jan drove him back to Riscombe, where Ben was cooking supper. They had agreed to wait until after they'd eaten before telling him any of the details regarding Colonel Gilbert's wishes for Dowerhouse Farm.

'I wonder if Dad knows the reason already, though,' Ben had said to Jan earlier.

If he did know, Reg said little. Instead he became very tight-lipped and his offspring quickly got the message that he didn't want to talk about the legacy or the reasons behind it. After Reg had gone to bed, Ben saw his sister out to the car.

'He knows, doesn't he?' Ben said, holding open the driver's door.

Jan got in and pushed the key into the ignition.

'Something, maybe. But he's not saying. Anyway, it's upsetting him, whatever it is.'

'Well, he's already fretting about Mum being in hospital—'

'Yes, I know, but what I mean is something about *this* is aggravating him even further.'

She twisted the key and the engine rattled into life.

'Well, we'll all know tomorrow, I guess,' she added as she released the handbrake.

❦

The next morning Ben deposited Reg by Mary's bedside and drove on to Broadway, where he had arranged to meet Jan in the pub overlooking the green. The bank holding many secrets was nearby on the High Street. Following a couple of bloody marys for Dutch courage, they set off together to arrive at the appointed time.

The manager, Mr Draper, greeted them in his office positioned above the banking hall. John Mellor was already there, sipping from his coffee cup, his little finger cocked at an awkward angle. Draper was a red-faced, jolly figure in a brass-buttoned blazer, a blue shirt and an overly loud tie. Whereas the moustached Mellor reminded Jan of a rabbit, with prominent buck teeth, curly hair and a hawk-eyed watchfulness, as if he were constantly on the lookout for surprises, or sudden danger.

Jan and Ben refused the offer of coffee and Draper rubbed his hands together in a decisive manner.

'So, let's get down to business. Firstly, we must descend to the bowels of the earth.'

He picked up a ring binder and a bunch of keys from his desk and led them down the stairs, continuing past the ground floor until they reached the basement. There, off the stairwell, was a room full of metal filing cabinets, ranged around the walls and in a block down the centre. Draper walked round these and approached a heavy steel door on the other side, unlocking it with one of the keys from his bunch. Then, with what seemed like an exaggerated effort, he heaved it open and leant inside to find the switch on the strip lighting. With a series of buzzes, clicks and strobe-like flickers, the interior burst into light.

Draper made a grandiose flourish with his right arm.

'My vault!'

Never having been in a strongroom before, Jan had envisaged a dungeon-like room, hung with cobwebs and smelling of damp. In fact this was no more than a large-sized, beige-carpeted, stone-walled cupboard. Entering behind the others, she saw that, apart from a single Formica-topped table in the centre of the space, it contained nothing but metal-doored deposit boxes, lining three walls from floor to ceiling, and a huge safe with combination locks set into the fourth wall. Each deposit box was equipped with two conventional locks and identified by a number. Draper checked the contents of the ring binder, running an index finger down the list of depositors with the numbers of their individual boxes next to them. He shuffled a few inches and tapped on one of the metal doors.

'This is the one. You have the colonel's other key, don't you, John?'

Mellor produced a key from his pocket, while Draper tucked the ring binder under his arm and selected another from the bunch in his hand. They fitted their keys into the locks and turned them. As Draper tugged the door open they all peered inside.

The large black deposit box contained a small green deed box, which the manager pulled reverently into the light. Now, as he laid it on the table, Jan could see the painted lettering on the lid, identifying it as the property of 'Colonel G. Gilbert MC.' The bank manager also recovered a small brown Manila envelope which had originally been Sellotaped on top of the box. On this were inked the words 'Key to Box 66098'. Draper handed the envelope to Ben, who slipped it into his pocket.

'Is this deed box all he kept here?' Ben enquired.

'There were several other papers,' confirmed Mellor, 'but we cleared them out following his death. I was just checking we hadn't missed anything this time round. Not knowing what was in this deed box, we left it here for safe-keeping until probate was granted. Now if you could just sign here, Mr Pritchard – I need to make sure my paperwork is in order.'

'Well,' said Draper, glancing at his watch. 'That would seem to conclude our business. Will you be taking the box away with you, Mr Pritchard? Or would you like to open a deposit of your own? We'd be delighted to look after it for you.'

Ben lifted the box, weighing it in his hands.

'No, that will be fine, thanks. I'm taking it with me, but if I do change my mind of course I'll let you know, Mr Draper.'

As they filed out, Jan murmured to Ben, 'Is it heavy?'

Ben shook his head. 'Not particularly. I'd say there's not a lot in it.'

As they reached groundfloor level, a secretary bustled down the stairs and interrupted them.

'Would you be Mr Pritchard and Mrs Hardy?'

'Yes, I'm Mrs Hardy,' said Jan.

'Oh good. We've had a phone message from Cheltenham General Hospital – from a Mr Reg Pritchard?'

Ben and Jan exchanged fearful glances.

'What is it?' asked Ben.

'It's your mother. He says there's been a change in her condition and asked if you could hurry.'

9

'Come on, Sis, hurry up,' Ben shouted over his shoulder as they ran from the bank.

'Hold on, my car's this way,' Jan said breathlessly.

'Never mind your old crate, jump in mine. We can pick yours up later, and if it gets a ticket, tough.'

Ben drove fast and they spoke little, both of them worrying about their mother. It had been impossible to tell, from the message left by the hospital, whether the news about Mary would be good or bad. There had been a 'change', but what kind of change? Skirting the Common, they plunged down Cleeve Hill towards the racecourse and the town of Cheltenham. Whenever she passed the spot, Jan thought of the accident a year and a half before, in which Eddie had so nearly been killed. For a few tense days he had been in a coma not unlike the one Mary was in now, before gradually recovering. Jan wished she could be sure her mother would do the same.

Meeting increasingly dense traffic in Cheltenham, Ben was forced to slow down.

As they waited at a set of traffic lights, he said, 'What shall we say about the Dowerhouse and this deed box?'

'To Dad?' Jan hesitated. 'I suppose there's nothing we can say that's worth saying – not until you have opened that box. He doesn't really want to discuss it, anyway.'

'But what about Mum? If she has returned to this world, I mean, she might want to.'

Jan contemplated the consequences.

'I think she could be told the outline, but only if she's better and when Dad's not there. There's something weird about all this that's upsetting him like hell and we don't need to add to his troubles right now. But Mum would never forgive us if we deliberately kept from her that you are the new owner of Dowerhouse Farm, that's for sure.'

As the traffic lights changed, Ben drove forward, concentrating on his choice of lane and did not answer straight away.

'Yes, I agree,' he said when he'd found the right junction. 'But we don't have to tell her right now, do we?'

'If she's come round and is feeling better, she'll have visitors from Riscombe soon enough. There's Rosemary Sterry, for a start. I wouldn't be at all surprised if it's not the first thing she brings up.'

'OK, Sis, I see your point. So, will you tell her?'

He looked at Jan with appealing eyes.

'Why don't you?' she asked. 'It's your legacy.'

'Yes, but you'll do it far better. If I take Dad off for a walk around the grounds at some point. You could tell her then.'

Jan sighed. 'OK, but only if Mum's in a condition to be told, I'll speak to the medics and decide then. The most important thing to deal with at this moment in time is helping Mum to get better, whatever that takes.'

On the ward the doctors told Ben and Jan that their mother had overcome her 'vegetative state' and might well go on to make dramatic progress. But they warned she might just as easily suffer another stroke, or remain in her present state indefinitely. What was the point in passing this information on to Mary? They decided the only thing to do was to remain positive.

They found their mother sleeping, with Reg looking fearful and drawn at her side. Jan knew immediately this wasn't the time to talk about Ben's inheritance.

Jan had been away from the yard for several hours and needed to get back to Edge Farm in time for evening stables, but she needed to go via Broadway to collect her car. Ben said he would take her and, despite looking tired, Reg decided to stay at the hospital until one of them could collect him later.

As Jan and Ben were leaving the hospital foyer Jan suddenly stopped.

'Oh, blast, Ben. You get the car, I've left my handbag by Mum's bed.'

'Leave it, Sis. We can get it when we collect Dad later.'

'No, I can't. It's got my house and car keys in it. I won't be a minute.' As Jan approached Mary's room she could see through the observation window Reg gently patting her mother's hand and although she was asleep he was talking to her. Jan could clearly see her dad had tears in his eyes. She pushed the door slightly ajar to hear Reg's words.

'Now don't you fret, my old lovely, the kids are all excited about this inheritance. I know the truth will come out, but you let me deal with it. I'll sort it, you just rest easy and get better. I ain't nothing without you, Mary Pritchard, so don't you go leaving me.'

With tears streaming down her face, Jan pushed the door open and wrapped her arms around Reg.

'Oh, Dad, we love you and Mum so much. We've got to be strong for one another.' She kissed her dad on top of his head, something he had always done to her as a child to reassure her. 'Dad, I don't want to leave, but I have to deal with the horses and that's Ben blasting the car horn. We will be back to collect you later. Try and have a nap in the chair, if you can.'

On the way to Broadway Jan and Ben talked for a while about their mother and the various ways of interpreting the medical reports. But it was not long before the colonel's deed box with its secrets, locked in the car boot, returned to their minds.

'I'm sorry,' Ben said, 'I know this sounds callous with Mum so ill and all that, but I have to know what's in that sodding box.'

'Of course,' Jan said, as they approached the car park in Broadway where hers had been left. 'Come back to Edge. We can do it there if you still want me to be there when you open it.'

❧

It was mid-afternoon when the two cars pulled up the drive and the house was unusually quiet. Fran, the housekeeper, had gone shopping and would collect Megan and Matty from school on her way home. Jan led Ben into the sitting room, where he laid the deed box on the low, glass-topped table that occupied the space between sofa and fireplace. He fished in his pocket and brought out the grimy beige envelope in which the key had been deposited.

They sat side by side on the sofa. Jan bit her lip as Ben, with a solemn look on his face, slipped the key from the envelope and into the keyhole. The mechanism unlocked with a loud click and he raised the lid.

At first sight the box contained a litter of used envelopes, old and lying face down. On top of these was a newer envelope with Ben's name on. It looked very much as if this was the last thing the colonel had put inside the box before finally locking it up.

Jan touched the inscription of Ben's name with her index finger. It was in blue ink, written with a fountain pen.

'That's the colonel's handwriting, no question.'

Ben picked up the envelope and turned it over. The flap was sealed. He and Jan exchanged looks, then without a word Ben inserted a thumb under the flap and tore it open. He felt inside and eased out a thick, folded sheaf of notepaper covered in the same blue-ink handwriting.

'It's dated three years ago.'

'That's when he made the codicil, isn't it?'

'Exactly. Shall I read it out loud?'

'Yes, please.'

'All right, here goes.'

Sitting forward on the sofa, with the sheets of paper laid on the table he took the first leaf and began to read the letter in his deep, resonant voice.

'Dear Ben,

'You will, I am sure, have been more than a little surprised upon receiving news from my solicitors of the legacy I have set aside for you in my will.

'I will try to explain, but I beg you to consider carefully how much of this information you make public.

'You must at least be aware, if your mother has told you anything about her childhood in Riscombe, that she and I knew one another at the age of five or six. We were just playmates, but as time went by Mary Collins and I developed a deep friendship which was solely based on enjoyment of each other's company. Maybe I found her more interesting because I knew how much my parents disapproved of me playing with the village children, even though I had no one in the family close to me in age (my brother was six years younger), but I have no idea what Mary saw in me.

'Without a doubt these are some of the happiest memories of my early childhood. But the innocent friendship between us was cut short when I was removed from the village school and sent to a preparatory school on the south coast. It was then that I lost touch with Mary for several years.

'But Jack Collins, your grandfather, was the best farrier in the area, so we used to see quite a lot of him and, as I was completely besotted with horses, I was keen to cultivate his acquaintance when he was doing his rounds. Especially as I heard news of his daughter, how she was doing at school and suchlike. Truth to tell, these things didn't much interest me at first, but there comes a time in a young man's life when the other gender strikes you as being worthwhile. One morning much later, during my Easter holidays from Rugby when I was sixteen, I was hanging around the stables waiting for Jack the farrier, who was coming over to shoe my hunter. But he didn't arrive: it was Mary who suddenly appeared, handing me a message to say her father was sick with the 'flu. In my impatience to have my horse shod I was angry and cursed him for being a lazy so-and-so. Instantly Mary came right up to me with her hands on her hips and her eyes flashing. She was a sight to behold. I'll never forget the words she used. "Deepest shame on you, George Gilbert. It's selfish, rude and ignorant to speak like that about my father, who is the most conscientious man that ever lived and the finest farrier for a hundred miles in any direction." Having delivered these scathing words, she stormed off.

'From that moment Mary Collins was on my mind every day. I found it impossible to get to sleep at night for thinking about her. I admired the spirit she had shown in facing up to me, and, I have to admit, what she said to me so outspokenly was quite true at the time. And of course I liked her pretty face. Eventually I wrote her a note to apologize and to ask if she would meet me. Thankfully she agreed. We met and went for a walk in Riscombe Woods, it was there I kissed her for the first time.

'So now, you can see, for the first time in my life, I was hopelessly in love and so, it seemed, was Mary. During termtime we wrote to each other constantly. In the holidays we spent as much time together as possible. We were determined to get married, if necessary by eloping to Gretna Green. But the whole affair had to be kept secret. We knew for certain my parents would never approve of me carrying on 'beneath myself', and it was a fair bet the Collinses would not approve the relationship either. So we decided, immediately after I left school, just a few weeks past my eighteenth birthday and your mother's seventeenth, to make our move. I packed a suitcase, and had some money for the journey. But the day before we could elope it all came out. Mary had confided in a close friend, who told her mother. She went round to see Mary's mother, who at once charged up to the manor to have it out with my father.

'The next thing I knew I'd been packed off to London to stay with my aunt and uncle while it was decided how to end our romance. Shortly afterwards I found myself in France, living with a family who kept their eye on me for the rest of the summer. Then I was dispatched to Sandhurst. Mary too was sent away for a time to stay with relations, I didn't know where. We had been forced apart quite brutally. Our letters were intercepted and returned unopened, and from that time onwards we were forbidden to meet.

'With the heaviest of hearts I accepted the situation. Then, two years later, came Korea and I could forget Mary Collins at last by immersing myself in war and the need to stay alive. For the next ten years I was a professional soldier and deliberately stayed as far away from Riscombe as I could. I served all around the world and relished the most hazardous postings – after Korea came Malaya, Cyprus, Kenya, every one of them a war zone. So it wasn't until my father died in the late fifties that I left the regular army and came home to manage Riscombe.

'By now, of course, I was married to my dutiful wife, Clare, and we already had our daughter, Virginia. I found when I returned, that your mother had married Reg and had a little girl, your elder sister, Jan, who has been like a daughter to me. Reg and Mary were tenants in one of my cottages and your mother worked at the manor as one of our dailies. We were, I would say, terribly British about the situation and never mentioned our earlier relationship. We had both, it seemed, put the past behind us and made different lives. That, I think, is how we considered the matter best dealt with.

'But as I get older, with my wife deceased and my children now adults, I dwell on times gone by and dear Mary Collins, my first love. Now I want to honour her, but without embarrassing either her or indeed her family. So nothing will happen until I have passed on, and possibly by that time she will have too. Nevertheless, that is the reason I have left you Dowerhouse Farm. From the little that I know of you (I've made a few discreet enquiries!) I think you will be able to make good use of it. I trust you will do so honourably and (if this isn't too old-fashioned a word) like a gentleman. <u>Wrongs were done</u>, though I hope and believe this bequest can go some way towards putting them right.

'I'm sorry if you think I have rambled on, but I need you to understand my position. It has taken me all night to write this letter, now I am exhausted and must close. The next person to read these words will be the new owner of Dowerhouse Farm. I send you my very best wishes.

'Yours sincerely,

George Gilbert

'PS: I am sure Jan will be a huge support.'

Slowly, Ben refolded the pages of the colonel's letter and slid them back into the envelope, which he placed on the table. Then he eased himself back until he rested against the sofa cushions, closing his eyes.

'But why me and not you, Jan, when it's clear he thought the world of you? That's what I would really like to know.' He sighed.

Jan felt her heart beating unnaturally hard. It was as if she had been a little girl again, and had ventured into a forbidden room in the house.

'I don't know, but I guess this explains Mum's behaviour after the colonel died,' she said, after a while. 'It clearly brought it all back to her.'

'But Mum loves Dad,' objected Ben. 'She worships him. Everybody knows that.'

'I'm not saying she doesn't. It was the colonel's death that jolted her into remembering a time before Dad and her first love. We all know about that – you never really forget . . .'

'You've got to admit, though, it is a fairly dramatic story, getting set to elope to Gretna Green and all that!'

'And later the colonel hurling himself into battle to erase the painful memories. Although, of course, he wasn't a colonel until much later on,' Jan added.

Ben suddenly jumped to his feet, picked up the envelope with the letter inside and made for the door.

'Sis, I've got to go and find Annabel,' he said. 'I need to talk to her and tell her about this crazy stuff!'

When he had gone Jan continued to sit in the silent room. The colonel's story didn't fully explain the reason for Mary's anxiety after his death, though it might account for Reg's peculiar attitude towards the legacy, and his adamant refusal to discuss it. Or might it not? Of course, he must have heard about George Gilbert and Mary Collins years ago. But, knowing her father as she did, Jan felt this was something he could have lived with, even laughed off. After all it was he, not the colonel, who had won the prize in the end. There had to be something more to all this. What on earth did the colonel mean when he wrote the words 'Wrongs were done' and underlined them? Was he only referring to the way in which the love affair had been cut short? OK, that had been pretty brutal. But did it really come under the heading of a wrong crying out for atonement? And even if it did, what other wrongs did the colonel mean? It seemed as if he was referring to more than one.

Jan began idly sifting through some of the other papers in the deed box. She half pulled one package of papers out of the envelope that enclosed it. It was held together by a red ribbon. She immediately recognized that these were letters, written in a slightly unformed version of her mother's own handwriting. So, there they were. The colonel had hung onto the love letters Mary had written to him while he was at school all those years ago. Jan didn't untie the ribbon, or try and read any of the words visible to her. Instead she pushed the bundle back into its envelope, returned it to the box and dropped the lid. To read the letters would be a violation, Jan thought.

10

Ben was in the middle of recording a new Band of Brothers album and on Tuesday he had no choice but to go back to London for an all-night session. Jan was saddened he couldn't stay down in the country, but Mary's stay in hospital was indefinite for the time being and Ben couldn't hang around at Riscombe and Cheltenham on that basis. A spell of compassionate leave was not an option for him as the studio had already been booked and paid for.

Reg had found Mary's sudden hospitalization stressful, but he was getting more used to the predicament, and it was a good sign that by Tuesday he had insisted he was perfectly capable of driving himself, in his own battered Daihatsu, to and from Cheltenham. Although he was approaching eighty Reg was an independent, strong-minded Cotswold farmer and, like all farmers, he believed difficulties must be faced squarely and in person.

And Reg felt the disaster of Mary's stroke fell into the same category. Coming and going to her bedside as he liked meant he was still his own man, still doing what was necessary. It also signalled his understanding of Ben's position – and Jan's. Like her brother, she had no choice but to attend to her business. Even though her mother lay desperately ill, the daily routine of the yard, going racing and overseeing the visits of vets and farriers and the work of the staff, could not simply be laid aside to be dealt with at a more convenient time. Annabel was a highly competent assistant, but to leave all these responsibilities to her would be too big a burden. And there was still the job of being a mother to Megan and Matty, which no one else could do. Jan felt at times like this that the pressure of being a one-parent family was immense and to get the balance right was nigh on impossible.

Even so, the next afternoon Jan spent two hours with her mother. Reg had been there in the morning, but had gone to meet a man about moving his sheep to their winter grazing. Mary was much as she had been on Jan's previous visit two days earlier – still unable to talk, or move any part of her body to a significant degree except her eyes and fingers, but Jan felt sure that the movement in her mother's hand had grown stronger during the last week. This aided communication as now she was able to squeeze Jan's hand with more emphasis.

Mary liked to hear about the comings and goings at the yard.

'Remember that new owner of mine, Bobby Montana, who sent us two horses from America? He said they're worth a fortune, but I have serious doubts about that. We ran one of them at Towcester last week and a clothes horse would have beaten him. Bobby's other is the one with navicular disease. We've been pulling out all the stops for him. Shirley the vet has been great. She's got Mickey Reid shaping his hoof in a special way to relieve as much pressure on the bone as possible. I expect Grandad Collins must have seen quite a few cases like that, in his time. I wish he was here now – I bet some of his old methods were as successful as the new ones.'

Jan stroked her mother's hand, feeling the fingers tighten a little as Mary confirmed she was listening and that, yes, her father had indeed known all about navicular disease.

'So! What else has been happening?' Jan said after a few moments. 'Oh, yes, I heard that the portrait of Russian Eagle's finished. The artist, Horace Pursival, rang up to ask if we want a formal presentation. Apparently a lot of clients like to host a reception, where their new painting gets formally unveiled. I told him to contact A.D. O'Hagan as he's his client, not me. But I reckon the old boy just wanted an excuse for a party, especially one in which he's the centre of attention and he can get sozzled at someone else's expense.'

Jan decided not to broach the subject of Eddie and the ending of their engagement, or the incident with Jason Cobb. She was determined to stick to light, amusing and unthreatening topics. So she began to tell Mary about some of her owners. Toby Waller had phoned from Hong Kong to say he was planning to be back in the UK by Christmas in time to see one of his horses run at Kempton Park on Boxing Day. Then there were the Band of Brothers, who were making a new album with Ben – their horse, Teenage Red, she told her mother, had already won twice this season – and Bernie Sutcliffe had finally agreed to retire his horse Arctic Hay, thank God.

'He calls him his "Grand National hero" because he completed the course last year. He ran a blinder for first circuit this year until he collided with a loose horse and unshipped his jockey at the Canal Turn. Even so, Bernie had been on and on at me to keep him in training for another crack at Aintree, but I told him no, definitely no, forget it. I wouldn't enter a horse at the age of fourteen in a race like that, or any other race, for that matter. So he's agreed that the old horse can go hunting and take life a bit easier, which will be a great way for him to semi-retire. At least he won't be just chucked out in a field in the cold and rain.'

Jan was interrupted by the clump of footsteps approaching the bed and, looking up, she saw it was the smiling figure of Rosemary Sterry, coming towards them with a bag of grapes at the ready. Jan stood and greeted her mother's friend, who took a seat on the other side of Mary's bed. Jan could tell from her mother's eyes how pleased she was that Rosemary had come to visit.

Jan started a conversation across the bed about events in Riscombe over the previous week. The exchanges were rather stilted as they were not really about communication between themselves, but a way of entertaining and informing Mary, even though she could do little more than listen. After half an hour of this slightly forced conversation, Jan excused herself and slipped out of the ward to let the two friends have some time alone. She spent a few minutes chatting at the nurses' station. Then she wandered down to the ground-floor cafeteria and had a cup of tea.

By now half an hour had passed and Jan decided to return to the ward. There she found Rosemary already standing and buttoning her coat.

'Jan, I've got to go. I'm catching the bus to Broadway. It arrives just in time to pick up the vicar's minibus home.'

'Oh, don't you worry about that, Rosemary. I can give you a lift. It's time I was getting back too.'

Jan went to Mary's side and kissed her lightly on the forehead before tidying and smoothing down the bedclothes. She explained why she had to get back, and that she would definitely return on Sunday with clean nighties, all freshly ironed. Mary's eyes looked at her steadily.

'Well, just fancy the colonel leaving Dowerhouse Farm to your brother,' said Rosemary as she sat beside Jan in the car. 'They reckon the Gilberts are furious – the news is all round the village.'

It was not yet Cheltenham's rush hour and having whisked through the outskirts of town they had made good time and were now approaching Riscombe.

'He was a dark one, that Colonel Gilbert,' Rosemary went on, 'and no mistake. Still waters run deep, I always say.'

'You're the same age as Mum, aren't you, Rosemary?'

'Rose, dear. Everyone who's a friend calls me Rose. Yes, we're almost exactly the same age, except I was born a month earlier, but we grew up together.'

'So did you know about her getting involved with George Gilbert when they were teenagers?'

'At the time? Oh yes, I knew all about it, being Mary's special friend, you see. You know what it's like when you have a secret boyfriend. You've got to confide in someone. We didn't have secrets, we used to tell one another everything. We were that close.'

Suddenly a thought struck Jan. 'So, was it you who let the cat out of the bag?' she asked.

'I'm sorry, dear?'

'Well, I gather it was one of my mother's friends who told *her* mother about the affair, and that's how the news reached the ears of old Mr Gilbert, that his son George was planning to elope with the farrier's daughter.'

Rosemary laughed, a nervous giggle.

'Oh! You've heard about that then. It was my mother – she wormed it out of me. I had this lovely print dress, see, that I used to go dancing in and Mary had always envied me in it. So, as we were about the same size in them days, I gave it to her. For her trousseau, I said. Anyway my mother noticed the dress was missing from my wardrobe. She went berserk and that's how she got the story out of me.'

Rosemary sighed deeply.

'At the time I was in such a state about what I'd done I thought I'd die. But Mary was most understanding. Anyway, she was soon packed off to Yorkshire, to a cousin of your grandad's, until things quietened down. When she came back I thought she would never want to speak to me again, but not a bit of it. All she said was, "Rose, it was my fault for coveting that dress of yours. I should have realized the trouble it would cause if I accepted it."'

'Was she very upset?'

'About losing George Gilbert? Oh yes, cried on and off for weeks, she did. And for a long time she wrote to him, but all the letters came back unopened. Gradually she got over it, of course, and in my opinion it was for the best. They were still only kids, you see. I couldn't see it lasting, not with such big differences in their circumstances. Anyway, by the time your father took the lease on Vale Farm and started walking out with Mary, she was more mature. And it was more suitable, in a way, Reg being a good bit older than her, and a steadying influence. Still, only the good Lord knows what would've happened eventually if she had run off and wed the squire's son.'

Well, I wouldn't exist for starters, Jan thought, but decided against putting it into words.

'Are you saying Mum was a little wild when she was young, Rose? I can't imagine that for one minute.'

Rosemary thought for a moment, trying to find the right word.

'No, not wild, wilful. One thing about her was, she spoke her mind and didn't give a fig who heard. In fact it got her into real trouble a few times, I don't mind telling you.'

'Oh, really? What kind of trouble?'

Suddenly it appeared that Rosemary did mind telling, because instead of replying she just stared at the road ahead, tutting and shaking her head a couple of times.

They arrived at Rosemary's home, a pretty terraced cottage in Cotswold stone. It, like most of the houses in the village, belonged to the Riscombe estate. She had lived there all her married life, staying on with Herb after the death of her husband Martin, seven years earlier.

'Won't you come in and have a cuppa? I've got a nice jam sponge that I made this morning.'

Jan thought of evening stables, but remembered Annabel was already half-expecting to cover for her. Besides, Rosemary's revelations were enthralling and she wanted to hear more.

'I'd love to,' she replied.

The front door of Rosemary Sterry's home opened straight into a small, impeccably tidy sitting room, which had an open fireplace and two armchairs with the chintz upholstery heavily frayed and worn. The room was dominated by a large Welsh dresser, behind which a box staircase rose to the floor above.

'Sit yourself down,' Rosemary said before disappearing through the rear door, which led to a small kitchen.

'Can I give you a hand?' Jan enquired.

'No thanks, I can manage. There's not enough room to swing a cat in here, as it is. Can you remember coming here as a little girl, both you and Ben? You'd call in on your way home from school and I'd give you a slice of cake and, if it was a hot day, a glass of pop. Who'd have thought one day those two little mites would be so successful?'

Rosemary soon reappeared and as Jan bit into the delicious sponge cake she remembered those times. She could even recall the prickling in her nose caused by bubbles from the dandelion and burdock that Rosemary used to give them. It was excessively sweet, but to small children it was quite delightful.

'Was that when you and Mum were working up at the manor?'

Rosemary looked pensive as she sipped her tea.

'I was still doing mornings, but not your mum. She finished when she fell pregnant with Ben.'

'The colonel's wife, what was she like? What was it like working there?'

Rosemary wrinkled her nose as she thought back.

'Mrs Gilbert, she was a proper tartar. Working at the manor was very hard on you. Nothing was ever done right in her eyes. Either it was the stair banisters not polished properly, or the table not set right – nothing you did ever suited her. I don't think the colonel had it particularly easy either. Old Martha the cook used to say she was a general's daughter and that was the reason she was so strict.'

'Was she good-looking when she was young? I only remember her as an invalid.'

'Yes, she did get old before her time. Originally she was . . . but look, you can see for yourself. I've got a picture of her somewhere.'

Rosemary heaved herself up and crossed to the dresser, where she opened one of the cupboard doors. She stooped and pulled out a thick album, bound in black. Breathing hard, she returned to her chair and plonked herself down. She opened the book on her knee while Jan got up and stood behind her. Rosemary's fingers, which were chafed and misshapen by years of hard work, turned quickly past the early pages. Occasionally Jan glimpsed stiff-collared, hoop-skirted and long-dead Sterrys, posing self-consciously for the camera. The sepia-tinted portraits gave way after a few pages to smaller black-and-white pictures, many of them tilting or blurred when the subject had moved at the wrong time. These were less formal images of mothers and babies, beach picnics, children setting off for their first day at school, and other memorable occasions, obviously snapped with the family's Box Brownie. As Rosemary turned one of these pages, a single rather larger photograph fluttered out and fell at Jan's feet. She picked it up and studied it.

This was not quite a professional picture, but nor was it a snapshot. A group of people stood in a field, behind them a downland ridge covered in furze and bracken. It was obvious the central characters were gentry. The half-dozen men, all in tweeds, carried twelve-bore shotguns broken open and nestling in the crooks of their arms. The five women standing with them were also tweedy, but only one had a gun on her arm. In the foreground the morning's bag of partridge and a few duck had been laid out in rows on the ground. They were flanked by an assortment of gun dogs with lolling tongues, mostly spaniels and Labradors.

Behind this group stood the estate workers – farm hands and domestics enjoying a day off from their normal duties to act as beaters or to help with the shoot picnic. Jan quickly spotted her mother wearing an overcoat and scarf, the wind blowing her ample fair hair across her face. She cut a trim, decidedly pretty figure.

Jan showed Rosemary.

'Isn't Mrs Gilbert the woman with the gun?'

Rosemary picked up her glasses and inspected the picture carefully.

'Oh yes, that's her, I remember it well. We were all given one. It was taken by Mr Kenworthy, the old estate manager. That was his hobby, photography. This was – what? – the first shooting party of the season in nineteen . . .'

She stared into the air, and screwed up her eyes.

'Oh! I don't know, late fifties, early sixties, something like that. That's me. There's my Martin there. And here's your mum, so good-looking she was in them days. And yes, that's Mrs Gilbert. Keen on shooting, she was, before her illness set in. You can see she was dark and not bad looking, but a little what I'd call scrawny, pinched maybe. Her daughter Virginia takes after her in that way – not to mention in others.'

'Who are the rest of them?'

'Well, here's the colonel, though, come to think of it, he was probably only a major then. I think his promotion to colonel came later, through the territorial army. These others are various friends come down for the weekend. I've no idea who they are.'

But one young man in the party especially struck Jan. He stood slightly apart from the rest of the group, with a cheroot dangling from his lips. There was something vaguely familiar about him and she wondered if he was an actor, or a celebrity who used to get into the newspapers. He was blond and more elegantly dressed than the others, and had a look on his face that could only be described as a smirk.

'I've a feeling I've seen this chap somewhere before,' said Jan, pointing him out to Rosemary. 'I wonder who he is.'

Rosemary was now breathing even more heavily, as if this reminiscing was tiring her out.

'Oh well, that's the colonel's brother, Mr Hugo we used to call him.'

'Hugo? I don't think I met him did I?'

While Jan was speaking Rosemary dropped the photo back between the pages and slammed the book too.

'No, I shouldn't think so, he went abroad years ago,' she said. 'And the less said about that the better. Put this back in the dresser, would you, dear?'

Jan took the album, returned it to its place and carefully shut the cupboard door.

'When did you and my mum first start working at the manor?' she asked, lingering by the dresser.

'Oh, that was way back in the old squire's time. It was easier then, in a way. Him and his lady were no pushovers, mind, but their hearts were in the right place.'

'But they were tough enough on their son, wouldn't you say?'

'Ah, I suppose. They wouldn't let him follow his heart's desire, would they?'

'And now it seems as if he never really got over it. Making that legacy to my brother, I mean.'

'But he *did* get over it. Or so we all assumed. When he came back from the army to take over the estate he was quite different, a married man with decorations and so on.'

'But how was he with my mother? How did he treat her?'

'Absolutely correct. He behaved very honourably towards your dad too, when he had quite a bad accident on the farm. The colonel paid for him to have medical attention in Harley Street, we heard. Nothing but the best, see?'

'Might that have been because he still had a soft spot for my mum, though?'

'I'm sure he did have. But his behaviour was always honourable, that's what I'm saying. Not like some I could mention.'

The last remark was made with a certain amount of bitterness. Jan was just about to ask what she meant by it when Rosemary suddenly pulled herself to her feet and rapidly piled the used crockery onto the tray. Her meaning was clear. Jan glanced at the mantel clock, and saw how late it was.

'My goodness,' she exclaimed. 'Is that the time? I should go.'

As Jan drove up the track towards Edge, she saw a car racing towards her. The headlights flashed into her eyes as the vehicle bounced in and out of the potholes. Seemingly oblivious to Jan's approach, the driver made no attempt to slow down. It was only by wrenching the wheel and skidding onto the grass verge that Jan avoided a collision.

She was furious as she jumped out of the car by the entrance to the yard. There she found Annabel on her way up to the house, with an arm full of jockeys' silks and other washing wrapped in a large bundle. Jan stood in her path, pointing with an angry, straight-arm gesture down the track.

'Who the sodding hell was that?' she shouted. 'He drove me off the road, the stupid bastard!'

Annabel did not answer. Instead she pushed the washing into Jan's arms.

'Here, you take these, I'll go back and get the rest.'

Jan steadied the unexpected bundle with her chin. After a few steps towards the house she stopped and called out, 'So who *was* it?'

'Bobby Montana, who else?' Annabel shouted back as she disappeared under the archway and into the yard.

As they loaded the washing machine a couple of minutes later, Annabel told Jan about Montana's visit.

'He happened to be passing, so he said, and took the chance to visit his little darlings.'

'What was his hurry? He was driving like a maniac.'

'He said he was late and had to be somewhere double quick. In actual fact he hardly had time to look at the horses properly.'

'Well, I wish I'd seen him. He already owes us a stack of money, the original advance ran out ages ago. I keep sending him bills, but nothing comes back.'

'Don't worry. On past form he'll be returning. I think we see more of him than the rest of the owners put together. Mr Montana can't stay away, it seems.'

'Well, his two aren't exactly fit for racing, are they?'

'No, and that's another thing. How in God's name can they be worth what he reckons, especially the condition they're in? It's not as if they arrived in good nick either. It's obvious they had been in a sorry state for some time, especially the one with navicular disease.'

'I have been thinking about that myself,' said Jan. 'It's really odd, he comes here and seems genuinely fond of his horses, but he never goes racing. How do you work that one out?'

11

Jan's point was underlined the next morning when, after exercising first lot, she was going from box to box checking the legs of each horse. Big Freeze was still a semi-invalid, and she could clearly see how unhappy he was. Next door was Spring Blow, who was being dressed over by Connor, one of Jan's three Irish lads.

'Phwaw! Christ, Con, what did you have for dinner last night?'

'Curry, Mrs H.'

'That explains it. This place stinks of garlic. How's Spring Blow today?'

'Terrible. Miserable as sin he is. He can hardly lift his head to the manger. And he has a touch of diarrhoea. It's him who stinks, Mrs H, not me.'

'That's interesting,' Jan continued, 'Well, he's going backwards on the gallops that's for sure. What the hell are we going to do with him?'

'I'd get the vet. He's sick, if you ask me.'

'I had him scoped weeks ago and the sample came up normal.'

'Perhaps he can't stand the sight of his owner. He always reacts badly when that feller's been here.'

Jan looked into the horse's eyes and nostrils, then she bent down and felt his knees, running her hand down to the hoof before passing behind to the tendons and down to the fetlock joints. She felt along the horse's back and ribcage before she moved on to the hind legs, paying particular attention to the joints. Were these a little swollen? She couldn't be certain.

'We'll put him back on road work for the time being,' she said, making a mental note to call Shirley on Monday. She sighed and moved on to the next horse, A.D. O'Hagan's Galway Fox. He had been a difficult horse to train until they'd found a problem with his teeth. With that sorted, he'd improved out of all recognition and during the last two seasons he had turned out to be a very useful two-mile chaser. Unlike Spring Blow, he was alert, his ears and eyes moving in co-ordination as he took in every movement around him.

On Friday evening Ben rang to invite Jan and the kids to join him and Annabel for Sunday lunch. This was to be a picnic in the grounds of Dowerhouse Farm. They had set a date for their wedding early next summer and had decided they would move into the house afterwards. This was the first chance they'd had to get a really good look at what would be their home.

'Wouldn't you two prefer to have the place to yourselves?' Jan suggested. 'I don't want to muscle in.'

'Sis, don't worry about that, it'll be fun. Dad's coming and a mate of mine, an architect, who's going to advise us on the work that needs doing. I need your advice about the gallop anyway. The colonel's instructions were to maintain it, but I'd like to take a closer look at what's involved. And, we need to talk about you using it for the Edge Farm horses, so why don't you and the kids ride over?'

After sitting for a couple of hours with her mother on Sunday morning, Jan drove back to Edge, where Megan, one of life's organizers, had her Monarch and Matty's pony Rocket tacked up and ready to go. Jan found that her own mount was also already saddled, thanks to Roz, who was to play concierge at the yard for the afternoon. They set off at a quiet walk, before trotting into the valley and up the slope of Riscombe Down on the other side. Twenty minutes later, they were clattering into the cobbled yard of Ben and Annabel's future home.

It was not as festive an occasion as they would have liked. The food was good – Annabel had laid on Reg's bantam eggs and sausage rolls, Wiltshire ham in baps and a nice Chablis. But except for

Larry, Ben's lanky, curly-haired architect friend, they were all thinking of picnics past, when it would have been Mary who boiled the eggs and filled the baps. Now the thought of her lying in hospital, unable to speak, was extremely hard to take in.

After the picnic they wandered around the house, discussing the essential work and other things that might be done by way of conversion. It was a roomy, stone-built, Georgian house, originally the dower house to Riscombe Manor, built in the eighteenth century for the use of the young squire's widowed mother, should she have need of a home. Facing towards the road was a door, with an imposing stone porch, which looked as if it had hardly been used during its later years as a farmhouse. This led into a hallway, where an elegant flight of stairs rose to the first floor, while a lateral corridor crossed it at the back, running almost the length of the building. Branching off this were airy rooms, adaptable for a variety of uses, Ben suggested. At one end stood a big sitting room, and at the other a large dilapidated kitchen. The arrangement of the rooms had been unchanged in the lifetime of the house, and the kitchen was almost exactly as it had been in the nineteen thirties, Larry thought. Another outside door opened directly into the farmyard itself.

'The ideal,' said Larry, 'would be to take it back to what it was and bring it up to date at the same time. Of course, that would be impossible. So what we need to look for is the right balance.'

Stabbing the window frames with his penknife, and testing the exterior walls with a meter, Larry diagnosed no serious ailments and was able to pronounce the place in good basic health, though it had not had a tenant for some four or five years as a complete refurbishment would have been far too costly, when set against any income generated from rent. There was evidence that some re-roofing had been carried out quite recently, proof that the colonel had been keeping a close eye on his empty property once he had earmarked it for Ben.

After they'd eaten, with Annabel's help Larry set to work measuring up the rooms, to enable him to make accurate drawings and a plan for the work they had been discussing. Reg, Jan and Ben, accompanied by Megan and Matty on their ponies, walked out to the fields below Riscombe Down, where the grass gallop was laid out. This consisted of two tracks. One was a loop which covered a mile and encircled an area of ploughland at present leased to a neighbouring farmer. Branching off from this was a second strip of turf in a spur; at first it went in a straight line, then turned into a shallow bend that resembled the shape of a sickle. Stretching for almost a mile, and starting on level ground, the gallop rose gradually as it met the lower slope of the Downs. At the end a bridle path led back towards the starting point.

As soon as they stepped onto the hallowed turf, Megan, with a sudden shout, rousted Monarch and set off at a gallop along the sickle-shaped track. Not wanting to be left behind, Matty kicked Rocket on and pursued her.

'So, what do you make of it, Jan?' Ben asked.

'It's bloody fantastic. Don't you think so, Dad? It feels like a top-quality carpet.'

Reg grunted as he jabbed in his heel to test the resilience of the turf.

'Yes, it's as good as I heard it was. They knew what they were doing when they laid this down, and that was a while ago now.'

'So when the colonel's will says I've got to maintain it, what does that mean? What would I have to do?' asked Ben.

'Not that much, really,' said Jan. 'The main thing is to keep it topped and only use it for its intended purpose. But you will need to watch out for any obvious invaders such as moles and thistles, though not many of those are going to get established here, this grass is so thick and well rooted.'

'So what are the possibilities of you using it from Edge Farm? We're not too far away, are we?'

'No, it will slightly increase the time it takes to complete our morning exercise. But basically I can't wait.'

'What about sharing it with Virginia Gilbert?'

Jan made a face. 'Oh, I wouldn't be very keen to do that.'

'Jan, I'm afraid you're going to have to.'

'Oh, Ben, there's bound to be trouble. You know what she's like. There's plenty of land. Why can't she just lay out some new gallops of her own?'

Ben put a hand on his sister's shoulder.

'You know I can't throw her off, Sis. She'll have to pay, which will be bad enough in her book. But if you're going to come here yourself, it's got to be on the basis of sharing with Virginia. If for no other reason than that's what the colonel wanted. I have my hands tied to a certain extent anyway because of the terms of the codicil.'

In frustration, Jan kicked a tussock of grass.

'Oh, all right, but don't expect me to be nice to her. And I want first use every morning.'

Ben chuckled. 'First use it is then. Hey! Look at those kids go.'

He pointed at Megan and Monarch, who were now moving away from them at a fair rate of knots. The smaller Rocket couldn't match Monarch's pace, so Matty urged him on until Rocket was galloping flat out. At the same moment his small rider lifted his bottom and lowered his chin, just like the jockeys he'd seen in action on television.

'Oh my God, he's not supposed to gallop! He's only six.'

Aghast, Jan began to run after them, shouting in vain as her cries were caught and whipped away by the breeze. Matty seemed to be working his hands up and down the pony's neck, urging him to go faster. Seconds later she saw him teetering in the saddle, and then topple off sideways. Jan shrieked as he bounced on the springy turf and lay stock still.

To her amazement, as Jan panted up to him, Matty was lying on his back with a broad grin on his face.

'Did you see, Mum? Me and Rocket were galloping. I was just like a jockey riding in a race.'

'Matty! I've told you before not to do that, you're not old enough.'

'But it was brilliant, Mum.'

'It wouldn't have been if you'd broken your neck. You can stick to riding a finish on the back of the settee for the time being.'

Hearing her mother's shouts, Megan had wheeled Monarch round, and was trotting over to collect the loose pony. She led him back by the reins to rejoin his unseated rider. Matty rolled over and got to his feet as Jan waved to Ben and Reg, who were making their way towards them, signalling that all was well.

'Anyway you're all right this time, thank goodness,' she told Matty. 'Let's lead him back shall we?'

'No! No!' he shouted. 'I want to get back up. Please, Mum! I want to get *back up on him now*.'

That evening, in Megan's room, Jan read aloud to the children for longer than usual. They had reached the last-but-one chapter of *The Story of Dr Dolittle* when both Megan and Matty had pleaded with her, as if it were a desperate matter of life and death, to go on to the end of the book, breaking their usual rule of one chapter per night. Jan was tired but she gave in rather easily, because all her old love of Hugh Lofting's books had been brought magically back to her over the last two weeks of reading.

'"And when the Winter came again,"' she read, '"and the snow flew against the kitchen-window . . ."' She turned at last to the final page, suppressing a yawn, '"the Doctor and his animals would sit round the big, warm fire after supper; and he would read aloud to them out of his books . . ."'

'They're like us,' said Megan, removing her thumb from her mouth. 'Only we're not animals.'

'Don't you be so sure,' said Jan, laughing and reading on. '"But far away in Africa where before the monkeys went to bed under the big yellow moon, they would say to one another, 'Do you think he will ever come back?' And the crocodile would grunt up at them from the black mud of the river, 'I'm SURE he will – go to sleep!' The End."

'And that goes for you two. It's late and you will be tired in the morning.'

She kissed Megan and carried Matty, already practically asleep, into his own room. As she tucked him up he murmured, 'Mum, you talk to the horses, don't you?'

'Do I?'

'Yes, I heard you. Talking to them, just like Dr Dolittle.'

She kissed him and stroked his cheek.

'Well, yes, I suppose I do.'

'Do they talk back?'

'Yes, they talk back in their own way.'

'I thought so. Rocket talks to me sometimes.'

She kissed him again and said goodnight from the door, but he was already asleep. Going down the stairs she reflected how much he had changed, how much more confident he had become, since starting full-time school. Until recently he had been the baby of the family; now he was becoming a man, he thought!

The phone on the small table near the bottom of the stairs was ringing. She picked it up.

'Hello?'

'Jan?'

It was Ben. She was aware of an unusual element in his tone of voice – tightness, strain, pain, something like that.

'Where are you? Is something the matter?'

'I'm with Dad at the hospital.'

It was then that Jan's heart jolted.

'It's Mum, isn't it?'

'Yes.'

Jan shut her eyes tightly, waiting for Ben to go on.

'I brought Dad back to Cheltenham after we left Dowerhouse. He insisted, he said he had to see Mum, that something was wrong. It was intuition. When we arrived, we found she'd had another stroke and was unconscious.'

Still Jan didn't speak. She knew now with an icy, unreal clarity what Ben was going to say next, but it was important to wait for the actual words, it was important not to anticipate them. The line was very clear and she could hear hurried footsteps in the hospital corridor, and odd snatches of conversation. Ben was breathing deeply.

At last he said, 'Sis, I hate having to tell you this, but Mum died a quarter of an hour ago.'

Jan's legs almost gave way. She put out her arm and steadied herself against the wall.

'Jan? Are you there? Please speak to me.'

A kind of numbness had begun to steal over Jan's entire body and she wanted more than anything to sit down. But she managed to say, 'Yes, Ben, I heard. I'll come over?'

'No,' he said, 'you've got the children to think of. There's nothing we can do tonight anyway except to take Dad home.'

'Right. I'll be over first thing tomorrow then.'

She hung up without waiting for Ben's reply and suddenly she was choking, hardly able to draw breath, tears flooding down her cheeks. She felt very alone.

12

Work is the best way to cure weeping. It had been one of Mary Pritchard's favourite sayings, often heard by Jan in her own childish outbursts, when a cherished plan failed or a playground friendship cooled off. But for her mother this was more than a glib proverb to be trotted out whenever a difficult situation arose. Mary had lived her life on the principle that one should never have an idle minute and that the needs of other people should always come before one's own. Jan knew she would honour her mother's memory much more by proving herself in the stable yard, on the gallops or at the racecourse than she ever could by moping around feeling sorry for herself. Besides, she was determined not to display any weakness in front of stewards, trainers and jockeys, who were ninety-five per cent male and in a few cases all too eager to see a female come a cropper at the slightest hint of emotional upset.

So carrying on with work, proving these dinosaurs wrong, was Jan's way of curing her grief.

For three days that short fit of crying after she'd put the receiver down on her brother were the only tears she shed. The numb, almost unreal sensation that had possessed her when she heard the news of Mary's death still persisted, however, as, in a fog, she helped Ben make the funeral arrangements. She tried to comfort Reg while running the yard and taking horses to Newton Abbot and Ludlow. Throughout this time she found the loss of her mother to be quite a different feeling from the death of her husband, John. This time, underlying her inability to mourn for her mother, she felt a sense of anger and of dread. Unpleasant though this feeling was, Jan was for some reason reluctant to let go of it and she held back the flood of grief that might wash it away and allow her to move on.

It was Tuesday when Jan took a call in the office. A.D. O'Hagan was on the line, his voice as always warm, yet measured.

'I heard of your loss, Jan. I am truly sorry. I had a long chat with your mother at the races, Stratford, I think it was. She was a fine woman altogether. Is there anything I can do to help out?'

How typical of A.D., Jan thought, that he should be the first of her owners to phone up to offer sympathy. She felt a sudden surge of gratitude towards him – for his past support and his kind and tactful dealings with her family. At the same time, however pleasant she found her most important owner, A.D. was another of *those* men in racing. So now she was not going to weep on his shoulder, or let him see any of her cracks under pressure.

'Thanks, A.D.,' she said with false cheerfulness. 'I appreciate the offer. But no, there's really nothing you can do. Thankfully, I have the funeral arrangements well in hand with the help of my brother. The staff have been a great help too, especially Annabel. So, the work of the yard goes on as before.'

'I don't doubt it, but this is a time when a person must also look after their own needs. Don't neglect that aspect, Jan.'

'I'll try not to, A.D. And thanks very much for ringing, it really is appreciated.'

'I'll just mention something else, if I may. It's not the reason for my call, I don't want you to think that. Anyway, I'd better explain. You'll be getting a glossy brochure through the post any day now. No pressure, but I thought you should be kept fully informed.'

'A brochure? What of?'

'Tumblewind Grange Stables. All the development plans. I think you'll find it interesting reading, if nothing else.'

Perhaps it was just another manifestation of A.D.'s nice social touch. He had been on at Jan for a long time now to become the guvnor at his proposed new training complex near Lambourn, a scheme still at the planning stage. But reminding her of this now, underlining the fact that he still valued her services and skills, was just the kind of support Jan needed at the moment.

On the other hand, he would probably have been sending her that brochure anyway . . .

🏇

They arrived back from Ludlow early, having had runners in the first and third races. Before evening stables, as Fran was giving the children their tea, Jan wanted to check on the four horses turned out in one of the paddocks. Although still in training, they had been turned out for the afternoon with their rugs on to have a play and relax from the rigours of training. It helped keep their minds fresh. She set off down the track, hugely relieved at last to be alone. After three days of continuous activity, she had had enough. It had been a good day at Ludlow, her horses coming in first and third. But she'd taken no pleasure in it.

Jan let herself into the paddock. The four horses she'd come to see were cropping grass in a group towards the far side, where several bales of straw she had been using to school the youngsters over had been left in the centre. Instead of moving over to the grazing horses, Jan walked across to the bales and sat down. She was engulfed by a sense of emptiness. Looking across the valley towards the wooded crest of Riscombe Down, she thought of the village in the next valley where she had been born, and where her mother too had been born and lived all her life, and *her* mother before that. When Jan thought about the continuities of rural life she found them deeply moving, but with that emotion came huge sadness. Country life at its most basic level was about seasonal repetition, the cycles and circles of life. That was why people from the countryside were usually conservative at heart: sudden, radical change was not natural and rarely worked in the interest of the farming industry or the wildlife. But the threat of change was always there and it usually brought heartache.

Her mother's death, which had been as certain as her life, was a sudden change and a rupturing loss. But it was a natural one too, a part of nature's cycle. This thought brought a surge of emotion and tears again stung Jan's eyes. The landscape laid out before her was misting over and distorting her vision. Suddenly, without further

119

warning, the dam burst and Jan was overwhelmed by grief; huge, racking sobs, like an erupting volcano, swept through her body. She had no choice but to give in to the emotion, losing herself in it. A few minutes later the sadness began to subside. There was no one near, no one to see or hear her, so it had been all right to let go, she thought.

Unexpectedly, Jan felt a sharp nudge in the middle of her back. She whipped around and found that the four horses had wandered over and that the leader – the one who had shoved her with his nose – was A.D.'s Morning Glory. Shaking her head to clear it, sniffing, and wiping the tears from her face with a sleeve, Jan was surprised that the most inquisitive horse had turned out to be MG, particularly as he had needed a considerable emotional rescue by his gifted lad Patsy Keating before showing his true ability on the racecourse. Even now, he was an extremely withdrawn and reticent animal. But something had compelled him to lead the others over in order to give the crying Jan a hefty nudge with his muzzle.

'Hey! Behave yourself, MG. This is not the time for playing games.'

Looking at her watch, Jan realized evening stables would already have started. She lingered for a moment or two longer, then stretched and set off back towards the paddock gate. Halfway across the paddock something made her turn and she saw that, led by MG, the four horses were walking solemnly behind her in Indian file, their heads lowered so far towards the ground that their nostrils almost touched the grass. It was quite different from the way the horses normally walked.

When Jan stopped, the horses stopped too. It was like a game of Grandmother's Footsteps. They waited in their line-ahead formation, as if holding themselves in some kind of readiness, their heads all the time submissively lowered.

'What're you up to?' she challenged. 'What's this all about, eh?'

She set off once more. Again the horses came along in her wake and this time she let them. Reaching the gate, she turned and rubbed MG's nose, then produced some Polos from her pocket for each of the animals. OK, that could be the explanation for this peculiar behaviour – the hope of a Polo to crunch. But somehow

Jan didn't believe it. She'd never seen horses behave like this – it was as if they were actually sharing *her* sadness. Now her heart lightened for the first time since the death of her mother.

What was it Matty had wanted to know the other night? Did she talk to the horses, like Dr Dolittle? She did, of course, but this was something very different. This was the horses talking to her, sympathizing with her, feeling what she felt.

On her way back up the track towards the yard, Jan felt the dark cloud of fear and anger that had enveloped her beginning to lift. She had been wondering how she would ever face the funeral. Now she felt that the church service would be bearable, and so would the gathering back at Vale Farm.

Jan turned and looked back at the paddock she had just visited. The dusk was thickening, but she could see the horses still assembled at the gate, still gazing after her, their breath smoking gently in the cold evening air. 'I love you, boys,' she said quietly.

The funeral took place on the Friday after Mary's death. Edge Farm Stables had withdrawn all its runners for the day as a mark of respect, and the entire staff were gathered at Riscombe's parish church of St Stephen for the ceremony. The lads looked unnatural in suits and sober ties with their hair wetted and combed flat. The smartly dressed girls were even less recognizable without their jodhpurs and jeans.

Reg always said you could tell a person's worth by the numbers who turned up to their funeral. By this measure Mary's stock was high, for the church was packed. The entire local branch of the Women's Institute was there, Mary's 'jam-making friends' as Reg sometimes called them jokingly, many with their husbands also on parade. Local figures such as Terry Clarke, landlord of the Fox & Pheasant, and the butcher, George Machin, turned up, as did most of the Riscombe Manor estate workers, even the manager, Fred Messiter, and his wife, Gillian. The vicar was able to speak warmly and from personal knowledge of the woman who had at different times over the years cleaned the church, polished the brasses and the carved bench ends, arranged flowers, run fête stalls, and in her earlier days even joined the bell-ringing team – though only for long enough to convince Reg that he should be doing it in her place.

'To call Mary Pritchard a stalwart of this parish would be true enough,' the vicar said when summing up, 'but it would not do full justice to the qualities of goodness and Christian love with which she touched all our lives. Mary was such a selfless, unobtrusive person that she sometimes went unnoticed. Such people are often literally unnoticed until they leave us, and then their absence loudly proclaims them, and how much we depended on them.'

He cleared his throat, settled his spectacles on his nose, before continuing. 'Let us pray, and give thanks for the life of Mary Pritchard.'

After the final hymn, the procession to the graveside and the interment, Jan stood with her father and Ben at the church gate, shaking hands and making sure that everyone in the congregation knew they were invited back to Riscombe Vale Farm for sandwiches and a drink. Reg had got through the service with fortitude, merely wiping an occasional tear. Jan cried a little, along with most of the other women, as she could clearly see from the parade of red-rimmed eyes that passed her. She was just thanking Gillian Messiter for arranging the beautiful flowers in the church when she felt a tap on her shoulder.

'Hello, Jan.'

She quickly turned and her jaw dropped in amazement.

'Eddie! I didn't expect to see you here.'

'How are you coping?' he asked. 'Your mother was such a sweet, good person. I felt I had to come.'

'Thank you, Eddie. Thanks, that was really kind. I'm fine. I had three days when it felt like my guts had dropped out. But that's over now. What are you doing? Have you found Ron?'

Eddie sighed. 'No, I'm afraid we haven't, so it looks as if we've both lost a parent.'

'You may still find yours, though.'

'I live in hope, Jan. That's all I can do.'

'What are you doing, otherwise?'

'I'm about to take a new job, I think.'

'Oh yes? Where?'

He looked at her and she saw hesitation in his eyes. 'It's not quite settled,' he said evasively. 'Better not go into details just yet.'

'Right.'

But the pause spoke volumes. Both knew that many things were still unsaid between them that might have been better out in the open. But all in all, Jan thought, perhaps they were best left.

'It's been really nice seeing you again. Bye, Jan.'

'Goodbye, Eddie.'

Then he was gone.

13

Jan's rehabilitation continued through the next week, but the children remained a little bewildered following the death of their grandmother and needed all the attention she could give them. The yard, too, was busy, as the first important race meetings loomed and she hoped several of her better horses would be contenders for some serious prize money. Jan still felt a surprising sense of well-being, which even Eddie's brief reappearance had not quashed. Since her experience down in the paddock with Morning Glory and the others, she found herself drawing a new strength from the horses, and one or two reasons why she had chosen such a demanding way of life had suddenly become clear to her. She did not waste this new revelation, and the heavy workload seemed less of a burden than it had in the immediate aftermath of Mary's death.

In the early morning, seven days later, a large Manila envelope with an Irish stamp dropped through the letterbox. It contained A.D. O'Hagan's brochure, a glossy, expensive production showing an artist's impression of the Tumblewind Grange estate seen from the air. Jan had visited the place when it was a derelict house surrounded by overgrown gardens and collapsing outbuildings. The bird's eye view imagined by A.D.'s watercolourist was almost unrecognizable as the same property.

The house, Jacobean on one side, neo-classical in the other wing, was an incredibly spruced-up version of the ruin Jan had seen earlier. The wrecked outbuildings had been replaced by two stable blocks, built in the traditional English pattern of a courtyard entered through an archway. The boxes, offices and storerooms were roofed with red tiles and ranged along all four sides. Surrounded by landscaped gardens, avenues of newly planted trees and white-railed paddocks, the Grange now looked like a fantasy racing yard, an idealized vision where there were none of the normal problems to distract a harassed trainer – no rain seeping into the boxes or tack room, no potholes in the drive, no patches of docks or nettles that someone would have to get round to digging out eventually.

Looking inside the prospectus, Jan began to read:

> Tumblewind Grange is designed to facilitate the training of around a hundred National Hunt horses, and will combine the best traditions, developed over centuries in the British Isles, with the latest in modern design and technology. This concept includes a range of all-weather gallops, a swimming pool, two automated horse-walkers and an indoor schooling barn. The veterinary facilities are superb and will include a state-of-the-art laboratory, a range of 'hospital' boxes as well as an isolation yard, and a forge for the farrier, which will enable him to hot shoe.

The text went on to describe plans for what amounted to a half-size National Hunt racecourse on the estate, with a complete range of fences and hurdles in various sizes. The investment seemed phenomenal, and the ambition limitless – and what's more A.D. wanted *her* to run it!

Jan closed the brochure and slid it back into its envelope. The place hadn't been built yet. Maybe it never would be. In the meantime she had more pressing concerns than making up her mind about whether she really wanted to be the employee of such a powerful man, with the opportunity to work in one of the most modern training establishments in the world, or to remain the boss of a small-scale, hand-to-mouth, make-do-and-mend yard like Edge Farm, in charge of her own decisions and destiny.

She sighed as she picked up the phone and dialled Gerry Harris's number. I really must get him to come over and deal with that leak into the tack-room, she thought.

🐎

Although Jan was a frequent visitor to Yorkshire's premier blood-stock sales, held at Doncaster, she had not sent many runners to the race meetings at Wetherby, and had not won an event in the county since her days point-to-pointing. This season she intended to put that right.

'I want to aim Magic Maestro at the Charlie Hall,' she had told A.D. O'Hagan back in September, during one of their weekly phone conferences. 'I think he'll like the track.'

'And the distance,' agreed A.D. 'I think he probably wants three miles now he's older and a bit more settled. You're of the opinion he's good enough, but will he be ready?'

'Yes, he'll certainly be ready – that run he had over hurdles should have put him spot on. He won the Cathcart at Cheltenham eighteen months ago, so I think he'll handle the extra half mile for sure, and I've never had a problem of any sort with him on the gallops. He's as genuine as they come.'

There was a momentary pause as A.D.'s mind worked. 'OK, Jan, let's go for it,' he said.

When the entries for the race, which had to be made three weeks before the event, appeared in the racing press, Michael Soley, racing correspondent from the *Daily Tribune*, phoned just as Jan was devouring the remnants of a luke-warm piece of toast and an equally tepid cup of tea.

'Is that Mrs Hardy?' his voice boomed.

'Yes, who's that?' Jan enquired.

'Mike Soley, *Daily Tribune*. Why have you entered Magic Maestro in the Charlie Hall? He's got no chance, he's a two-and-a-half miler – he won't get three miles in a horsebox with that class of field, and he wouldn't beat Mrs Dickler's horse if he started the day before. Her horse performs a stone better at Wetherby than any other racecourse in the country.'

'Oh, really,' mused Jan, the hackles rising on the back of her neck. 'And how many winners have you trained?'

Soley began to splutter down the phone.

'Well, none, actually, but everyone's talking about it. You really have cocked it up this time.'

'Look, Michael, I don't want to be rude, but I suggest you stick to writing about racing and leave me to train my horses. Goodbye.'

Jan was seething at the cheek of the man. 'How dare he tell me how to do my job? Right, Maestro,' she muttered. 'We'll bloody show them.'

On the morning of the race, the Edge Farm horsebox made an early start, trundling up the motorway, through the suburbs of the Midlands and south Yorkshire, before joining the Great North Road. It arrived at Wetherby three hours before the race and in plenty of time for Jan to walk the course, as she always did when she had a runner at a relatively unfamiliar venue or when there were any question marks about the going.

A.D. had assembled a party of friends for the event. This would not have excited much comment at Cheltenham or Aintree, but, in the more modest confines of Wetherby, it quickly set rumours flying that the legendary Irish gambler had placed a large bet and was expecting to collect. As a consequence it looked as though Maestro would start one of the favourites. This increased the pressure on Jan and she felt herself becoming tense as she joined her owner for lunch in his hospitality box.

'How are you, Jan? You look as nervous as a cat's tail in a room full of rocking chairs.'

She laughed. 'It wouldn't be so bad if they weren't rocking quite so energetically. You've got the whole place talking about Magic Maestro.'

'Me?' said A.D. innocently. 'Why on earth would I do such a thing?'

'Just by being here.' Jan didn't mention to A.D. the phone call she'd had from Michael Soley. She felt under enough pressure as it was.

At lunch she sat next to Baron Guy de Vilmorin, a white-haired banker from Geneva carefully dressed in what was considered on the continent to be the ultimate in English style – a tweed jacket, yellow waistcoat and starched shirt, with carefully pressed cavalry-twill trousers and brogues. He also had a neat beard and a precise command of the English language.

'I have placed a bet on your horse, Mrs Hardy,' he told her, with the air of someone who had managed a difficult feat. 'I hope it will succeed in gaining the prize.'

'That goes for the two of us.'

'Have you made a wager yourself?'

'No, I don't bet. There's enough uncertainty in this game as it is, and I really don't need the added pressure.'

'For you, I can see that might be so. But as an ordinary racegoer one requires the extra excitement.'

He produced a betting ticket from the fob pocket of his waistcoat.

'I entrusted my money to those bookmaker fellows. We do not have such creatures in Europe, you know, only the Pari-mutuel, the Totalizator. But I love your English way of doing things.'

'Well, you don't hear *that* said too often on an English race-course,' she replied.

She knew, at least by sight, most of the others present. There were the usual members of the O'Hagan team, such as the hard-drinking Jimmy O'Driscoll, A.D.'s racing manager, and a small group of the billionaire's relatives from Kerry. But she did not recognize one member of the party, who was talking quietly to Siobhan O'Hagan, A.D.'s serene and beautiful wife. Jan couldn't hear what the two were discussing because O'Driscoll, sitting between her and them, began telling a joke.

'There was this feller went into the presbytery, d'you see, and asked the priest if he would say mass for his dead dog . . .'

Jan had heard this joke before, and was more interested in the handsome stranger on her right. Having heard him speak earlier, she knew he was Irish and put him as somewhere in his late thirties.

'Well, the priest shook his head and none too politely pointed the gentleman in the direction of the Protestant church down the road. At this the feller slipped his wallet from his pocket and took out a couple of tenners, whereupon the priest's eyes lit up like a couple of sparklers . . .'

Throughout all this, the stranger was listening with close attention not to O'Driscoll but to the famous international mezzo-soprano. Jan could see from his body language that theirs was not quite a relationship of equals. Was he a journalist? Or someone who operated down the bloodstock supply chain – an agent perhaps, or breeder?

'"Now, why didn't you tell me in the first place that the dog was a Catholic?" said the priest.'

Laughter gusted round the table as O'Driscoll lifted his glass and took a swig.

'Is our horse a good Catholic, Jan?' enquired A.D. leaning forward to talk to her.

'Yes, did you make sure he said his rosary before coming away to the races today?' O'Driscoll added.

Jan had noticed that Irishmen tended to conceal their religious feelings under a cloak of humour. But she had decided a long time ago that, as an outsider, it was not particularly wise to join in with the joking. She ignored O'Driscoll, saying only, 'He was born in Ireland, A.D., so I guess he must be.'

The rest of the lunch passed quickly enough before Jan had to go downstairs to the weighing room, where she met her jockey and collected the tack before making her way to the saddling boxes on the far side of the parade ring. There she made sure everything was done, then double-checked, to make sure her charge was ready to line up for the Charlie Hall Pattern Chase, which was the fourth race on the card.

In the parade ring, as the saddled but unmounted runners circled the perimeter, owners, trainers and jockeys assembled on the grass in the centre. Jan discussed tactics with A.D. and her jockey, who on this occasion was Murty McGrath.

'I've walked the course,' she told them, 'and the going's good almost everywhere except for a patch of soft ground over on the far side.'

Murty, who had already ridden in two races that afternoon, confirmed this.

'That's a bit wet, for sure. But you're through it in a few strides. Nothing too serious.'

'I know, but as it's on the turn and only about three feet from the running rail there's always the danger of a horse slipping,' Jan pointed out. 'I think it's best to move to the outside there to avoid any trouble. And for God's sake don't drop him out at the back of the field. He needs to be up with the pace or he'll lose interest. You won't get a sudden burst of acceleration out of him at the finish, so don't be afraid to push on as you turn into the straight and head for home.'

Murty nodded. A man of few words, he was one of the most skilled jockeys in the country as well as one of the most productive. In Jan's experience, some of the riders either had cloth ears or thought they knew better than she did, but Murty generally followed her instructions. At the same time he could be a brilliant improviser if, for one reason or another, a race plan went awry. This combination of modest good sense and necessary initiative was what had made him successful in Ireland too.

A.D., beaming with pleasure in anticipation of the race to come, patted his jockey on the shoulder. 'And don't forget, this feller jumps for fun, Murty, so over these big fences you might be in for an exciting couple of circuits.'

🐎

Jan stood high up in the stands, alongside A.D., as the runners were called into line. When the field of seven came streaming past them for the first time, Jan's binoculars were fixed on hers – though no bigger than average, but still a powerfully built, athletic horse, he was moving easily. On the first bend one of the contenders pulled its way to the front and kept going to establish a fifteen-length lead. The rest of the pack stayed in a group, refusing to be rattled by the front runner. At this stage Murty did nothing remarkable, but sat quietly and let Magic Maestro settle in fourth place, one away from the running rail, exactly as Jan had requested. As A.D. said, Maestro seemed to revel in the big, black Wetherby fences, even though they were some of the stiffest in the country. With each leap he flew past his rivals, and on landing Murty had to restrain him.

As the field pounded past the stands for a second time and began the final circuit, a flurry of dry mud flew up from under the horses' hooves to create a blurry screen around the harlequin display of racing silks. By now the leader had predictably come back to the pursuing pack, and quickly dropped away through the field, his energy spent. Magic Maestro was disputing second place with another horse on his inside, which seemed to be full of running.

Approaching the next fence, an open ditch, Jan felt her throat constrict as a loose horse came flying up Murty's inside in such a way that Maestro's rival blundered into the ditch and tipped his jockey onto the other side of the fence. At the next, the culprit, jumping as enthusiastically as Maestro, but without the guidance of a jockey, leapt the fence on the diagonal across Murty's path, dramatically forcing him to switch inside to avoid a collision. Fortunately, by the time they had reached the last plain fence on the far side, the loose horses had run onto the hurdle course out of harm's way. Approaching the patch of false ground on the bend, Jan saw the maroon and gold stripes of A.D.'s colours bobbing up and down alongside the running rail – in the very position she had asked Murty not to be.

Jan's fears regarding the isolated patch of sodden ground were soon realized. Murty was trapped. He couldn't manoeuvre Maestro onto the drier narrow strip of ground because another horse had beaten him to it. Instead Murty edged right, further away from the rail. But he didn't have time to get out far enough. Jan gasped as she saw Maestro's feet slide under him as they hit the slippery turf. Murty immediately brought his centre of gravity down, crouching low in the saddle in anticipation of looming disaster.

Maestro's rear end slewed sideways towards another challenger moving up on the outside. Maestro's haunches cannoned into the other horse, making contact with his shoulder, and the impact was forceful enough to bounce Maestro back onto an even keel. As he took another stride, his hind legs cleared the slithery turf and he quickly found safe purchase on the better ground.

Maestro seemed none the worse for his momentary loss of traction and the leader was now within striking distance. As they entered the home straight, Murty let his horse carry him up to the heels of the leader. At the second last fence Maestro gave another exuberant leap as Murty crouched low in the saddle. By the time he passed the winning post, he had four lengths in hand.

A.D. unhooked his binoculars from around his neck and slowly wrapped the strap around the bridge between the eyepieces.

'Ours was half a stone superior to everything else in the race, and they weren't a bad bunch. What've you been putting in his feed, Jan? Spinach or what?'

'Nothing untoward, A.D., I can assure you of that.'

'Do you think there'll be a stewards' enquiry or an objection over that slip on the far side, when we barged the other horse out of it?' A.D. asked.

'No, it happened too far out. There was contact all right, but it was a complete accident and if anything the fault of the racecourse. They should have dolled that area off,' Jan said confidently.

As A.D.'s entourage followed Maestro into the winner's circle, where the horse received a tremendous round of applause from a knowing Yorkshire crowd in appreciation of a good race and a fine performance, Jan caught sight of Michael Soley's face in the rugby scrum of press which had now gathered around.

'Great performance, Mrs H, any chance he could go for the King George Chase?' said one scribe.

'I don't know, you had better ask Michael Soley. He knows all the answers, don't you Michael?' Jan's smile widened and she winked in the direction of the crestfallen lead writer. 'We will have to wait and see how the horse is after this race and when I've had a chance to discuss it with Mr O'Hagan.'

There was no enquiry and, after the post-race formalities, they reassembled in A.D.'s box for a celebratory drink, the guests all applauding Jan as she came in. A television in the corner was show-ing a race at Ascot, a valuable hurdle in which Virginia Gilbert's Velvet Dynasty was running. The hubbub in the box quietened as they watched Virginia's horse mow down its opposition with the utmost ease and professionalism. A.D. nodded towards the screen, which showed Virginia leading Velvet Dynasty towards the unsad-dling enclosure, her arm pumping the air in triumph.

'I wouldn't mind getting my hands on that horse, Jan. He's improved by a good few pounds since we saw him last. He could do anything now and I'm not sure our Morning Glory would beat him again.'

'As a matter of fact there's a whisper he may soon be on the market,' Jan said. 'Virginia and her brother have got a shed load of inheritance tax to pay. The talk at Riscombe is they haven't got the cash and apparently this is the only horse her father left her whose sale price would cover the amount owed. After that performance I expect they might decide this is the moment to turn him into readies.'

'Is that a fact?' There was a momentary pause as A.D. made a mental note of what she had told him. Then he beckoned her to come with him. 'Now, Jan, I want you to meet someone. Michael Finnegan, this is Jan Hardy. I've just brought Michael in as my project manager at Tumblewind Grange.'

It was the stranger from lunch. Finnegan held out his hand as his face split into a broad grin, showing lovely even white teeth.

'I've been looking forward to the chance to make myself known to you, Mrs Hardy. That was a damn fine win of Maestro's. You must be feeling very proud of him.'

Jan nodded at the television screen. 'Yes, I am, of course, but what did you think of that hurdler at Ascot? He used to be one of mine. I bought him too.'

'Did you indeed? He's a crackerjack.'

'And what's more,' put in A.D., 'Jan thinks that particular crackerjack might be coming on the market.'

'Well, in that case, maybe we can get him back for you,' said Michael, turning back to her.

'When did you come in on Tumblewind?' Jan asked, as A.D. moved away to speak to the baron.

'A while ago. I've been working in racing in America, but I used to know the boss back in Ireland when I was growing up. I rode a few as an amateur for him till I got too tall.'

'What brought you back from the States?'

His mouth twitched and he looked suddenly uncomfortable, as if her question had touched a nerve. 'Oh, you know, the pull of the oul' country . . . that kind of thing.'

He recovered instantly from the uneasy moment, waving his arm with an airy negligence. But there was more to his return than homesickness, Jan felt sure.

'And Tumblewind Grange?' she resumed. 'I've seen the brochure. It's going to be fantastic.'

'Yes. We still have the hell of a lot to do, but when we've finished there'll be nowhere like it. Well, in Dubai maybe. But not in Europe.'

He smiled that attractive, warm, engulfing smile again.

'I sound like a salesman, don't I? Actually I'm just the guy who makes sure the hod carriers turn up on time. But you do know A.D.'s mad to have you installed as the guvnor of Tumblewind, don't you? He wants to know what he can do to persuade you.'

'Oh, he told you about that, did he?' Jan sighed. 'He's been badgering me about this for a long time. But I value my independence too much, that's the problem.'

Michael Finnegan smiled.

'So do I. But a job's a job and the boss is a first-class employer. Still, I don't need to tell you that, do I?'

Jan giggled. 'Now *that* sounds like a sales pitch.'

'Well, it happens to be true,' Finnegan said earnestly.

'Will you go on working for him after this project is finished?'

'I hope so. My true vocation is with the horses rather than the hod carriers. So it depends on what comes up.'

'By the way, Michael,' she said, 'one other thing. When you were working in the States, did you ever come across a chap called Bobby Montana? An owner and a wealthy member of the Cherokee tribe, or so he says.'

Michael thought for a moment, then he shook his head.

'No, I don't think so. I reckon I might remember someone like that.'

'What about a Canadian trainer called Mervyn Sawyer?'

Michael rubbed his chin.

'That rings a bell. I probably saw his horses run, maybe just on the TV. But I don't know anything about him. Why do you ask?'

'Nothing that should worry you, Michael. It was just a thought. See you.' Jan smiled and waved as she walked away.

On the drive home that evening she really hoped it wouldn't be too long before she did.

14

The satellite racing channel that Jan had installed on the television in the office had proved an invaluable piece of equipment as she could record all her races and review the horses' performances, good or bad, and analyse any fallers.

Watching the videotape again on Sunday afternoon, Magic Maestro's performance at Wetherby looked even better. Jan was particularly interested to study the incident on the far side of the course, where A.D.'s horse had slipped on the patch of false ground. She was struck immediately by Murty's horsemanship, and how he had coped with the unwelcome intervention of the loose horse. Luck had played its part – Maestro might have gone down altogether if he hadn't bounced off the other runner – but Murty McGrath's cool head and the horse's natural athleticism had done the rest, as he kept himself and his horse balanced, then cleared the slithery patch and powered away.

Often, as a little girl, Jan had curled up on her father's knee to watch the racing on television. Once a horse whose name she had liked was pulled up at the halfway point, and she had complained bitterly.

'It's the jockey's job to be in charge and do the right thing,' she remembered Reg telling her. 'If his horse goes lame or he breaks a blood vessel, he's got to pull up. Don't forget, it's not a merry-go-round. That's real flesh and blood. Bones do get broke sometimes. Horses get frightened, some of 'em. So do jockeys.'

'Don't the horses like racing then?' she had asked.

'Oh, yes, I think they do most of the time. But remember, they're charging around the track as fast as they can in the middle of a pack of strangers, all different shapes and sizes, and different characters even. And there's not much time to think either. When something unexpected happens, the rider's got to keep cool.'

Jan thought that if anyone could be relied on to keep his head, when all around were losing theirs, it was Murty McGrath.

The tape was a recording of an entire afternoon's racing, a transmission that had been shared that day with the meeting at Ascot. So, after she'd rewound the video and looked at the Wetherby race a second time, Jan fast-forwarded to the Ascot hurdle event in which Velvet Dynasty had triumphed so easily. As she watched the gelding skipping up the straight all on his own with a dozen rivals toiling in his wake, she remembered the day she'd first seen him on television in a minor flat race. He'd performed that day like a drunken duck, but she'd realized what a good National Hunt prospect he might be, given the right handling. Later that year she had been delighted to get the chance to buy him at the Newmarket sales for Colonel Gilbert, who had sent a few horses to Jan even though his own daughter was a trainer. Following the sudden and unexpected death of the old man, Virginia had removed Velvet Dynasty from Edge Farm and taken him to Riscombe. Despite taking Velvet Dynasty on head to head in Ireland with A.D.'s Morning Glory and coming home victorious, Jan had always felt indignant at the loss of her future champion. Velvet Dynasty, she felt, was hers – her discovery, her baby, and she wanted him back.

🐎

A few days later A.D. O'Hagan telephoned to make an appointment for one of his periodic stable visits. Apart from making a careful inspection of the ten valuable animals he kept under Jan's care, he was to take possession of Horace Pursival's portrait of Russian Eagle. He asked Jan to organize some champagne one Sunday for the stable staff in celebration of the occasion, and Maestro's win at Wetherby. The guests of honour were to be Russian Eagle, Annabel, the artist and Magic Maestro.

It was a relatively warm day, with the low autumn sun shining from a crystalline sky. Pursival had arrived early and set up a large easel in the stable yard next to Eagle's box. There he placed his still-unseen painting, covered by a velvet drape, after issuing dire warnings to any passing lads about what would happen if they peeped.

Pursival was in a feverish state of excitement by the time the O'Hagan party turned up, but was quickly put at ease by A.D., who was as suave and charming as ever, as they chatted at some length about art and horses. Once the staff had finished their duties they assembled in the yard with the other guests, including important figures like Mickey the farrier, Shirley McGregor and the ever-devoted Gerry Harris. When everyone was ready with glass in hand, and in the company of Russian Eagle peering curiously over the bottom half of his door, A.D. made a short speech about the horse, the yard and the people who had made it what it was. He then stepped aside to allow his wife, Siobhan, to unveil the great work.

There were a few seconds of complete silence and breath-holding while they waited to see the fruits of Pursival's labours, then at the very moment Siobhan whipped the cloth away to reveal his image, Eagle snorted loudly.

'Well, we all know what *he* thinks of it!' said A.D.

Everyone laughed and as they stepped forward to cluster round the easel there were murmurs, and a few gasps, which to Pursival's delight seemed to signify approval.

Although in the painting Annabel was wearing long black riding boots and denim jeans, she did not look, at least to Jan, like a groom, or any kind of horsewoman. Pursival, she thought, had somehow, quite subtly, re-imagined Annabel as a photographic model, a film star even, a girl with a striking pose that could almost have been for a publicity shot. She looked beautiful in real life, but in the painting she seemed a good deal more sexy.

Jan looked at Annabel, and then at Ben, who was holding her hand. He grinned, moved her hand to his mouth and kissed the back of it lightly, then whispered in her ear. Annabel blushed and turned crimson at the remark, then shook her head. Now it was clear the image had not filled them with complete horror Jan could relax.

A few minutes later, as they walked across the yard, Jan was dying to ask A.D. what he thought of the painting, but he was already thinking about something else.

'I have Michael Finnegan installed in one of the old cottages at Tumblewind,' he told her. 'He keeps a good eye on the work in progress, but he's getting ants in his pants because he's not seeing any horses. You wouldn't be kind enough to let him come over here a couple of times a week, would you? You'll find he's a highly competent work rider.'

'Do you mean give him a job?' she asked cautiously, though her heart was racing.

'No, no, this would be strictly as a favour to me. You wouldn't have to pay him or anything. I'll take care of that.'

'Well, I'd like that very much. We can always do with more help.'

'You could call it staff training, if you like. I see it as a sort of refresher course. I think after being in America he needs to connect up again with the way we do things in British racing. So I want him to ride work, go to the races, see how you do entries, attend the sales, things like that. Anything you can do to help would be a bonus.'

'I don't see any problem with that,' said Jan. 'Provided he's prepared and willing to make himself useful, we'd welcome him.'

'Good. I'll get him to give you a ring and you can make the arrangements between you. Now, who do we have here? Ah yes, it's my old friend Tom's Touch.'

By the time they had visited every horse, the party around Pursival's painting had thinned out. Gerry and Daragh, A.D.'s driver, had taken the canvas off the easel and were carrying it with agonizing care across the yard and up to the house, where it would await the services of a specialized packaging firm. It would then travel across the Irish Sea to take its place in the gallery at Aigmont.

'So, what's the verdict?' Jan asked A.D. quietly, nodding towards the canvas as it disappeared through the yard's archway. 'Are you happy with the efforts of Mr Pursival?'

'The horse is grand and everything I would ask for. But between you, me and that weathercock up there, he's got just a tiny bit carried away over the "groom", wouldn't you say? But I'm inclined

to forgive him. It's not too obvious and, anyway, entirely under-
standable to my way of thinking. Your brother is a very lucky man.'

🐎

Michael Finnegan worked out well from the start. Jan watched him
carefully on the first morning, but he handled his mount with
thorough confidence – a quality she liked to see in a work rider, as
long as it fell short of recklessness. After that he came over from
Lambourn three times a week for the early morning gallops, which
now took place at Dowerhouse. He had to drive almost forty miles,
but he never turned up late or seemed hungover, like some work
riders she had employed in the past. Finnegan was in fact a model
pupil with a quiet good humour, yet he possessed an authoritative
presence that at first put the girls, Roz and Emma, into a state of
giggly awe whenever he was near them. At the same time he got on
well with Declan and Connor, managing to come up with jokes
even they had not heard before, which was no mean feat. Of the
regular staff only Patsy seemed a little wary of Michael: but then
again, Jan thought, he's wary of everyone but me.

Even the children took a shine to Michael. He was infinitely
tolerant of Matty's tendency to break into song with 'There was an
old man called Michael Finnegan', followed by searching interro-
gations as to why this Michael Finnegan didn't have whiskers on his
chinnegan. Michael and Megan enjoyed long conversations about
horses, and she became enthralled with tales of his early adventures
in three-day-eventing around County Cork, and of his first pony,
Misty. So it was not long before Michael was accepted as a regular
member of the Edge Farm team, which Jan found herself quietly
pleased about.

🐎

December came and there was no news of Ron Sullivan. As for
Eddie, Jan still had no idea what his veiled remark at Mary's funeral
had meant. She filled her days with work and the children, hardly
seeing anyone outside the racing world or her family.

The building work on the conversion of Dowerhouse Farm had
made progress, but the place was still a long way from being

habitable, and when Ben was in the country he stayed at Annabel's cottage. It was far too small to host a large party, so Jan invited them to join her and Reg at Edge Farm for Christmas Day. In her solitary moments she had been dreading Christmas without her mother. There were times during the days before when she felt tearful and alone, as she doggedly made mince pies and chestnut stuffing to store away in the freezer for use on the day. But she kept in mind the strength she had received from her horses on that memorable afternoon following Mary's death. Scolding herself for feeling weak, and remembering that she was her mother's daughter, she carried on.

One Friday morning, as they were tacking up the horses, she asked Michael what he was doing for Christmas.

'I thought I might go up to London, stay in a hotel, maybe, and see a few shows.'

'Have you friends in London?'

'No, I don't know a soul.'

Jan was horrified.

'But you can't spend Christmas by yourself in a hotel, for God's sake. Haven't you got any family?'

'Ah, no, they're all dead. Well, I've an uncle in Limerick, but he's a priest. He's too busy that time of year to be entertaining an old nephew.'

'Look, forget London,' Jan said enthusiastically. 'You must come to lunch with us. There's loads of room and, I can promise you, plenty of food.'

Michael protested, saying that he wouldn't want to impose. But Jan could see he really wanted to say yes and found herself insisting until he did.

🐎

The day went as well as she had dared to hope. Michael joined them after church, where they'd sung carols vigorously before going home to exchange presents. He went with them on a frosty ride to Riscombe before they all returned to Edge Farm for the huge traditional dinner. Afterwards they played Scrabble (at which Michael proved to be unbeatable) and watched *National Velvet* on the box for the umpteenth time.

Later in the evening Ben played his guitar and sang – first some of his own songs, then old favourites which everyone could join in. After some determined persuasion, Michael too agreed to sing a solo. His gentle but true tenor voice sweetened the melancholy of the song and produced a thumping round of applause. But he wouldn't sing another, pretending that he couldn't remember any more songs by heart.

Later that night Jan went out with him to his car before he set off back to the building site at Tumblewind Grange. As he said goodbye he held both her hands tightly and for a moment she thought he might try to kiss her. But he didn't. Instead he said, 'That was a marvellous day. The best Christmas I've had in years. And thank you for the tie too, by the way.'

'It was my pleasure and don't be silly. I just hope it was better than some poxy hotel in London.'

'Yes, a better class of company altogether, I'd say. And with all the turkey I could eat and the chance to show off my Scrabble skills – what more could any man want?'

As he drove away she waved to him, although, in the darkness, she realized he could hardly have seen her.

What more *could* any man want? As she turned back to the house she wondered if, in Michael's case, the answer to that question was quite as easy as the one that would normally spring to a man's mind.

15

The financial crisis at Virginia Gilbert's yard came to a head in January. Local whispers indicated that the Inland Revenue had given Virginia and Harry until the end of the month to pay their arrears in full. Jan felt the rumour was decisively confirmed when she saw Lot 829 in the catalogue of Doncaster's horses-in-training sale, scheduled for the end of the month. Her stomach flipped when she read the name Velvet Dynasty.

Jan's heart was pounding as she immediately reached for the phone and spoke to A.D. He authorized her to bid up to one hundred thousand guineas for the horse and suggested she take Michael with her. So, with what seemed like a staggering amount of money at their disposal, they set off in the lorry, full of confidence that by the evening Velvet Dynasty would be installed once again in his old stable back at Edge Farm.

As she walked around the sales complex with Michael, scrutinizing the animals on offer or simply studying them from the seated area, he impressed her. It was evident he had a clear knowledge of young horses. He easily identified possible defects in conformation and behaviour, and spoke with confidence regarding what he liked to see in a prospective purchase. Jan wasn't always of the same opinion – but then again most horse people never quite agree on what makes a perfect thoroughbred, which makes the game all the more enthralling – but she could tell his thoughts and ideas came from experience and weren't just hot air.

'Come on,' said Jan, when they'd been taking in the atmosphere for a couple of hours. 'We still haven't seen our fellow.'

She checked in the catalogue for the exact location of Lot 829, which was due to appear in the ring mid-afternoon. As they made their way through the network of wooden boxes, they passed a group of Americans and Michael suddenly stopped and slapped his forehead.

'Oh hell, Jan, I meant to tell you. Remember you asked me about that Yank the first time we met at Wetherby.'

'Bobby Montana?'

'Yes, and Mervyn Sawyer, the trainer.'

They were just nearing the box where Velvet Dynasty was stationed.

'Oh, have you got any news?' she said eagerly, her ears pricked in anticipation.

'Well, I put a call through to one of my friends in the States. He said he'd let me know if he heard anything, but he didn't get back to me for ages so I rather forgot about it. But now he's come up with some very interesting information. It seems that—'

'Oh Christ!'

By now they had arrived at their destination and Jan was peering into the stable. Her interruption was loud and had come with an odd crack in her voice, and not a simple expression of surprise. Michael leant in to see what she was looking at. A young man was grooming the horse, working hard and cursing at the effort he was forced to put in. Suddenly he stood up, stretching his back as he checked out the two figures who were now blocking the doorway.

'Jan?' he said, with a puzzled look on his face.

'Eddie!' she gasped. 'What the bloody hell are you doing here?'

He smiled in recognition, but this was not his usual breezy, self-confident grin. It was defensive, apologetic even.

'I could ask you the same question,' he said guardedly.

'Me? I've come for the sale. That's my job. But what about you?' Eddie gestured towards the horse.

'Well, it's my job. In a different capacity, I agree, but I'm working too. I told you about it, didn't I?'

'You talked about *a* job. But what the heck are you doing at the sales and grooming Velvet Dynasty *of all horses*?' Her voice tailed off.

Jan was not thinking straight. She had formed a dim idea that Eddie must have taken a job connected with the auction.

'Like I said,' he replied, 'it's my job.'

'I don't get it. Why are you—? Oh my God, I do get it. Tell me it's not true! You're . . . with that ghastly Virginia Gilbert, aren't you?' she challenged. 'You're actually *working* for her.'

Eddie shrugged. 'Of all the loose boxes in all the world—' he began.

'Don't be such a prat, Eddie,' Jan interrupted. 'After all I've been through with that beastly woman, you have to go and work for her. I can't believe it.'

'I've only been doing odds and sods, travelling stuff mainly. I'm really based in London. I have to live, Jan.'

'Well, obviously, and if you'd been based in Riscombe, we would have heard by now, wouldn't we? Especially now Virginia and I are cosily sharing the Dowerhouse gallops. But for Christ's sake, Eddie! I don't know what to say any more. This is just . . .'

Unable to express what she felt, Jan spun away from the door.

Eddie immediately called after her, in a desolate voice. 'Jan, please don't go! It's not my fault, it was Virginia who approached me. I was in London at the time. She offered me the job. I couldn't refuse, I needed – I *need* – the money.'

Briefly Jan had caught sight of Michael's face – baffled, embarrassed and concerned, with perhaps the slightest touch of amusement. Quickly, she held up her hand to prevent him intervening. 'Michael, why don't you stay and have a proper look at Velvet Dynasty? Check his tendons thoroughly. I know him well enough. I'll see you in the cafeteria.'

She marched stiffly away by herself, with her arms wrapped tightly around her body. For several minutes she wandered aimlessly around in the throng of prospective buyers with their opened catalogues, drifting from one lot to another. The main question hammering away in her brain was – How could he? How could he? How *could* he?

🐎

Eddie knew every facet of the vendetta between Jan and Virginia Gilbert. OK, he and Jan were no longer engaged, but there had been no bitter war between the two of them and no blood-letting hostilities that could justify Eddie doing something like this. The engagement had finally ended because their attraction for one another was not such a strong bond as they, or at least she, had been hoping for. But now Jan saw this as an act of betrayal – that was how strongly she felt – and it was forcing her to revalue everything she had ever thought about him, everything they had ever done together. She accepted that he was no longer her lover. She could come to terms with the possibility that he was no longer a friend, *but was he even a human being*? Had he just been using her all along?

It was a while before Jan calmed down. She took a few deep breaths and began to look at the situation more realistically. Why was she not altogether surprised by Eddie's behaviour? Men were men and not too many would feel they owed a sense of loyalty and duty to a former girlfriend. Virginia was a bitch, that was for sure, and the admission that she had personally head-hunted Eddie in London was a riveting bit of information. Was there anything she wouldn't attempt to make Jan's life more difficult?

As Jan approached the cafeteria, she caught a glimpse of Michael through the door as he wandered around looking for a table. He was balancing a cup of tea in each hand while holding a pack of biscuits in his teeth. The sight of him cheered her up immensely. Did it really matter what Eddie was doing? It would only play into Virginia's hand if Jan let this piece of vindictiveness weaken her. Right now she had new friends and fresh challenges, and what's more she had a business to run, which made her even more determined to stop moping and carry on regardless.

'I'm sorry about that, Michael,' she said, joining him at a table he'd found on the far side of the room. 'Eddie and I used to be engaged. It was just a bit of a shock to see him here, working for my rival. You can imagine.'

If Michael Finnegan had felt any embarrassment before, he was entirely unembarrassed now.

'Yes, I can,' he said simply. 'I'd heard about it, of course.'

'About what?'

'How your engagement went pear shaped.'

'Did you indeed?'

'Well, it's a small world. And almost everyone who drinks in the pub I go to in Lambourn works in racing.'

'I hate the thought of being talked about in every bloody pub in the county. Why the hell is it anyone else's business anyway?'

Michael slid Jan's tea across the table towards her and tore open the biscuit wrapper.

'People seem to enjoy the misfortunes of others and they like to gossip – it's human nature. Look at the papers. You won't find much good news there.'

'And there's not much that's true in them, either. Most of it's exaggerated beyond belief.'

'You can rest assured I wouldn't allow any lies to be told about you, Jan. I am a jealous guardian of your reputation.'

'Oh, really. In what way?'

Michael looked at her seriously with steady brown eyes.

'I'd never put up with anyone saying bad things about you, that's all.'

Jan thought she was blushing. She picked up her cup and hurriedly took a sip of tea.

'Well, thank you, kind sir,' she said skittishly, as she lowered the cup. 'Does the opportunity to defend my honour arise very often?'

Michael's eyes crinkled attractively as he smiled.

'Like I said. Just once or twice in the pub. Here, have a digestive.'

When Velvet Dynasty, Lot 829, came up they were ready for action and deliberately sitting on opposite sides of the sales ring in cloak-and-dagger style. Michael had agreed to do the bidding on Jan's behalf according to the signals she made. It gave the buyer a certain advantage to be an anonymous player on these occasions.

This was the second time Jan had bid for Velvet Dynasty. The first was at Newmarket more than a year ago when, at four years old, the horse was still untried as a National Hunt prospect and she had paid eighteen thousand of Colonel Gilbert's guineas for him. That, it turned out, had been a bargain. The horse now had victories at Stratford, Cheltenham and Ascot under his girth strap, and also a run in a sensational race at Leopardstown against Morning Glory, passing the post first but being subsequently disqualified. It was obvious he had become a live contender for some of the biggest hurdling prizes around and, with his build, might well convert into a top-class chaser.

Leading him round the ring, Eddie looked vaguely shifty, as if aware of the eyes of the crowd, and of Jan in particular, boring into him. He tried to compensate by walking with a nonchalant saunter, but his slight limp spoiled the effect.

Jan wished she'd had a pee before taking her seat at the edge of the sales ring. Was it because of nerves, excitement or anticipation that she might just get Velvet Dynasty back? All thoughts of Eddie temporarily disappeared as the bidding started in earnest. The auctioneer was rapidly taking bids from around the arena until he began to slow at forty thousand guineas. Jan had told Michael not to make his move until the auctioneer shouted, 'He's on the market,' which indicated the horse had now reached its reserve, which was exactly what the man with the gavel shouted when the bidding reached fifty thousand. Jan's lip quivered and her throat suddenly went dry as she realized the short, stocky man increasing the bidding was the champion jumps trainer, Fred Gallagher. He had plenty of owners with pockets as deep as A.D. O'Hagan's.

Michael matched Fred bid for bid until the price had reached eighty-eight thousand guineas. Jan held her breath – this was her last chance to get Velvet Dynasty back.

'The bid's against you, sir,' the auctioneer said as he turned to Michael. 'Will you fill him up to ninety thousand? I can't dwell. Yes? Yes?' Michael slowly nodded his head. 'Ninety thousand it is.' The auctioneer wheeled back to Fred Gallagher. 'One more, sir?' Fred nonchalantly moved his hand to his flat cap.

'*Oh no,*' Jan whispered and closed her eyes to say a silent prayer. Fred pulled his cap down, looked squarely at the auctioneer, then shook his head from side to side and marched out of the sale ring.

'Sold at ninety thousand guineas to you, sir,' the auctioneer shouted as he banged his gavel and pointed at Michael. 'And the very best of luck with him.'

Jan leapt to her feet, gave Michael the thumbs up and rushed out of the sales ring to meet Velvet Dynasty as he was being led back to his stable. Jan seemed oblivious to Eddie's sour face as she threw her arms round Velvet's neck and planted a big kiss on his nose.

'I remember when you used to do that to me,' he muttered gruffly.

'You had your chance, Eddie Sullivan,' Jan snapped back. 'It was you who walked away, which is exactly what I'm going to do now. I've got another horse to bid for. Maybe if you have time you could give me a ring and tell me what's been happening.'

Michael went off to phone A.D. to let him know the good news but Jan returned to the sale ring to bid for an unnamed five-year-old gelding that had attracted her attention earlier in the day. She thought he would make a decent chaser for Toby Waller, who had recently called her to say he had made so much money in Hong Kong that he felt like rewarding himself with another horse.

Toby had set a limit of thirty thousand and, bidding herself this time, Jan was disappointed to find another energetic bidder coming in against her. This individual, probably a bloodstock agent, seemed determined to secure the horse at any cost. Thirty thousand guineas came and went, and the agent was still active. Jan dropped out disappointed and a few seconds later the lot was knocked down at thirty-five thousand. Minutes later a woman, wafting the aroma of a very expensive perfume, sat down beside her. She looked curiously at Jan.

'Hi, I just bought a horse. And I have you to thank for having paid so much for it,' she said brightly in a strong Yorkshire Dales accent.

There was nothing hostile in her voice and it was stated as a matter of fact.

'Me?'

'Yes, dear, you. That *was* you bidding against my chap for the five-year-old, wasn't it?'

Jan admitted that she was the underbidder.

'Well, there's no need to be sorry,' the woman continued. 'I'm going to give you the chance to redeem yourself, if you would like to.'

Jan looked with renewed interest at this straight-talking, pushy stranger, who was clearly capable of extracting fun from anything she did. The woman was probably in her fifties but very glamorous. Her hair was a vibrant chestnut red, and coiffured to look slightly windswept. The woollen jacket and skirt had been styled to fit her excellent figure to perfection. Her matching shoes and bag looked as if they had been purchased from an exclusive Italian boutique.

'That sounds like an opportunity I ought not to turn down,' Jan said.

'That's exactly what I hoped you might say. Would you like to train the horse for me?'

The question was so direct that it took Jan completely by surprise.

'*Sorry?*'

'You are Jan Hardy, the racehorse trainer, aren't you?'

'Yes, yes, I am.'

'Then I'd like you to train my horse. It's not my first, but I got cheesed off with the chap at Malton who had the other one. He kept saying the horse was a good 'un, but it wasn't. I only came to the sales today to see it sold off. Then this other little beggar took my fancy, and when something does that there's not a lot that anyone can do about it. Anyway, after I'd seen you bidding I reckoned I might have chosen well. So here we are.'

'He looks a nice horse, all right.'

'So that's it, then. You'll train him for me? By the way, my name's Nina Clark. I'm from Harrogate. I have a hairdressing business with shops all round this area.'

She held out her hand and Jan, still faintly bewildered by the speed of this new development, shook it.

'Right,' Nina Clark went on. 'Now we've shaken on it we can take that as settled. You can take him back in your horsebox tonight, I suppose?'

🐎

Without a deposit, Jan would normally have taken a few soundings before accepting a complete stranger as an owner. But Nina Clark had been so dynamic and likeable that she'd allowed herself to be swept along without a murmur into agreeing to transport the as-yet-unnamed horse back to Edge Farm, along with Velvet Dynasty.

'It's weird,' said Jan to Michael, who was behind the wheel of the lorry as it swung out through the sale gates and onto the highway. 'I'd just been thinking about how I could attract new owners, when this un-horsy-looking woman came and plonked herself down right next to me. She'd seen me bidding against her and said she thought it was a good omen, just like that, and would I train it for her. So in a flash I agreed. I hope she doesn't turn out like Bobby Montana.'

'Oh yes! Montana. I knew there was something I meant to tell you,' he said, banging the steering wheel as he remembered what he'd started to say earlier in the day. 'I was about to tell you that I had found something out when we were interrupted.'

By now Bobby Montana had become a real pain in Jan's arse. He had not paid another penny in fees either to her or the vet. His horses, which he continued to visit, were not well. One still showed the symptoms of navicular disease, while the other remained listless and impossible to enter for any races.

'Did you say it was from America?'

'That's right. It's only a titbit, I'm afraid, but it seems that Mervyn Sawyer's being investigated by the Illinois state attorney's office for fraud.'

'Christ, what kind of fraud? Race fixing?'

'My friend wasn't sure of the exact details. Apparently Sawyer doesn't race outside Fairmount Park, so he's not that well known at the other racing centres.'

Jan mulled over this information, which didn't look good for Bobby Montana's future.

'Montana called Sawyer a "genius trainer".'

Michael laughed.

'Genius takes many forms. How much does Mr Montana owe right now?'

'Over eight thousand.'

'That's quite a tab.'

'I know. I think I'm going to have to take some serious measures to curb Mr Montana. I'm going to apply to the Jockey Club to have him placed on the forfeit list.'

'Really? What does that mean in English?'

'It's basically a black list. He won't be able to run a horse anywhere until he coughs up what he owes. The next step, I suppose, would be to get a lien against the horses. But I'll start by getting him onto the forfeit list, I think, and take it from there.'

When they arrived back at Edge Farm they saw the hire car that was always used by Bobby Montana parked next to the yard gate.

'Talk of the devil,' said Jan as Michael pulled alongside the loading ramp.

She leapt from the cab and hurried off in search of her renegade owner. She found him leaning over the door of Spring Blow's box, muttering as he stroked the horse's nose. As Jan approached, she heard the crunching of the sugar lump Montana had given Spring Blow.

'Ah, there you are,' she said, striding purposefully towards him. 'I hope you've brought a cheque to settle your account.'

Montana swivelled round to face her.

'No, ma'am. I'm sorry. Don't seem to be able to remember anything right now. Next time I visit, you will be fully paid up.'

'That's not good enough. I've lost track of how many times you've promised to pay your bills. I'm sorry, but unless I receive payment by this time tomorrow I'm going to apply to the Jockey Club to have your name placed on the forfeit list.'

Montana shrugged.

'Really. Well, I don't know what this forfeit list of yours is and I'll stay off it if I can. But, if not, I guess I'll just have to live with it.'

'Mr Montana, are you telling me you don't have the money?'

'I'm not saying I do, and I'm not saying I don't. I'm saying I can live with being on this list of yours.'

'It would mean you wouldn't be able to run these horses, or any others, for that matter.'

Jan knew that in their present state of health there was not much of a possibility of this anyway, but it was the only sanction exacted under the forfeiture system. Montana, however, seemed completely unworried by the threat and shrugged his huge shoulders again.

'Like I said, I'm sure I can live with that if I have to, Mrs Hardy. But the money's definitely coming, maybe tomorrow, maybe next week, no problem.'

'Mr Montana, as long as you don't pay your fees I'm feeding and medicating these animals out of my own pocket, and I just can't afford to carry on doing that.'

'Hey, Mrs Hardy, don't get all riled up. Old Bobby'll pay you your money.'

Later that night, just after supper, the phone rang.

'This is Bobby Montana.'

'Well, I hope you're ringing to tell me the cheque's in the post.'

Montana ignored her and continued in a vaguely threatening tone. 'What I want to say, Mrs Hardy, is don't put me on no forfeit list. Bottom line is I can't be on no forfeit list. Do you understand what I'm saying, Mrs Hardy?'

'But I explained it to you this afternoon. I have no choice. You have to pay your bills, and if you don't the Jockey Club will put you on the list. I'm telling you now, I have no other choice.'

'No, I'm tellin' *you*. I don't want to be on no goddamn fuckin' forfeit list. I'll deem it as an unfriendly act to be put on that faggot list. I'll be real mad at you, Mrs Hardy. And most people where I come from would say they don't like to see Bobby Montana real mad at them. Because that can be kinda messy, you know what I'm saying?'

'Yes, I think I do, Mr Montana. I think you're threatening me.'

'I'm not threatening you, Mrs Hardy. I'm *warning* you. No frigging forfeit list, no way. OK?'

Then he hung up.

16

For the best part of January the cold northerly winds had rocked the bare trees and shaken the hedgerows throughout the Cotswolds, and liberal quantities of snow had fallen on the higher ground. Several days' racing were lost due to extreme frosts.

The routine at the yard was constantly made more difficult as each day any fallen snow needed to be shifted before the yards could be salted, which meant longer hours for everyone. Accidents had to be avoided at all costs and Jan didn't want any of her precious horses to slip over, either on their way to the gallops or during any other exercise. Gerry the builder, who was very adept with a shovel, came in extremely handy at such times and willingly lent a hand. With the Cheltenham Festival only six weeks away, it was of paramount importance to keep the horses on the move. Jan did her best to keep everyone's spirits up by supplying them with mugs of Fran's steaming home-made soup, whilst reminding the staff that A.D. O'Hagan's horses, the ones which held entries, all had serious each-way chances, which would mean a massive boost to their pooled share of the prize money.

It was a particularly frosty day when Toby Waller paid Edge Farm a visit. The plump, balding, pink-cheeked merchant banker was not the most dashing bachelor ever to have patronized Jan's yard, but he was easily the most popular. He never forgot to bring chocolates and biscuits for the staff and the boot of his car always seemed well stocked with assorted bottles of wine 'in case a celebration was called for', he said.

Following the Doncaster sale, Jan had kept her eyes peeled for a suitable chaser that Toby might buy, and when she heard on the grapevine that a six-year-old hurdler named Balladur was up for sale from a yard in Wiltshire, she thought she might have at last found the right one. On the two occasions Jan had seen the horse run, he had looked to have far better prospects over the larger fences than he had over hurdles. Today Toby and his trainer were to drive south to look at Balladur more closely and see if they could strike a deal.

The fifty-mile journey took them south along the old ruler-straight Roman road across Salisbury Plain and within two miles of Stonehenge. At the wheel of his latest toy, a custom-tweaked sports car, Toby told Jan about his nine months in Hong Kong. He was full of entertaining tales of pink Rolls Royces with matching fur coats, and the unique Happy Valley race track, a green oval oasis in the middle of one of the world's most densely populated islands.

When they arrived at their destination, they were met by a tall man. Peter Tilley was around forty years old with grey curly hair, a bulbous nose and purple cheeks. Jan had spoken to him the previous day to arrange the visit. He'd held a trainer's licence for fifteen years or more, but many thought it was his wife Sally who really ran the business.

'Hi, it's a pleasure to see you, Jan,' he said cheerily.

His eyes looked warm and twinkly and gave a very different image from that of the crusty military man which the tabloids liked to give him.

'Likewise,' said Jan. 'This is Toby Waller, one of my longest-standing owners – that is if we haven't been celebrating,' she teased.

Peter nodded approvingly towards the car.

'Nice wheels you've got, Toby,' he commented.

Suddenly Jan regretted not using her battered Shogun. Toby's car made him look like a reckless spender, which in fact he wasn't. The impression could easily push up Tilley's idea of his horse's value.

'Shall we go down to the yard and look at the beast in question?' Peter Tilley went on smoothly. 'I must say I'll be really sorry to lose him. I know he's not won anything too competitive yet, but I'm bloody certain his day will come.'

'So why is he for sale?' asked Jan, when they reached the horse's stable.

'The owner died. That was old Lord Quantock, you know. Very sad, but then he was ninety-five. We were awfully fond of the old goat. He was a great supporter of racing and had been all his life. We sold the horse to him after buying it as an unbroken three-year-old in Ireland. Lord Q was already well over ninety by then and this was the last of his horses.'

Peter beckoned to one of his staff to bring the prospective purchase into the middle of the yard. Jan cast a critical eye over him and watched closely as the horse was led at a walk and then trotted in straight lines. She realized almost immediately that he was a good sort and the kind of horse she really liked – butty, sixteen-two hands high, with good hocks, a nice rounded backside and bright, willing eyes.

The group chatted about Balladur's recent form and breeding for a while until suddenly Tilley intervened.

'That's it, we've seen enough. Come on, let's get into the house for a jar. Sal's in there making marmalade.'

An acrid smell of burnt sugar and orange met them as they stepped through the kitchen door. Sally Tilley, 'Mustang Sally' the red-top press called her, was peering into a large smoking pot on the stove.

'Sod this!' she said, pushing her blonde hair back from her round face. 'I think I've burnt the bastard.'

'She does that every year,' said Peter with a wink at Jan. 'It's still the best marmalade in the county.'

'What do you think of Balladur?' Sally said, killing the heat under the boiling marmalade and stirring in a measure of cold water. 'He's quite a character, that one, did Peter tell you? You need to watch him. If he's in a wicked mood he'll take a bite out of your arse. He's even done it to Lord Quantock. Do you know what his lordship said?' She put on a flutey, upper-class accent. '"Dash it,"' he said. '"If me bum's to be bitten, it rahlly ought to be by a filly, eh what?"'

Over coffee in what Peter graciously called the drawing room Jan broached the subject of the asking price for Balladur. No actual sum had been mentioned yet, but Jan had hoped for a bargain. She'd heard Lord Q's only surviving child Frederick, who was now sole owner of the horse, was also a bishop and had never got on too well with his father. Preferring to be known as Bishop Fred, his views against drink and gambling were well known, as were some of his unorthodox and radical opinions on theology. Given this information, Jan was calculating that Bishop Fred would be only too pleased to get shot of his father's racehorse in the most discreet way possible.

However, she soon learnt this was not quite how Peter Tilley viewed the situation.

'The owner's bound to want a good price. I'd say seventy thousand would satisfy him though,' he crowed.

Jan gasped and looked at Toby in dismay. Now she regretted even more arriving in the flashy sports car. He must be nuts or on wacky backy, she was thinking, as seventy grand for Balladur was way over the top. She was just about to say so when Sally broke in ahead of her.

'Seventy thou?' she said, mocking. 'What a load of balls. Just tell me how he can be worth that amount. What's he won to justify it?'

'Well, he's got potential.' Peter said in a defensive manner.

'Please don't insult Jan's and Toby's intelligence, Peter. He's probably worth around twenty.'

'Oh come, come, that's absurd,' said Peter, his voice cracking in outrage. 'All right, maybe sixty-five. But the horse has a great career ahead of him. His breeding alone—'

'Sod the breeding, I say, look at the form, a fair price is twenty-five thousand max.'

'OK,' her husband retaliated, 'sixty, possibly. But look at him. Where can you find a strapping young horse with great breeding like it? He's never done anything wrong in his life, and he's a great chasing prospect, any fool can see that.'

Jan and Toby sat listening in total amazement to this bizarre round of bidding while the Tilleys carried on, the wife arguing for the lower amount, but gradually creeping up, while the husband with apparent reluctance lowered his own estimate bit by bit. In the end, rather predictably, they compromised on forty-five thousand pounds as the desired amount.

At this point Toby got to his feet in a decisive manner.

'Well, thanks. I'm very grateful for the coffee and the chance to look at Balladur. It's rather more than I wanted to spend, but I am still interested, and will need to give it further thought. So I'll get back to you. Oh! There's just one more thing. You do have authority to sell the horse do you, or would, er, Bishop Fred have the final say?'

Toby had asked in the friendliest tone, yet the question was loaded. He was wondering if he'd be better off dealing directly with the owner of Balladur rather than with the bizarre double act.

'Well, as a matter of fact,' said Peter, 'the bishop did say he wants to approve the sale. But I can put any offer to him on your behalf, of course.'

Toby drew his car keys out of his pocket.

'As I said, I need to mull it over. I'll be in touch soon. And meanwhile thanks again for the coffee.'

Driving back to Edge Farm, Jan and Toby laughed at the way the Tilleys had debated the value of the horse. But neither thought the argument had been in any way sincere, in spite of the couple's battling reputation.

'It was a ploy,' concluded Toby. 'And rather a transparent one, if you ask me. They were play-acting to try and convince me to part with forty-five thousand quid. Am I right in assuming that would still be rather too much money?'

'Well, I reckon so,' Jan said. 'It looks as if you might have to go up to your limit of thirty. But the horse really does look a nice prospect.'

'Why do you think they were talking up the price, though? Bishop Fred gets the money, not them.'

'They might get some of it, I suppose, as they sold the horse to Lord Q in the first place. A percentage on the difference between the original purchase price and the eventual selling price isn't an uncommon agreement for transactions like that.'

'I see, a sort of incentive scheme. The trainer gets a bonus for increasing the resale value of the horse – payment by results, is that what you mean?'

'Exactly. So if Tilley can persuade someone to pay forty-five thousand pounds, he would expect to be in for at least two. It will depend on the original agreement they signed.'

'The better the price, bigger the commission.'

'Precisely.'

After a while the conversation turned to past events in Jan's yard, and she told Toby about Bobby Montana and her unsuccessful attempts to get him to pay his fees.

'It's really very odd. At first he says he doesn't give a toss if he's put on the forfeit list, then a few hours later he rings me up and warns me quite threateningly not to do it.'

'What's the penalty of being on the list? What can't he do?'

'Run any horse under the rules of racing. But his horses aren't fit to run anyway, and they're not likely to be in the near future either, which is why I thought he was so relaxed about it.'

'But what if he had another horse in training, with its fees paid up to date? Could he run that?'

'No, it's a total ban. But there *is* no other horse. At least I don't think so.'

'I wonder,' said Toby.

A few days later Toby rang Edge Farm with triumph in his voice.

'Jan, I've contacted Bishop Fred and it's great news. He's accepted my offer of thirty thousand. He thinks even that's a ridiculously high price to pay for a horse.'

Jan laughed. 'That'll educate the Tilleys. Has he told them he's selling?'

'I guess he will have done by now. We've already shaken on the deal, as it were.'

Toby lowered his voice. 'By the way, remember that conversation we had about your owner, Bobby Montana. Well, I have a friend who's a dedicated poker player, and he says he met the bloke recently at his club in London. My friend says Montana owns a flat horse, a filly – I can't remember the horse's name – but he thinks the trainer might be someone called Doug Shaw at Newmarket.'

'That's very interesting,' said Jan. 'Thanks a lot, I'll explore that further. But, meantime, what are we doing about the Tilleys' horse? Can I contact them right away?'

They chatted on for a few more minutes about Toby's new horse, but Jan was itching to hang up. She wanted to lose no time in phoning Doug Shaw.

Jan found the number through *The Directory of the Turf* and dialled, her heart pounding.

'Hello? Doug Shaw here.'

The voice was hearty and well fed. Jan had never met Shaw, but she had seen him interviewed on television and recognized the voice instantly.

'Doug? It's Jan Hardy.'

It took just a second or two for Shaw to grasp the reason for her call.

'Oh, hello, Jan,' he said, as some of the jollity drained from his voice. 'I, er, guess this is about Mr Montana, right?'

'Yes, you know him then?'

'Of course. I've got a filly of his.'

'Does he pay his fees on time?'

'Jan, I wouldn't answer that question even if he didn't.'

'Well, I don't mind telling you that he's in default over the two horses he has here with me. In fact he's several months behind. Has he mentioned that to you?'

'He did say something about it, yes.'

Jan realized Montana must have spoken to Shaw after she had mentioned the forfeit list, and that would explain why he had changed his mind so quickly and warned her to back off.

'What did he say exactly?' she continued.

'He told me you're talking about going to the Jockey Club.'

'Yes, I want him put on the forfeit list. I've got no choice, I've tried everything else and he still won't cough up.'

'Yes, well, I've been meaning to speak to you myself about that.'

'To back me up, I hope. It would be in your interest if he owes you also.'

'That's the problem, it wouldn't benefit me. In fact it would be bloody disastrous.'

'How's that?'

'Because if he's on the forfeit list I can't run his filly in the spring.'

'So? Hopefully it'll persuade him to pay up what he owes you. What's disastrous about that?'

'Mr Montana wants to sell her eventually. Running the filly will enable him to make some dough.'

'If she wins, that is.'

'I think she will,' Shaw replied confidently.

'Which could indeed be really profitable for you.' If the filly came out of the shadows and won a competitive race, Shaw and his owner could take some big money out of the betting ring, in addition to the prize money. Of course, Doug Shaw could also have an interest in the filly besides being her trainer and then, like the Tilleys, he would be due to collect a percentage of the filly's price at auction.

'Would I be right in guessing you sold the horse to Bobby Montana?' Jan enquired innocently.

'That's right, I did, a couple of months ago. I was bloody amazed at what he was prepared to pay, especially as she did nothing last season when she was a two-year-old. But she's beautifully bred, you know, and since he bought her she's been flying on the gallops.'

'I see.'

'Do me a favour, Jan. Please don't put Montana on the forfeit list.'

'Doug, I'm not aware that I owe you any favours and at the present time I am owed over eight thousand pounds. So I don't really have any other choice.'

'You do. You can back my filly. She'll be any price.'

'I don't bet. And I don't train horses for free either. I can't afford to, I've got bills to pay no matter what.'

'Oh, Jan! Can't you see the position I'm in?'

Shaw sounded almost distraught and Jan even felt a twinge of sympathy for him.

'Look, I've had an idea. I'll tell you what I'm prepared to do,' she said. 'You want to keep him off the forfeit list in order to run your filly, right? So why don't you guarantee to pay me any overdue training fees owed by Mr Montana yourself? In return I won't apply to the Jockey Club to have him blacklisted.'

There was a moment's pause while Shaw considered the proposition.

'I can certainly make sure you get paid *after* the filly wins,' he said guardedly. 'She's in a couple of the classics, so there'll be all sorts of money flying around if she's as good as I think she is.'

'Doug, you're not listening and that is not what I'm offering. I'm asking you to step up to the plate. Give me an undertaking, in writing, that you will personally guarantee those debts, irrespective of whether this filly wins her race or not. Then my side of the bargain will be to hold off speaking to the Jockey Club.'

Another long pause followed, before Shaw continued, 'OK, fine, have it your way, Jan. No problem. I have total confidence in my horse.'

'You'll write me a letter?' she urged.

'Sure, like I said, no problem, Jan.'

But his tone of voice was less convincing.

Two days later Bobby Montana made one of his lightning visits to Edge Farm. Jan was at the races at the time and so, frustratingly, she missed the opportunity to question him about the filly he had in training with Doug Shaw, and whether they had discussed the proposed guarantee. But the next morning there was a dramatic development as Patsy Keating rushed into the office.

'I'm dead worried about Spring Blow. His joints have all swollen and he's not eaten a thing. He looks really sick, Mrs H.'

Jan raced across the yard to the horse's box, where she found Spring Blow hanging his head and drooling from the mouth. The box stank and she noticed he had diarrhoea. He presented a picture of sheer misery and seemed unable to lift his head any higher than six inches.

'God, you're right, Patsy. This horse is very sick indeed.'

Jan contacted the veterinary practice and asked for an emergency call, but neither Shirley McGregor nor any of her colleagues would be available until later in the day.

In desperation she went to the bookcase in her office and took down one she often consulted, Horace Hayes's *Veterinary Notes for Horse Owners*, a five-hundred page volume first published more than a century ago, but stuffed full of useful information. She was reading with concentration and muttering to herself, 'It'll be in here somewhere, I just need to find it,' when Annabel came in.

'What do you need to find? Have you seen Spring Blow?' her assistant asked.

'Yes, and it looks bad. The vet can't come till later and in my opinion that horse could be dead by then. I've been looking up his symptoms in here. Horses are horses at the end of the day and some of the stuff in here is as good, if not better, than modern-day treatments. The problem is I don't really know what I'm looking for.'

'That book's a bit out of date, isn't it?'

'Old Horace has never let me down yet,' Jan said without lifting her head. 'Hang on a minute, I think I'm onto something. It says here the symptoms are consistent with poisoning. Probably arsenic.'

'Arsenic poisoning? How on earth could the horse get arsenic?'

'Bel, I can think of a few ways. But let's not worry about that for now. I need to see Patsy.'

Jan left the office with the thick book under her arm and five minutes later Patsy set off from the yard on his clapped-out moped, with an empty plastic container strapped onto the pannier.

'Where's he going in such a hurry?' Annabel asked.

'The farrier's'

'Mickey Reid's. What for?'

'A miracle cure, with a bit of luck chucked in for good measure, I hope.'

17

Less than an hour later Patsy returned, crunching the old and rusty moped's clutch as he forced it up the Edge Farm track, while the contents of the canister sloshed around inside.

'I got the stuff,' he yelled to Jan, who was already coming out of the office. 'A whole load of it. He thought I was joshin' till I told him what it was for. He soon copped on then, for sure.'

'What's going on?' asked Annabel, who now joined them. 'Where've you been, Patsy?'

'I sent him to get some of Mickey Reid's water,' Jan said, reaching down for a bucket. 'It's an idea I got from Horace Hayes.'

She hurried across the yard with the bucket, with Annabel following, now more puzzled than ever.

'Mickey Reid's *water*? What on earth are you going on about? Do you mean pee?'

Jan laughed out loud.

'I've just realized what I said. No, not *that* kind of water. This is water for drinking. But it's no ordinary drinking water, Bel. It's going to be Spring Blow's tonic, or so Horace says.'

As she reached the horse's stable, Jan took the bucket inside and poured most of it into Spring Blow's trough.

'There you are, old lad,' she said, patting the distressed animal gently on the neck. 'Drink up. It can only do you good.'

'I still don't get it,' Annabel said, looking even more perplexed.

'Don't look so worried. Come on, I'll show you.'

Jan led her assistant back to the office, where the *Veterinary Notes for Horse Owners* lay open on the desk. Jan picked it up and showed Annabel the page, pointing to the section labelled 'Arsenic'.

'Look. This is how the Victorians treated arsenic poisoning.'

Annabel took the book and read the sentence out loud.

' "Give two pints of the water in which the farrier cools down his irons." Are you sure about this?' Bel queried. 'It looks like some dodgy folk remedy.'

'No, it's not,' said Jan. 'The point is that the blacksmith's water is rich in iron, and apparently that counteracts the effect of the poison. Spring Blow's been showing, I believe, the symptoms of arsenic poisoning, even down to the smell of garlic on his breath that old Horace mentions further up the page. I'd noticed the smell a few times, but I thought it was because the lads had been eating curry.'

'But how can he have been getting arsenic? Has he been licking paint or something?'

Jan shrugged. 'Is there arsenic in paint these days? I don't know for sure. I think we'd better check it out with Gerry.'

That afternoon Reg drove over, his old car sagging on its suspension under the weight of a bootload of roofing slates, which he had been storing in the barn at Riscombe. They were for Jan's builder to use in repairing the old barn's roof at Edge, whose leak could now no longer be ignored.

While Gerry was unloading the slates, Jan took her father down to the office for a cup of tea. Considering the years they had spent together, Reg had recovered well from the shock of his wife's death, though the absence of her cooking had left him looking a whole lot thinner.

'Are you eating properly, Dad? You ought to come over here to eat. You could come every day, if you want.'

'No, no, not every day, Jan. From time to time maybe, that'd be nice. What I believe is, if you don't eat in a house, you don't live in it. So I'll make do at home, if you don't mind. I can manage most days. I'm not useless, you know. But you're very good, especially sending me that stew last week.'

'I just wanted to make certain you're not going short. Have you been going down to the churchyard to Mum's grave?'

'Aye, every day. It's bare enough now but come spring it'll look a treat.'

'Do you think of her a lot, Dad?' Jan asked. 'I do.'

'Aye. Most of every day. But not sadly, like, not any more – not in a weeping way. I look at it like this. Your mum's just started a new life, that's all. She's still here, you know.' He said, tapping his heart. 'I talk to her and I wonder if she's thinking about things, and what she would say when I'm cooking my bit of dinner. No, she may be dead but her life's not over. She's still around keeping an eye on us.'

They both wiped away a tear and after a few minutes strolled out into the yard and across to Spring Blow's box. Jan wanted to show her father the troubled patient.

'I know this may sound daft and Victorian, Dad, but I think he could have arsenic poisoning.'

'Arsenic? Where on earth did you get that idea?'

'I looked up the symptoms in Hayes's *Veterinary Notes* – you know the book.'

Reg chuckled.

'I was brought up on it. Your grandad's copy was so broke apart I think it ended up in three or four bits, he read it that often.'

'Well, Hayes's description and the symptoms of arsenic are very like this horse's. And he says the water used by the farrier to cool his irons down is an antidote – it contains a lot of iron, see, and apparently the iron acts as an antidote.'

Reg nodded approvingly. 'That's clever, that is.'

'Do you ever remember a case of a horse with poisoning?'

Reg considered.

'Yes, it happened from time to time, I reckon. The stuff was still used around the farm many years back – pesticide, weed control, for killing rats and such. In my grandad's day some bloody fools used it for a sheep dip, against warble fly. They didn't think what'd happen when it rained.'

'What did happen?'

'Arsenic washed off the wool and into the grass and the sheep ate it. Whole flocks were wiped out, see.'

'God, how awful.'

'It took years before them boffins worked it out. But that was the way of it then. It takes a power of living to get a pinch of learning, and some folk never do.'

He sighed reflectively. 'Anyway,' he went on, 'there's not likely to be any call for arsenic now. Not in a place like this, any road. That horse never got poisoned from pesticide, not on the land here. You can be sure of that.'

'Well, no, I'd never have anything here with arsenic in it, at least not knowingly. Annabel thought it could be in the paint somewhere.'

'Aye, like as not. I've heard tell it was used in paint manufacture once, but I'd have thought that's long gone.'

'But where would he be getting in contact with old paint anyway? We built the boxes from scratch. I know the barn's old, but we stripped that out when we came to live here.'

Leaning over the bottom door of the horse's stable, Reg fished in his pocket and brought out an enormous carrot.

'Here you are, old chap,' he wheedled, holding out the carrot for Spring Blow, who was standing at the back of the box, staring moodily at the floor. At the sound of Reg's cajoling voice he raised his head and then, with a slow, unsteady movement, he stepped forward and took the carrot in his mouth. He crunched then, almost eagerly, he took another bite.

'Well, good boy,' said Jan in surprise. 'He enjoyed that! He's been off his feed for the last couple of days.'

'Maybe your forge water's doing the job, then,' said Reg.

'Let's hope so,' said Jan, feeling mightily relieved.

At first, when she called later that day, Shirley McGregor was extremely sceptical about Jan's diagnosis of Spring Blow's illness, but after making a careful examination of the patient she agreed to run tests for toxicity, paying particular attention to the likelihood of arsenic. Taking away hair and dung samples, she promised to phone as soon as she had the result. The call came through two days later and the vet was hardly able to conceal her astonishment.

'Jan, I must say I'm finding this really hard to believe, never mind explain. The test's come up positive for arsenic. The horse has a serious concentration of the stuff in him – it's built up in the tissues, so he must have been consuming it for some time. Do you have any idea how he got hold of it?'

'No, none whatsoever. It can't possibly be in the feed. We're incredibly careful with that.'

'No, you're right, it won't be the feed, unless you're giving him an exclusive diet. Anyway, all your other horses would be affected too, if that were the case.'

'He gets what the others get. Except he's been off his. Anyway, he's hardly eaten a thing lately, though he has been a bit better since we dosed him with Mickey Reid's magic water.'

'Has he been turned out on his own somewhere? Maybe he cropped some contaminated grass.'

'No, definitely not. He's not been well enough to turn out and I thought he was colicky a couple of days ago.'

'Look, as far as treatment's concerned, I'll come over later and give him an injection. Give him a warm mash as and when he needs it. And plenty of water. He needs all the fluids you can get into him. I can put him on a drip if you like.'

'That's a good idea, but what about the forge water? It seems to be doing him good.'

'You can keep on with it, but go easy. Give him a couple of pints a day for the next few days. No more than that or he'll end up magnetic. I'll see you later. Bye.'

A few mornings later Joe Paley turned up for work even later than usual and delayed the departure of the string by several minutes. But it was still a surprise, on arriving at the Dowerhouse gallops, to find that the Gilbert horses had got there first. They were not supposed to appear until three-quarters of an hour after Edge Farm's kick-off.

'Hey!' Jan shouted furiously as she spotted them. She could see they were preparing themselves to work in pairs up the hallowed turf, with Scottie Venables, Riscombe's head lad supervising. Jan immediately booted her hack forward, waving her arm in an attempt to head them off.

'Scottie, what the hell do you think you're doing? Your lot shouldn't be up here until I've finished working mine.'

A lively young chaser was about to lead off the Gilbert string. But when he saw Jan heading in his direction, he jinked and neatly dumped his lad onto the turf, before careering off loose in the direction of his stable. Scottie reacted swiftly, roaring a succession of Glaswegian expletives.

'Don't you dare swear at me, Venables,' yelled Jan. 'You know I've got first use of these gallops.'

By now the lad who had been unceremoniously decked had gathered himself up. He was as white as a ghost and was breathing heavily. As Jan drew near, she could hear quite distinctly his lungs wheezing, making the exact same sound that Matty made when he had one of his asthma attacks. It seemed the boy must be asthmatic too, and the shock of his fall or fearing the wrath of Jan, not to mention Scottie Venables, had brought on a serious attack. Jan's assessment was confirmed when she saw him pull out an inhaler and suck deeply to ease his constricted lungs.

'Are you all right?' she asked.

'What you do that for? You ought to know better,' he said in an aggrieved tone, tucking the inhaler back into his jeans pocket. 'He's a right bastard, that horse. You got to approach him careful, like.'

'Well, he shouldn't be here at all. Nor should any of you, for that matter, not yet anyway,' Jan said a little more sympathetically. 'I'm sorry you got chucked, though, and you've got a long walk home.'

Having satisfied herself the lad would be all right, Jan jogged her mount back down the gallop to confront Scottie.

'You'll have to back off and wait your turn,' she told him. 'I'm going first. And, by the way, where's Miss Gilbert? I want a word with her.'

'At the top,' the head lad said in surly tones. 'You'll have her to answer to for barging in like this.'

'Get stuffed, I'm not barging in. It's you who's done that,' Jan countered, her anger increasing by the second.

With obvious reluctance Scottie motioned his work riders to wheel their horses round and, without another word, they all moved quietly away in the direction they'd come from, though she could hear muttered swear words drifting through the air. Jan decided to ignore their churlish behaviour and, looking up, located the silhouette of Virginia's Land Rover almost a mile away, at the far end of the gallop. It was the best place to view the horses extending themselves in the final stage of their exercise, and the very place Jan had intended to supervise this morning's work from. She told Annabel to wait with the Edge Farm horses while she got into position, and then let them work in pairs up the curved track, gradually increasing the pace until they finished at full stretch.

Jan wondered why Virginia had chosen this moment to make more waves. Until now, the sharing arrangement had worked well, though she guessed Virginia must have been chafing about it. This was the morning, it seemed, that the ghastly Virginia had decided to engineer a confrontation.

'OK, if that's the way you want it,' Jan muttered to herself, 'that's the way you can have it.'

Jan found her rival sitting in the driving seat of her vehicle. She trotted the hack up to the Land Rover and dismounted.

Virginia had slid the window open and was leaning her bony elbow on the sill, but made no comment as Jan approached.

'You've broken the agreement. You go after me, not before,' Jan said angrily.

Virginia did not look at her. 'You were late,' she said cuttingly.

'Five minutes, that's all. And you know damn well that I require a minimum of forty minutes to work my horses.'

'Get lost. You weren't here so I thought with this frost you were using your famous all-weather gallop.'

Her tone was one of bored superiority, as if dealing with this problem was beneath her and of no interest.

'What frost?' retorted Jan. 'The ground's not frozen. There isn't a sodding frost.'

Virginia shrugged. 'Well, as I said, you weren't here. How could I know why? And what's more I don't take kindly to you coming along and muscling my guys out of the way.'

'I had every right. So kindly stick to the arrangements in future.'

This time Virginia made no attempt to reply and Jan turned away. She could hear the drumming of hooves on the turf as the first pair of horses approached at speed. Morning Glory and Velvet Dynasty flashed past. Once rivals, the two horses now exercised together and were the two fastest horses in the yard by far.

With a smile Jan remembered the tense, nip-and-tuck meetings between the two during the previous season. In speed and ability they had appeared to be very much on a par, but after only a couple of weeks under Jan's care Velvet Dynasty had been thriving, and she wanted to see how he measured up now, at level weights, against his old adversary.

What she had just seen delighted her and a warm feeling flooded her soul. She had told Michael Finnegan and Patsy to ride out, just hands and heels over the last furlong. For a second Patsy on Morning Glory got his horse's head in front and was about to pull away when suddenly Velvet Dynasty picked up, finding another gear, and with silky smooth, deceptive ease he lengthened his stride, took up the running and finished a length to the good.

'If that was Morning Glory in second place, I suppose you fixed that gallop on purpose.'

It was Virginia's voice, which came from a place almost immediately behind Jan. She too, had seen the exceptional way the two horses had worked.

'Really, why would I do that?'

'To score another point. To get me to watch the horse you took from *me* doing well. You're pathetic.'

'I don't fix my horses' exercise – as you call it – for any reason except to see how they're working for myself,' Jan stated, turning to face Virginia. 'I've got too much respect for them, which is more than I can say about you.'

'Respect?' spat Virginia. 'Don't make me vomit. You only bought that horse to spite me.'

'I didn't buy him. He belongs to A.D. O'Hagan, who knows a

useful horse when he sees one. Your loss is my gain. Life can be a bitch at times, Virginia.'

'Well, you wouldn't have got hold of him at all, if your bloody rat-faced brother hadn't been a complete bastard.'

'Ben has acted absolutely correctly. He's honoured your father's wishes.'

'He's still a bastard.'

'Virginia, I doubt if he's going to lose any sleep over what you think of him.'

Suddenly Virginia held out the palm of one hand and tapped it with the index finger of the other.

'No, Jan, you don't get it, do you? It's not what I'm thinking. It's what I know for a fact. Your brother is a real bastard.'

Jan looked at Virginia in bewilderment. 'Virginia, what on earth are you trying to say?'

The woman had a smirk on her face now, the spiteful smirk of a child about to reveal a shameful playground secret.

'Well, I'm not *trying* to say anything. I'm telling you how it is. How pathetic you are with your illusions about your comfy family. Ben's a bastard. Not in the same way that you're a bloody cow, but like he is, in actual fact, the brat of the village whore. Do you understand me now? She was anybody's, and as for your darling brother he's the result. You could be too, for all I know. But he certainly is.'

Jan was aware of cold anger stealing over her. She let go of her horse and without precisely knowing what she was doing, she made a hard fist and swung it with all her might at Virginia's grinning face. Her knuckles cracked into Virginia's nose, who staggered sideways from the impact, letting out a harsh cry of pain. She barely kept her footing as she clapped her hand to her face.

'You will regret that, you bitch,' Virginia snapped as she regained her balance. A trickle of blood was oozing down from her nose. 'That's just about your level, isn't it? Violence. You're an ill-bred, common cow.'

Jan didn't trust herself to speak. She swivelled on her heels and marched away, trembling with rage as she worked the fingers of her hand to ease the self-inflicted pain. Now she could hear the sound of hooves, like distant thunder, as the rest of her string came up the incline of the gallop in one group. The sound almost muffled the last snarling remark that Virginia hurled at her.

'I'll have you for this,' Virginia said. 'I'll see you in court and then in jail, as God is my witness.'

18

It had been a long time since Jan had actually hit someone in anger, even though the wallop that had landed on Virginia's leering face was richly deserved, and she felt there was no dishonour in defending her dead mother when she was being vilified. All the same, Jan regretted losing control because it gave the advantage to Virginia. It would enable her, like a villain in a melodrama, to have the last word by threatening Jan with a lawsuit.

However, Jan believed there were many reasons for Virginia not to take this step. For one thing she didn't appear to have much money, or at least not the ready cash needed to risk funding a legal case. For another, she would not want the world to know what a vicious, spiteful, underhanded shrew she was.

It was several hours later when Jan rang Bob Warren, her solicitor, to ask his opinion, after telling him of Virginia's threat to take her to court.

'And did you?'

'Did I what?'

'Hit her or assault her in any way?'

'Yes, of course I did, and I would do it again. So would you if you'd heard the things she said about my mother.'

'What damage did you do?'

'Um, I gave her a bloody nose, and probably a black eye as well. But she wasn't spitting out teeth.'

'And you would be prepared to admit that in court, would you?'

'Well, Bob, you know that I always prefer to tell the truth.'

'Then I'm afraid she would almost certainly win a civil case. But, given Miss Gilbert's provocation, I doubt she'd be awarded much by way of damages and I suspect a competent solicitor in possession of all the circumstances would advise her against serving a writ. There is one other thing, though.'

'What?'

'Assault is a criminal offence. She doesn't have to sue you in the civil court – she can make a complaint to the police.'

Jan hadn't thought of that. 'Ah . . . well, yes, I suppose she could.'

'Were there any witnesses?'

'No, not that I know of.'

'That helps. But again, you'd be on a loser in front of the magistrate if you admitted it. On the other hand, the same proviso applies about the relative credibility of the complainant. A sympathetic magistrate might take a very lenient view, given Miss Gilbert's past record. Do you think she might actually pursue a complaint?'

'If you tied me to a tree and put a gun to my head, I'd say she won't.'

He laughed, sounding relieved.

'We'll just have to wait and see, then. Don't hesitate to call me if she does. Bye – take care and do please try and stay out of trouble.'

🐎

When Jan saw Virginia at the races two days later she was wearing a large pair of sunglasses with impenetrable lenses, but seemed otherwise unaffected by their antler clash on the gallops. As they usually did in public, the two women did their best to avoid being in close proximity to one another. At the same time it seemed as though the threat of legal action had receded as Jan had heard nothing from the police or from Virginia's lawyer.

🐎

On the way home from the track, with Declan ensconced at the wheel of the lorry, Jan was thoughtful and tried again to understand the extraordinary and incredible statements Virginia had made to her about the Pritchard family. Ben, her brother, was illegitimate and their mother had been promiscuous – not a chance. There could be no basis whatsoever for this horrible charge. Absolutely nobody who knew Mary could possibly entertain such an idea even for a moment. But, on the other hand, Jan knew her mother's teenage fling with George Gilbert was real enough. True, it had been more than a decade before her birth and even longer before Ben's, for that matter. But suppose the affair had been revived in some way when the young officer returned from the army. Was that what Virginia had been getting at? Was Ben the colonel's illegitimate son? Was that the reason he'd inherited Dowerhouse Farm?

Suddenly Jan remembered her conversation with Rosemary Sterry. 'His behaviour was honourable always,' she had said.

Was that really true, though? Both George Gilbert and Mary had married other people, and Mary had Reg's child when George came back. Nevertheless it seemed that George still secretly carried a torch for his first love. Had Mary reciprocated that love? And had their first meeting for ten or more years rekindled those old feelings?

'Shit,' Jan said out loud. 'Could the colonel have been Ben's real father?'

'What'd you say, Mrs H?'

'Oh, nothing, Dec. Just a thought.'

These unanswered questions charged round Jan's mind wildly and were still a long way from establishing that Mary was promiscuous, but they hacked away cruelly at the foundations of Jan's own family, which she had always assumed to be rock solid. And now that she was examining them, she knew she was going to have to find the answers, one way or another, as soon as possible.

❦

That evening, after Fran had agreed to stay on with the children for a couple of hours, Jan drove to Riscombe via Stanfield and parked outside Rosemary Sterry's cottage, which stood on the edge of the village. The porch light was on, as was the light in the window of the sitting room. But was Rosemary alone? Jan had some very difficult and private matters to discuss and she didn't want Herb Sterry hovering around.

She was still sitting in her Shogun when a man in jeans and

bomber jacket, leading a scruffy dog, turned through the Sterry's front gate and sauntered up to the cottage. He pressed the bell and Jan faintly heard the notes of the door chime inside. After a moment Herb appeared, wearing a fluffy bobble hat and pulling on a parka. The man with the dog slapped Herb on the back and they set off together, their breath steaming in the chilly night air, in the direction of the pub.

A few minutes later Jan herself was standing on Rosemary Sterry's doorstep. She thumbed the button and again heard the door chime, followed by a creaking hinge and a slight bump as Rosemary pulled open the door.

'Oh, Jan! It's you,' she said, in a tone that seemed not entirely pleased.

'Hello, Rose,' Jan said brightly, ignoring the manner. 'Have you a few minutes? I need a chat.'

'I was just sitting down to watch— oh well, never mind. Come in, dear.'

She pulled the door wider and stood back for her unexpected visitor to enter. On the television a soap opera's theme music was playing as the opening titles rolled. Rosemary banged shut the front door and returned to her armchair by the fire, where she groped among the cushions for the remote control. Having found it, she took careful aim at the TV screen and blanked it with the press of a button.

'Don't you watch *Corrie*?'

Jan shook her head. 'I'm sure I'm missing out,' she said, not wishing to be rude about what was obviously one of Rosemary's keenest interests. 'But no, I never seem to have time. I'm sorry if I've interrupted your viewing.'

'No, no. Never mind. There's a repeat later in the week. Tea, or something a bit stronger?'

Jan said yes to the tea ritual and, as before, she stood looking at the array of framed photographs on Rosemary's dresser while her hostess clattered around in the kitchen.

'Now, dear, what can I do for you?' said Rosemary when she had returned and they were both sitting down. 'You wanted a word, you said.'

'Yes, it's, er, about my mum.'

'Oh yes? I've not seen you since the funeral, have I? Lovely service, dear. The vicar spoke beautifully. Even my Herb said so, and he normally never notices such things.'

'Yes, it was very moving. But it's not about that. Do you remember when I was here last, you were telling me about Mum and the colonel when they were both young?'

The look on Rosemary's face suddenly altered and she appeared uneasy, a bit like a witness in court who had already said too much, and did not want to be cross-examined again.

'*Yees*, I remember,' she said warily.

'Well, I was wondering if there was any possibility that their relationship could have started up again? I mean after he came back from the army.'

Rosemary had been bringing her cup to her lips, but now she trembled so badly she needed to check herself and after a moment she returned the cup to the saucer. Her answer was rather rapid and breathless Jan thought, and was delivered with a frown and a slight paling around her mouth.

'No, dear, that's definite. As I told you, it had finished long before. Mary was married to Reg by then and she already had you. Mr George – the colonel – was married too. Not very happily as it turned out, but married nevertheless.'

'But are you sure?' Jan pressed. 'Rose, this is important. Some things have been said. I'm sorry I can't go into it in detail, but I would like to know a bit more about why Ben received such a large and generous legacy from George Gilbert. You see, I think it's about more than just the colonel feeling nostalgic for his first love, or even having a touch of guilt over what happened when they were forced to separate . . .'

Jan dried up, trying to grasp what she actually did think about the inheritance. What if it was not about any of these things?

'Go on,' prompted Rosemary. 'What is it you are thinking?'

'God, this is awful. I'm thinking maybe it's something to do with my brother and his parentage. That's what I'm thinking.'

There was an extended silence while the two women stared at each other.

'With Ben's parentage?' Rosemary repeated blankly, after several seconds.

Jan was sure Rosemary was stonewalling her, trying to put off the moment when she would have to declare what she knew. Jan cleared her throat.

'Rose, please, just tell me. Was Ben in fact . . . I mean, is he actually, or could he be, the colonel's son?'

Very deliberately, Rosemary stretched forward and placed her cup and saucer on the low table in front of her. She smoothed the dress across her knees with the palms of her hands and stared into the middle distance for a moment, as if composing herself. Then she spoke.

'Maybe the time has come to tell, make a clean breast of it, so to speak. You're shooting in the dark, Jan. Making two and two add up to six, or whatever it is. I don't know about Ben, whether he should know the truth or not, you will have to decide that for yourself, but maybe it's best if it comes out now.'

'What, Rose? What should I know? What needs to come out now?'

'There wasn't an affair with Mr George, you see. It was Mr Hugo.'

'Hugo? But he's the colonel's younger brother?'

'Yes, him. He was a wrong 'un.'

'You mean *he* had an affair with my mother?'

'No, no, dear me. It wasn't like that. It takes . . . well, it takes a deal of explaining.'

'Tell me. I need to know everything that happened.'

Rosemary settled in her chair. Jan could see from the way she composed herself she had made up her mind.

'Do you remember the photograph we were looking at when you were here before? Well, it was at a shooting party, just like the one in that picture. It could even have been the same one, I think. The Gilberts used to have their friends over at the beginning of September for the start of the partridge season. Mr Hugo wasn't living at home then. They said he spent most of his time abroad, but he came home for the shooting party every year.'

'What did he do? For a living, I mean.'

Rosemary grimaced.

'Mr Hugo? Oh, nothing much. He spent money, he didn't earn it. That was his claim. He never had a job, as far as I know, but lived off the family. Gambling, drinking and women, that was how he spent much of his time. Anyway, on this particular day we came back from serving the picnic lunch at the shoot. The guns weren't back yet. Mrs Gilbert told Mary and me to go up and get the guest rooms ready, put in clean towels and so on. When the shoot came back, it was obvious Mr Hugo was drunk. You could hear him from upstairs as they came in. I was working in the Blue Room and Mary was in Mr Hugo's. The next thing I heard Mr Hugo on the stairs, shouting something, before he came up and went into his room. Then I heard the door slam.

'Well, I finished preparing the Blue Room and I was just passing Mr Hugo's door. Although it was closed tight, I could hear his voice inside. He was laughing, and it was then I realized Mary was still in there because I heard her voice too. She sounded distressed, pleading like, but he just went on laughing. I thought of knocking on the door, but I didn't like to, not with Mr Hugo in the state he was in. He could be very threatening, you know, if you crossed him. To this day I can't forgive myself that I didn't do something – God help me. I just walked by and went downstairs to the kitchen. It haunts me to this day, Jan, honest it does.'

'But what on earth was happening?' Jan asked, her mind full of dread.

Rosemary lowered her voice.

'Mr Hugo forced himself on your mother, Jan. That's what happened.'

Jan frowned.

'You mean . . . ?'

Rosemary nodded slowly and pulled a hankie from her cardigan pocket to wipe away the tears that rolled down her face.

'He raped her.'

Jan gasped.

'Oh my God!'

This vile information was impossible to take in. Jan just sat and stared at Rosemary in total disbelief. She had had no idea, not the slightest.

'But h . . . h . . . how, Rose?' she stammered eventually. 'How could it happen? In a house full of people.'

Rosemary shrugged.

'The two of them were alone in the room, the door was shut. It doesn't take long, a thing like that. And Mr Hugo, he was a big man, cunning too, one of those who always thought he could get away with anything.'

Jan closed her eyes. She felt cold and a shiver ran right through her. Then she felt her gore rising. It was totally unthinkable. Mary had never dropped the slightest hint, not in her whole life, that she had gone through such a dreadful experience. To live all her life and say nothing was incredible.

'Anyway,' Rosemary continued, 'Mary came running down to the kitchen. Her clothes were all messed up and she was distraught. There was just two of us in there, me and Martha the cook. We comforted her as best we could, but we didn't catch on to what had happened, not at first. She was too upset and she couldn't talk straight.'

'Didn't anyone call the police?'

'Oh, no. At first, like I said, we couldn't get any sense out of her. Then, when we worked it out, and what Mr Hugo had done and all that, it was sort of hushed up. We were told not to say anything and that Mr George would be dealing with his brother personally. I don't think I've ever known anybody to be as angry as Mr George was. He almost killed his brother there and then, so I heard. He started to throttle him, but the other guests pulled him off. But he gave him a right pasting all the same.'

'What about my father? What did he do?'

'Reg was very, very grieved. Absolutely beside himself he was. But that was later. He didn't know a thing about it until some way into the evening. He stormed in to see Mr George and they were closeted in the library together talking, for a long time. By then Mr Hugo had gone, vanished. They spirited him away. One of the party – a Dr Shoemark it was, from Harley Street, a great shooting friend of Mr George – drove him, so we heard.'

'Where?'

'I wouldn't know. But we never ever saw him again in the house or in the village. The story was he'd been sent on a ship to South America and told never to return.'

There was a long silence. Jan rose from her chair and went to the window, staring out into the dark, still struggling to absorb the truth.

At long last she turned and said quietly, 'Do you know if Hugo Gilbert is still alive?'

Rosemary shook her head slowly.

'I doubt it, the way he lived his life. But who knows? Gone to his maker long since, most like. Or to hell, if there's any justice. He was not one for repenting his sins, if you ask me.'

Suddenly Jan felt hot, claustrophobic even. She gabbled something about the children and began searching in her bag for the keys to the Shogun.

At the cottage door Rosemary took Jan's arm for a moment, her eyes still full of tears. 'I'm really sorry, dear, that you had to find out like this.'

But as she stood in the doorway Jan remembered why she had come here in the first place. It had been to ask if Ben was Colonel Gilbert's son. Instead she was coming away with the knowledge that her mother had been raped by his brother, Hugo Gilbert.

'Rose, I've just had another thought. I asked you if there was any possibility the colonel might be Ben's real father and you said no definitely. Then you told me about all this. Do I take it to mean that Hugo . . . that *he* might be?'

Rosemary took her hand off Jan's arm and stroked the back of her fingers in a brief, tender gesture across Jan's cheek.

'Oh that's not for me to say, dear. I think you'd better ask your father.'

🐎

On the short drive home, Jan pulled over, retching. Her head was buzzing. The image that kept reappearing in her mind was Virginia's face, distorted by loathing, hissing, *Your brother is a bastard.*

Jan knew, if it were true her brother was conceived as a result of Hugo's criminal action, that it would explain the codicil to the colonel's will. It was not just a matter of making some kind of delayed recompense. It was that Ben carried the Gilbert genes and would have had some claim, a moral one, if not a legal one, on the family property. The colonel hadn't explained this in his letter to Ben, though. He could have done, but he had chosen not to. Perhaps such a shameful act against his family honour couldn't ever be openly admitted, even after his death. Or perhaps George Gilbert was still trying to protect Mary and assumed she would be alive when the will was read.

It was obvious from what Virginia had said to Jan on the gallops that she knew something about it. But her version and the true facts of the matter had been mangled out of all recognition to make Mary the guilty party. Had Virginia twisted the truth herself in the recesses of her own sick mind, or had it been twisted for her? Jan didn't think the colonel would have divulged the facts, especially to his daughter. And if he had, he would certainly not have made up such a catalogue of lies.

In a flash Jan thought of the mother. Rosemary Sterry had said Virginia took after Clare Gilbert and had the same mannerisms. Had she been the source of her daughter's nasty, monstrous lie – that it had been Mary Pritchard who seduced Hugo Gilbert, like a sultry temptress, and conceived his child?

Jan turned at last into the gateway of Edge Farm and the car began bouncing up the rutted track towards the yard, then she slowed and stopped right opposite the spot where she had been at her lowest ebb after her mother's death. Out there, in the field, her horses had comforted her, and what she had told herself then was still true – in fact, truer than ever. She had to get through this. Grief was necessary, good even, but she couldn't let it take over her life. Now she had to take on board the truth and move on.

But before she could do that there was still one question that needed to be answered. Was Ben really the child of Hugo Gilbert?

The fact that he had raped Mary did not make it definite. And, as Rosemary had gently put it, there was only one person alive who could tell her the real truth.

But how on earth was Jan going to approach Reg?

19

By the time Jan had finished evening stables and had written her riding-out list for the next day, Fran had usually got the children bathed and into their pyjamas. Tonight their mother was only too glad to take over the rest of the bedtime palaver and willingly poured glasses of milk and supervised their tooth brushing, before she finally read them a few pages of a carefully chosen tale. As usual, this brought their day to a satisfying conclusion. And those precious moments also negated Jan's own anxieties.

Jan was not overly sugary or starry-eyed about children. She had soon learnt how manipulative and crafty they could be, even at a very early age, though she firmly believed this only became troublesome when adults failed to show their offspring love and taught them their own bad habits instead.

Reg had related one of his parables in a similar fashion to her once. It was when Jan first discovered she was pregnant with Megan, and had travelled to her old home in Riscombe to tell her folks they were about to become grandparents. Before she left to return home to John Hardy, Jan and her father had taken a walk together on Riscombe Down. It was autumn and they passed under a copse of beech trees that had just finished shedding their foliage. Reg crouched down and stirred the orange-brown carpet of leaves with his finger until he found one of the little husks, matted with stiff, curly spines, which contained the kernel. He prised it open with his thumb to reveal the shiny brown nut inside. Picking it out, he showed it to Jan, holding the uniquely shaped triangular object to the light between finger and thumb.

'It's amazing to me,' he said, 'how a tiny bonny little thing like this can become a massive tree as big as that.'

He gestured at the towering beech that loomed above them.

'Nature does it better with trees, I reckon, than with people. But you'll be all right with your little ones, Jan, because I know you. Some folk teach their young 'uns all wrong, they don't look after them and they grow up crooked. Then they blame someone else when a crime's been committed – the schools and police usually.'

He let the beech nut fall to the ground and stood up straight staring out across the valley in the cold, damp, aromatic air.

'I worked it out for myself, years ago, and it seems to me it's a fact. When you get kiddies, and it doesn't matter how you get 'em, there's a contract that you sign. It's a contract with nature. It says you've got to pay for those kiddies with love. Money ain't no use on its own.'

He looked at his daughter earnestly to impress on her how much he believed in this.

Jan smiled at her father's passion. 'But it's not a heavy price, Dad. It's instinct, isn't it? Genetic, I suppose.'

'No, it's not.'

Suddenly, and to Jan's complete surprise, Reg was agitated.

'No, it's *not* bloody genetic,' he said vehemently. 'It's about caring and loving. Them are things you gather up early in life, like a harvest, to get you through. They're not in any damn genes, so you can forget that. First you've got to gather them up and later you give them out again. That's how it works.'

Reg fell silent for a moment, breathing heavily and thinking.

'And there's some folk,' he went on, 'that don't have enough love in them. When their turn comes to be parents they forget their side of the bargain. They won't do it, some can't – it just ain't in 'em. And that's when them children become damaged goods.'

He sighed.

'I've seen it happen afore.'

Jan had never forgotten how Reg had stood at that moment, as if he was carved of granite, looking out over the landscape, completely lost in thought. Suddenly he'd come back to himself and laughed, pointing again at the ancient beech towering above.

'So them trees have got it lucky, eh, lass? They don't have feelings the way us people do.'

Jan lifted Matty into his bed, kissing him as she smoothed down the covers. Megan wanted to read for a while, so Jan kissed her too before going down to the sitting room to throw more wood onto the fire. As she leaned into the wicker basket standing alongside the inglenook fireplace, Jan noticed something black and metallic peeping out of the hollow recess that had been built into the fireplace wall. It was Colonel Gilbert's deed box. Instantly Jan remembered that she had placed it there out of the way after they read the colonel's letter. Neither of them had touched it since.

Strictly speaking, the box belonged to Ben, but he'd left it with her deliberately, and had shown no further interest in the contents since. In fact he had been extremely reticent about the papers inside, telling Jan he might go through them some day. Whether he was actually afraid of what he might find, or simply did not think there would be any benefit, she couldn't tell. Either way, Jan felt she would not be trespassing if she examined the items now. After what Rosemary had told her, she thought, there might be additional clues to the events at that shooting party thirty-odd years ago. And, if there were, she intended to unearth them.

Jan poured herself a glass of wine and placed the box on the rug in front of the fire. She plonked herself down and removed the key that was Sellotaped to the side. She put it in the lock and heard a click as the lock was released. She noticed her hands were trembling as she lifted the lid and saw the colonel's last letter to Ben was no longer on top of the pile. Her brother must have taken it away with him, she decided. She took a deep breath as she saw the ribbon-tied letters, addressed to George Gilbert in Mary's handwriting. She undid the knot and opened the first letter, scanning it quickly, almost guiltily, feeling she was breaking into something private and painful. Her eye caught a few phrases – 'with love always', 'long to be with you' – and knew at once that she would not be able to read the contents further.

Lower down there were several Manila envelopes, some

addressed to 'George Gilbert Esq.', others to 'Lt G. Gilbert' and 'Capt. G. Gilbert' at various British Forces Post Offices around the world, from Hong Kong to Nairobi. Some had been stuffed with photographs and memorabilia, apparently collected at different stages during the early years of the colonel's service. Jan began to remove these from the box in turn, putting them aside without consideration. She was desperate to see what lay below.

Eventually she came to one addressed to 'Major George Gilbert', Riscombe Manor. This, Jan concluded, might indicate the contents could date from the period after his return home. Jan could hear her heart beating as she slid the contents out of the envelope and began to rummage through them.

The first thing she came across was a print of the exact same photograph she had seen at Rosemary Sterry's cottage – the group portrait taken by old Kenworthy, Riscombe's estate manager. She flipped it over and saw a date had been scrawled in pencil on the back: 3 September 1960. Jan's heart thudded even more loudly. She knew that the partridge season began on 1 September, so this must be the original shooting party that Rosemary had described, the photo probably taken on the very day Mary was brutalized.

Jan pressed her finger on the figure of Hugo Gilbert, while studying his face. He did not look particularly brutal – but then, what did a rapist look like? For a while Jan thought she could detect some slight resemblance to her brother in the handsome, self-satisfied features, but the impression grew less clear the longer she stared. The peak of Hugo's tweed cap shadowed his face, making it too difficult for her to be certain. She laid the photo down and picked up the next item.

It was three slimline pocket books, held together in a bundle by a rotting elastic band, which snapped as she tried to tug it off. The books it seemed were made by the same manufacturer, all covered in green leather with the words *GAME AND FISHING RECORDS* stamped on the front in faded gilt lettering. As she opened the first, Jan found George Gilbert's personal and meticulously compiled list of game bags and fishing catches taken on the estate, from the first day he came into his inheritance: every gun and rod was personally named, and the particulars of their success itemized, including, in the case of the fish, the name of the fly on which they had been caught. Each entry was brought to a conclusion with an abrupt summary of the day's sport. 'Ghastly day, incessant rain,' said one. 'Good conditions early, too hot later. My Purdeys misfiring,' read another. The first record was written in 1959.

Jan continued leafing through the flimsy pages until she reached 3 September 1960, the date on the back of the photo. There she found the number of birds shot by each member of the party, all had been identified by name. She saw that, out of a total bag Colonel Gilbert had shot five, Mrs Gilbert three, Hugo Gilbert one and the other guns between two and six. Dr Shoemark, who later was to drive Hugo away from the manor in shame and disgrace, had scored four. Underneath, in the colonel's neat handwriting, was a solitary, bleak comment: 'Good shooting, day best forgotten.'

Now with her eyes standing out on stalks Jan carefully unfolded a yellowed clipping from what looked like the local paper. It was a column of christening announcements; one of the entries under-lined in blue ink read: *Benjamin James son of Reginald and Mary Pritchard of Riscombe Vale Farm, at St Stephen's Church, Riscombe.* Jan tried to recall Ben's birth. She had been only four at the time and had little recollection of it, except for a vague memory of standing on tiptoe to peer into a cot in a darkened room, and being told she had a new baby brother. Had Ben been born prematurely, or gone full term? Jan couldn't remember her parents even talking about this, but his birthday was 26 May 1961, so if he had been born at around the expected time he must have been conceived in late August or early September 1960.

Jan's stomach lurched and a hollow feeling of dread began to develop. She grabbed the glass of wine and took another gulp. None of this meant that Hugo Gilbert really was Ben's father, but the circumstantial evidence that he might have been was beginning to build. And the saved cutting from the christening announcements showed that Colonel Gilbert had taken an interest himself in Ben from the very start.

The next thing Jan unfolded was a clipping from a paper dated 31 August 1964. Yellowed and beginning to crumble, it showed several photographs under the headline *RISCOMBE FETE RAISES*

£60. One was of Colonel Gilbert opening the event. A second showed the old priest, Joseph Clifford, who had served as vicar for most of Jan's childhood, handing out prizes, while a third was a shot of the skittles, manned, as they always used to be, by the landlord of the Gilbert Arms, a former Spitfire pilot with a spectacular handlebar moustache. But it was the fourth much smaller picture that made Jan's heart ache. It was of the Women's Institute stall and showed her mother in a floral print dress standing proudly behind a trestle table that groaned with home-made jams, marmalade, biscuits and fancy cakes. In her arms she had a small boy wearing a navy blue sailor suit with the collar edged in white, grinning gap-toothed for the camera. It was Jan's blond, spiky-haired little brother, Benjamin James.

She stared at the pictures as tears stung her eyes, almost in a trance, as a series of forgotten details from her childhood raced back into her mind. Eventually she refolded the article and slid it back into the Manila envelope.

Only one more item remained at the bottom of the box, another envelope, a white one of superior quality. It was addressed to Major G. Gilbert MC, and was typewritten. The postmark was illegible. Jan lifted the flap and drew the folded paper out from the envelope.

It was a bill, from a Dr Walter Shoemark, MD, FRCP, which gave his address as Harley Street, London. Underneath, the date was inscribed at the top of the page as 16 April 1960. Lower down, the amount requested was five guineas for 'private consultation for Mr Reginald Pritchard'. Jan quickly looked on the back of the bill, and in the envelope, in the hope of finding more. But there was nothing.

She took another swig and stared at the fire. The logs she had added earlier were now sizzling and spitting, as flames pushed up the chimney. Why on earth, she wondered, would her father have visited Dr Shoemark? And in Harley Street of all places? Reg liked London even less than Jan did, and would go to almost any lengths to avoid the place. Besides, there were doctors in the Cotswolds whose services would have cost nothing.

Reg's medical history had been uncomplicated, as far as Jan knew. She remembered he'd had a hernia operation back in the seventies, and there had been the odd period of bed rest when he'd strained his back. Apart from these and the occasional bout of flu, her father had been exceedingly healthy. Yet here was the colonel paying for his tenant to visit a posh metropolitan doctor. So why? That's what Jan wanted to know. Why hadn't she heard about this before? It was the kind of thing that, in normal circumstances, Reg would have told stories about in that gently self-mocking way of his. She could imagine him dressing up the whole adventure and taking the part of a character from one of his favourite books. But, as far as she could recall, the trip to see Dr Shoemark had never ever been mentioned.

Now she looked down at the various heaps of paper that she had scattered all over the carpet. They meant something significant, that was for sure. They were not a random collection of memorabilia, but a series of clues, signposts, designed for someone – Ben, presumably – to follow up. But what was the conclusion? What was it pointing to? Did the colonel really want Ben to know the truth, the reason why he had become one of the Gilbert heirs? And, if so, did he really want this to be connected with the fact that Mary had been raped by Hugo? Or, on the other hand, was he trying to conceal that event by drawing attention to his own forlorn love of Mary?

George Gilbert might not have been able to spell out in words of one syllable why he had left Dowerhouse Farm to a young man he hardly knew, but it certainly looked as if he was now pointing the way to the real motive.

Jan gathered up the strewn papers and replaced them carefully in the order she had found them. She locked the deed box and slipped it back into the recess. Questions still buzzed around her brain like a swarm of bees. She took a deep gulp and swallowed the last of the wine, hoping to quell her thoughts, but she knew they would keep her awake late into the night.

<h1>20</h1>

Jan had tossed and turned for most of the night and was slightly hungover while riding out with first lot the next morning. Impatient though she was to get answers, Jan knew she wouldn't get any further without first tackling Reg. It was a prospect she dreaded and she wished there was someone to talk it over with. To go to Ben was obviously out of the question as he didn't even know about the attack on his mother, let alone its possible consequences. Jan had no idea how she would tell him, or even if she should. Normally something like this would have necessitated a heart to heart with Annabel. But it seemed cruel to burden Bel with dark questions about the paternity of the man she was about to marry. The only other person who Jan could trust to be understanding and sympathetic was Toby Waller, but he was out of the country for the time being.

Jan stood banging her rain-soaked jacket against the wall by the back door to the house. It had been a filthy but satisfying morning's work on the gallops.

'Cor, I hope you've got the kettle on, Fran. I'm bloody freezing.'

'Cuppa coming up, Mrs H, and breakfast won't be long,' Fran replied as she slapped the frying pan onto the Aga. 'Oh, by the way, I was Hoovering the sitting room while you were out and I found this tucked under the rug by the fireplace. I don't know if it's important.'

As Jan look quizzically at the tatty piece of paper, her face froze for a second or two.

'Thanks, Fran, it's nothing major. I was just going through some old papers last night, chucking some out, I must have missed the bin.' But Jan's face told a different story. The document was an invoice from the P&O shipping line for a one-way ticket to South America and the passenger's name was Hugo Gilbert. Jan moved swiftly through to the sitting room to check she hadn't left any more bits scattered around. She hurriedly undid the black box and popped the receipt inside.

'What an idiot,' she said, rollicking herself, 'there's enough speculation going on around here without adding to it.'

Jan decided that as the events of the shooting party had already been kept dark for thirty years and she had more than enough on her plate already if she was to get her horses prepared for Cheltenham, she would do nothing about Rosemary Sterry's revelations, or the secrets of Colonel Gilbert's deed box, until after the Festival.

In the past Bobby Montana had been a regular visitor, but now he was making himself scarce. A few days earlier Jan had called to tell him about Spring Blow and the arsenic poisoning, reassuring him that it must have been discharged accidentally and she would thoroughly investigate how it had got into the horse's system. But Spring Blow seemed to have turned the corner and looked much better now they knew what they were treating. Montana had seemed angry rather than distressed to hear the news, and he was even angrier when Jan mentioned the long-drawn-out business of his unpaid bills. Instead of his usual humble tactic when confronted, apologizing for his forgetfulness or inefficiency, he chose a different technique and went on the attack.

'Let me tell you something, Jan Hardy,' he snapped. 'You get my horses ready to win on the track then I'll pay my dues.'

Jan replied firmly, but had no intention of being drawn into a full-blown row.

'I'm sorry, Mr Montana, that won't wash. The money is owed whether they run or not. And there is in fact very little chance of them running for quite some time.'

Montana tried to interrupt, but Jan refused to let him. 'As you have been informed from the outset, Spring Blow is ill. Big Freeze has been making progress, but the outcome of his case is still uncertain and you have to face the possibility that he may never race again.'

'The hell with it, I'd rather he was dead,' screamed Montana as he slammed down the receiver.

He had not been seen in the yard since.

🐎

In the middle of March Jan took Pat's Gem, a new horse of A.D.'s which he had recently sent to Edge Farm, to the St David's Day meeting at Chepstow. The owner had told Jan he would be there to see his latest prodigy in action.

A stiff breeze was blowing, whipping A.D.'s long dark raincoat about his legs as he approached the stable in the security yard, where Roz Stoddard was working tirelessly on Pat's Gem, determined to win the prize for the best-turned-out horse. Jan had just returned from the declarations office and had signed her owner in.

'Your horse looks better than you, thank goodness,' she teased. 'You must have had a rough crossing.'

'We certainly did. Daragh was as sick as a dog.'

'So why on earth don't you fly?'

A.D. never used aeroplanes and, ever since she'd known him, Jan had been longing to ask him the reason.

'I reckon,' he said, 'if the good Lord had meant us to he'd have given us epidermis filled with gas. Now I've met many with rubber necks, but not skins. So how's the horse? What'll he do today?'

As he stroked the horse's nose, Jan remembered Eddie's reluctance to admit to his own fear of flying. With A.D. it was clearly not a subject for discussion.

'Oh, I'm quite optimistic,' she said. 'Especially as the wind's dried the ground out a bit.'

'So we'll tell Murty to lie up with the pace, I suppose?'

Jan nodded. 'Yes, that's what Pat's Gem needs. He could even make the running, if he has to.'

'That's good. We don't want him laying too far out of his ground.'

A.D. rubbed the palms of his hands together, then extended an arm in the direction of the grandstand.

'Come over for a drink with me, why don't you? You've plenty of time.'

Jan left the horse's preparation in Roz's capable hands and headed back with A.D. For once he was racing without his usual entourage and when they reached the hospitality box she found only Daragh there. He was still looking more than a little queasy as he studied the *Racing Post*.

'Has Michael been telling you how things are going at Tumble-wind?' A.D. asked, after he had poured Jan a glass of white wine.

'Oh, I hear bits and pieces,' said Jan casually, not wishing to sound over-enthusiastic, or let slip that she really liked Michael. 'He says renovations to the house are well under way, and they've started on the stable yard now.'

'Yes, the old barns and outbuildings are down. We've cleared that site completely and laid the foundations of the new yard already. I'm on my way there myself tomorrow, for a site meeting.'

He said no more about the grandiose project at Lambourn, and they moved on to analyse in detail their runners' chances at the Cheltenham Festival.

When Jan's horses raced she was not able to watch in complete serenity. But Pat's Gem's performance that day was a pleasure from start to finish. He took total command of the race from the off and, with Murty McGrath's expertise and guidance, won it readily. Afterwards, the journalists who approached Jan for a quote were very complimentary.

'It looks like your horses are bang in form, Mrs Hardy,' said one. 'I hear you have a strong hand and are expecting some winners at Cheltenham – is that right?'

'I never *expect* winners,' said Jan firmly. 'Nobody can in this game – you can only hope. If we come back with some place money I'll feel we've played our part.'

Next day she read the journalist's report under the headline: JAN HARDY CLAIMS A STRONG CHELTENHAM HAND. They were his words not hers, but with newspapers she'd learnt it wasn't unusual for words to be taken out of context.

🏇

On the Sunday evening before the Cheltenham Festival, Jan had settled in front of the television for what she hoped would be a quiet night after a busy day in the yard and entertaining the kids all afternoon.

'Peace at last,' she thought as she switched the TV on. Slowly, as the embers of the log fire began to die down, Jan drifted off to sleep, only to be woken by the sharp trill of the phone. Jolting upright on the settee, she fumbled for the source of the disturbance.

'Hello,' Jan said abruptly, 'Who is it?'

'A.D.,' came the reply. 'Sorry to ring you so late on a Sunday, but I've got some good news.'

'Oh really, I could do with some.'

'Well,' said A.D. 'I ran into an old friend yesterday, Demi Flatterly – we were pals way back in the early days. He owned a horse called Moonstone Magic, one of the favourites for Wednesday's Champion Chase, and I've just bought the horse off him.'

'You're joking,' exclaimed Jan.

'No, Demi was telling me his business has hit the skids and he needs some cash quickly but quietly, so I agreed a deal over the horse there and then, subject to the vet, of course. Listen,' A.D. went on, 'he's passed the vet this morning and he's on his way to you now. Eddie Brennan's shipping him. Jimmy, the travelling groom, reckons they should be with you about four o'clock in the morning.'

'Bloody hell, A.D. Excuse my French,' Jan said. 'This is quick.'

'It had to be, there was no time to lose over the deal, that's why I'm ringing you at this time of night.'

'A.D., that's brilliant, I saw the horse win the A.I.G. Chase at Leopardstown in January. He's one of the best-looking greys I've ever seen. Look, I'll get Patsy to give me a hand to set a stable fair for him right now. Do you want me to ring you when he arrives?'

'Not at that time of the morning. But I'm very excited about this feller.'

'I'm trembling with excitement, I can tell you,' Jan replied. 'I'll ring you at breakfast. Bye.'

As soon as Patsy had set the stable fair, Jan returned to the kitchen armed with a cup full of linseed that had been soaking in the feed room for twelve hours and two jugs of barley, which she immediately put in the slow cooker. This would boil up into a lovely gooey porridge, ideal for Moonstone Magic's breakfast.

By quarter-past four Jan had been lying awake for what seemed hours. She heard the power of the horsebox engine as it pulled into the yard. She quickly put her jacket over the top of her pink pyjamas and hurried down the slope.

'You made good time,' she declared to the driver.

'Always easier off the night ferry, Mrs H. Road's a lot clearer as well. Yer man has travelled like a baby. Not heard a peep out of him,' he said in a soft Irish lilt.

'Good,' said Jan. 'We'll get him settled and I'll make you lads a cup of tea and some toast.'

At nine o'clock precisely Jan rang A.D.

'He's arrived safely and he's bloody gorgeous. We'll give him some electrolytes later and a fairly easy day, just a canter this afternoon. He'll need a blow-out up the gallops on Tuesday as he runs on Wednesday.'

'Good morning, Jan,' came the reply. 'I take it from all that information you just told me in one breath that you're happy with our new arrival then.'

'Too right I am! Roll on Wednesday. I hope you've booked Murty to ride him.'

'I have indeed. He didn't need asking twice. Jan, I've got to go, see you at the races.'

The week of the Cheltenham Festival began in sunshine, which greened the grass and gladdened the racegoers who gathered in their thousands like pilgrims at the temple of the racing god. The fine spring weather continued through the week and, as Jan walked the course on the Wednesday morning, prodding the ground with one of Reg's old walking sticks, she found the turf had stood up well to Tuesday's action and the going was perfect: she paused at the top of the back straight, looking across to the already packed, sun-brightened enclosures, and felt a rush of well-being, tinged with slight panic.

How would Moonstone Magic handle these undulations, she

thought, before she moved on, heading down towards the third last fence, a big open ditch.

'Murty will need to keep hold of Moonstone's head and get him back on his hocks here,' she said to Annabel, who was accompanying her, 'or they will end up A over T.'

It was only as they completed the circuit and were approaching the grandstands that Jan's mood changed. She glimpsed the bookmakers setting up their pitches on the tarmac between the stands and the course, and a new bout of anxiety began to gnaw at her. She thought of the enormous bet A.D. O'Hagan would have had on Moonstone – in an attempt to recoup the purchase price – and suddenly prospects for the afternoon's sport seemed less enjoyable.

Going into the weighing room half an hour later to declare her runners, Jan was about to push through the door when it was suddenly yanked open from the inside, releasing a blast of chatter from the inner sanctum. Virginia Gilbert stood, with her hands on her hips, blocking Jan's path. She was dressed in a tweed suit, beautifully cut but hanging a little oddly from her bony frame, as if it had been made for a different woman entirely. With a tiny modicum of satisfaction, Jan thought she could detect the yellowish remnants of a black eye at the top of Virginia's left cheek. No action had materialized from the fracas on the gallops and the two women had not communicated since. For a moment it seemed Virginia was about to speak. Instead an extraordinary look crossed her face, as if the features were being twisted from within by the force of malice, stretching her mouth into a snarl.

Jan met her opponent's glare with an indifferent look and said lightly, 'Excuse me. I didn't know they served lemons in here.'

Virginia scowled and held her position for a moment longer, then barged past Jan without a word.

Jan had heard many old jockeys reminisce, declaring the Queen Mother Champion Chase the most thrilling, heart-pumping, white-knuckle journey of them all. The competition was fierce, over the minimum two-mile trip and the pace akin to that of a helter-skelter, with no chance to take a breather. Some mistakes were inevitable and were magnified by the speed, so a skilled rider with plenty of nerve was essential.

Murty McGrath was that rider and, despite the stampede to the first fence, he quickly got his mount settled in a mid-field position. By the time the fence had been cleared, a small group of runners had opened up a lead of four or five lengths. But Murty knew about pace and made sure he led the chasing pack, with enough room in front to enable the horse to see the obstacles and adjust his stride. Watching from the stands, Jan's trembling, clammy hands were clasped tightly around the binoculars as if they were a lifebelt in a rough sea. Jan could see how well Moonstone was jumping, gaining ground in the air, springing straight back into his stride as he touched down on the landing side.

After a mile the pace slackened. As they neared the top of the hill, Moonstone Magic and the big black horse alongside him, in the colours of Pat Whelan, better known in the world of greyhound racing, were disputing the lead. The watching crowd, largely silent until now, began to stir as the complexion of the race changed. Moonstone Magic's rival was a well-known, high-class chaser and, with three seasons behind him, had already won this race twice before.

Four fences from home Moonstone made his first mistake. Taking off too soon, he dragged his hind legs through the birch and stumbled on landing. Depending on where their money lay, the crowd groaned or cheered as the black gelding took command, immediately going into a two-length lead. But Murty remained calm and unflustered: gathering the horse together, he gave him a sharp slap down the neck with his whip to remind him of the job in hand. Now the field turned out of the back straight and swept downhill towards the third last. It was always a particularly difficult fence to negotiate and one at which a big jump could have a decisive effect. Whelan's horse met it all wrong and ploughed into the top of the fence, checking his momentum so sharply he almost lost his jockey on landing. But Murty had conjured a soaring leap out of Moonstone and they sailed past their rival in a flash.

Now the noise of the crowd had increased, winding itself up to a climax until it reached the usual celebrated Cheltenham roar.

It was a unique sound, with agony and acclaim roughly divided between fifty thousand throats, as they bellowed their favourite horses over the last two fences, urging them on up the long and, at times, seemingly never-ending hill towards the winning post. Full of running, Moonstone Magic bounded over the second last fence and approached the last unchallenged. Murty risked a look behind and saw Whelan's horse struggling in his wake, but a horse from Ireland, ridden by Timmy Connelly, had emerged from the pursuing pack and was beginning to close him down.

Whether it was because he was tiring, or because he sensed the approach of a new challenger, Moonstone Magic made a complete hash of the final fence. Completely misjudging it, he hardly lifted a limb and blundered badly. Miraculously he somehow managed to stay on his feet, as Murty performed a remarkable feat of horsemanship and stayed in the saddle. But, by the time he had re-gathered his reins, Timmy Connelly had gone flying past.

Now Jan saw a new aspect of Moonstone Magic as, with his ears lying flat, he began to give chase with grim determination. Slowly, with each weary stride, he began to reduce the leader's advantage. By now the crowd was frantic and the roar deafening, as the whole racecourse realized they were about to be treated to a finish truly worthy of a championship event.

With two hundred yards to go, Moonstone Magic had reached the leader's quarters. Murty continued to push, desperately trying to lengthen his horse's stride to its maximum, forcing him forward up the unforgiving hill until he was back on level terms. The last hundred yards were complete torment for anyone with an interest in either horse, as first one, and then the other, seemed to lead, their necks fully stretched. By now Jan's legs had completely gone and it was only the crush of the crowd – packed in the owners' and trainers' stand like sardines in a tin – that was holding her up.

The result of the ensuing photo finish confirmed what almost everyone knew. A.D. O'Hagan's horse had taken the Champion Chase by a whisker.

21

Jan was on auto-pilot as she went through the post-race ceremonies, television interviews and presentation of the trophies. This was the best and most prestigious memento she had ever won – a large Waterford crystal bowl inscribed with the title of the race. Later, her name, A.D.'s and that of the horse would be added to the base.

Jan was very self-conscious when she was beckoned forward to meet the Queen Mother and knew she must curtsy.

'Christ, I haven't done this before,' she whispered to Bel. 'I hope I get it right.'

Annabel grabbed her friend's hand and gave it a squeeze.

'Here, let me straighten your scarf,' she said softly. 'You'll be fine, just be yourself.'

Jan's ordeal was mercifully brief and was quickly followed by a visit to the dope testing unit, where the official racecourse vet would be taking a sample from Moonstone Magic, which would then be sent to a laboratory in Newmarket for the technicians to test for any prohibited substances. Jan always tried to be present when the sample was taken. After she'd checked the horse thoroughly for any injury she was still on a high as she made her way through the thronging crowds and put in an appearance at A.D.'s private box to drink a celebratory glass of champagne.

'Well done, Jan,' A.D. said as he gave her a hug and a kiss. 'I think we have a star on our hands.'

'It's well done to you, A.D. You did the deal and bought the horse, then had the courage to send him to me.'

'It was all about being in the right place at the right time. The good Lord must have been smiling on me that day. A bit like Murty was in the race today.'

After a few minutes, Jan excused herself and made her way back down to the saddling boxes to tack up the Galway Fox for the Coral Cup, a two-mile five-furlong hurdle race.

After the delirium of victory came disappointment. The Galway Fox's performance had been abysmal. Usually he was a straight-forward animal, but today the enormous crowd and the fevered atmosphere it generated got to him. In the parade ring he was lathered in sweat and even the presence of Patsy Keating did not calm him.

During the race he ran erratically and refused to settle for Murty, expending all his energy over the first mile. At the business end of the race he had nothing left to give and finished in the ruck. As standard procedure, the stewards called Jan in to explain his per-formance, as he had started the race as one of the better-fancied horses. Jan told them anyone with eyes could have seen the horse was boiling over in the paddock and that he was normally a well-behaved individual, but he had never been exposed to a riotous occasion like Cheltenham before and had simply reacted badly to the tension and the raucous crowd. The officials accepted the explanation and dismissed her without any further questioning. They did, however, order the horse to be dope tested as a matter of course. So now two samples from the Edge Farm runners were being couriered to the testing centre in Newmarket.

Toby had returned to England specifically to attend all three days of the Cheltenham Festival, and he took the opportunity to invite Jan to dine with him that night at a new gourmet restaurant near the hotel where he was staying at Stow-on-the-Wold.

Jan insisted she would need to return home before meeting Toby again that night and the atmosphere back at the yard was exhilarating, with the promise of another exciting day tomorrow. Having checked all she needed to do, Jan practically skipped up to the house to be greeted by Megan and Matty, who threw themselves into her arms.

'They've been like this ever since Moony won, Jan. And when they saw you curtsy to the Queen Mum, well! Megan's been practising ever since,' Fran told her.

Jan laughed as the kids mimicked her and curtseyed once more.

'Come on, you two scallywags, I've got to have a bath, I'm in a hurry. I'm meeting Toby Waller for supper at eight thirty. Scram. Go and have your tea then you can stay up for another hour if you're good, then bed. OK?'

'OK, your majesty.' Megan curtsied once more. 'Come on, servant,' she said to Matty. 'Let's go and feed our ponies before Fran catches us.'

Following the excitement of the race and a ten-minute soak in the bath, a rejuvenated Jan walked confidently into the restaurant – something she had not always found easy – to be greeted by the ever-smiling Toby Waller.

'What a fantastic day, Jan. I have a lovely table in the window –' he gestured – 'so I can show you off.'

'Toby! Stop it,' Jan whispered, flushing with embarrassment. 'I'm nearly as red as the curtains.'

'Nonsense,' Toby chortled as Jan slid self-consciously into the seat opposite.

Having ordered their food and one of the better wines on the list, Toby asked Jan about the yard. He wanted to know if the matter of Bobby Montana had been resolved.

'It hasn't. He's not paid a single penny towards his fees, which by the way are now well past the ten-thousand-pound mark, and from what Doug Shaw has told me he's very unlikely to, at least until the flat season starts.'

'The flat season?'

'Yes. This filly he owns, the one you found out about, they want to make a killing with her. Shaw's confident she will win a classic and once she's got black type after her name Montana will be able to sell her at a vast profit. He also dropped a few hints that the chap might struggle to find a hundred pounds right now, let alone ten thousand.'

'I see. So if you put Montana on the forfeit list that would stop him from running the filly and effectively block his chance of cashing her in.'

'Exactly. It's a real dilemma: letting the filly run could mean there's a possibility I might be paid. I'm really worried, though, because it's dragged on so long and I'm stuck between a rock and a hard place. What do you think?'

Toby pondered for a moment, then suddenly made up his mind.

'I wouldn't trust him. Not for a moment. My guess is he's some kind of crook or a con man.'

'Well, it's interesting you should say that,' Jan said, lowering her voice, 'because there's something else I found out about him, at least about a friend of his, a Canadian trainer called Mervyn Sawyer, who had handled the two horses last summer. Anyway, the point is, Sawyer's been investigated for fraud.'

'Do you know any details?'

Jan shook her head.

'It might be worth finding out,' said Toby. 'But in the meantime you really must go ahead and apply to have Montana placed on the forfeit list. If running this flat horse means so much to him, he'll come up with your fees somehow, won't he? You can't be sure he'll pay you a single penny unless he's forced to – even after he's made this so-called *killing*. By the way, do you think he hopes to pull a similar stunt with your two horses?'

Jan winced. 'Not a chance. They're invalids. He claims they're worth a lot but, let me tell you, he wouldn't get the price of a bag of chips for them right now. One of them's had navicular disease and the other's recovering from arsenic poisoning.'

'Arsenic? How on earth?'

'We have no idea.'

'Deliberate poisoning, do you think?'

'I don't see how. It couldn't be anyone on my staff, I'm sure of that. It has to be accidental. It might have happened before the horse came into the yard, an accumulation already in his body which was triggered in some way to make him even more sick. Of course, I'm only guessing, I don't know for sure. But at least he's on the mend now.'

The main course arrived, providing a natural moment for the subject to change.

'You implied earlier there was something else you wanted to talk to Uncle Toby about. So let's have it.' He grinned.

'Yes, but it's really delicate . . .' Jan said with a forlorn look.

Hesitantly at first, she outlined the story of Ben's legacy from the colonel, the old man's letter and the Gilbert family's dark secret which Rosemary Sterry had revealed to Jan. Toby listened with concentration.

'You mean your mother was actually attacked by this brother of Colonel Gilbert's.'

'Yes. She was raped. Can you imagine how dreadful it must have been? And to have kept it a secret all these years.' Tears filled her eyes. 'I wish I'd known before, Toby, I really do.'

'But surely there was police action?'

'They were never told. It seems everything was just brushed under the carpet and Hugo Gilbert got packed off to South America. What do you think was going on?'

Toby took a sip of wine and swallowed it slowly before replying.

'I'd say George Gilbert, who already carried a bit of a torch for your mum, became absorbed with guilt about his part in hushing up the rape. So much so that he split his estate to compensate your mother – it seems he couldn't bring himself to do it in his lifetime so he did it through his will.'

Jan tapped the table between them.

'Yes, but that's the point. He split the Gilbert inheritance. Would he do that for someone *outside* the family?'

Jan left the question hanging while Toby frowned.

'I see. You're wondering if Ben might in fact be the colonel's nephew. Is that it?' he asked.

'Yes. I'm hoping it's not true, of course. But yes, that's what I'm saying. I did ask Rosemary Sterry if she thought he was, but she said I would have to ask my father. And that's where I'm stuck. I just don't know how to do it.'

'Well, I don't see how you can avoid it. I think you've got to go to your father and tell him everything you know.'

'But he's going to *hate* it! He's always been like a clam about anything to do with sex, unless it's his livestock.'

'You're both adults now, Jan.'

She took a forkful of food and contemplated for a moment.

'But somehow, when I'm with him, I don't feel like one.'

She placed the loaded fork back on the plate. Toby was about to speak, but Jan held up her hand like a policeman to stop him.

'There's something else I've got to ask Dad about, though.'

She told Toby about the contents of the deed box, and her feeling that the colonel had left it as a trail of clues through which Ben, if he wished, could find out the truth.

'At the very bottom there was a medical bill for a consultation with a Harley Street doctor called Walter Shoemark, who was one of the shooting party on the day Mum was attacked. But this was dated sometime before.'

'How long before?'

'Several months.'

'And you don't know what this consultation was about?'

'No. All I know is it cost five guineas and the colonel paid.'

'Hmm. It does look significant, if only because the colonel put it in the deed box for Ben to find. But your father alone can tell you why he visited the specialist, Jan. Unless, that is, the doctor is still around. What age would he be now?'

'In the photograph he looked late thirties, I suppose. That was 1960. So if he's alive now he's seventy-five or so.'

Toby poured some more wine.

'Well, you know how much I like a spot of detective work. I'll see if I can find him for you, shall I?'

'Do you think I should go and speak to my dad first?'

'Not yet. Let's wait and see if the good doctor turns up. You'll find it easier to tackle Reg if you know all the facts.'

By now they had both cleared their plates and Toby called the waitress.

'Let's order some revoltingly sticky pudding, yes? Then you can tell me all about how my lovely new horse is coming along.'

🐎

On Thursday, back at Cheltenham racecourse, the action continued. Velvet Dynasty found one better than him in his race, though Jan swore he'd beat the winner all ends up on a different course. Cheltenham is left-handed, and Velvet's tendency to jump slightly right at each hurdle, put him at an accumulating disadvantage as Murty hauled him back on an even keel. Magic Maestro, ran bravely in the Gold Cup, as Jan knew he would, jumping round safely, but never able to catch the leading bunch. He ran on well to finish in fifth place. On another day, with softer ground, he might have gone one or two places better. But in that field of runners, he was never quite good enough.

At the day's end, and before setting off home, Jan paid a last visit to A.D. O'Hagan's private box.

'You had a good Cheltenham, Jan. A first, a second and a fifth in the big one – that's quite an achievement with only a small string of horses.'

'Oh, I don't know, A.D. It's thanks to you I've got some really good ones.'

'They still have to be handled right. But I wonder if we'll ever win a big one here with that Velvet Dynasty. Can't you tell him to jump straight?'

Jan laughed. 'I'll have a word with him in the morning. Look, I'd better be going, A.D. It's late.'

'Well, bye for now, Jan, and thanks for winning the Champion Chase for me.'

'The pleasure was all mine. And I mean that most sincerely.'

The buzz at Edge Farm continued for a few days after Moonstone Magic's victory. Jan had a lot of press interest and was well supported and popular in the locality, where apparently most of her neighbours had lumped on Moony as if he had been a nailed-on certainty. The fact that they'd done the same with Magic Maestro hardly seemed to dampen the outbreak of high spirits, and Jan was left wondering what it would have been like if Maestro had, by some amazing chance, won the Gold Cup as well.

'All hell would have broken loose,' she told Bel warmly.

By the following week the euphoria had subsided, as Jan and her staff went back to the daily grind. She took a couple of horses to a meeting at Exeter, where one fell and the other, the fancied Trojan Banquet, ran out a ten-lengths winner, only to lose the race in the stewards' room when he was disqualified on a technicality as his jockey had weighed in more than two pounds heavier than he weighed out.

Declan, who looked after Trojan, was spitting with rage as they drove home that evening.

'The horse did nothin' wrong. So tell me, Mrs H, why did they take it off him?'

Jan did her best to explain.

'Maybe the jockey had put on a different pair of boots or an extra sweater or he could have taken a diuretic and had a cup of tea after being weighed out, the silly sod. But rules are there to be adhered to and that's why we got disqualified. Except I've now got to ring the horse's owner and try to clear up what happened. That will be fun – I don't think!'

'Jobsworths. If he's heavier, what does it matter? They're like teachers confiscating sweets. They love taking races off us. It's a bloody scam, so it is,' Dec fumed.

'No, it's not. It's life. But we can take some comfort in the thought that we won the Champion Chase. The trophy's sitting on my sideboard. At least they can't take that away.'

It was only an hour after they had arrived home, as the runners from Exeter were being rugged up and given a feed, that the phone in the office rang. Jan dashed in to pick it up.

'Mrs Hardy?' said a throaty male voice.

'Speaking.'

'Jack Smallgrass here – Jockey Club.'

'Oh yes?'

'It's about the sample which was taken from your horse at Cheltenham last week.'

'Oh really, what about it?'

'I'm afraid we've found something.'

'Found something, like what?'

'I regret to say it's something that might have affected the horse's performance.'

Jan immediately thought of Galway Fox in the paddock, his coat awash with foam, and did not find it entirely surprising that he had given an unusual blood test.

Speaking with a funeral director's gravity, Smallgrass chose his words with care, as if following a carefully written script.

'The sample contained traces of a prohibited substance.'

'A prohibited substance? He couldn't have. What was it?'

'We'll send you a copy of the report. We have already communicated the matter to the Cheltenham stewards and we will, of course, be carrying out our own investigation.'

Jan's mind was in a complete whirl.

'I know we've had a case of poisoning in the yard recently,' she said hurriedly. 'I suppose I should have reported it. Maybe this horse picked up the same stuff. God, I hope not. I am at a loss to explain how it got into his system, and it's true he was in a state on the course. He ran a terrible race and I would be the first to admit it.'

There was the hint of a hesitation before Smallgrass responded, 'A terrible race, Mrs Hardy?'

'Yes. He certainly ran like something was amiss, but nothing has come to light since the race.'

'But he won.'

'No, he didn't! Not the Galway Fox – he finished way down the field.'

Like the 'prohibited' substance found in her horse's bloodstream, Smallgrass's voice now contained a trace of incredulity.

'Mrs Hardy,' he continued quietly, 'I wonder if we are talking at cross-purposes here. I'm not referring to the Galway Fox's test. It's Moonstone Magic, your Champion Chase winner, who's tested positive.'

22

As Jan put down the receiver, the dire implications of what she had just been told were sinking in. Obviously there would be a thorough investigation, with Jockey Club snoops coming into the yard to interview everyone who worked there. If the allegation was true the Jockey Club would be obliged to strip the horse of his victory and the race records would be amended, wiping out Moonstone Magic's achievement as if it had never happened.

Suddenly Jan felt a desperate need for air. Fleeing the stuffy office, she crossed to Moony's stable door. She stood there, feeling queasy, and held out a trembling hand to stroke her horse's nose.

'It's not your fault,' she told him. 'I know you did everything you could. So who gave you this substance, and what's more, *how?*'

From across the yard she heard the office phone ring out, but in her miserable state she decided to ignore it.

'And what was it, anyway?' she asked looking deeply into his eyes. 'You'd say if you could, wouldn't you?'

Moonstone Magic delivered a long snort and shook his head. He obviously agreed with Jan on this matter.

'Phone for you, Mrs H,' called Declan, who had dodged into the office to pick up the call.

Jan gave Moonstone Magic a final caress, then turned and retraced her way to the office.

'Hello?'

'It's Henry Pickles, Mrs Hardy.'

For a moment Jan couldn't place the name.

'I'm sorry, Mr Pickles, I'm not quite with it. Do I know you?'

'I'm the engraver. It's about your trophy. When shall I come over and collect it?'

Then she remembered. She had contacted Pickles to have the inscription on the Champion Chase Trophy completed.

'Mr Pickles, there's been a . . . a change of plan. I won't be having the piece engraved for the time being. I'll have to get back to you about it.'

Jan knew she needed to phone A.D. immediately to give him the news. He had contacts everywhere and the last thing she wanted was for him to read or hear it through a leak to the newspapers. Worried about A.D.'s reaction, Jan prepared in her mind how she would impart the news. Fortunately he picked up the phone almost immediately.

'Hi, Jan, I was just about to call you myself. How's Moonstone?'

'Actually, it's about Moony I'm ringing.'

'Oh, not bad news I hope.'

'It's worse than bad,' Jan blurted out. 'He's failed his dope test for some reason. The Jockey Club called just a minute ago – they are going to have an investigation, then hold an official enquiry. God, A.D., it's awful. I really don't understand it.'

'Oh. That's a shock to the system – but it can't be your end, Jan, can it? The horse was only with you for a couple of days and all your foodstuff is analysed, I know. Have they said why he failed the test?'

'Apparently it showed positive traces of some sort of steroid,' Jan said in disbelief. 'How do you want me to play this, A.D.? I expect the press will be onto it soon via a mole. They have them everywhere, as you already know.'

'Tell them the facts, Jan, that's all you can do. Meanwhile, I'll have a word with the horse's previous owner and trainer to see if they can shed some light on it. Don't worry, Jan, we'll get through this. Just keep a cool head, cooperate fully and be as helpful as you can to the Jockey Club, I'll ring you if I get any news.'

'Thanks, A.D., for taking it so well. I'll ring you with any developments this end. Bye for now.'

The next day two brown-suited men arrived from Portman Square, the Jockey Club's headquarters. The older one, a heavy-breathing cigarette smoker, introduced himself as Jack Smallgrass. His shorter, slighter, ginger-haired colleague was Gus Foley. They had come to discuss the failed dope test.

'Just a preliminary meeting, Mrs Hardy,' said Smallgrass, in an ingratiating tone, after Connor, who'd found them wandering around the yard, showed them into her office.

Jan was sitting at the desk, checking some paperwork. She pushed back her chair and inclined her head, indicating two more chairs by the wall.

'Take a seat. So what do you mean by preliminary?'

Smallgrass lowered himself onto one of the chairs with a laboured grunt, as if it hurt him to take his ease.

'Just to lay down the parameters of our investigation. Nothing heavy. Look around the yard, inspect your medical cupboard, that kind of thing. You'll hardly know we're here.'

As he spoke, Gus Foley dragged the second chair away from the wall. He sat down and drew a biro and a small black and red notebook from his breast pocket. He smoothed the notebook open against his knee at a blank page, and clicked the biro ready for action.

'I see,' said Jan. 'Well I'm a busy person, Mr Smallgrass, but I'll do what I can to help.'

'Jack, please.'

'Jack, then.'

Jan realized she must tread carefully. Whatever she thought of the heavy mob from Portman Square she could ill afford to alienate them. These men wielded considerable power over her livelihood, should they choose to use it.

'You realize I haven't seen the result of the blood test myself yet, so I'm completely in the dark.'

Smallgrass delved with a podgy hand into the case he was carrying. He tugged out a typed document, its pages secured by a staple. He placed it with a magician's flourish on the desk in front of Jan.

'I have it here, take a look for yourself.'

Jan picked it up and flicked through the pages. She noticed the name of one chemical appeared several times.

'I'll have to study this. I won't be able to answer any questions until I've read it and taken some professional advice.'

'Of course not,' said Smallgrass. 'And I'm not here to ask questions, not in a forensic way. I mean, we're not the inquisition.'

He chortled wheezily, and was then shaken by a series of coughs registering high on the Richter scale.

'Let me give you a timescale,' he managed as his gasps subsided. 'The investigation will take three or four weeks. Obviously, with a race as high profile as this we don't want undue delay, but at the same time we mustn't rush things. You will need time to gather your own evidence, I'm sure.'

'What is the object of your investigation, exactly?'

'To find out how, when, why and by whom this substance was administered, if we can. Then there'll be a full hearing by the discipline committee at headquarters, probably in around six weeks' time. You'll be able to give your evidence then. And they'll come to a decision on any sanctions, etcetera, very shortly after that.'

Sanctions? What the hell was he talking about? Incensed, Jan felt the hackles on the back of her neck begin to rise.

'But I haven't done anything wrong, you know that. This yard is Persil white. I have always thought using drugs on a horse for any reason except a therapeutic one is criminal. I'm not a criminal, nor do I employ criminals. I hope I've made myself clear, Mr Smallgrass.'

Instead of replying, but with a movement halfway between a shrug and a gesture of support, Smallgrass smiled and opened the palms of his hands. Jan glanced across at young Foley, who was hurriedly writing remarks into his notebook.

'And what will you do today?' Jan continued, her face now flushed bright red. How long will you be here?'

'As I said, just a quick look round. And I'd be grateful if you would provide me with a list of your employees and anyone else who works here who is self-employed. And all your regular professional visitors – farriers, vets and the like – with their contact details.'

Jan half-closed her eyes and sighed. What had he said at the start? You'll hardly know we're here. Oh yeah, she thought. Movements were going to be logged. Visitors quizzed. Race results and betting patterns checked. Feed records, prescriptions and medication protocols analysed. The whole place was going to be turned over while Laurel and bloody Hardy here made as much of a pain in the arse of themselves as they could. And there was bugger all she could do about it.

Four days later an envelope arrived in the post addressed in Toby's unmistakably untidy handwriting. It contained a compliments slip from the bank where he worked and a scrawled message:

> *Dr Walter Shoemark*
> *The Laurels, Sandmount Lane, Leamington Spa.*
>
> *I'm just off on my travels again, so this is in haste.*
> *Good luck!*
> *Toby*

Directory enquiries gave Jan the number and she dialled it immediately. Shoemark sounded decidedly wary on hearing that Jan wanted to speak to him about one of his old cases. But he perked up and said, 'Oh!', when she mentioned her name. He would be delighted to see her, he said more cheerily, on the following Sunday.

The Laurels was a detached red-brick house in the suburbs of Leamington, dating, Jan guessed, from the end of the nineteenth century. It overlooked a golf course, on the fairways and greens of which, no doubt, the good doctor had passed many agreeable hours since his retirement.

'Let's hope he hasn't lost his marbles,' Jan prayed as she waited for an answer to her ring on the bell push.

The figure who eventually opened the green wooden door was still recognizable as a shrunken version of the man in the 1960 shooting party. He flashed a gleaming set of false teeth at his visitor.

'Come in, come in,' he said. 'You must be *the* Jan Hardy, I wondered if you were. I saw your horse on the television the other day winning at Cheltenham. What a wonderful performance, you must be delighted.'

So far so good. She smiled back. The marbles seemed all present and correct.

Dr Shoemark shuffled ahead of her, leading the way through a hall decorated with an assortment of sporting prints. The lounge was chintzy but spacious, with French windows leading onto a well-tended lawn, beyond which Jan glimpsed a tennis court and greenhouse. There was a grand piano at one end of the room, but it was dominated by something even grander: a gigantic stuffed brown trout in a glass case, set as if lying by the water's edge on a bed of pebbles, and surrounded by preserved foliage. He noticed her looking at it.

'I caught him in Ireland, on Lough Corrib,' he said with pride. 'Twenty-three pounder. Hell of a struggle I had, you can imagine. Played the beggar for almost two hours, while he dragged the boat around the lake like a mad thing. Got him in the end, though. Can't fish any more. Can't hold the rod.'

He held up his hands, disfigured and clawlike from arthritis. He nodded towards one of the armchairs.

'Do have a seat.'

He did not offer Jan refreshment, but sat opposite her, his arthritic fingertips touching, regarding her over the rim of a pair of half-moon spectacles.

'So, what on earth can I do for you,' he asked, 'that has necessitated your journey all the way from Gloucestershire?'

Jan took an envelope from her bag and slipped out old Mr Kenworthy's photograph. She laid the envelope on her lap and passed the photo across.

'I wonder if you remember this being taken, Dr Shoemark.'

For an instant he looked at it blankly, and then Jan saw a moment of unwelcome recognition bring a twitch to his cheek.

'Well, yes, yes,' he said slowly. 'At least, I can tell you where it was. This is me, and that's my wife Pamela. I used to shoot all over the place in the old days, but this must be Riscombe Manor, old

George Gilbert's place. That's him in the middle. Died last year, didn't he? I couldn't get to the funeral.'

'Can you remember any of the events of that particular weekend?'

Shoemark did not take his eyes off the photograph.

'I, er, don't think I can. When was it now? We were down there so often for shooting parties. I couldn't be precise.'

'It was nineteen sixty,' said Jan. 'The third of September.'

Shoemark looked startled.

'How do you know that?'

'The date's on the back.'

Shoemark flipped the photo over to verify this, then looked back at Jan, his eyes suddenly fearful.

'So it is,' he said flatly. 'Nineteen sixty. September that would be. The first shoot of the partridge season.'

'Do you remember the man in the flat cap on the left?'

Glumly, as if his worst fears were about to be realized, Dr Shoemark nodded. He did not look again at the photograph.

'I'm afraid I do. It's Hugo Gilbert.'

'And do you remember what Hugo did later that day, after you all came back to the manor?'

With an almost convulsive movement the doctor rose from his chair and stepped towards Jan, thrusting the photograph at her with repulsion, as if it might be coated in anthrax.

'Now look here, Mrs Hardy, this is all ancient history. I want to know what business you have with it.'

His voice was shaking and high pitched, almost squeaking

Jan took the picture and turned it so he could see it again. Then she pointed to Mary, standing demurely in her overcoat as the wind swept through her hair, disarranging it.

'I used to be Jan Pritchard,' she said simply. 'That is my mother.'

The instant he heard Jan's declaration, the fight went out of Dr Shoemark, like the air in a punctured ball. He turned away and slumped weakly back into his chair. He sat tapping nervously with his damaged fingers on the armrests.

'It's a long time ago,' he said quietly. 'I suppose most of the people in that picture are dead now, or ga-ga.'

'Tell me what happened.'

Shoemark leant back against the cushions and fixed his eyes on the ceiling. He bared his perfect dentures in a grimace, as he steeled himself to tell a story he had kept secret for thirty years. Jan gave him time.

'It's probably against my Hippocratic oath, but as I'm not about to divulge any medical facts about the man involved, what the hell! Hugo was drunk, as usual,' he began at last. 'That chap had absolutely no idea how to behave properly. As you can see from the picture, they'd brought lunch out to us, and straight away he started making suggestive remarks to the girl, the pretty one – your mother. Then later, after we got back to the house, he went up to his room and found her there. Perfectly innocently. She'd just gone to turn down the bed or something. Anyway, we never found out precisely what happened but clearly he . . . Well, he took advantage, it's as simple as that. Took advantage in the worst possible way.'

His voice had sunk almost to a hoarse whisper as he came to the ugly heart of the story. Now, clearing his throat, he went on a little more firmly.

'As soon as he let go of her, the girl came running down in a hysterical state and told the cook, who took the matter straight to Clare Gilbert. There was an almighty row, an eruption. At first Hugo denied he'd done anything wrong but, of course, being the swine that he was, he later condemned himself out of his own mouth. He said something like, well, of course he'd had her, it was his right, but she'd invited it anyway, led him on, he claimed. I've never seen old George so angry, beside himself he was. He damn near strangled Hugo and, I think, would have done had I not pulled him off.

'Things calmed down a little then, and we had a conflab. It was decided the only thing to do was spirit Hugo away. I agreed, God help me, to drive the chap to a little cottage I had in Hampshire while George somehow pacified the girl's husband – sorry, I mean your father. He'd come up to the house in a furious state of mind and, though I don't know how he did it, George got him to agree not to go to the police. Meanwhile Hugo lay low in Hampshire until George arranged a passage by ship to South America – Rio, I think it was. That was nothing but good riddance. Hugo never came back, and several years later George wrote to me to say his brother had died of drink. A fitting end, if you ask me, and no loss to the world.'

A silence fell between them as Dr Shoemark recalled those long-distant, shadowy events.

Finally Jan broke in on his brooding. 'But why did you do it?' she demanded. 'You, of all people, covered up a rape. You helped the man go scot-free.'

Shoemark sighed, a deep, shuddering exhalation. He was evidently close to tears.

'Friendship. Comradeship. It wasn't because I had any feelings for Hugo, you can be sure of that. I'd never liked the chap. But I was a great friend of George's. We'd known one another in Korea when I was in the Medical Corps. I stitched him back together after he got cut up at Imjin, a God-awful battle. He said the family would not be able to suffer the dishonour of having its name dragged through a trial. His old mother was alive at the time and he said it would kill her. He was probably right too.'

He looked at Jan in a kind of desperate appeal, as if begging forgiveness.

'I know it was wrong. And sometimes . . . well, it's haunted me ever since. And it killed my friendship with George. Though we wrote a bit, we never actually saw one another again. But your mother, is she—?'

'She died recently.'

'Oh.'

'Did you know she'd had a child, a son? About nine months after.'

'Yes I, er, did hear something.'

Jan slipped her fingers into the envelope, which still lay in her lap.

'There's something else I need to know. The colonel left some papers when he died. It seems as if he wanted the truth to come out, but he couldn't openly admit it and only wanted us to find out after his death. Among the papers was this.'

She handed Dr Shoemark the bill for her father's consultation in

Harley Street. He unfolded it with a kind of resignation, as if he already knew what was to come.

'I think it's possibly connected with what the colonel wanted us to discover. Can you tell me about it?' Jan went on.

The old man let out another feathery sigh.

'Yes, I thought we might be getting to this. I shouldn't really tell you. Patient confidentiality and all that.'

Suddenly Jan felt angry.

'To hell with bloody patient confidentiality,' she burst out. 'This is my family and I need to know.'

Shoemark suddenly held up his knotted, trembling hand in defeat.

'All right, all right. I'll tell you. It's so long ago, I don't suppose it matters now. It was a few months beforehand. Your father had been badly hurt in an accident on the farm. He was kicked by a cow in his groin and it did irreparable damage. George Gilbert always took a pride in looking after his tenants, you know. So he sent your father to me for some tests after he'd more or less recovered.'

'What kind of tests?'

'They were afraid the kick had done permanent damage – that it had made him infertile, as a matter of fact.'

'Infertile?' she gasped.

The word hit Jan like a punch in the stomach.

'You mean he thought he couldn't—?'

'Exactly. And so it proved, Mrs Hardy. Your father couldn't have children after that. The son your mother conceived, well, he couldn't have been her husband's, you see.'

Jan leaned forward and buried her face into her hands. She was conscious of rocking slightly, to and fro. So it was true. This was the reason for the colonel's legacy, the whole explanation. It was all true.

For a while nothing was said and the silence hung heavily in the room. All of a sudden Jan got to her feet and snatched the paper from the quivering Dr Shoemark's fingers.

'I'm going now. I really don't know what to say. I'm glad you told me what happened, but in a way I wish you hadn't. Ben, my brother, is thirty. He doesn't know anything about this, and now I'm going to have to decide what to do for the best.'

The doctor stood at the door watching Jan go down the path. She was halfway to the gate when he called out.

'Mrs Hardy?'

She turned for a moment. He was a pathetic sight, woeful and exhausted.

'Can you forgive me?' His voice quavered.

She hesitated. She almost felt sorry for him. But no. Old man or not, he didn't deserve it.

She turned back and strode on down the path, slamming the gate as she left.

23

During the drive home Jan felt uneasy, and tried desperately hard to work out in her mind how her sensitive, complicated brother would take news that she was finding extremely difficult to absorb herself. For Ben to learn, without warning, that he was not who he had always thought he was would be a complete nightmare, that was for certain.

If Ben was going to be told, how should it be done? And who on earth would want to deliver such a devastating blow? Jan felt in her heart the news really should come from Reg, but he was an old man and had borne the secret for three decades. Was it fair to force him into a confession now?

After a restless night, Jan phoned her father to say she was popping over to see him, and half an hour later she arrived at Riscombe.

'You'll have a coffee,' Reg said as Jan bent forward to kiss him on the cheek.

It was a statement, not a question, and, while he was rattling around in the kitchen, Jan cleared the coffee table and set out the documents she had found in the colonel's deed box. Then, with a heavy feeling in her heart, she went into the kitchen to collect the mug of coffee.

'Dad, I've brought some things to show you.'

'Oh, really. What sort of things?'

'I've put them in the sitting room. You'll need your reading glasses.'

Reg followed her through and pulled out a chair. He sat, looking bewildered at the papers laid out on the table before him.

'What's all this about, girl?'

Jan, rarely at a loss for words, suddenly found it difficult to speak. She cleared her throat.

'Dad, it's papers from the deed box. You know, the one Colonel Gilbert left to Ben regarding his will.'

'Oh yes, I remember. What's in 'em, then?' Reg reached for the nearest item. 'Ah, that's old Mr Kenworthy's photograph. I've seen it a'fore.'

'Well, for a start,' Jan began, her voice a little hesitant, 'it contained the colonel's letter explaining about the, er, er, relationship with Mum when they were teenagers. Ben thinks that's the reason he's been left the Dowerhouse, and he says he's not interested in the rest of the stuff. I think he believes it's just a lot of adolescent love letters and thought they would be too embarrassing to read. But when I sorted through the contents myself I realized the colonel was sending Ben a message: the real reason for his inheritance or, at least, the most important one.'

Reg's eyes narrowed as he studied his daughter's face.

'How d'you mean, the most important reason?'

'I mean blood ties, Dad. I'm really sorry to have to say this, but it can't stay hidden forever, not now anyway.'

For several endless seconds Reg continued to stare at his daughter. Then with a huge sigh he took his reading glasses from his shirt pocket, carefully unfolded them and perched them on his nose. With silent concentration he scanned Kenworthy's photograph, then put it down and shifted his attention to the green-covered pocket book and the christening announcement. Finally he came to Dr Shoemark's bill for the Harley Street consultation. He looked at it briefly, then set it down again. Leaning back in the chair, he slowly removed his glasses and rubbed his eyes.

'And there was me thinking it was all over and you and Ben would never need to know,' he said quietly. 'But I can see now it was bound to come out some day, and rightly so. You know the reason why I went to see this doctor, I suppose?'

Jan nodded.

'Then you know the truth.'

'Yes. I'm just sorry it was me, Dad: I mean, that I had to bring it all out in the open.'

'Have you told Ben yet?'

'No, I haven't mentioned it. I don't think it's for me to tell him, I think you should. But how you go about it heaven only knows.'

'You're right o'course.' Reg gave another deep sigh. 'Perhaps he ought to know now before he gets wed. But it won't be easy, a thing like this, especially when I've kept it from him all these years. I don't know that I'll be able to find the right words, for a start.'

'But, Dad, you've never been afraid of the truth.'

'Aye, but the truth can be bloody cruel at times, it can cut to the quick. I'm not his dad, see. Never could have been. It's been bad enough over the years for your mother and me, knowing how it happened in the first place. I don't want to hurt Ben now, do I?'

Jan shook her head.

'Don't be silly, of course you're his dad. I mean, it was you and Mum that loved him and brought him up. That's the only thing that counts. Ben will see it that way too, I'm sure.'

One evening a few days later the phone in the house rang.

'Hello, Jan. It's Toby.'

'Hi, Toby, it's good to hear from you. Are you back?'

'No, afraid not, I'm in the States, doing a stretch at our office on Wall Street. I've got a meeting in a few minutes, but I have to tell you something first.'

'Great, fire away.'

'Yesterday a gang of us went to Belmont Park and I met a man from Chicago who's a great racing fan over in Illinois. It seems he knew all about the trainer you mentioned, Mervyn Sawyer. As you already know, the guy's been indicted for fraud, but that's not the whole story. It was, by all accounts, an insurance scam. Apparently what he did was inflate the value of some horses, insure them for "all risk mortality" and then he allegedly fed them rat poison.'

'Oh God, that's awful!'

'Yes. If what they're saying is true, that guy's a horse killer. Apparently his partner's in on the scam too, someone callcd

Jerry Pace. There was no mention of Bobby Montana, but, by all accounts, this Pace chap disappeared, leaving Sawyer to face the music on his own.'

'Do you know what Jerry Pace looks like?'

'No, but here's the sting: it seems he's an American Indian who made his money running gambling houses on the reservations. Jan, he could be *your* man, or a brother, perhaps, or an associate. Anyway, think about it. If he is connected in any way to what I've been told, Montana could be very dangerous. You should be extremely careful, Jan.'

'Thanks, Toby. Don't worry, I'll keep it in mind.'

'What's happened about the forfeit list?'

'I've already made an application – filled in the forms and everything – but it takes weeks. However, I did notice that the filly he's got in training with Doug Shaw has been entered in the One Thousand Guineas, so we'll have to wait and see if she will be allowed to run. If my request comes through before then, Bobby Montana will have to pay the money he owes me first and that could be a deciding factor.'

'Well, I'll be back in the UK by then, so I'll be able to see it for myself. Look, Jan, I've got to go, but there's one thing I almost forgot to mention. The poison involved in the scam at Fairmount Park – guess what?'

'It wasn't arsenic, by any chance?'

'Spot on or, as they say in ten-pin bowling, that's a strike.'

During early-morning exercise every hand at Edge Farm Stables was required for riding duty, especially on work days when the fitter horses were taken over to the Dowerhouse to be galloped.

Shortly after dawn, on a breezy spring morning a few days after Toby's call, Bobby Montana turned up at the yard. With Jan's string already out on the gallops, Montana had clearly felt confident of avoiding human contact, but by a lucky coincidence Jack Smallgrass and Gus Foley were pursuing their interest in Edge Farm's daily routine, and were working in the office when the first lot of horses pulled out.

An hour and a half later, when the horses clattered back up the track, Jan noticed Smallgrass pacing up and down on the forecourt.

'We've had a spot of excitement while you were out,' he said as she approached. 'An intruder in your yard. Foley saw him through the office window. Crouching along by the stables he was. When we went out to ask him what the 'eck he thought he was doing he looked real shifty. He's a wrong 'un, if you ask me.'

'What did he say?'

'Said he was an owner. Not very likely, I thought. A scruffy Yank with a ponytail, probably some sort of tout. I bet you get them hanging around all the time, Jan.'

'No, no, it's Bobby Montana!' Jan exclaimed, springing down quickly from her saddle. 'As a matter of fact he *is* an owner, but he's a very shifty character. Have you still got him here?' she asked urgently.

At that moment Smallgrass's jowly face began to look extremely uncomfortable.

'No, I'm afraid we haven't. When we challenged him, he said he was just visiting his horses. Often did, so he claimed. He even showed us a couple of sugar lumps he was going to give them. I said he'd better stay away from the horses until you returned and could vouch for him. He said no way: he was in a right old huff. He swore a few times, chucked away the sugar lumps, and stormed off back to his car. Next thing he'd driven off.'

'For God's sake, why didn't you detain him?'

Smallgrass looked crestfallen.

'I should have, I suppose. But he moved too damn quickly.'

'You're sure he never got near any of the horses?'

'Absolutely sure, Jan. We'd never have allowed that. After all, it's our job, keeping racehorses safe. That's what we're paid for.'

🐎

Ten minutes later Michael Finnegan knocked on the office door, interrupting Jan, who was once again closeted with the two Jockey Club officials who were now scrutinizing the diet of her horses.

'I heard Mr Smallgrass mention that your man chucked these away,' he said quietly, holding out two brown sugar lumps. 'I found them in the corner of the yard. Thought I'd better pick them up in case, you know, one of the dogs . . .'

At that precise moment, and in a flash, Jan saw the whole plot laid out, as neatly as the papers she had displayed on her father's table only a few days earlier. Of course, if it hadn't been for the information she had received from Toby Waller she probably would not have twigged even now. His phone call had left her with the clear suspicion that Spring Blow had been poisoned by the last person she would have suspected – his owner. Montana would have been giving the same stuff to Big Freeze too, she thought, if he hadn't believed that navicular disease would bring the animal's life to a premature end.

Jan concluded Montana's original plan must have been to kill the horse slowly, but he had been forced to abandon this idea and had stopped visiting the yard altogether when Jan told him she knew arsenic was in Spring Blow's system. He must have been desperate for money; like most gamblers, he had probably been hoping to reverse his fortunes with some inspired play at poker or in the betting shop. Instead, Jan guessed, things had only got worse, and now Montana's last hope was for the Doug Shaw-trained filly to run in the classic at Newmarket. But first he had to make sure of avoiding the Jockey Club forfeit list – which he would if the horses at Edge Farm died soon and he cashed in his insurance policies to pay off his outstanding debts.

Jan felt a huge surge of anger towards Bobby Montana, and almost as much towards the two clowns from Portman Square. Keeping racehorses safe, my arse, she thought as she yanked at the desk drawer and took out a clean envelope. She held it open for Michael, who tipped the suspect cubes inside. Then she pressed down the flap, carefully sealing it with tape.

'Thanks, Michael. I owe you. And as for you two – 'she waved the envelope in the direction of Smallgrass and Foley – 'these sugar cubes are almost certainly lethal. Any of my animals could easily have picked them up off the ground. But instead of gathering them up and putting them in a safe place yourself, what did you do? Brewed more coffee, I wouldn't wonder, and put your feet up on my sodding desk, by the look of it!'

She wiped the top of the desk with her sleeve then leant back in her chair and glared, first at one then the other.

'We, er, thought he was a bad lot, Jan,' Smallgrass blustered. 'We prevented the worst, at any rate. We did see him off—'

But Jan wasn't listening any more. She had picked up the phone and was dialling the police.

24

By the end of April, despite the formal complaint Jan had lodged against Bobby Montana, the Gloucestershire Constabulary had still not tracked him down. Meanwhile, Smallgrass and Foley had arranged for the sugar lumps to be tested at the Jockey Club's laboratory, and the results showed they were indeed doctored with arsenic. Thankfully, pending the police investigation, the Jockey Club agreed to accelerate Jan's application and Montana's name was at last placed on the register of blacklisted owners.

For now it felt like a small victory in a much bigger war, since Jan still had her appointment with the Jockey Club Disciplinary Committee hanging over her, which was just a few days after Ben and Annabel's wedding. Jan had tried lobbying Jack Smallgrass to find out how his investigation was progressing, but he was evasive and would only say that he had concluded his observations at Edge Farm and would not require any more information or feed samples. In fact, he and Foley would probably not need to return at all.

🐎

Jan decided to contact Bob Warren, the solicitor who had been so helpful when Eddie had been in trouble with the police the previous year and after she had hit Virginia.

'I've got to appear before a Jockey Club enquiry and I need someone to represent me,' she told him. 'How are you fixed?'

'The thing is', he said hesitantly, 'I've not done this type of work before.'

'Bob, I trust you. You were brilliant with Eddie last year.'

'That was a very different type of case, Jan. Sorry, but I'll have to decline on this occasion. It would be like asking a squash player to win Wimbledon. You need a specialist.'

'You don't know of anyone, by any chance?'

'Actually, I do. His name's Peter McCormick. He's a mate of mine and I know for a fact that he's represented several trainers at Jockey Club enquiries. Would you like his number?'

🐎

Jan met McCormick at his office a few days later. He was an ebullient type who sported a beard. He probably had the loudest laugh in the Rotary Club and the broadest smile on the golf course, but Jan knew shrewdness when she saw it and McCormick did not look as if he missed too many tricks.

'In all, I've done five cases like this before,' he told her after she had explained the circumstances. 'In essence it's not terribly different from the magistrate's court.'

'Well, I really do hope they don't send me to jail, as much as some of them might like to,' Jan said light-heartedly.

McCormick laughed, but his face immediately grew more serious.

'No, they certainly can't do that. But I have to say what they can do might feel very nearly as bad. The committee has draconian powers and, given the fact that the Champion Chase is an extremely high-profile race, the members might, just might, feel compelled to crack down heavily. They could levy a large fine or even withdraw your licence for a period. How would that impact on you, Mrs Hardy?'

Jan winced. Given Edge Farm's situation with the bank she would almost certainly be out of business.

'There's no way I can pay a large fine,' she said. 'And, if they banned me, the owners would almost certainly move their horses elsewhere. So, as you can see, my cash flow would stop like a tap being turned off and I'd be crippled financially.'

'In which case we must stop it coming to that,' said McCormick briskly. 'What about this steroid in the horse's bloodstream? How did it get there?'

'I really don't know. I didn't put it there and nor did any member of my staff. I can vouch for them all.'

'Well, I suggest you try and find out what you can. Since no one at Edge Farm doped the horse, there are only two other possibilities. It was someone else – an outsider – or it was an accident. The point I'm making is you need an explanation – or at least a plausible theory – that you can put before the committee in support of your innocence. They'll be very unimpressed if all you can say when they ask is that you have no idea. Now, we have a lot of ground to cover and very little time to cover it, so we had better get a move on. So tell me . . .'

The following Sunday, with Peter McCormick's advice still ringing in her ears, Jan got out the videotape of Moonstone Magic's Cheltenham victory. She ran the whole race, over and over again, first at normal speed then in slow motion. She had been staring at the screen for over two hours, and was about to give up when she noticed something especially interesting happen after the horses had crossed the winning line.

On the way back to the unsaddling enclosure Moonstone Magic had been surrounded by over-excited racegoers. There was a brief moment when he had to stand stock still while the path in front of him was cleared. Suddenly someone from the crowd lurched forward and gave him a pat on the nose. Jan noticed the horse's objection as he gave a sharp upwards jerk of his head before walking briskly on again.

'What're you watching, Mum?'

Jan stopped the tape and sighed, puzzled by what she had just seen.

'Oh, it's only Moonstone Magic's race and the presentation afterwards.'

Matty sat down beside her. He had a brown plastic object in his hand. He removed the cap and put the mouthpiece to his lips. Suddenly Jan made a vital connection.

'Matty, can I look at your inhaler?' It was an everyday object, used by thousands of asthmatics.

She quickly leapt up from the settee and went in to the kitchen, where she rooted around for the box in which the inhaler had originally been packed. Finding it at last, she extracted the printed leaflet. To her shame she had never read this fully before, but now she scrutinized its contents with feverish interest. The medication the inhaler delivered, she read, 'belongs to a group of drugs known as steroids called beclomethasone dipropionate', whatever that means in English, she thought.

Could the substance found in Moonstone have been the same drug and have been administered from an inhaler? Jan hurried back to the television and ran again the horse's walk back to the unsaddling enclosure, freezing the tape at the moment Moonstone seemed to receive a pat from the over-enthusiastic racegoer. The man who had delivered the caress wore a dark suit and had a healthy head of hair. But, apart from that, he was unidentifiable. By now Jan was down on her knees only inches away from the television screen. Was he holding something? Was the man's hand near her horse's nose at the same time as Moonstone tossed his head? No matter how many times she re-ran the tape, she couldn't be certain.

There was another question: why? Jan's mind scurried back to the incident on the Dowerhouse gallops. If Virginia had wanted revenge for that slap across her face, she just might arrange—

'Oh, my God!'

In a flash Jan remembered the lad from the Gilbert yard who had fallen off his horse near the start of the gallop. The shock of his fall had triggered an asthma attack and Jan had clearly seen him using an inhaler exactly like Matty's. He could have been the guy who gave the Judas pat to Moonstone.

It was only a theory. But Jan believed it already.

In the evening Jan phoned A.D. and told him of her suspicions.

'I'm thinking this might be some kind of revenge attack,' she told him. 'Is there anyone else you can think of who might want to damage your reputation in some way?'

'There might be one or two, right enough,' admitted A.D. 'I suppose not everyone thinks I'm God's gift. You know how it is,

Jan, people can become envious and that drives them into doing all sorts of things.'

'But if we can show the stuff was administered after the finish of the race, for malicious purposes or whatever, that must affect the enquiry, surely. It must help us.'

A.D. thought for a moment.

'Jan, I just don't know. At the least I don't think it's going to be possible for us to keep the race. There's a thing called strict liability, which applies in these cases. Which means no excuses are accepted.'

'But that's ridiculous if we can prove it wasn't our fault.'

'Let's have another look at the tape. I'll get my laboratory to run a test to see if we can say positively whether this stuff in Moonstone's system is the same as the asthma treatment your boy uses. It would be good for the truth to come out, anyway.'

'You can say that again. My reputation's on the line here, A.D. I'm desperate.'

25

Jan was thankful she still had a busy yard to run. Every three or four days horses set off to the race track, and there were constant routine stable matters to deal with, as well as the never-ending family ones: keeping a close eye on Reg, vetting the children's homework, even doing the supermarket run. These, and the increasing number of preparations as Ben and Annabel's wedding drew near, kept Jan from dwelling too much on her impending visit to the Jockey Club.

With the yard's income as precarious as ever, Jan phoned the Gloucestershire police several times to ask if they had found Bobby Montana, hoping that his capture might allow her to recoup some of his outstanding debt. The reply as usual was unforthcoming. Could it be the police had no real idea where he was? At least, while the American evaded the law, his horses continued to do well. Now the small but regular dose of arsenic had been stopped, Spring Blow's health was measurably brighter; even his coat had begun to recover and take on a bit of sheen. Big Freeze's improvement from navicular disease, too, was steady. Shirley was treating him with supplementary minerals in the diet in an effort to restore calcium in the diseased bone, and judging by how much more easily he was walking it looked like her regime, combined with Mickey Reid's careful paring and shoeing of the affected hooves, was beginning to get results. If all other efforts at debt recovery failed, Jan would need to get a lien on Montana's animals and sell them for whatever price she could, in which case she would need them to be as healthy as possible and back in full working order.

The Cotswolds had recently been enjoying a prolonged spell of clear spring weather, but unexpectedly one morning the sky darkened and sleet fell, turning into rain. It poured for hour after hour with such force that the next day's racing was almost certain to be a washout. Jan had declared Gylippus for a race she felt sure he would win. But at around eleven, just as she was about to turn in for the night, she pulled back a sitting-room curtain and peered out. The downpour was unrelenting, even building in strength, drumming on the roof and lashing the windowpanes.

'Just my bloody luck,' she cursed. 'Who says April showers bring spring flowers? This is more likely to flatten the poor bastards.'

Jan was about to redraw the curtains when something registered through the rain, a shadow moving across the forecourt. She turned and quickly killed all the lights until the room was illuminated only by the fire's flicker. Back at the window she looked out again, narrowing her eyes to accustom them to the rain-soaked darkness.

There it was, this time she was sure: a skulking figure merging into the shadows of the old caravan, which was empty at the moment. It was unlikely that her workers would be lurking around particularly on such a wet night.

Jan let the curtain fall back into place and made her way into the hall. She picked up the heavy torch that she always kept there, clicked it on and found her wellies, before cautiously opening the front door.

'Who's out there?' she yelled into the rain. 'Bloody show yourself. I've called the police already. They're on their way.'

She waited, unwilling at this stage to go further, straining her eyes as she scanned the area around the caravan. But, through a screen of rain, and with hardly any light coming from the house, the darkness was impenetrable. For a few moments nothing happened. Jan began to think the intruder must have slunk off, then, within the rain's hiss, she heard the faint crunch of a footstep on gravel. Her thumb moved on the torch and its beam of light flashed upwards.

Jan gasped. 'Oh, my God! What the hell are you doing here?'

'Hello, Jan. I hope you haven't really called the police.'

Eddie was standing in the open space immediately in front of the house. The rain continued to beat down, plastering his hair to his scalp. It ran off his nose and chin. Pinched, pale, saturated and shivering, he looked more than miserable: he looked desperately ill.

'For God's sake,' Jan said, beckoning to him, 'come in quickly. I don't need a corpse on my doorstep.'

Before any explanations were given, Jan insisted that Eddie have a hot bath while she made coffee, with a large measure of brandy in it. Back in front of the revived sitting-room fire, wearing some old clothes he'd left behind last year, he drank the coffee with noisy, appreciative slurps. It was a well-remembered habit which, when living with him, had been irksome. Now it made Jan nostalgic.

Hardly daring to prompt Eddie, Jan played the attentive listener, and waited patiently for the whole story to unfold.

'You see, I was wrong all the time. Wrong, bloody wrong, all along. The old man was found dead on Bodmin moor. It was mad of me to think he could have pissed off up to London. You know, anything could have happened on that bloody awful moor. It's such a desolate place in the winter. Anyway, some rambler stumbled on what was left of him. I don't know why the cops couldn't find him before, when there was more of him to find. They had enough sodding sniffer dogs farting about out there. But no, it was some old geezer from Bristol walking his retired greyhound who found him. Called the police, he did. They took him down to the mortuary in Truro, or what's left of him more like, then they phoned me. I went in. God, it was vile, Jan. It wasn't like my dad. It was something out of hell – a horror movie.'

Jan could see he was close to tears.

'They identified him from the clothes – there wasn't much left of him, you see. Animals had got him . . . wild animals, or maybe the beast of Bodmin, for all I know. Or it was his criminal friends in the first place, teaching him a lesson. I just puked all over the mortuary floor, I couldn't bloody help it. Anyway, they did a post-mortem and the inquest's tomorrow. I've got to go and give evidence, of course. I haven't a clue what I'm going to say, Jan. I'm sorry, but I'm feeling kind of strange right now. Maybe my evidence is going to be important. Maybe there's certain people who won't want me to give it. I really do feel weird, like it's all on my shoulders. I can't take much more, that's one thing I am certain about.'

At that moment Jan felt desperately sorry for him, but there was really nothing she could do to help him.

'Eddie, I can see that. I think you need help. You should see a doctor, check yourself into a clinic or something.'

Jan could tell immediately she had said the wrong thing. Eddie's eyes filled with tears and he looked at her wildly.

'Don't be bloody stupid. A clinic? I've got to be on hand to support my mother. Anyway, what makes you think I'm a nutcase? It's a case of shock, that's all it is. There's fuck all wrong with me that a good night's sleep won't cure.'

'So why did you come back here?' Jan asked him gently.

Eddie paused, reflecting on Jan's question, then he shook his head in a dazed manner. It seemed he didn't even know himself why he had homed in on Edge Farm. He'd found himself at Gloucester railway station and had taken a taxi to Stanfield on impulse. He'd been standing around outside Edge Farm in the pouring rain for an hour, not knowing what to do next.

'OK, that's enough. I'll tell you what you're going to do right now,' said Jan when she'd heard him out. 'You're staying the night here and it's not up for discussion.'

She hurried off to collect some bedding, which she brought back and dumped on the sofa.

'You can sleep here. I'll chuck a couple of logs on the fire. You'll be as warm as toast in no time.'

In the morning Jan returned from the gallops to find Eddie already standing outside the front door, waiting for a taxi. In daylight he looked gaunt and sallow, even jaundiced. He cut a pathetic figure.

'Eddie, have you had some breakfast? You can't leave with an empty stomach,' she asked concerned.

'I've got to get off,' he said, in a low voice. 'I'm due in Truro by eleven: it's the inquest, see. I'll get something on the train, I promise.'

As he spoke he stared at his hands, as if he were unable to look Jan in the face.

'I shouldn't have turned up, not without warning, anyway. How could I have been so daft? It all got on top of me – the accident, my dad being found all chewed up and you not giving a shite about me any more.'

Jan coloured and raised her hand to shut him up.

'Eddie, I can't believe I'm hearing you say this! It was *you* who walked out on me. Then it was *you* who went and worked for that ghastly Virginia Gilbert.'

Her outburst reduced Eddie to a grumpy silence. Jan stood around, feeling awkward. Should she wait with him for the taxi to arrive or go about her business? Trust him to wrong-foot her again, she thought.

When at last the car turned up, Jan felt a stab of relief. In the aftermath of their road accident two years ago, Eddie had shown a new and much less attractive side to himself, full of aggression and self-disgust. As he recovered from injury, these traits had gradually lightened until they seemed to disappear completely. But now, in his distress over Ron, they were back in full force. Thinking regretfully of better times, Jan waved as the taxi finally drove Eddie away.

A red Mercedes sports car drew up in front of the house before Jan could even make a cup of tea to calm herself down after Eddie's departure. From it emerged Nina Clark, the glamorous hairdresser who, having outbid Jan for a horse at Doncaster in January, had then asked her to be its trainer. Nina had phoned just over a week ago to arrange to drop in and see her new baby.

'Shit, I forgot she was coming today,' said Jan, and hurried out the door to greet her latest owner.

Taking Nina back down to the yard to look at her new purchase, Jan went through the usual drill of having Declan bring the gelding out and walk him up and down the yard on a lead rein.

'He's been so full of beans,' she assured the owner. 'Last week's fine weather and plenty of good grooming have really brought him on.'

Nina patted the horse's neck fondly as her face took on an adoring expression.

'He's such a pet. Look at his seductive eyes. How would you like to wake up every morning with those staring back at you? When's he going to race?'

Jan stifled a giggle as she pictured the horse asleep in Nina's bed. She was suddenly glad to see her; the perfect antidote to Eddie's moroseness.

They talked about the horse's prospects, with Jan outlining the autumn campaign of novice hurdling that she had already planned.

'At this stage he could be anything,' she continued. 'He's been schooling over hurdles and jumps pretty well. He needs a bit more practice, of course, but I can assure you he's got a touch of class. Takes after his owner, I guess. Then it's just a question of how he responds on the racecourse. Most blossom after a couple of runs, but not all. Anyway, it's a bit of a waiting game for the time being.'

Jan said nothing about the fact that come the autumn she might not even have a trainer's licence.

'By the way, it's time you gave him a name. He's called Billy around here, for some reason. But I will need to register a proper name before he can race.'

'Call him Pat's Fantasy,' said Nina, decisively. 'That's what I am to my old man. We don't always see eye to eye, though, if you know what I'm saying.'

Jan couldn't help smiling.

'Yes, I think I do,' she said.

It was Sunday morning and Jan's skeleton staff were sitting and chatting noisily over their breakfast in the kitchen. Declan and Connor, always the noisiest, were talking as they crammed forksful of bacon and egg into their mouths and boasted about their social activities the night before. While the girls listened sceptically Patsy, always the quiet one, was studying the racing page of the *Sunday People*. The nine o'clock news played on the small kitchen television, which stood on the counter.

Giving the screen a passing glance while she dropped slices of bread into the toaster, Jan caught a still shot of someone she thought she recognized.

'Shut up, all of you. Listen to this.'

The news reporter was standing in a London street, with the morning traffic passing in a steady stream behind him. A commissionaire in a braided cap and wearing a dark blue frock coat stood self-consciously just beyond him.

'I'm outside one of London's most prestigious hotels, where, at eleven thirty last night, police were called out to an incident. One of the guests, believed to be an American businessman, had barricaded himself inside his room, claiming he had a female hostage whom he threatened to shoot if his demands were not met.'

The shot cut to a scene obviously filmed sometime during the night. The facade was lit up by brilliant arc lights, red and white cordon tape had been stretched across the road and blue police-car beacons were flashing. An officer was using a loudhailer, while passers-by stood around in groups looking up at the building. The report continued in voice-over.

'For several hours police negotiators tried to talk to the man as marksmen took up positions around the building. Then at around three thirty a loud report, believed to be from a shotgun, was heard from inside the room. It was then that a decision was made to storm the room. In a dramatic operation the door was blasted open by controlled detonation and a suspect was arrested. He had apparently been wounded by his own gun. No hostage was in fact present.'

The film cut away to a shot of the hotel entrance, as the prisoner was brought out between two burly uniformed officers, with one of his hands heavily bandaged. He was blinking in the harsh light, his eyes darting from side to side. Suddenly he saw the television cameras and ducked his head, but in the Edge Farm kitchen they had already recognized him.

'That's him, Mrs H! That's Montana!' shouted Connor. 'They finally got the dirty bastard!'

🐎

Sitting round the table, the staff applauded as the programme moved on to the next story.

'What's he owing you now, Mrs H?' asked Declan.

'Never you mind,' said Jan sternly. 'But it's a lot. Anyway, I've been thinking. If that guy goes to jail, which he sure as eggs will do now, I'll be able to get a lien on his two horses.'

'A what?' asked Connor.

'It's a legal term which means I can take the horses instead of what he owes, since I'm obviously never going to be paid in cash. So, this is what I'm planning to do. I'll find a race for Spring Blow, and you, Declan, are going to wind him up to run the race of his life. If he does well, it'll raise his price well past what the jailbird owes.'

Declan touched his forehead. 'No problem, Mrs H.'

'What about Big Freeze?' Roz wanted to know.

Jan shook her head sadly.

'We just can't afford to keep him. He's months from making a full recovery and, even then, I doubt I could ever race him. The only thing to do is find somebody who'll take him on and be kind to him. What's that, Patsy?'

Patsy was holding up the racing results page of the *Sunday People*.

'Take a look at this, Mrs H.'

Jan leant across to read the item he was pointing at, the result of the previous day's classic for three-year-old fillies at Newmarket. It had been won by the Hawk at seven to one.

'Well!' exclaimed Jan in surprise. 'What do you know? That filly was a top-class horse after all, just as Doug Shaw said she was.'

🐎

Doug Shaw was primarily a flat trainer but he had two or three dual-purpose runners in his yard, stayers on the flat who could also perform over hurdles. So it was not a complete surprise when Jan spotted Shaw's sandy-coloured, combed-over hair and short, brick-shaped figure in the owners' and trainers' bar at Towcester on the following day, the May bank holiday.

'Wotcher, Jan. Can I buy you a drink?'

She accepted a glass of wine.

'So our mutual owner's enjoying a spot of chokey,' Shaw went on. 'I suppose you heard.'

'Yes, I saw the news. I also saw you got a result with the Hawk. Congratulations.'

'Thanks. It was really ironic that it happened on the same day as Bobby was collared, wasn't it? As far as I'm concerned, the whole thing couldn't have turned out better.'

'What do you mean?'

'I mean I did all right personally.'

'Lucky you. I'm still owed a stack of training fees.'

Shaw waved his hand as if training fees were a secondary consideration in the great game of horse racing.

'See, I'd already got Bobby to sign over Hawky to me. It was a question of the late-entry fee for the Newmarket race. He couldn't stump up, so I arranged for another of my owners to take a majority share in the horse in partnership with me. Bobby was only due a fifteen-K contingency fee if the filly won the race.'

He took a deep draught of his beer, smacking his lips with satisfaction.

'Fifteen thousand?' said Jan. 'That's good. He can pay me what he owes.'

Shaw sniggered.

'I doubt it. Why should we pay him now he's banged up?'

Jan looked doubtfully at Shaw.

'Don't you think you should?'

Now Shaw laughed openly, almost cruelly.

'Don't be so naive, Jan. It was only a gentleman's agreement. Anyway, he was no effing gentleman. He was an out-and-out crook. I heard on the grapevine he was into killing horses for the insurance. No, no. He doesn't get a bean out of this.'

'I see. Well, thanks for the drink,' said Jan, draining her glass and placing it firmly back on the bar.

As she walked away she was boiling with rage. Yes, Montana was a fraud and a horse-killing criminal. But was the slippery, scheming Doug Shaw any better? In her opinion, not much.

26

As the fine bank-holiday weather promised to continue, Ben and Annabel decided to hold a family barbecue in the evening at the Dowerhouse. When Jan and the children arrived, they found Annabel chopping salad in the kitchen.

'Where's my little brother?' Jan teased.

'He's gone off with Reg to see a chap about buying some sheep.'

'I don't believe it. Ben buying sheep? What on earth for?'

'I know, I can hardly believe it myself. He's got a crazy idea of putting a small flock in the top field. I said to him, what do we know about sheep? But his point was how can we go wrong as long as we have Reg to advise us? Which is fair enough, I suppose. The land's got to be grazed apparently or it will sour, which was news to me.'

Jan picked up a knife and joined her best friend at the chopping board while the children ran outside.

'Remember that Sunday when we had the picnic here?' said Annabel. 'The place was derelict. I could hardly visualize it as my home then, but just look at it now. It couldn't have worked out better.'

Annabel was right. Since she and Ben had moved in, although several rooms remained unpainted and others lacked furniture, the old dilapidated house looked more like a home. The kitchen was now completely modernized, but so discreetly that much of the original appearance was retained. The sitting room was comfortable and upstairs the main bedroom and bathroom were complete but for a few minor details.

Annabel suddenly looked at her watch.

'The men said they'd be back by four thirty – but they're an hour and a half late already. Look, this salad's almost done. You couldn't go out and get the barbecue started, could you? I know firing up charcoal is supposed to be men's work and all that, but they're not here so we'll have to do it ourselves.'

Jan went out onto the paved area between the house and the garden, where Ben had had a permanent barbecue built, a solid structure made of local Cotswold stone. With Megan and Matty as her helpers, Jan had soon got a good flame going under the nuggets of charcoal when she heard Ben's car pull up in the yard on the other side of the house and the doors slam shut.

A few minutes later, as she made her way back into the kitchen, Jan was aware of a complete change in the atmosphere. Ben had not come into the house and Reg immediately excused himself and went upstairs to lie down in the guest room.

'What's the matter?' asked Jan anxiously. 'What's happened?'

'I'm not sure. Reg said he's a bit tired,' Annabel told her. 'He certainly seems subdued – I hope he's not sickening for something.'

'But what about Ben? Where's he gone?'

Annabel shrugged and said she hadn't seen him.

Jan hurried back outside and, shading her eyes from the low evening sun, could see her younger brother about three hundred yards away, striding with dogged determination up the track which led to the top field. With a feeling of dread, Jan set off in pursuit.

When she caught up with him, Ben was leaning on the field gate, staring towards the setting sun, as it inched towards the bottom of the downs.

'He's told you, hasn't he?' she said simply when she joined him at the gate.

'Yes, he's told me all right.' Ben gave a short sharp laugh. 'We all realize life's going to be full of surprises, right? But there can't be many as bad as this one, Sis, wouldn't you say?'

Jan noticed as he pushed the hair away from his eyes that his hand was trembling.

'So what happened between you and Dad?' Jan asked gently.

'Oh, we were just driving back slowly after looking at the sheep I'm thinking of buying, then suddenly Dad suggested a drink, so a

few minutes later we pulled into this pub by the road. I thought it
was a bit strange, Dad wanting a drink, but he said he needed to
have a chat. So we did. A real father-to-son thing. I don't think I've
ever seen him so emotional.'

Ben swallowed hard and looked up at the sky, narrowing his eyes
in an attempt to control his own feelings.

'Ben, are you sure you want to talk about this right now?' Jan
asked.

'Yes, definitely. I need to tell you what happened,' Ben said
fiercely. 'So, anyway, Dad said he'd been carrying the terrible
burden of a big secret for thirty-odd years. It wasn't something you
could talk to a child about, he said, but I was an adult now, and
soon to be a husband and probably a father myself. Then he rambled
on about Mum no longer being with us and he thought it was time
I was told.'

He lapsed into silence.

'Go on,' Jan prompted.

'Well, then he asked if I knew about the love affair between
young George Gilbert and Mother when they were teenagers. I said
yes, of course I did, because it was in the colonel's letter explaining
why he left me the house and land. Dad said that wasn't the real
reason for the legacy. He said that was – his atonement. I said, what
are you talking about? What do you mean atonement? And then it
all came tumbling out, the story I suppose you already know –
Dad's accident on the farm, the shooting party, Hugo Gilbert, and
the news that my biological father isn't who I always thought he
was. For Christ's sake, Jan, it's like reading a novel.'

'How did you feel? I mean when he actually told you.'

'Numb at first, completely confused. Dad told me the colonel
had promised him, immediately after the . . . whole thing happened,
that he'd do all he could to compensate us, but on condition that
the Gilbert family honour was preserved. That was when Dad
started crying. The next thing I was blubbing too. I mean, there we
are, two grown men in a nearly empty pub with a couple of pints in
front of us, crying our eyes out. I've no idea what the landlord must
have thought.' He smiled wryly.

'Then suddenly Dad started to apologize, saying he had often wondered what right he had to keep it all from me. He said he didn't give a bugger about the Gilbert family honour and he'd have killed that man if he could have got near him. I think even now he wishes he had done something. But Hugo Gilbert was spirited away, disappeared without trace, it seems.

'I told Dad he had to stop blaming himself. It doesn't matter that he didn't give Hugo a hiding. What would it have achieved, anyway? It makes no difference. Reg is still my Dad, I told him that. It's certainly not that scumbag Gilbert. Reg's name's on my birth certificate. He and Mum brought me up and loved me like a real son. He *is* my dad, isn't he, Jan? I mean there couldn't be any other, could there?'

'Of course he is, in exactly the same way as he is mine. He loves us both and that's all that matters.'

Dusk was falling now and birdsong could be heard echoing from higher up on the ridge.

Ben said nothing more but turned and embraced Jan, squeezing most of the breath out of her. 'I just want to say thanks, Sis. Thanks for finding out about this and thanks too for letting Dad tell me himself. That was important.'

'I guess it took a lot out of him,' said Jan when Ben finally let her go. 'Last I heard, he'd taken to your spare room for a rest.'

Reg rejoined them for supper and, although he looked drained, the faint smile on his face reflected the weight that had been lifted from his mind. At the end of the evening, as Jan prepared to give Reg a lift home, Ben gave his father a big hug and a kiss on the cheek.

'I love you, Dad, I always will.'

Jan choked back a tear as Annabel looked a little perplexed. Ben now had the job of explaining everything to Bel.

27

By the end of the month the rain had blown itself out completely and calm blue skies returned. So, amid a blaze of May flowers, and in a shower only of rice and confetti, Annabel and Ben were married, bathed in warm sunshine. Annabel looked more beautiful than ever in her traditional satin wedding dress, her head covered by a delicate lace veil. Bridesmaid Megan and pageboy Matty thoroughly enjoyed the theatre of it all – the elegant bride floating up the aisle, the tension before the ring was found, the lifting of the veil and the bridegroom's kiss, and the clangour of the bells ringing to announce the marriage to the world. Walking out of church behind the newly weds with Annabel's mother on his arm, Reg looked pleased as Punch in his rented tails. Escorted down the aisle by Ben's father-in-law, Jan felt more than pleased with the new suit she'd treated herself to in Broadway.

Of all the guests, only Major Halstead refrained from entering into the spirit of the day. He maintained consistently, as Annabel had confided privately (and bitterly) to Jan a few days earlier, that he was giving his only daughter away to a social inferior and a confounded *musician* at that. Leaving the church beside the major, Jan noted the bristling moustache, the tight-drawn lips and the long nose cocked at a superior angle, as if to avoid the surrounding smell of peasantry. Rather than anger, Jan felt pity that someone could be so mentally bitter and stuck so far back in the past.

By contrast, Annabel's mother enjoyed herself thoroughly. She wept in church and laughed riotously as the speeches were made in the marquee in the garden of Stanfield's Fox & Pheasant pub. Then, as a small jazz band began to play, she insisted on dancing one after another with each of Annabel's ex-boyfriends, before moving on to the lads from Jan's yard. When she finally approached the scarlet-cheeked Patsy, he shuffled Mrs Halstead once around the floor in a state of deep embarrassment, before making his excuses and darting out of the tent as if pursued by hornets.

Jan sat watching all this with her father.

'She hasn't danced with you, yet, has she, Dad?'

'No, though she asked me all right.' Reg stuck a finger into his dress-shirt collar to pull it loose. 'I told her I retired from dancing after the Silver Jubilee.'

He turned and pointed to Ben and Annabel. 'But they make a grand couple, don't they, Jan? I meant what I said in my speech. As genuine and handsome a couple as has ever graced Stanfield church, any church, for that matter.'

Reg sat tapping his foot to the beat of the music.

'Yes,' said Jan, 'you're so right. I just wish Major Halstead could see it that way.'

'Oh, don't worry about him. His head's so far up his own backside he can probably see his own tonsils. He's no more use than a penny-farthing bike. You'd never guess he was Annabel's dad, would you?'

Jan laughed and kissed her father on the cheek.

'No. But you'll always be Ben's dad. He's such a credit to you. To you and Mum.'

'She'd be proud today, all right. I was just thinking of that time when he walked home from Riscombe Down carrying that injured lamb he found. He could have been no more than six year old at the time.'

'I remember. It had broken its leg, hadn't it?'

'Aye, it had. I can see him now, staggering into the kitchen with it. No son of Hugo Gilbert would've done that, eh Jan? Walk two mile to save a baby lamb.'

'No, Dad. I don't think he would. But it's just the sort of thing a son of Reg Pritchard would do.'

Reg chuckled and squeezed Jan's hand.

'Aye, lass, so I would hope.'

There was one other unhappy guest at the party, though he, unlike Major Halstead, concealed his misery under a cloak of good humour. It was only a short time after the couple had driven away in a vintage Rolls, to begin their honeymoon, that Jan found the forlorn Toby Waller sitting on a child's swing in the pub garden, with a distant, rueful smile on his face, cradling a bottle of Krug in his arms. The jazz band had by now given way to the rock 'n' roll rhythms of a group made up of Ben's closest friends.

'The end of my hopes,' said Toby gloomily as Jan slid onto the swing next to his.

'There'll be others,' she said tenderly.

'Not like her there won't. I'm just thankful she's ended up with Ben. He's a good man. A very good man.'

As the two of them swung back and forth, Jan thought of her own hopes only a few months earlier. It could have been her, with Eddie by her side, driving off in that Rolls, piled high with flowers and ribbons and dragging a cacophony of empty tins along the road.

'What a pair we are,' she said.

Toby gave out an explosive laugh.

'Now that's a thought.'

'I didn't mean—'

Toby clambered off the swing, but even on his feet he was still swaying. In his quiet, dignified way he was completely sozzled.

''Course you didn't,' he said, waving the champagne bottle in the direction of the marquee. 'But come and dance anyway. We embittered old battleaxes have got to stick together, you know.'

🐎

A while later Jan found herself alone with Michael.

'Weddings always make me feel differently,' he said, breathing in the garden's sweet night air.

'Differently? How do you mean differently?'

'From what I usually think about the institution of marriage.'

He said the word carefully – in-sti-tu-tion – as if afraid of slurring it. Michael, too, was a little squiffy.

'Come on, spit it out.'

'What I mean is whenever I go to a wedding my outlook on marriage changes, you see. I find myself seeing it through rose-coloured lenses. I get seduced by all the ceremonial and the fuzzy warm feelings everybody shares.'

'But you've never been married yourself, have you?'

'God, no. Though I came close a couple of times. But that's what I'm saying. I may get seduced by the idea, but the next day, when the stardust has blown away, I'm back enjoying being fancy-free again.'

'What *is* it with you men and commitment?' Jan challenged. 'Why do you have so much trouble with it?'

'Oh, in my case it's cultural. Irish men our age are always terrified of giving a ring to a woman. You wouldn't normally do it until after your ma dies because it's then you need someone to cook your eggs and rashers.'

'Now come on, Michael,' said Jan severely. 'Even I know that's a myth, I know loads of happily married Irishmen. I'm surprised at you.'

Michael laughed.

'Yes, but like all stereotypes there's more than a smidgen of truth in it. Traditionally, a country boy in Ireland wouldn't marry till he'd got his hands on the farm. That might only be when he's fifty or more. So maybe marrying late's in the Paddy genes.'

'So, is there a farm to get your hands on one day in County Cork?'

Michael shook his head.

'Ah, no. My father had a livery yard and a taxi business combined. Best of both worlds, as he always said, though he never made any money from either one of them. It's probably all down the bookies, if the truth were told, so there's nothing for me to inherit. When I get Tumblewind finished, I'll be at a bit of a loose end. But I'm not thinking about that for now.'

'Is Tumblewind very important to you?'

They had been standing for some time at the far end of the pub garden, looking out over a large acreage of wheat, and at the dark line of the Riscombe Downs on the horizon beyond.

'Right now Tumblewind is *everything* to me,' Michael replied with an unexpected passion. 'And I haven't a clue how it'll be with me when it's all done and dusted.'

He turned round and began making for the marquee.

'Let's forget about tomorrow, eh? Come on, let's go and have another drink.'

Jan hurried after him.

'Forgetting about tomorrow's easy,' she said, 'but not the day after.'

He turned again and waited.

'The Jockey Club you mean?' he asked gently.

'Yup. That's when my future as a trainer will be decided.'

Michael flashed Jan a smile. 'It'll be a doddle, so it will, you'll have Uncle Michael with you as chauffeur, adviser, and pressure-release valve. So you don't need to worry now, do you?'

'Thanks, Michael. Thanks for agreeing to drive me to London. It's beyond the call of duty, it really is.'

'Ah, no!' he said briskly. 'A.D. had already asked me to do it, but I'd have volunteered for the job anyway. Come on inside now and put it out of your mind. I think we both need a drop more of the hard stuff. There's still the rest of the evening to enjoy, so there is.'

28

As they swung round the Oxford ring road at nine o'clock on Monday morning and approached the London-bound M40, Michael and Jan were congratulating themselves that they had made good time and still had an hour and a half in which to complete the remaining forty miles, park the car and present themselves unruffled in Portman Square. The motorway was busy enough, but the traffic kept flowing at a reasonable pace and, for ten minutes, they hummed along in the fast lane. Shortly after passing the sign for Stokenchurch, Jan noticed their speed slacken as vehicles bunched up around them. Soon the traffic was reduced to a ten-mile-an-hour crawl in all three lanes.

'Oh shit, what's all this about?' Jan asked with a certain amount of tension in her voice.

'Don't worry, it's just volume of traffic,' Michael replied calmly, manoeuvring expertly into the middle lane and then into the inside lane, where the traffic seemed to be moving the fastest. 'There's no cause for alarm.'

But in the next stop–start mile they were almost down to walking pace and Jan noticed Michael flicking an anxious glance at the dashboard clock. As he did so, the vehicles ahead stopped dead, choking all three lanes. Michael stamped on the brake and he, too, ground to a halt.

'Don't panic. It may be nothing. This traffic can move off just as quickly as it stops.'

While Michael pretended an air of calmness, he was concerned enough to flick on the car radio and search for a channel that might provide news of the local traffic conditions. Several times rock music swamped the interior of the car, which he instantly tamed with a twist of the volume control.

Anxiously Jan checked the time. It was not quite half-past nine.

'We're still in good shape,' said Michael. 'It's only about twenty-five miles, thirty max, and we've got more than an hour to do it in.'

'But we've got to meet Peter McCormick and go through the final evidence.'

They had arranged to meet Jan's lawyer at ten a.m. in the Churchill Hotel across the square from the Jockey Club offices.

'Jan, trust me. There's bags of time. It won't do you one bit of good getting wound up.'

They sat in silence as a singer on the radio caterwauled about the two-timing exploits of her boyfriend. But Jan wasn't listening, she could only think about the threat of the proceedings that lay ahead.

'Mike, how do you think it's going to pan out?' she asked. 'I want you to be honest with me.'

'Honestly, like I said the other night, I think they'll go easy on you. If they've got any sort of moral conscience, anyway. There's no evidence you doped the horse – actually, all the facts point the other way. Those scenes after the Champion Chase, with the crowd clambering all over Moony were a potential danger both to the horse and the public, and the Jockey Club'll have to admit it when they see the video.'

Jan had the video in her briefcase with the other papers.

'Yes, I would hope so,' she said, but she couldn't help adding grimly, 'if we get there in time to show it.'

The music had ended and another more pleasant tune, with a country twang to it, began.

'It's also occurred to me,' Jan went on, 'that something could have happened on the ferry when Moony came over from Ireland.'

'How do you mean?'

'Well, look at it this way. He's in the transporter on the car deck and no one is allowed to stay with him. All passengers are supposed to go to the upper decks while the ferry is at sea, but someone could have sneaked down easily. Apparently there's no security to stop people doing that. I did hear one groom was so concerned about leaving his horse that he hid in one of the empty stalls on the horsebox for the whole journey.'

Michael nodded.

'Yes, I can see it's a possibility.'

On the radio the country music was interrupted by a special road report.

'News is coming in,' the announcer said, 'of a serious accident on the M40 around junction four, High Wycombe. A tanker has apparently overturned, leading to severe delays in both directions. We'll bring you more information as we get it, but in the meantime drivers are advised to steer clear of the area and find an alternative route.'

'Oh no!' gasped Jan, overcome with emotion. 'What next?'

Michael opened his door and stood on the sill to scan the road ahead. He dropped back inside with a sigh.

'It's rock solid. No one's moving.'

He was looking increasingly grim. Both of them knew that motorway tailbacks behind accidents sometimes took hours to clear.

'What the hell's going to happen if we're late? Will they start without us?'

'If they do, it won't be good. They'll automatically assume you're guilty. Have you got the mobile?'

Jan groaned. The stable's only mobile phone had been left with Annabel, and Michael had no car phone, so all they could do now was sit and sweat it out.

A couple of minutes later, the annoyingly perky announcer was back on the radio with more news.

'Back to that blockage on the M40,' he said breezily. 'We understand that several cars have crashed and that ambulances are on their way to the scene. So stand by for long delays there!'

At that moment a police siren was heard and a patrolman's motorbike zipped past on the hard shoulder, its blue light flashing. Jan peered into the wing mirror on her side and saw that a second bike was now approaching, this time with an ambulance behind it.

'Sod it,' she said. 'I'm going to do something. I can't just sit here with my whole life about to disappear down the pan.'

Jan flung open the car door and made to get out onto the hard shoulder.

'Jan, for God's sake get in before you get nicked,' Michael shouted. 'I've just checked the map – we're only half a mile from the next exit at High Wycombe.'

'We might as well be a hundred miles away,' Jan moaned as she slumped back in the seat. 'Oh, Michael, what a cock-up, everything's bound to be lost now.'

'No, it isn't, Jan. Look, the police are directing the inside lane onto the hard shoulder; we'll be at High Wycombe soon. It's going to be OK.'

🐎

'What are you going to tell the hearing, Mrs Hardy? Do you expect to get off, Mrs Hardy? Who do you think doped Moonstone Magic, Mrs Hardy?'

The barrage of questions filled the air as Jan and Michael pushed their way through the throng of reporters who had already gathered outside the Jockey Club's London headquarters. Even if they had been able to answer all the questions, they wouldn't have had the breath to do so.

Peter McCormick was sitting in the anteroom outside the Disciplinary Committee Room. He jumped up as Jan came rushing through the door.

'You're late,' he said abruptly, until Jan gasped out the reason for their delay, 'I guessed so, which is why I didn't hang around in the Churchill. In fact, I've already told the committee we can't be responsible for Britain's motorways. They're in session now, waiting for us minions to appear. I expect they won't be in the best of tempers. We'd better crack on, we don't want to antagonize them further.'

Jan swallowed hard and tried to control her breathing.

'But we haven't had our preliminary meeting,' she said. 'Didn't you say we have things to discuss?'

'It's not necessary. I think we've already covered everything they can throw at us. You just answer the questions. I'll jab you with my foot under the table if I want you to shut up. Now, let's get in there and win.'

The committee room was dominated by a horseshoe-shaped table laden with reams of paper, pencils, tumblers and jugs of water. The three Jockey Club stewards, the tribunal who would decide the case, sat at the head, with a fourth, rather ashen-faced man, alongside them. On their left sat Jack Smallgrass and Gus Foley with a large bundle of typed-out papers set in an orderly fashion on the table in front of them.

Behind the three stewards was a smoked-glass window with a recording and projection control room on the other side. On the wall in front of them was a big screen on which film or video could be shown.

The senior member of the tribunal, a tall, gaunt, grey-haired man in his sixties, looked up as Jan and Peter entered, almost in surprise.

'Ah! Mrs Hardy, Peter, you're here at last. We were beginning to wonder if we should begin without you. Happily we shall not have to now. Please take a seat.'

Obviously in a hurry to get proceedings under way, he waved them into the two chairs on the opposite side of the table from Smallgrass and Foley and, when they were settled, twisted round in his seat, nodding towards the control room.

'Robin, can we start the recording?'

He turned back and cleared his throat. 'We are convened to enquire into the circumstances of the running of Moonstone Magic in the Champion Chase at Cheltenham on the seventeenth of March this year. I am Henry Jeevons, chairman of the Disciplinary Committee. On my right is Lord Welwyn and on my left the Honourable Thomas Bowlby, stewards of the Jockey Club and members of the committee. Also present are Mr Robin Jones, the committee's legal adviser, and Mr Jack Smallgrass and Mr Gus Foley of the club's security department. Finally we have Mrs Jan Hardy, the trainer of Moonstone Magic, who is attending at our invitation. She has exercised her right to be legally represented by Mr Peter McCormick. Good to see you, Peter.

'Now, I should add that, for evidential purposes, this session is being sound-recorded only. Is everybody happy?'

He looked round and everyone nodded their agreement.

'Right. Let's begin. Mr Smallgrass?'

Jack Smallgrass selected a document from the bundle in front of him and began to outline the charge against Jan, namely that she ran Moonstone Magic in the Champion Chase with a banned substance in his bloodstream. Smallgrass reminded the committee that it was a high-profile race, then went on. 'I should emphasize, however, that this offence is contrary to the Rules of Racing in any event, whether it is a bumper at Bangor or the Epsom Derby itself.

'So let me turn to what happened on the seventeenth of March last, when Moonstone Magic won the Champion Chase at Cheltenham. Subsequent to his run, following unsaddling, he was subject to a urine sample in the designated testing area. The sample was taken by the racecourse official and labelled with the security code DC4792. It was then dispatched to the testing centre at Newmarket with other test samples taken during the course of the day. The results of the test on sample DC4792 showed traces of a steroid, specifically beclomethasone dipropionate in a concentration of 0.005 micrograms per millilitre. This steroid is on the list of prohibited substances issued by the Jockey Club as an addendum to the Rules of Racing. You have a copy of the lab report, as well as a copy of the list of prohibited substances, before you.'

Jan quickly sorted through the sheaf of papers before her and found the long alphabetical list of banned chemicals on several sheets of paper. Beclomethasone dipropionate was highlighted in yellow on page one.

'On receipt of the report from the testing centre on the twenty-second of March, the Cheltenham stewards convened and matched the security code to the sample obtained from Moonstone Magic. The horse was automatically disqualified from the race and Mrs Hardy was informed. Mr Foley here and I subsequently paid a number of visits to the yard of Mrs Hardy to investigate the matter further, but she was unable to offer any explanation for the presence of this steroid in her horse's body.'

As Smallgrass's prosecuting speech unfolded, Jan studied the faces of the three men who held her fate in their hands. Jeevons looked impenetrable, a deadpan racing bureaucrat who gave nothing away. The decidedly podgy and relatively young Lord Welwyn looked as if he was only half listening. The Hon. Thomas Bowlby, by contrast, gave every appearance of attending carefully to Smallgrass's every utterance. He was probably in his fifties, a handsome, foxy-looking type with jet black hair, bushy eyebrows and a distinct five o'clock shadow. Jan decided he was probably the most dangerous of the three. She had already detected hostility in his eyes.

Meanwhile Smallgrass droned on.

'So this is the substance of the charge against Mrs Hardy. I should just remind the committee that cases like these are ones of strict liability, which means that the race must be forfeited under all circumstances, including one of accidental administration of the drug, or administration of it by an unknown party. I would also remind the committee that it is within their power to allocate responsibility for this breach of the rules and that any person found so responsible can be subject to whatsoever sanctions the committee decides, up to and including permanent disqualification from taking part in racing or holding any licence issued under the aegis of the Jockey Club.'

Smallgrass fell silent and Jeevons, with a thin smile, thanked him before turning to Jan.

'Now, Mrs Hardy, you have heard the substance of the case against you. It seems to me that the nub of this matter is whether this drug was knowingly administered to the horse by you, or alternatively given as a result of negligence by yourself or your staff. I take it you accept the results of the blood test on this horse?'

Suddenly Jan felt hot as she struggled to control her temper. Who were these people to make such allegations? Her stable was clean! One thing was certain, she and her staff were honest people! How dare Jack Smallgrass accuse them like this?

She was about to give vent to her feelings when she felt a sharp tap on her ankle. She looked down to see Peter McCormick's foot poised to strike again if she should so much as open her mouth. With a considerable effort she clammed up.

Peter quickly took control and spoke instead.

'My client does not deny that this steroid appears on the test report, and that code number DC4792 correlates with the horse Moonstone Magic. She does, however, vigorously deny any involvement in the administration of the substance named. Mr Smallgrass, during your thorough investigation of Mrs Hardy's yard, did you find any irregularity in relation to Moonstone Magic, either in his feed or his training regime or the conditions in which he was kept?'

'Er, no, not with that horse. We did find another matter which—'

McCormick seized the moment – the last thing he wanted was to have the activities of Bobby Montana brought in to muddy the waters – and interrupted ruthlessly.

'No, no, no, Mr Smallgrass, we are only concerned with Moonstone Magic, are we not? And you found nothing untoward there, I take it?'

'No. No we didn't.'

Peter sifted his papers and selected several sheets, which he passed around the table.

'My client has made a short deposition, which I submit for the consideration of the committee. As you will see, she is of the opinion that the substance was administered by a person or persons unknown, for malicious reasons, in the certain knowledge that it would be detected, and that the purpose of this action was to discredit and damage Mrs Hardy's reputation and to deprive her and the horse's owner Mr A.D. O'Hagan of substantial prize money.'

'Who on earth would want to do that?'

It was his lordship who spoke, his voice squeaky as if personally affronted by this suggestion.

Again Jan was about to burst out, with Virginia Gilbert's name on the tip of her tongue, when she felt another sharp jab on her ankle.

'Mrs Hardy has no idea who it might be,' said Peter innocently. 'But, as the committee must be constantly aware, racing is a sport in which there are keen rivalries and jealousy also, unfortunately. Many people believe they have scores to settle.'

He passed out more papers.

'I turn briefly to the nature of the steroid in question. This is a leaflet enclosed by the manufacturers with a common asthma inhaler. The committee will see that the active steroid is beclomethasone dipropionate. Thus the substance apparently found in Moonstone Magic is commonly and easily available to anyone who happens to receive asthma treatment – which is a considerable proportion of the population. I'm sure you will agree on that point.'

Peter went on to outline two occasions during which time the stable could have had no control over the horse, each providing someone the opportunity to administer a substance maliciously. He described how Moonstone Magic had been brought over on the ferry from Ireland three days before the race and explained that stable staff were prohibited from the car deck while at sea. He distributed an affidavit from the ferry company confirming this.

'But *if* no one was allowed on the car deck,' piped up Lord Welwyn, 'then no one could have interfered with the horse, could they?'

'Well, what we are actually saying is someone might easily have concealed themselves on the car deck specifically for this purpose. It seems it is a potentially huge problem, which cannot be discounted.'

'Ah.'

Lord Welwyn sighed, waving his hand, beckoning for Peter to continue.

'We would like to offer the video evidence now,' he stated.

The curtains were drawn and Jan's video was played, showing the horse's progress towards the unsaddling enclosure after his victory in the Champion Chase. At the instant in which the racegoer appeared to pat the horse's muzzle, the lawyer said, 'Freeze the frame! This is the other time when we believe someone had the opportunity to administer the drug, this time with the use of a commonly used inhaler. Again, the trainer cannot be expected to be able to protect her horse from such an attack, given the circumstances and the large boisterous crowd who have no security barriers to keep them back.'

Peter finished by arguing that, whether the drug was given on the ferry, or on the way to the unsaddling enclosure, Jan Hardy could in neither case be held responsible. He then asked the committee to note that, if the drug got into the horse as a result of lax security on the course following the race, or indeed on the ferry, then perhaps they should make further recommendations. The criticism of the ferry companies, which carried many fancied runners to English race tracks, and the racecourses themselves, did not go unnoticed, and Jan saw Bowlby's eyes narrow in response.

'Thank you, Mr McCormick – Peter,' said Jeevons. 'Would you kindly wait outside, where you will I hope find tea and coffee? We will let you know as soon as we've reached a decision.'

Michael was pacing up and down the corridor outside the anteroom waiting for them, having just sunk his fourth cup of coffee.

When she had given him a full account of what happened, Jan shut her eyes. 'I felt sure that man Bowlby was against me.'

'Jan, you're imagining it. Lord Welwyn kept making remarks,' said Peter. 'Bowlby said nothing.'

'Exactly. Silent but deadly.'

For thirty minutes they paced around the room, drinking coffee but saying little. Finally they were called back by the stewards' secretary.

'Please be seated,' said Jeevons, settling himself to read from a typed piece of paper. By now Jan's heart was thumping like a jackhammer.

'We confirm the Cheltenham stewards' disqualification of Moonstone Magic in the Champion Chase. We further find Mrs Jan Hardy responsible, either deliberately or negligently, for the administration of a prohibited substance. We do not find evidence that anyone else outside her yard was involved, nor is there any evidence against anyone within the yard. Therefore, as proprietor of the licensed yard, the weight of responsibility falls solely on Mrs Hardy's shoulders. This is our finding.'

Jan was outraged. She flushed crimson.

'I don't believe you can do this!' she cried. 'It's absolutely— Ow!'

The sharpest kick she had yet felt smashed into her shin as Peter McCormick quickly cut in.

'May I make some remarks to the committee in mitigation?'

Jeevons inclined his head and Peter launched into a speech extolling Jan's previous record, as well as detailing the hard road she had followed to success as a trainer since being widowed: starting from scratch in a new yard, which she had built mostly herself, and turning it into a centre of excellence. He said nothing, however, about one thing, because Jan had expressly forbidden him in advance to raise it.

'You'll say nothing about me being a woman,' she'd said. 'I know they'll probably already think I'm a weakling, but it cannot and must not form any part of the defence. I compete in this job as an equal.'

When Peter finished his submission, he and Jan were invited to step outside for a brief interlude while the committee deliberated further.

🐎

'I just can't believe they've found me guilty,' exclaimed Jan as the waiting time lengthened. 'It's completely and totally unjust.'

'But it was only on a technicality,' said Michael sympathetically. 'Everyone will understand that.'

'Bollocks they will; it's a bloody travesty, that's what it is. What the hell are they doing in there now, Peter? What's taking them so long? Having their frigging lunch, I expect.'

'Jan, you really are going to have to calm down. Throwing your toys out of the pram won't help matters—'

Suddenly the door opened and they were called in at last to hear Jan's fate. The slight headache she had earlier worsened. The throbbing was unbearable and made Jan feel light-headed. As if from a great distance Jan heard Jeevons intoning the public statement the committee had prepared.

'Prohibited substance found . . . Rules of Racing must be upheld . . . Mrs Hardy's grave responsibility . . . disqualification of the horse . . . on hearing evidence in mitigation . . . committee inclined to leniency . . . minimum fine of two hundred and fifty pounds . . . The committee sincerely hopes Mrs Hardy and other trainers will learn lessons from this case . . . Thank you for attending this hearing Mrs Hardy, Peter.'

Tears filled her eyes and a single thought came into focus. It was OK. It was absolutely OK. She was a trainer still. Edge Farm was not out of business. She wasn't destitute.

🐎

'I never thought I'd thank someone for kicking my shins black and blue.' Jan hugged Peter McCormick when they were back in the anteroom. 'But you were great. Thanks. At least I don't have to resort to begging.'

'I'm only sorry we didn't win it. I think we did, actually, in a moral sense. It really galls me you have to pay a fine. Still there it is. You'll just have to put in extra hours!' he teased.

Suddenly the door burst open and Jack Smallgrass stood before them.

'I thought you should know,' he said, in a confidential voice that reeked of insincerity, 'the press are waiting out there, a mob of them, with photographers. I suggest you make your way out by the back door, through the underground car park.'

'That's a good idea,' said Peter. 'I tell you what. I'll go out the front and fend them off. In fact, I'll make a statement – you're completely innocent, but you accept the verdict of the committee on the basis of liability. And I'll emphasize that their levying of a minimum fine proves they don't think you did anything untoward. OK? I've got to get off to another meeting, so I'll speak to you in the morning.'

They all shook hands and Smallgrass directed Jan and Michael down a passage and past a kitchen area. Soon the pair emerged into a yard lined with huge rubbish bins and from there through a gate into the street. The first person Jan saw was a large figure loitering across the road.

'Shit, that looks like Soley from the *Tribune*. How the hell did *he* know . . . ?'

With a snide grin the reporter held up his mobile phone.

Jan crooked her finger at him. 'Come here, you cretin, you

disgrace to humanity,' she barked. 'If you don't want to be scooped by your mates, then I strongly suggest you slither back to the front entrance, you disgusting little toad. My lawyer is making a statement there and it will be my *only* statement. So get lost!'

Scurrying away like a whipped dog, Soley disappeared around the corner at the double, while Jan and Michael burst out laughing and made their way to the Churchill Hotel.

'That bloody Smallgrass. I'd bet my house it was him who tipped that ghastly little reptile off.'

'Never mind them,' Michael soothed. 'You saw him off in style.'

In the hotel lounge Michael found two comfortable armchairs in a quiet corner and ordered a pint and a large gin.

'Time for a toast,' he said. 'You've had a result in anybody's language. Your training licence is secure and you won't lose any owners. It's brilliant. The best news ever.'

Though she admitted to enormous relief, Jan was not completely pacified.

'It's still a bloody travesty,' she said. 'You know I did nothing wrong. I accept I need to tighten up our security. A.D. will be on my back about it now, that's for certain. I suppose you've got a huge system in place at Tumblewind – money-no-object sort of thing, I expect.'

'You bet. It's electronic, with guards also present as back-up. After all, A.D.'s going to have all his key horses there before long. So we can't take any chances.'

'Like Moony,' said Jan, with a sigh. 'And Galway Fox and all the others, I expect. All my stars.'

Michael, who was sitting opposite her, leant forward.

'Listen, Jan. This case – it's a kind of a warning. You're made for bigger things. You're too vulnerable operating a small yard like this on your own. You deserve to be in the big time, and the only way to be there is by joining up with A.D. as his private trainer at Tumblewind. It's you he wants, you know.'

'But are you sure? I have a feeling he thinks you could do it just as well.'

Michael shrugged. 'Who knows? If I don't make a complete balls of this building work, maybe I'll get the chance. It's true I've always wanted to train racehorses. I couldn't deny it.'

'Now's your chance, then. You'll do a great job.'

'Not as well as you, Jan. You know that as well as A.D. I don't have the experience, at least not at this stage. But I'm sure of one thing.'

Jan was struck by a change in Michael's voice. He was speaking now in absolute earnest.

'What?' she asked.

'I could do it brilliantly as your assistant trainer, Jan. We'd make a great team.'

Jan was completely taken aback.

'What on earth do you mean?'

'What I'm saying is, why don't we do it together? We'd be an unbeatable partnership, I know we would.'

The almost painful sincerity suddenly gave way to a broad smile, and Michael winked. Then he jerked his thumb back over his shoulder.

'I've got to call the site. I'll use the phone over there.'

As he left, Jan felt an odd rush in the pit of her stomach. Maybe this case really had revealed her vulnerability. Maybe she owed it to her family before anything else to consolidate her position and go along with A.D.'s plans. But deep down there was more, there was Michael. He was a man who, time and again, had had a calming and wise effect on her life, and he was really good with the horses. But no doubt once his beloved Tumblewind was finished he would be gone from her life and with A.D.'s horses withdrawn from Edge Farm, there'd be no reason for him to ride out. Like a bolt out of the blue, Jan realized how much she would really miss him.

She looked across to where Michael was making his call. Suddenly she saw him start up, his voice rise and his hand clamp on the back of his neck. He barked several questions into the receiver, listened to the answers and strode back to Jan, his face aghast. She could see something was very wrong indeed. Michael sank down in the chair and bent forward with his head in his hands.

'What on earth's the matter? You look like you've seen the devil.'

'Maybe I have, Jan. Or maybe I'm about to. Either way I've got to get back to Lambourn immediately.'

A chill shiver ran through Jan.

'Why? For God's sake, tell me what's happened.'

Michael looked up, his expression grim, Jan could see tears forming in his eyes as, almost choking on the words, he told her.

'I can't believe it, they've just told me the place is on fire. All my work's gone up in flames. The new stable block's burning. The entire bloody place, Jan – it's gone – I'm probably finished!'

Jan leant forward and took Michael's hands into her own.

'No, you're not, Michael. You have to believe that. You have been so kind, so helpful and understanding to me. Now it's my turn. I will be there for you, I promise.'